THE
CASANOVA

OTHER TITLES BY T L SWAN

THE
CASANOVA

THE MILES HIGH CLUB

T L SWAN

 Montlake

Published by Montlake, Seattle

www.apub.com

Amazon, the Amazon logo, and Montlake are trademarks of Amazon.com, Inc., or its affiliates.

ISBN-13: 9781542028073
ISBN-10: 1542028078

Cover design by Plum5 Limited

Cover photography by Wander Aguiar Photography

Printed in the United States of America

GRATITUDE
The quality of being thankful; readiness to show appreciation for, and to return kindness.

I would like to dedicate this book to the alphabet.
For those twenty-six letters have changed my life.
Within those twenty-six letters, I found myself and
live my dream.
Next time you say the alphabet,
remember its power.
I do every day.

Prologue

Elliot

I stare at the numbers above the door as they go down with each floor I drop; my phone vibrates in my pocket, I take it out, it's from Christopher.

Warning!
Witch is looking for you.

Fuck.

I stuff my phone back in my pocket and exhale heavily, not in the mood for her shit today. The elevator doors open and I stride out, glance up, and catch her in my peripheral vision. I pretend not to see her and turn toward Courtney, my PA.

"Mr. Miles," I hear her call from behind.

I keep walking.

"Ahem." She clears her throat. "Mr. Miles. Don't ignore me."

I feel my temperature rise.

My nostrils flare and I turn toward the voice, and there she stands. The most infuriating staff member to have ever walked the earth.

Intelligent, bossy, arrogant, and fucking annoying.

Kathryn Landon, my arch nemesis.

The official wicked witch of the west.

A title well deserved.

I fake a smile. "Good morning, Kathryn."

"A word?"

"It's nine a.m. on a Monday morning," I snap. "Now is not the time for"—I put up my fingers to do fake quotation marks—"a word."

I swear she spends all weekend brainstorming ways to fuck up my Mondays.

"Make time," she barks.

I run my tongue over my teeth: this bitch has me over a barrel and she knows it. A complete computer geek, she designed our new software. She knows she's indispensable and holy fuck, does she ride my ass.

She marches to her office and opens the door in a rush. "I'll be quick."

"Of course you will." I fake a smile, imagine myself slamming her head in the door as I walk through it.

She sits down behind her desk. "Please, take a seat."

"No, I'm fine standing. You're being quick, remember?" She raises her eyebrow and I glare right back at her. "What is it?"

"It has been brought to my attention that I won't be getting my four new interns this year. Why not?"

"Don't play games, Kathryn, you obviously already know the answer to that question."

"Why would you give those traineeships to offshore employees?"

"Because it's my company."

"That isn't a good enough answer."

I begin to hear my heartbeat in my ears as I tilt my chin to the sky; nobody riles me up like this woman. "Miss Landon, I don't have to justify any decisions on the running of Miles Media to you. I report to the board, and the board only. Although, I do have to wonder about your intentions."

She narrows her eyes. "What does that mean?"

"Well, if you are so unhappy here, why do you stay?"

"What?"

"There are a million other companies that you could go and work for and yet you insist on staying here and complaining about every little thing. I'm not going to lie, it's getting very old."

"How dare you!"

"I think you should remember that nobody is indispensable. I'm more than happy to accept your resignation at any time. Hell, I'll even pay you a bonus to leave."

She puts her hands on her hips. "I want a written report on the internships you have taken from the London office and the reasons why. Your excuse is not good enough and I will be presenting this issue to the board myself."

Of course she will. My fury bubbles.

"And don't roll your eyes at me," she huffs.

"Kathryn, I need a damn retina transplant from all the eye rolling you cause."

"Well, that makes two of us."

We glare at each other and I don't know if I've ever hated someone like I do her.

Knock, knock, sounds at the door.

"Come in," she yells.

Christopher comes into view, just like I knew he would. He always interrupts my meetings with Kathryn moments before my impending explosion. "Elliot, can I see you?" he asks. He nods to her with a smile. "Morning, Kathryn."

"We're not finished, Christopher, you will have to wait," she snaps.

"We are finished." I turn. "If you have any more complaints, which no doubt you will, take it up with HR."

"I won't be doing that," she snaps again. "You are the CEO and I will be taking up any issues I have with you. Stop wasting my time, Mr. Miles. I'm more than happy to report to the board on your incompetence. Lord knows there's enough of it. I want those intern positions returned to the London office immediately."

"Not happening."

She shuffles the papers on her desk. "Fine, see you on Tuesday next week."

The board meeting.

I glare at her as I begin to hear my heartbeat in my ears.

Fucking bitch.

"Ahh . . . Elliot," Christopher prompts me. "We have to go."

I clench my jaw as I glare at her. "Name your price to resign."

"Go to hell."

"I will not be accosted with your trivial complaints every single time I walk through my office," I growl.

"Then stop making stupid decisions."

Our eyes are locked.

"Goodbye, Mr. Miles, close the door on your way out." She smiles sweetly. "See you at the board meeting."

I inhale sharply as I grapple with control.

"Elliot," Christopher prompts me again. "This way."

I storm from her office straight into the elevator. Christopher is hot on my heels and the doors close behind us.

"Holy fuck. I hate that woman," I whisper angrily.

4

"If it makes you feel any better"—he smirks—"she hates you more."

I loosen my tie with a hard jerk. "Is it too early for a Scotch?" I ask.

Christopher looks at his watch. "It's nine-fifteen a.m."

I inhale heavily as I try to calm myself down.

"Who fucking cares."

Chapter 1

KATE

I throw my lunch into a bag and look around for my keys. "I'm leaving," I call to Rebecca.

Beck pops her head around the bathroom door; she's wrapped in a white towel with another around her head. "Make sure you're not home late tonight. I don't want it to seem awkward and weird when he gets here."

"Yeah, yeah."

"I mean it, I want him to feel welcome, and you know, it would be nice for us both to be here to settle Daniel in."

I roll my eyes as I look for my keys. Where are they? "What makes you think that he wants us to settle him in?"

"I just think it would be nice to give a good first impression."

"Okay, I get it." I spot my keys in the small basket on the coffee table.

"I'm picking up our netball uniforms today on my lunch break," she calls.

I smirk; God help us, we're starting to play indoor netball this week. My first competitive sporting activity since high school. "I can't wait," I call back. "Hopefully they come standard with defibrillators. I'm so unfit I might have a heart attack."

Rebecca laughs as she unwraps the towel from her head. "You have a gym in your building at work, why don't you use it?"

I make my way toward the door. "I know, I really should stop being so lazy."

"Do you think I should cook Daniel dinner tonight?" she asks.

I screw up my face. "Why are you breaking your neck to be so nice to this guy?"

"I'm not."

"Do you fancy him or something?" I widen my eyes. "I didn't see you going to all these lengths for our last flatmate."

"Yeah, because she was a pain in my ass, and besides, Daniel is new in town, just arriving today, and he knows nobody. I feel sorry for him."

"He's a personal stylist, I'm pretty sure he has his own wanky friends to hang out with," I mutter dryly.

"Correction, he's a fashion graduate who has moved to London because he wants to be a stylist, there's a big difference."

I roll my eyes. "Whatever, see you tonight."

I take the stairs and three flights later I'm in the street and walking toward the train station. It's only three stops until the Central line but still, too far to walk.

I wait on the platform, and right on schedule along comes my train. I climb on and take a seat.

I've come to the realization that this is the weirdest twenty minutes of my day. It's like a time tunnel; I take a seat, I look around, and the next minute I'm miraculously there. I must fall into this catatonic state—I don't know what I think about, I don't know where the time goes. I just know that somehow, every day I lose twenty minutes thinking about subjects that I can't remember.

I get off the train and make my way to the office. I work in central London, and there's a small coffee shop diagonally across from the Miles Media building; it's busy and bustling as people rush in and out on their way to work.

"Hey, beautiful girl," says Mike.

"Hi." I smile happily. Mike is the barista who works here; also he's had a low-key crush on me for a few years. He's sweet and cute and unfortunately I feel absolutely nothing every time he speaks to me.

It sucks, because he's a really great guy. If ever there was someone that I knew would be good for me, it would be Mike. I wish I could pick who I was attracted to; it definitely would make things a lot easier in my life.

"The usual?" Mike asks.

I take a seat by the window. "Yes please." I look around.

Mike makes my coffee and comes over and sits it down in front of me. "What's new?" he asks.

"Not much." I pick up my coffee, steam floats to the ceiling, and I blow on it. "I'm thinking of joining the gym at work."

"Yeah?" Mike's gaze looks over to the building across the street. "You have a gym in there?"

"A huge one, on level fourteen."

"Ha, who knew? Do you have to pay?"

"No, it's free for employees." I take a sip of my coffee.

Mike chuckles as he pretends to wipe down the table next to where I'm sitting.

"I can come with you," he offers with a cute wink.

"Sorry, it's for employees only and I can't afford to go to another gym."

Mike rolls his eyes.

Mike and I watch on as a black Bentley pulls up in front of the Miles Media building. The driver gets out of the car and opens the back door, and Elliot Miles climbs out. Like some kind of morning spectacle that I go through every day, my eyes roam up and down the man I despise. Today he's wearing a navy-blue pinstripe suit with a white shirt, his dark hair curled to just-fucked perfection. I watch him do up his jacket with one hand, his briefcase in his other. His back is ramrod-straight, his stance dominant.

Arrogance personified.

I sip my coffee as I watch him; it infuriates me that he's gorgeous.

It infuriates me that every woman stops dead in her tracks, and stares when he walks into a room. And more than anything, it infuriates me that he knows it.

Although I'd never admit it, I read the tabloids and gossip magazines, I see all the exotic parties he goes to and the beautiful women he dates.

I know more about Elliot Miles than I care to admit.

I mean, I should—I've hated the man for the whole seven years that I've worked for him.

I watch as he says something to his driver with a smile, then he walks into the Miles Media building as people turn their heads to watch him, and I feel the hackles on the back of my neck rise.

Elliot Miles, the epitome of a rich bastard . . . pisses me off.

It's just three in the afternoon and my email pings.

I open it.

Elliot Miles.

CEO Miles Media UK.

Kathryn,

Have you finalized the tracking report?

Asshole.
I clench my jaw and type my reply.

Dear Mr. Miles,

Good afternoon, always a pleasure to receive correspondence from you.

Your manners are as impeccable as ever.

The report isn't due until Tuesday next week, you will receive it then.

Perhaps if I had the adequate number of staff members, I could work to your unrealistic work schedule.

Enjoy the rest of your day.

Sincerely,
Kathryn.

I smirk and hit send; being a sarcastic bitch to Elliot Miles is my favorite hobby. A reply bounces straight back in.

Good afternoon Kathryn,

As always, your dramatics are unappreciated.

I didn't ask when I would receive the report, I asked if you had finished it.

Please pay attention to detail, I don't want to constantly repeat myself.

Have you finished the report or not?

I inhale sharply, this damn man drives me fucking crazy. I type my reply, hitting my keyboard so hard I'm surprised I don't break a finger.

Mr. Miles,

Of course the report is finalized. I am, as always, prepared for your inconsistencies in dates and timelines.

Thankfully, one of us is a professional.

Please find the attached report.

If you have trouble understanding it, I'm happy to take time out of my busy schedule to explain it before you meet the board.

I smirk as I keep typing, imagining the smoke coming out of his ears as he reads it.

Have a lovely afternoon, always a pleasure.

Kathryn Landon.

I sip my tea, feeling happy with myself—take that.

My email pings again and I open it.

> Miss Landon.
>
> Thank you.
>
> Have a safe trip home this afternoon, don't walk in front of a bus or anything.

I smile to myself. *Stupid twat* . . . you wish.

I stand and watch Rebecca run around the apartment like a chicken—Daniel is arriving at any moment. And boy oh boy, is Rebecca in overdrive.

"Don't just stand there," she snaps.

"What do you want me to do?" I look around the spotless apartment. "There is literally nothing left to clean. What is it with you and this guy?" I ask. "You're hell-bent on impressing him. The fact that he's gorgeous wouldn't have anything to do with it, would it?"

"Don't be ridiculous," she snaps again. "I have a boyfriend, remember?"

"Oh, I remember, but do you?"

"Shut up," she huffs.

The doorbell sounds and our eyes meet. "He's here," she whispers.

"Well." I gesture to the front door. "Go and let him in."

Rebecca nearly runs to the front door and opens it in a rush. "Hi." She smiles.

It's really hard not to roll my eyes.

"Hi." He smiles as he looks between us. He's got two big suitcases with him, he's tall and blond, and I have to admit, he really is quite handsome. I don't remember him being this good-looking when he came around to meet us before. No wonder Beck is breaking her back to impress him. "Here, let me help you with those," I offer.

Beck looks out onto the street. "Do you have any more things you want help with bringing in?"

"Thanks, I've just got another two suitcases in my car. I can get them."

"You remember Kate?" She gestures to me.

Daniel's eyes come to me. "Yes, of course I do. Nice to see you again, Kate."

I give an awkward smile—I'm always so weird in social situations. Until I get to know someone I'm really not friendly at all. Not by choice of course, shyness is a curse.

"This is your bedroom through here." Rebecca plays tour guide, leads him through and shows him his room. "And this is my bedroom. Come upstairs and I'll show you Kate's bedroom," she offers.

I follow them as she shows him around the apartment. My eyes roam up and down Daniel: he's wearing black trousers, a black knitted sweater, pointy shoes, and a bomber jacket in camo green. His clothes are expensive and trendy; he really does look the part of the personal stylist.

"When do you start work?" I ask as I try and make conversation.

"I have four clients next week, and I have to find about fifty more as soon as possible," he says.

I smile.

"But seriously, I start with Harrods next week, I'm going to be one of their in-house shoppers."

Oh, what a hellish job—shopping is my living nightmare. Unsure what to say and feeling awkward, I hunch my shoulders. "I've never met a personal shopper before."

Daniel smiles. "There aren't too many of us."

I take a suitcase from him and glance down at it: Louis Vuitton. Jeez . . . I think the suitcase is worth more than my car. He disappears down the front steps to the street and I peer out after him: he has a black new-model Audi. Why the hell is he sharing an apartment with two other people if he has all this expensive stuff?

Surely he would want to live alone?

I know I would.

He grabs another two suitcases from his car and once again they are beautiful black leather; I eye them suspiciously as he walks back up the steps. I wish I had good taste like this. I wouldn't know what to buy even if I did have the money.

Daniel wheels his suitcases into his bedroom and looks between us as he puts his hands on his hips. "Please tell me that you girls are taking me out tonight. There's no better way to get to know each other than over a few drinks."

Rebecca's eyes nearly pop from her head in excitement. "That sounds awesome." She glances over to me. "Doesn't it, Kate?"

Not really.

A fake smile. "Sure does."

"Shall we go?" he asks.

"Now?" I frown. "You don't want to put anything away first?"

"No, I'm good, it will still be there tomorrow and I have nothing to do until next week so it will give me a mission."

An hour later, we sit at the bar in a restaurant, wine firmly in hand.

"So?" Daniel looks between the two of us. "What's the story with you two, are you single or dating?"

"Well." Rebecca smiles. "I have a boyfriend, Brett. And Kathryn here is trying to get an honorary membership to the nunnery."

I laugh. "That's not true. I'm just very picky."

Daniel gives me a cute wink. "Nothing wrong with that. I'm quite picky myself actually."

"And what's your story?" Rebecca asks.

"Well . . ." Daniel pauses as if choosing the right words. "I am . . ." He pauses again.

"Gay?" I ask.

Daniel laughs. "I like women too much to title myself completely gay."

"So . . ." Rebecca screws up her face as she tries to make sense of that statement.

"You're bisexual?"

Daniel twists his lips as if thinking. "I wouldn't say I'm bisexual. My natural attraction is toward women. But lately . . ." His voice trails off.

"What?" I ask, fascinated.

"A few years back I was partying with a few guys that I didn't know that well in Ibiza. One of them was gay."

"How many were you away with?" I ask.

"There were four of us in total."

"So, three of you were straight?"

Daniel nods. "Maybe it was the sun, maybe it was the alcohol, or maybe it was the cocaine, I don't know, but something happened and we got a little randy, spent the weekend in bed, and now I have a bit of a fetish for men on the side."

Rebecca smiles dreamily over at Daniel, as if this is the best story that she's ever heard. And I can almost hear the cogs in her brain clicking, assessing how liberated he must be.

I sip my drink, equally fascinated with his story. "How does it feel to be sexual with somebody that isn't your natural inclination?"

"Good. Perhaps a little kinky." Daniel shrugs. "I think that's what it is for me, I feel like I'm doing something naughty, something that I shouldn't be doing but at the same time feels so natural. And I don't know how long I'll keep doing it, maybe not forever, maybe not much more at all. But whenever I do it, I don't regret it. It doesn't feel wrong, if that's what you mean."

"How many . . ." Rebecca's voice trails off as she stops herself.

"You can ask me anything," Daniel prompts her.

"How many men have you been with?"

Daniel narrows his eyes as he thinks. "Hmm, not many, I would say more than ten but less than twenty."

"Jeez." My eyebrows raise by themselves.

"What's that look for?" Daniel smiles.

"Well, you said that you haven't slept with many men. If that's a low number for you what's a high number? I mean . . . what are your numbers for women?"

Daniel laughs. "Too many to count, I'm afraid. I meet some beautiful people in my industry, sometimes the temptation is just too great."

Disappointment fills me and I screw up my napkin and throw it onto the table in disgust. "I wish I was more like you," I sigh.

"Meaning?"

"You know, all liberated and cool and"—I pause as I think of the right terminology—"I guess, free."

Daniel's face falls. "You don't feel free?"

Oh God, why did I say that? Now I sound like a freaking drama queen. "What I meant is, I guess I would like to be in your shoes, you know, sleeping with whoever I wanted to for fun."

"You don't have sex for fun?" Daniel frowns.

This is all coming out wrong. "I mean, I have in the past. I guess I just got out of the swing of it as I got older."

"How old are you?" he asks.

17

"Twenty-seven. I had a few boyfriends in high school and college, and then after that I had a long-term boyfriend. We broke up a year after my parents died."

"Your parents died?"

I sip my drink; how did we get onto this subject?

Why did I say that?

"They were involved in a head-on collision car crash," Rebecca replies; she knows how much I hate saying that out loud.

Daniel's eyes come to me in a question.

"My mother died at the scene, my father died on the way to hospital. The driver that hit them had a heart attack and veered onto the wrong side of the road." I feel the heaviness come over me as my chest constricts, and I glance up into the kind eyes of Rebecca, who gives me a soft smile and takes my hand across the table. I had just moved in with Rebecca at college when my parents died. She's been my rock and a wonderful friend and has been there for me on many lonely sad nights.

"I'm so sorry," Daniel whispers. "Do you have any other family?"

"Yes." I smile. "I have a wonderful brother, Brad, and I have a sister who . . ." My voice trails off.

"Who what?" Daniel asks.

"Is a raving bitch," Rebecca snaps. "I have no idea how the two of these girls are genetically related. They have nothing at all in common. Chalk and cheese."

Daniel smiles in surprise as he looks between us. "Why, what's she like?"

"Beautiful." I sip my drink.

"Entitled and mean," Rebecca interjects.

I smile sadly. "She's not so bad. She's taken our parents' death the hardest and somehow her personality changed overnight. Brad and I have held each other up and limped along and yet, all she

18

wanted to do is be on her own. She hasn't handled grief the same as we have."

"You don't see her at all?" Daniel asks.

"No, I do see her," I reply. "I'm just usually upset or ruffled after she leaves. You know when you spend time with someone and they kind of suck the life out of you. She likes money and fame and having the designer handbags and all her gorgeous boyfriends. I feel like"—I pause as I try to articulate myself—"I feel like she's replacing our parents' love with objects."

"You don't like designer things?"

"I guess." I shrug. "Everyone likes nice things, don't they? It's just not my priority."

"Kate is very good with her money," Rebecca interrupts.

"That's code for tight." Daniel laughs as his eyes flick to me. "Are you tight, Kate?"

"I am not tight."

"Oh, you are too," Rebecca scoffs. "She won't spend any money on herself at all and is always saving for a rainy day. She wears the same ten outfits and hides behind those big thick glasses."

"I need them to see, Rebecca," I announce, indignant. "And I just don't see the point in spending a fortune on clothes and dressing up fancy all the time."

"You work in central London with some of the hottest men in the capital and you're too busy wearing sensible office clothes to attract any of them."

I roll my eyes in disgust. "Trust me, there is no one at work worth impressing."

Daniel's eyes linger on me and, as amusement flashes across his face, he clinks his wineglass with mine.

"What?" I ask.

"I think I just found my new project."

Four hours and three bottles of wine later, and with Stevie Nicks playing in the background, Daniel says, "Then what will I write?" He laughs.

We are sitting on the couch still talking way too much nonsense, and filling in a profile on a dating app for Daniel on my computer. Apparently this is a priority when you move to a new city.

Who knew?

The question reads:

What are you looking for?

"*Hmm*, that's a hard one." Daniel inhales sharply as he does his best to think through the cloud of alcohol.

"Oh, I know. Write this," Rebecca says in her throaty, I'm-as-drunk-as-a-skunk voice. "Vagina or dick, short or tall, waxed or hairy, preferably hot."

"So basically"—I point to him with my wineglass—"you'll take anything."

"In a nutshell," Daniel replies as he types something in. "Scratch the preferably."

I laugh as I lie back; the room is beginning to spin. "I have to go to bed." I sigh. "I have to work tomorrow."

"Not so fast," Daniel says. "We're making you a profile next."

"I am *not* getting on a dating website. For your information," I slur, "there isn't a man on earth who could impress me in writing. And besides, I'm way too inebriated."

"Yes," he insists.

"Not right now, the timing isn't right."

Daniel types furiously. "You *have* to fill these things out while you're drunk, and there is no time like the present."

"What if someone found out it was me?" I asked, horrified. "I would never live it down."

"Nobody cares about dating apps, everybody does it," Rebecca scoffs as if I'm clueless. "Don't use your real name, then."

"Wouldn't that be weird, though?" I say. "Like I told him a fake name and then we're on a date and I have to say, sorry but this is my real name now, and I'm actually a liar."

"Well, you don't have to tell them straight up," Daniel says as he types. "You keep the fake name until you know if you like them and then you tell them your real name."

I smirk into my wineglass as I watch him and Rebecca go through the profile.

Daniel is fun.

He hands me my laptop. "You fill in the rest."

"Huh?"

"I filled it out for you, answer the next question."

"What?"

"We made you a profile," Rebecca informs me. "Just humor us, please."

Name	Pinkie Leroo
Height	5ft7
Weight	Just right
Appearance	Gorgeous
Hobbies	Gym and working out, laughing
Favorite pastime sex	Eating out and having

Profession	Computer analytics
Hair color	Sandy blonde
Eyes	Brown
Skin	Olive

What are you looking for?

"Pinkie Leroo?" I scoff. "Who the hell is that?"

"That's you."

"What?" I laugh. "You couldn't come up with a better fake name? I sound like a cheap bottle of wine."

"Men love that shit," Daniel replies.

"But, do they?" I read through the details they've added. "I thought we were lying on this thing?"

"We are."

"Well, I do like eating out and having sex, so . . ." I shrug.

"The gym and working out part?" Rebecca raises an impatient eyebrow.

"This is ridiculous." I slam my computer shut and stand. "I'm going to bed." I go up on to my tippy toes and kiss Daniel's cheek. "Goodnight, naughty boy."

"Night. Fill in that profile, I'm checking it in the morning."

I roll my eyes as I begin to walk up the stairs. "You just worry about your own profile, or more specifically, how easily pleased you are," I call. "You really should work on that. Up your standards a bit."

"Don't knock it till you try it," he calls back.

"Ugh." Rebecca winces. "I am never going down on a woman. Like fucking ever. It's just too . . . in your face . . . literally."

I get a really bad visual and I screw up my face with a laugh. "Stop," I cry.

Half an hour later, I lie on my bed. I'm wrapped in a towel after showering and Daniel's and Rebecca's words from earlier are running through my head, and more importantly my words: *I wish I was more like you.*

Who am I kidding, I *am* free.

I don't know where I get this notion that my hands are tied. It's men who have preconceived ideas on what they want; they're all just looking for the next Barbie doll.

I read over the profile they created and I smile as an idea rolls around in my head. I'm going to prove just how shallow and fickle men really are.

I open my computer, go back to the profile, and I change my answers.

Name	Pinkie Leroo
Height	On point
Weight	Pretty face
Appearance	Below average
Hobbies	Playing with my twelve cats
Favorite pastime	Washing my hair
Profession	Taxidermies

Hair color	Pink – notice my name (insert eye roll)
Eyes	Star struck
Skin	Pasty white

I go onto the internet and search for a picture of a cat, find an image of a huge fat one with bulging eyes. It's the ugliest cat I ever saw.

"Here, kitty, kitty." I smile as I upload it as my profile pic.

I read the question again:

What are you looking for?

I inhale deeply as I think, *hmm* . . . I want to write something that will show me what I already know, that nobody interests me at all. I twist my lips as I contemplate my words.

I'm looking for someone who is only one color,
but not one size. Stuck at the bottom, yet easily
flies. Present in sun, but not in rain.

Doing no harm, but feeling no pain.

I smile and hit submit: that will weed them out.
Nobody will respond.

It's Thursday, and it's been the best week I've had in a long time.

Daniel is hilarious, and we've been out to dinner every night, because apparently, he doesn't ever feel like anything home-cooked.

We have champagne taste on a beer budget.

He's announced that, by default, we are his official best friends now, seeing as he has nobody else in town. He even asked me to go to an event next week that he's been invited to. I'm going as his date, but there is no date, it's not like that between us.

I do have to admit though, he's great company.

Oh, and surprise, surprise . . . nobody has messaged me on my dating app.

Just like I knew they wouldn't.

I smile as I wriggle into my netball uniform.

I'm in the bathroom stall in my office building, work has finished for the day, and I'm playing netball at six-thirty, and there isn't enough time to go home and get back into town.

I slide it down over my shoulders and cringe as I look at myself. "Oh . . . yuck," I whisper. "This is hideous."

Skintight, bright red, the dress sticks to my body like super glue and it's super short.

I walk to the mirror to stare at my reflection. I look like a netball player in some sicko porn gang team skit.

I don't know whether to laugh or cry.

"Ugh, who picked these uniforms?" I sigh as I rearrange my boobs. "So ugly."

I shrug my shoulders. Oh well. I pull my hair up into a high ponytail and make my way back to my office. It's too early to go yet, so I'll finish up some odd jobs while I wait.

ELLIOT

I glance at my watch. Jameson and Tristan are here and have gone downstairs with Christopher. I'm just finishing up these reports and then we're heading out. Running the London arm of Miles Media, one of the biggest media companies in the world, has its trials and tribulations. I get to be the boss, but with that comes a never-ending sense of responsibility.

My brother Jameson is the CEO of the United States company, and I oversee UK and Germany. We run France together. It's a stressful role, but one that I enjoy immensely.

They've been ages, what the hell are they doing?

I click onto the security camera to see if they're close; a collage of pictures comes up on my computer screen. I glance through them to see that they are on level one, and am just about to click out of it when something bright flashes in the bottom left of the screen, catching my eye.

What's that?

I click to enlarge that screen for a closer investigation.

It's a woman wearing a high ponytail—she's in a bright red, Lycra sports dress . . . It's fitted and all-in-one and has a little short flared skirt . . . Huh?

She has her back to the camera and is standing at a photocopier.

I study the screen to try and make out where the footage is from. It looks like . . . a photocopy room, maybe. I can't quite place it, is she a cleaner or something? No, a cleaner wouldn't be photocopying.

I'm confused.

I turn up the audio of that camera and I hear music; a man's voice comes on.

"Good evening, you're listening to Disco with Dave."

The radio is playing.

"I've got your number tonight, groovy people. Get ready to party with the best disco tunes of all time," his voice continues.

A song comes on, it's catchy and familiar, although I can't place it.

The woman in the short Lycra dress begins to wiggle her behind to the beat; she double-bumps to one side and then the other.

Hmm, interesting.

Leaning on my desk, I press my index finger along my temple as I watch her moving to "Ring My Bell."

She's really dancing as she photocopies and I smirk; my eyes drop to her long legs, which are muscular and shapely. Her waist is small and the curve of her hips is accentuated by the way she sashays from side to side.

Hmm . . .

I run the side of my finger over my lips and sit back, totally distracted by the hot ass bumping in the red dress.

The way she bounces to the beat is so joyful . . . She's dancing like nobody is watching. Only I am, and it's very . . .

She drops one of her papers and bends over with straight legs to pick it up; I get a full view of her tight ass in her tiny red Lycra shorts.

My cock twitches, my eyebrows rise in surprise, and I sit forward in my seat, my interest officially piqued.

She rolls her hips and a wave of arousal runs through me; I begin to hear my pulse in my ears. The way she dances and moves is so . . .

Fucking hot.

My cock pitches a tent in my pants and I inhale sharply. I can't remember the last time a woman aroused me on sight alone.

She drops another file and wiggles down to pick it up, and once again I get a full view of her muscular legs and ass. I inhale sharply as she stands, my body imagines what she would feel like, and I rearrange myself in my pants.

Delicious.

She turns toward the camera and for the first time I see her face; I jump back from my computer.

What the fuck?

It's Kathryn . . .

"You ready?" Tristan's voice sounds from behind me.

I immediately click out of the footage and shuffle the papers on my desk, completely flustered.

"I'll meet you in the lobby," I stammer. "Just got to take care of something."

"Okay, don't be long, hey?" Jameson says.

I hear them leave in the elevator and I stare at my computer screen in shock.

No.

Couldn't be.

Kathryn's not hot, she's never been hot. I would have noticed if she was that fucking hot.

My cock is thumping, demanding attention, and I guiltily look back at the door to make sure my brothers are gone.

Just another quick look . . . Wouldn't hurt.

It probably wasn't even her.

I open the computer screen again and see the red dress bouncing to the beat.

It is her.

She's facing the camera now and my eyes roam over the way her breasts are bouncing. The curve in her neck, the cinch in her waist. The way her high ponytail moves as she dances.

I get a vision of wrapping that ponytail around my hand as I pull her down to suck me off.

My cock clenches. I shudder with a disgusted shake of my head.

Fuck . . .

I need to get laid.

Chapter 2

I pack up my desk with haste—I want to get far from my computer as quickly as possible. I close it down and with one last look around my office, I head to the elevator, hit the button with force, and exhale heavily.

I'm rattled: it's rare that a woman gives me a physical reaction anymore. Lately I've been struggling with attraction issues, nobody seems to be doing it for me, no matter how beautiful they are, and I have no idea why. Perhaps it's the fact that I've dated some of the most beautiful, extraordinary women in the world, and yet, still. I haven't found what I'm looking for. Perhaps my brothers are right about my standards being unrealistically high.

But, a rock-hard boner from an employee I despise, Kathryn Landon.

Just fucking no.

I march out of the elevator and into the lobby, and see Jameson, Tristan, and Christopher waiting out on the curb for me. Jay and Christopher are looking at something on Jameson's phone, deep in conversation.

"We going?" I snap impatiently. "Or what?"

Tristan looks up. "We're waiting for you, dick. What do you think?"

I roll my eyes as I run my hand through my hair. "Drinks?"

"Yeah," Jay mutters.

We turn the corner and begin to walk, and Tristan digs his phone out of his pocket; his eyes narrow when he sees the name on the screen.

"Who is it?" I ask.

"Malcolm, my neighbor at home." He answers it. "Hi Malcolm."

He listens as we walk and then he narrows his eyes at me and gives a subtle shake of his head.

"What?" I mouth.

"Harrison," he mouths.

I chuckle. Tristan's middle son is sending him grey.

Wild as a bear.

"Okay, thanks for letting me know, Malcolm, I'll take care of it from here." He listens. "No, I appreciate you not calling Claire, she has her hands full with the girls," he says. "Thanks again." He hangs up and immediately dials a number. "I'm going to kill this fucking kid with a smile on my face," he mutters under his breath.

I smile as I walk along and listen.

"Harrison," he barks. "Do you mind telling me why Malcolm just called to tell me that you were speeding down our street late last night? Said you were going way over the speed limit."

He listens.

"Listen," he barks. "I spoke to you about this only last week. You are driving way too fast for someone who only just got their license and I'm not putting up with it." He listens again. "Don't give me that bullshit. Why would Malcolm make this up?" He rolls his eyes in disgust. "Malcolm is not trying

31

to get you into trouble. No, I warned you. You've lost your car for a month."

He listens again, his face murderous.

I chuckle and turn to see Jay and Christopher trailing behind us, still looking at a phone. "What *are* you two doing?" I snap.

"Looking for something," Chris replies. He gestures at Tristan. "Who's he yelling at?"

"One guess." I sigh.

Jameson smirks. "What did Harry do now?"

"Speeding."

"Hand your keys over to your mother right now, young man . . . or I am getting on the first flight home," Tristan growls. "Do you understand me!"

He listens again.

"This may come as a shock to you, Harrison, but you are not invincible," he snaps. "You're going to cause an accident or, heaven forbid, kill yourself, and I'm not having it. Hand the damn keys over."

"Dramatic bitch," Jameson says as he rolls his eyes.

I laugh; watching Tristan navigate rebellious teenagers might just be my favorite pastime.

Tristan hangs up and stuffs his phone in his pocket, fuming mad. "That fucking kid, every single time I go away he gets into shit." He punches his hand into his fist.

We walk into a bar and take a seat at the back; the waitress approaches us. "What will it be?"

"I'll have a Blue Label Scotch please," Tristan replies way too fast. "Actually, make it a double."

"I'll have a Corona." I smile; nobody riles Tristan up like Harry does.

"Same," Christopher replies.

32

"Make that three," Jameson says.

Christopher laughs as they see something on Jameson's phone, and then they pass it over to me.

"What's this?" I ask as I take the phone from them. I look at the screen and see a photo of myself and frown as I try to make sense of it. "What is this?"

"This dating app is using your photograph." Christopher smirks.

"You have got to be kidding me," I snap. "Surely anyone with half a brain knows that I would never go on a dating app."

"Well, you look pretty and they're just using your image to hook up with chicks." Tristan smiles. "However, if they really wanted to pull the chicks they should have used my photo."

I scroll through the app angrily. "Where do I report this shit? I want this taken down immediately."

"There should be some kind of info or admin section," Christopher says as our drinks arrive. The boys fall into conversation and I keep flicking through the app as I look for a contact page where I can report this piece of shit. I'm scrolling through when something catches my eye, the ugliest cat I have ever seen, fat and hairy with bulging eyes. Who the fuck would use that as a profile picture on a dating app?

My eyes roam over the profile and the name Pinkie Leroo. Pinkie Leroo. I frown. What kind of name is that?

I read her ad.

Name	Pinkie Leroo
Height	On point
Weight	Pretty face

Appearance	**Below average**
Hobbies	**Playing with my twelve cats**
Favorite pastime	**Washing my hair**
Profession	**Taxidermies**
Hair color	**Pink – notice my name (insert eye roll)**
Eyes	**Star struck**
Skin	**Pasty white**

Below-average appearance . . . who says that?

Taxidermies . . . She stuffs dead animals for a living? Who is this freak? I've officially heard it all.

I can't believe that people actually find dates on this website . . . How?

I get a vision of a pasty-white, pink-haired woman sitting on a couch with twelve cats, surrounded by stuffed animal corpses, and I cringe.

Good grief.

I read on.

I'm looking for someone who is only one color, but not one size. Stuck at the bottom, yet easily flies. Present in sun, but not in rain.

Doing no harm, but feeling no pain.

Oh please. I roll my eyes.

I screenshot a picture of the profile that has been stolen from me and I send it to myself to deal with later.

It's late, after dinner and drinks with the boys, and I'm back in my apartment, unwinding. The moonlight streams through the window and I sip my Scotch and sit back in my armchair.

I stare at the colors, the way they fade into the darkness. The beams of light that filter down from the heavens.

I do this often, sit here late at night and inhale the beauty of the painting on my wall.

I read the title:

Fated

What was she thinking about when she painted this?

A possession, a situation. What was fated?

A person?

I lift the glass to my lips and feel the heat as the amber fluid slides down my throat.

Harriet Boucher . . . the woman I am enamored with, a woman I don't even know. As strange as it sounds, I feel like I do know her.

There's an honesty to the brushstrokes, a deeper connection to her emotion, something I don't feel from other paintings. It's the weirdest thing and something that I can't quite explain.

Looking at Harriet's paintings is like looking into her soul.

Breathtaking.

I smile as I imagine the older woman; I know she's beautiful, perhaps not physically any longer, but definitely spiritually . . . emotionally.

She's French from what I've heard and only recently came onto the scene. Harriet Boucher is an artist that I follow, I've got all of her paintings apart from three. There are only thirty in circulation, she's a recluse and nobody knows who she is—there are only whispers.

I only have interest in the finest, most unique pieces of art. I've spent millions of dollars and my collection is one of the best in the world.

But Harriet is the queen; she's the one whose work I chase.

I visualize her in a quaint French country town, painting outdoors on an easel. I wonder how many years ago she painted this and at what stage in her life she was at?

Was she young or old, in love?

And who was fated, the love of her life . . . and their child?

I exhale heavily as I stare at my beloved painting. I'm going to look deeper into this, I have this need to know who she is.

I own twenty-seven of her paintings, have spent a fortune, and yet the hunger to meet her still eats at me.

Why . . . I don't know.

What I do know is that I don't want to be thinking about Kathryn Landon, I need a distraction.

I'm going to make some calls on Monday to try and find out more.

I have to, it isn't even a choice anymore. I need to know the person who affects me so deeply . . . if only just to tell her so.

I open my phone and am reminded of the fake profile on that cheap and nasty dating app.

It's misleading, I have to get it taken down. I go to search on the app and it won't let me past the front page unless I join and make a profile.

I roll my eyes in disgust. Fuck's sake . . . what is this shit?

I lean on my hand as I watch the red skirt twirl, the way her hips move, the long legs, the sexuality of the whole package . . . I've replayed this security footage more than I care to admit, maybe on the hour. I can't stop watching it, again and again.

It's a guilty pleasure, the ultimate kink in porn.

Although I would like to, I can't deny it, Kathryn Landon turns me on.

A knock sounds at my door and I quickly minimize the screen. "Yes," I call.

Christopher puts his head around the door. "I'm going downstairs, want to come for a walk?"

"Where to?"

"IT."

My eyebrows rise. "IT?"

"Yeah, I have to check a few details with Kathryn on that report."

I'm standing before I have time to answer.

"You're coming?" he asks in surprise.

"Yeah, why not? I need to stretch my legs."

We take the elevator and two minutes later we arrive on level ten, the IT floor. There are workstations throughout and at the back are six offices with glass walls as partitions, slimline black venetian blinds offering privacy to each office.

I follow Christopher down the corridor as people dive for their desks and pretend to work. I never come to this floor. Never needed to; not exactly sure why I'm here now.

Christopher stops to talk to someone and I continue on, get to the first glass door and read the sign:

Kathryn Landon

Hmm, even reading her name leaves a bitter taste in my mouth. "Knock, knock."

"Come in."

I open the door. "Hello."

Kathryn looks up from her computer as if surprised. "Hello Mr. Miles, and to what do I owe this honor?"

I press my lips together so I don't say something snarky; this woman brings out the smart-ass in me tenfold. "Just doing a tour, thought I'd pop in."

She fakes a smile. "How lovely, the king has come to visit his faithful servants."

I glare at her as I clench my jaw.

How can someone who when she dances is so happy and joyful, not to mention insanely hot . . . be filled with pure venom?

I walk in and close the door behind me, take a seat at her desk and link my hands in front of me.

She stares at me as she waits for me to speak . . . I don't, we remain silent.

"Well?" She smiles.

I narrow my eyes as I stare at her; what is it with this fucking woman?

Nobody treats me the way she does, my mere existence pisses her off.

She smiles as if she's happy, but what comes out of her mouth is always low-key aggressive. She's the ultimate temper bait.

"Well what?" I reply.

"Are you going to talk to me on your visit?"

I dust my jacket off as I try to think of something to say. "How do you like working here?" I ask.

She rolls her eyes. "Are you going to try and pay me off to resign again?"

I wince. I did do that . . . didn't I?

"Of course not," I snap. "Don't be ridiculous."

She exhales heavily and turns back to her computer. "Well, do you want to discuss anything?"

That little red dress you own.

"Not particularly." I run my pointer finger back and forth over my lips as I stare at her.

"So . . ." She raises an eyebrow. "What is it?"

"What do you mean, what?"

"Why are you acting weird?" she asks.

"I'm not," I scoff as I stand. "I came to visit you, but obviously you don't want visitors."

"Mr. Miles."

"Elliot," I correct her.

She frowns as she stares at me. "Okay, you asking me to call you that is weird in itself. I've been here for seven years and never once have you asked me to call you that or bothered to visit me."

"I've been very busy," I fire back.

"For seven years?" She raises an eyebrow.

"Precisely." I move for the door. "And now I know why I've been so busy."

"Why is that?"

"Because you're a very bad host, Kathryn."

A trace of a smile crosses her face. "Are you high?"

"What?" I snap. "Of course I'm not fucking high."

"Okay . . ."

I inhale deeply as I try to think of something to rectify this fuckup of a conversation. "I'm leaving," I announce.

She smirks. "Okay . . ."

"Is that all you can say today . . . okay?"

She narrows her eyes. "Mr. Miles."

"Elliot," I correct her.

"Elliot, are you feeling alright?"

"I was until I visited you." I exhale heavily. "Now you've completely ruined my day."

She smiles as she puts her hand over her chest. "There he is, oh thank God, I thought I was going to have to call a doctor."

I glare at her. "Goodbye, Kathryn."

She smiles sweetly and waves with her fingertips. "Goodbye, have a nice day, my favorite boss ever."

"Don't patronize me," I snap.

She turns back to her computer. "Just being a good office host. How am I doing?"

"Failing miserably." I march out of her office and back to the elevator.

I push the button with force and clench my jaw as I try to think of a reasonable excuse as to why I came down here.

Nope . . .

I've got nothing.

The woman's a bona fide bitch.

Kate

I walk out of the front doors of my building an hour later to see Daniel's big smile: he's leaning against his parked car on the other side of the road.

I smile and wave and make my way over to him across one of the busiest streets in London. "How did you find a parking space here?"

"Just lucky, I guess." He winks. "I thought we could go shopping for a little bit." He throws his arm over my shoulders as we stroll along.

"Shopping?" I screw up my face. "Ugh, I don't want to go shopping, I can think of nothing worse. I'll meet you at home."

"Well . . ." He pauses as if getting the wording right in his head. "You know how I told you that I got invited to that function on Thursday night and I asked you to come with me?"

"Yeah."

"Well, I asked some questions and I've just been sent the guest list."

"So?"

"Every potential client in the entire world will be in that ballroom."

I screw up my face again. "Will you speak English, what the hell are you talking about?"

"You need to look fucking incredible."

"Me?" I scoff as I point to my chest. "Why me?"

"Because everyone will know that I styled you."

I stop on the spot. "I'm not being your walking billboard, Daniel," I snap. "I've changed my mind, I don't want to go anymore, take Rebecca instead. She can be your mannequin."

"No. I need you." He links his arm through mine and drags me along. "You have the look that I need and I know exactly what I'm doing with you. And don't worry, I'm footing the entire bill."

"Why would you offer to pay?"

"Well, I'm returning everything on Friday. Don't get excited, I'm not that nice."

"Isn't that, I don't know . . . a crime?" My eyes widen in exasperation.

"Only a little bit, and if you ruin anything, I'll kill you. Oh, and I've booked you in for a hair and makeup appointment."

"What's wrong with my hair?" I cry.

He runs his fingers over the top of my head and over the neat bun nestled tightly in the back. "Nothing . . . if you were ninety."

I roll my eyes as he drags me along.

"First stop, Givenchy." He smiles happily.

"Are you crazy?" I gasp. "You can't afford Givenchy."

"Oh, shut up already." He scoffs as he pulls me up the front steps of the swanky building. "I'm faking it till I make it, and if you're with me, so are you."

I look down at myself and throw my hands up in the air in surrender. "I look like a damn Christmas bauble."

Daniel on bended knee with a pin sticking out of his mouth. He sticks his hand up the bottom of my dress and fiddles with the hem. "Nothing about this outfit says Christmas." He huffs. "Name one thing that's Christmassy."

"Oh, I don't know." I glance up at my reflection in the mirror. "Maybe the painted nails, or the big red lips, perhaps the gold string stilettos . . . oh wait, what about the blazing bright gold fucking strapless dress."

"You look awesome, Kate, just admit it." Rebecca smiles dreamily as she lies on the carpeted floor.

I nervously glance up at myself in the mirror again and brush my hands over my hips. "But I don't look like me."

"That's the point," Daniel says as he stands and fluffs my hair. "Your hair is incredible at this length."

"I love the blonde highlights too," Beck chimes in. "How much did he cut off?"

"Four inches. It was way too long; did you wear it up every day?" Daniel asks.

"I wear it up for work, that's all."

"No more, you look ten times hotter with your hair down. If I see it up again I'm ripping it out, and I don't care where we are or who sees."

"You're beginning to become an annoying flatmate," I mutter dryly.

"Flattered." Daniel takes out his phone and begins to snap away.

"I don't want to be on your Instagram," I huff.

"Oh, will you shut up." He sighs as he snaps away. "Do you know how many women would kill to be styled like this?"

He's right.

I smirk.

"And for free, I might add," he says. "I'm very fucking expensive, you know?"

"Sorry." I give him a lopsided smile. "I'm just . . ."

"Just what, darling?"

"I feel very . . ." My voice trails off.

He drops his phone as he looks over the top of it. "Very what?"

43

I gesture to my boobs and then down to my hips. "Exposed."

Daniel smiles proudly as he holds his hands together. "Angel, if I had a figure like yours, I wouldn't bother with clothes at all."

I roll my eyes. "That's because you're a raving ho bag."

Daniel chuckles with a cheeky shrug of his shoulders. "I am, aren't I?"

"It's not a compliment," I reply as my attention turns back to the mirror.

My now shoulder-length hair is a honey blonde and set into big curls, my dress is strapless and gold—it fits like a glove and leaves nothing to the imagination. My makeup is smoky with big red lips. I don't look like me. I look like someone you would see in a magazine and that makes me nervous as all hell. I put my hand on my stomach. "I've got butterflies," I whisper.

Daniel holds his arm out and I link mine through it. "That's the universe's way of telling you that you look divine." He smiles proudly.

"Thanks." I look down at his black dinner suit. "You look pretty gorgeous yourself."

"I know, right?" He winks and passes his phone to Rebecca. "One for the gram."

Rebecca stands and takes a photo and Daniel's phone beeps a message, which he checks. "Our car is here," he announces.

He kisses Rebecca on the cheek. "Don't wait up, sweets, we'll be setting the town on fire all night long."

Rebecca smirks and I chuckle. "You're so dramatic."

He whisks me out the door. "Always, angel, always."

I link my arm through Daniel's as we walk into the ballroom. "I'm so nervous I feel like I may throw up any minute," I whisper as we walk through the beautiful-people crowd. Everyone is dressed to the nines in black tie; it really is spectacular.

"Why?" he whispers back. "Because you look hot for a change?"

He leads me through to the seating map and I glance over and see Elliot Miles. "Fuck," I whisper as I turn my head away in disgust.

"What now?"

"My fucking boss is here."

"So?"

"So . . . he's a giant twat," I whisper angrily. "I can't see him, looking like this."

Daniel looks over my shoulder in his direction. "Oh . . . hell," he whispers. "That's your . . . boss? Casanova Miles is your fucking boss . . . are you kidding me?"

"Why did you call him that?"

"That's the press's nickname for him. Well earned from what I hear."

I glance over my shoulder at him: Elliot is talking to his three brothers. Oh no, they're all here. "Don't be fooled by his good looks, he'd cut your kidneys out with a blink of an eye," I say.

"Baby . . . he could cut anything out and it would probably still feel good."

I roll my eyes in disgust.

"Let's go to the bar." Daniel smiles as he pulls me along by the hand.

We get our champagne and his eyes go back to the corner where the Miles brothers are standing; he lifts his glass to his lips. "Well, well, well, he sure does have some powerful friends."

"Who?"

"Your boss."

"Oh, him." I sip my champagne, wishing I could drain the entire glass. "Who cares?" I concentrate on sucking my stomach in. "This dress is suffocating me," I whisper.

"Look who he's talking to," he replies, totally distracted.

"Did you hear me? I can't breathe in these Spanx. Why did I need to wear this fucking ridiculous underwear?" I whisper.

"To hold your coochie in. He's talking to Julian Masters and Spencer Jones."

I laugh and snort my champagne up my nose. "Coochie?" I cough.

He slaps me on the back.

"What is a coochie?" I giggle.

His eyes stay fixed on the Miles brothers over my shoulder. "That hairy thing between your legs."

I burst out laughing. "What the hell?" I continue to choke while I laugh.

"Julian Masters comes from one of the wealthiest families in the world, he's a Supreme Court judge," he continues.

I sip my drink, uninterested. "For your information, my coochie isn't hairy and it most definitely doesn't need to be held in."

"Spencer Jones is a player, everything he does is across the tabloids." He sips his champagne. "All coochies need to be held in. Unsightly things in evening wear."

I giggle. "How many coochies have you seen through evening wear?"

"Too many to count, hideous mounds. Oh . . ." He lets out a low whistle. "And here comes Sebastian Garcia."

I frown, and glance over. I definitely know the name of the prime minister of the United Kingdom. "Maybe they're just seated together?"

"No, they're acting like long-lost friends."

I look around at all the beautiful people, so many gorgeous dresses. Imagine what it must be like to come to swanky events like this all the time.

"Oh, look," Daniel whispers. "He spotted you."

"Who?" I sip my drink.

"Elliot Miles." He smiles darkly. "And . . . he likes what he sees."

"What?" I frown.

"He's eyeing you up and down."

"What?" My eyes widen. "What do you mean?"

"I mean, he's fucking checking you out."

"Well, he won't see anything," I whisper. "Because my coochie is buried under the tightest underwear on earth."

Daniel chuckles and taps his glass on mine. "Touché."

"Where are we seated?" I ask.

"He's coming over."

"What?"

"With his brother."

Oh no.

"Kate." I hear a voice from behind me.

"Tristan." I smile.

He kisses both my cheeks. "Holy shit, when did you get so hot?" He laughs. "You look incredible."

I glance over his shoulder to Elliot standing there; he gives me a stifled smile with a curt nod. He's not friendly like his brother.

"Tristan, this is Daniel. Daniel, this is Tristan." They shake hands.

"Elliot, this is Daniel. Daniel, this is Elliot." Elliot gives him a nod and shakes his hand.

No smile, no greeting.

Eesh . . . *awkward.*

"I'm going to the bar," Daniel says.

"I'll come," Tristan replies, and they walk off together.

Oh no.

My eyes float to Elliot as he stares at me; there's this awkwardness between us. "Have you come to make fun of me dressed like this?" I ask.

47

"On the contrary, I came over to tell you that you look beautiful, but I'll take it back now. You obviously don't want to hear it."

I grip my champagne glass so tight that it might smash in my bare hands.

"Is he your boyfriend?" he asks.

"Um." I glance over to Daniel and Tristan at the bar. "Friend."

Elliot's eyes hold mine. "What kind of friend?"

"Not . . . that kind."

He nods once. "I see."

"Is your . . . girlfriend here?"

"I don't have a girlfriend."

"Wife?"

"No," he replies curtly.

"Oh."

An awkward silence falls between us and I see the muscles in his jaw clench as if he's uncomfortable too.

"Excuse me while I go to the bathroom." I smile.

He nods once.

"Lovely to see you, Mr. Miles."

"Elliot." His eyes hold mine. "Likewise."

Our gaze holds for a few seconds longer than it should.

What's going on here?

He's different.

The night has been a whirlwind. I haven't laughed so much for as long as I can remember. We've danced and drunk and Daniel has schmoozed with the women he needs to style and I've had a wonderful time. It's late and the night is coming to an end.

"Home time." He smiles as we sway to the music, then he looks across the room. "Kate . . . what is going on with you and your boss?"

"Nothing, why?"

"He hasn't taken his eyes off you all night."

"Don't be ridiculous," I scoff, but I do have to admit, every time I look Elliot's way, he's already looking at me. "He is not."

"I'm telling you, darling, I can read men's minds."

I giggle. "And what is his mind saying?"

"It's saying that he's going to bend you over his desk and fuck you hard."

I giggle again. "I don't think so."

"It's so unusual."

"What is?"

"Do you know the kind of women he usually dates?"

"No, and I don't care."

"Darling, you really need to keep up to date on current events. Don't you read the tabloids?"

"No, and I'm appalled that you do."

"He dated an acclaimed opera singer, an author, a humanitarian lawyer. He never dates run-of-the-mill women, and he wants you."

"Should I be flattered to be the run-of-the-mill woman, then?"

"You know what I mean." He gives me a cheeky wink.

I burst out laughing and he spins me around. I lock eyes with Elliot Miles and he gives me the best come-fuck-me look I have ever seen.

Our eyes lock and for a moment, time stops.

My stomach flutters and I snap my eyes away.

What the fuck was that?

It's late Tuesday night. I make a cup of tea and sit it on my bedside table, begin to flick through my phone, and click on the dating app.

You've got mail.

What?

I open the chat box and read the message.

> Dear Miss Leroo,
>
> You do sound very tempting indeed. Nevertheless, I have an allergy to cats and with twelve of your own, dating you is an impossibility.
>
> My best advice is to go outside and look to the ground, there you will find your one true love, although as we both know, dating a shadow would have its own obstacles.
>
> I'm sure you are attempting (very poorly, I may add) to be witty.
>
> Life must be pretty boring at your end.
>
> Good luck in your dating ventures, Miss Leroo. With pick-up lines such as yours, you're going to need it.
>
> Keep chasing that sun.
>
> Edgar Moffatt.

I click on his profile.

Name	Edgar Moffatt
Height	4ft2

Weight	Snack size
Appearance	Very handsome
Hobbies	Playing with my small dick
Favorite pastime	Watching porn
Profession	Garbologist / dick fondler
Hair color	Bald as a badger
Eyes	Green
Skin	All over my body

A goofy smile crosses my face and I slump back against my headboard as I reread the message.

Keep chasing that sun.

That's what I'm doing, Edgar Moffatt the dick fondler, that's what I'm doing.

I sit my head back against the wall as the sweat runs down my chest; it's around 8 p.m. on Wednesday night and after the longest day in history, I'm in the sauna at the gym.

It's hot and steamy and I let out a relaxed sigh.

The door opens and Elliot Miles appears with a white towel wrapped around his waist. He's naked from the waist up and tanned skin and muscles are all I see.

Oh crap.

I swallow the lump in my throat.

He glances up and his step falters as he sees me. "Kathryn." He takes a seat.

"Hi," I squeak.

The door opens and a man goes to walk in.

"This is full," Elliot snaps. "Come back later."

Chapter 3

I stare straight ahead. Shit . . . Don't look at him, don't look at him, *don't look at him*.

"I didn't know you used the gym at work?" he replies casually.

"Uh-huh." I smile awkwardly as I keep my eyes straight to the front. What is the correct etiquette for saunas? I mean, I've been in here a few times already and never once have I had to concentrate on not looking at anyone.

The air is thick and hot and I find a piece of wood on the back of the door and stare at it. Elliot's presence is all-consuming and taking up the small space; I can almost feel his nakedness under that towel from here.

Look straight ahead, I remind myself.

Don't give him the satisfaction of drooling over his muscles. Dammit, why does he have to have them?

"How was your day?" he asks.

"Fine thanks." I smile. "How was yours?"

"It just got a lot better, thank you."

My brow furrows, what does that mean? Does that mean it got better when he got in here with me? I run my finger in a circle on the wood on the bench beside me, unsure what to say or where to look.

Or what to think.

My mind wants to go to a dark place and glance over at the golden muscles that I can feel taunting me from my peripheral vision.

But I won't, I'll continue to stare straight ahead.

"Do you come to the gym often?" I ask to try and fill the awkward void between us.

"Not often enough," he says. "I have a gym at home and usually run there at night. But it's late tonight and I know once I get there I will want to relax. I did a quick half an hour on the treadmill."

I get a vision of him running, and the sweat dripping down his . . .

I grip the seat beneath me with white-knuckle force. "Oh" is all I can force out of my mouth. I glance down at myself: my black bikini top is covering all my bits.

Just.

What must he think?

"Do you always stare at the wall in the sauna?" Elliot asks

"Well, it's a square wooden box." I shrug. "What am I supposed to look at?"

Elliot lets out a low chuckle and I bite my lip to hide my embarrassed smile. He knows that I'm avoiding looking at him with all my might.

"I don't know, perhaps the person you're talking to?" he replies.

I drag my eyes over to him.

"That's better." His eyes hold mine and then he gives me a slow, sexy smile.

I feel it in the pit of my stomach as the butterflies flutter.

What the hell is going on here? I swear to God he's different, but I can't put my finger on why.

If I didn't know better, I would even say he's more than friendly, perhaps a tad flirty. It's like I've missed part of the conversation, but I'm really not sure what it is.

"Why would you like me to look at you, Elliot?" I ask as I focus on looking at his face.

It's been a long time between drinks for me, and by drinks, I mean sex. I hate to admit it, but after seeing Elliot Miles in his black dinner suit last week, he's run naked through my mind more than once.

Unable to help it, my gaze drops. Just as I suspected, a thick, broad chest with a scattering of dark hair, chiseled shoulders, and a fifty-pack of stomach muscles. His skin is a beautiful glowing tan. It makes the towel look fluorescent white.

We sit in silence for a few minutes. While he seems perfectly happy with the situation, I just want the earth to swallow me up so I can die. If I stand to leave he gets a full bird's-eye view of my body.

Warts and all.

I mean, I have a towel, but it's freaking tiny. Why did I have to be saving space in my damn gym bag?

He leans back and rests against the wall, his stomach muscles contracting as they catch the light.

Don't look down, whatever you do, don't fucking look down.

Well, this is just great. I come in here to relax, and instead get a bird's-eye view of my asshole boss's hot body.

"How long have you known Daniel?" he asks.

I frown, how does he even remember his name? "Not very long. Why do you ask?"

Elliot's eyes hold mine and he gives a gentle shrug. "No reason. You said that you were just friends—"

I cut him off. "We are just friends."

He raises an eyebrow. "He's very touchy."

"What? No he isn't. That's just his personality. He's very affectionate."

"I noticed," he says dryly.

I stare at him as my brain malfunctions. "Why would you notice that?" I ask. "And more importantly, why would it matter to you?"

"It doesn't," he fires back way too fast. "Merely an observation."

This is bizarre.

If I didn't know better, I would say he's a little jealous. But that's ridiculous and we both know he couldn't be.

I stare at him as I try to unravel the puzzle. "What's your problem?" I ask.

"No problem," he snaps. He stands in a rush, and for the first time I get a full view of his Adonis physique.

Jeez.

Elliot Miles may be a lot of things, but I can confirm with certainty that he looks good in a towel.

Not that I care, of course.

"So, I've been thinking about you," Daniel says as we walk down the street on our way to pick up our Thai takeout, his arm linked through mine.

"What about me?" I ask.

"Don't take offense at this."

I roll my eyes. "When someone says don't take offense, it means they're going to say something offensive."

He smiles and his eyes come over to me. "What were you like before your parents died?"

"What do you mean?"

"What were you like? Did you dress different? Did you have hobbies, were you social?"

I drop my head as we walk; nobody has ever asked me this before. "I guess I was . . ." My voice trails off as I shrug. "I don't know."

"Did you make an effort to look pretty every day?"

I think back and I nod. "Yes."

"Were you focused on work all the time?"

I shake my head sadly. "Not in the least."

"Did you have a boyfriend?"

"I did, but we broke up not long after they died."

"And you haven't had a long-term relationship since?"

I shrug.

"Baby." He leans down and kisses my shoulder. "I've been wondering why someone as beautiful as you . . . acts the way you do."

I frown in a question.

"You hide behind your grief, don't you?"

My eyes well with tears and I drop my head. To hear someone say it out loud . . .

I haven't been the same since that day, I know I haven't.

I miss my parents, I miss their unconditional love. And their deaths shouldn't be about me, but why did they leave me here all alone?

I get a lump in my throat.

I angrily wipe a lone tear away as it escapes. "Stop it, I don't want to talk about this."

Daniel kisses my shoulder again. "Okay. We won't. I should have got the spring rolls, I'm fucking starving," he says to change the subject. He squeezes my arm.

I fake a smile, and for the first time in a long time, I feel like someone gets me.

I twist the ring around my finger as I stare into space; I'm on the train and on my way home from work, and I'm trying to analyze the last few days. I've been busy and preoccupied, but for the life of me, I can't stop thinking about what Daniel said about me hiding behind my grief.

Is that why I'm so anal at work, because the alternative is to fall apart and lose my job?

If I don't look pretty, nobody will notice me . . . and my heart can never get broken again.

My mind is a clusterfuck of confusion and, through it all, I can't get the vision of Elliot Miles in a towel out of my head.

I think about those muscles when I wake up, I think about them when I go to work, I think about them when I go to sleep. In the shower, in the gym, alone in bed . . . you name it, I've thunk it. And trust me, the things I'm thinking are going to get me sent straight to hell. Let's just say that in my dreams Elliot Miles has spent a lot of time with his head between my legs, and boy is his tongue strong. I can almost see my arousal glistening on his lips as he looks up at me, feel the burn of his stubble on my inner thighs.

I keep fantasizing about being summoned to his office and getting bent over his desk while he has his wicked way with me, and it's hot and hard and sweaty.

And it goes on and on and on.

Jeez . . . what the hell is going on with me lately?

And the worst part of it is, I don't even like him. In fact, up until a week ago I would even say that I despised him.

But something is changing in me, and I don't know what it is or how to explain it.

My hormones are having some kind of meltdown and I've turned into one of those people who think about sex all the time.

That white towel is a damn troublemaker.

We approach my stop and I stand and catch a glimpse of my reflection in the glass door, feel disappointed with what I see. I look dowdy, and so different to how I looked the other night at the ball.

Maybe it's time.

I smile as I read the email from my place in bed, and I reply.

Dear Edgar,

Such a shame that you are not a cat person, you could have had a happy life filled with feline love.

I am fascinated though, what would you suggest I use for pick-up lines in the future?

As a dick fondler, your word is gospel.

I will wait for your reply with bated breath.

Pinkie Leroo

"Goodnight," Daniel says as he pokes his head around the door. I look up from my computer.

"Night."

"What are you doing?" he asks.

"Ah." I shrug bashfully. "Fooling around on the computer, what time did you get home?"

"Just now."

"How did today go?"

He leans on the doorjamb. "Well, today I styled the biggest pain in the ass that I've ever met."

"Why?"

"Tells me that she wants a complete new look but then hates everything I recommended and refuses to even try it on."

I smile. "Is that common?"

"Sometimes. Usually with people who haven't been styled before. Change is scary for some people."

"I guess."

"Not you though, you are a complete pro, look what you wore last week."

I smile bashfully, and an idea comes to mind. I hesitate as I look over at my closet. "Maybe I should get you to help me buy some new clothes."

"Well, well . . . well."

"I mean." I twist my fingers on my lap, embarrassed that I just said that out loud. "I mean . . ."

"You aren't superficial."

"Exactly."

"But you just need a few pointers."

"Yes." I smile, and think for a moment. "What would you wear to work tomorrow if you were me?"

Daniel's eyes hold mine. "If I wanted to . . . ?" His voice trails off.

"I don't know." I shrug. "Look nice."

"To impress a certain CEO?"

"No." I scoff. "This has nothing to do with Elliot Miles."

Daniel goes to my closet and begins to flick through the hangers. "Honey, it should." I hear him rattling around in there. "Where are your skirts?"

I frown and sit up onto my knees. "What do you mean?"

"Where are your work skirts?"

"Oh." I think for a moment. "I usually wear trousers."

He pokes his head around the corner of my closet. "Every day?"

I nod.

"You wear flats too, don't you?"

"Not . . . dead flat." I shrug.

He rolls his eyes and goes back into the closet.

"Well, I just don't see the point of being uncomfortable at work, you know?"

"No, I don't, and looking dreary is what should make you uncomfortable, Kate," he calls.

I roll my eyes.

A hanger with a shirt on it comes flying out and lands on the floor.

"What are you doing?" I frown.

"Cleaning out this shit-pile of a closet."

"Now? It's nine p.m."

"I can't find anything in here."

"What are you talking about? It's completely organized into sections," I fire back.

"There's the crap section and then there's the really crap section," he mutters dryly; another hanger comes flying out and lands on the floor. "What even is that?"

I listen to him rattle around in there, a pair of shoes comes out and then another few hangers. "What about shirts? Where are the shirts you wear?"

"For God's sake, are you blind?" I get out of bed, go in, and point to the shirt section. "Right here."

Daniel frowns as he looks through the choices. "*This* is it?"

"Aha."

"I'm taking you shopping as a matter of urgency."

"I can't afford Givenchy, Daniel." I sigh.

"You don't have to spend a fortune to look good, Kate." He curls his lip as if I'm clueless, then he holds up a shirt and looks at it and shakes his head. "Where the fuck did you get this?"

"College."

His eyes widen. "You've had this shirt since college?"

I shrug. "I guess."

"Dear God." He keeps flicking through and then pulls out a long black dress; it's fitted and sleeveless and in a casual material. He holds it up against my body. "This I can work with." He thinks for a moment. "Actually, I have a bag of samples in my car, I think there's a shirt in there." He rushes from the room, I hear him run down the stairs and the front door open. Moments later I hear him take the stairs two at a time. I smile; this really is his calling, he just loves it.

Back in my room, he unzips the bag and pulls out a black shirt and smiles. "This."

I frown as I stare at the shirt. "That?"

"Over the dress."

I screw up my face. "What?"

He grabs my shoulders and turns me back toward my bed. "Just trust me, I've got this."

I stare at myself in the elevator mirror. The image is unfamiliar. I'm wearing a long, black straight skirt that also moonlights as a dress. A black fitted button-up shirt over the top with a few buttons undone. A patent leather belt strategically placed to cinch in my waist, and black high heels from my cousin Mary's wedding.

My blonde hair is out and styled and I'm wearing makeup, not a lot, but more than usual. I don't dress up this much to go out, let alone for work.

And I don't know why I'm choosing now to do it . . . but I have . . .

I let out a shaky exhale as the nerves dance in my stomach.

I've got a meeting with Elliot this morning and am on my way up to his office right now. I glance back up at my reflection and I cringe. Oh, this is stupid, what the hell am I doing? I hit the level sixteen button, I need to get off. I can't see him looking like this.

He'll know.

The elevator flies past level sixteen and I close my eyes. *Shit.*

The doors open on the top floor and I drop my shoulders as I step out and into the reception area, all black with a trendy black timber feature wall. Huge gold letters tell me exactly where I am, as if I could ever forget.

MILES MEDIA

The flooring is black marble and, like everything up here, it just feels expensive.

"Hello Kathryn." Leonie smiles, she looks me up and down. "You look lovely today, dear."

"Thanks." I smile as I wish the earth would swallow me up. "I have something on . . . after work." I make an excuse for looking the way I do.

"I love it, you should wear this every day."

I fake a smile. *Kill me fucking now.*

"Just go through, he's expecting you."

I walk down the corridor and close my eyes. God, what was Daniel thinking making me wear this? It's too over the top. I knock softly on Elliot's door.

"Come in," his deep voice calls.

I close my eyes as I steel myself and I push the door open. "Hello."

Elliot glances up from his computer and then looks back down; he then does a double take and his eyes rise and look me up and down. He sits up as if suddenly interested, and holding a pen between his fingers he says, "Hello Kathryn."

I grip my folder with white-knuckle force. "Hello."

"Please." He gestures to the seat at his desk. "Come in."

I walk in as his eyes drop to my toes and then back up to my face for the second time today, and he leans back in his chair as if pleased about something.

I raise my eyebrow. "What?"

A trace of a smile crosses his face. "What, what?"

"Why do you look like that?" I ask.

"I was just going to ask you the same question."

"Oh." I glance down at myself and feel like I have to justify my choice of outfit. "I just—"

"Look lovely," he cuts me off.

I stare at him, unsure what to say next. I swallow the large lump that is lodged firmly in my throat. "The report?" I stammer.

"Yes." His eyes hold mine. "Let's do that." He points to the seat with his pen and rotates his chair back to his computer. "I wanted to go through a few points. I'm unsure how to read the data."

"Okay." I sink into the chair.

He looks up and narrows his eyes as if processing a new thought. "A new perfume."

"What?"

"You're wearing a new perfume today."

"No, I'm not," I snap. Oh, hell on a cracker . . . this trying to be sexy is a disaster.

"Yes . . . you are. I know your scent." His eyes hold mine. "And . . . today it's different."

He knows my scent . . . what the fuck?

I frown as I stare at him. "Umm . . . " I give a subtle shake of my head, completely flustered. "I don't know, maybe you haven't been around me when I've worn it before."

"What a shame."

I drop my head in confusion. *Is he flirting with me?*

I don't get it: for seven years I've known this man, despised him, and thankfully been immune to his charm. I've watched every woman around me in the office fall desperately in lust with Elliot Miles and I could never see the attraction.

For the life of me, I didn't get what they saw in him.

Today, I do.

I open my folder as a distraction.

Focus.

"So . . . the projected income is on the left-hand side of the graph here." I point to the pink line with my finger as I try to act professional. "This line here is the actual income of the UK office, and this line here is projected advertising costs, although we don't have all the data for France . . ." My eyes flick up to see if he's listening; he's sitting back in his chair, his thumb is under his chin, and his pointer finger is tracing over his lips as if he's thinking deeply.

"What are you doing?" he asks.

"I'm . . ." I pause. Huh? "I'm explaining the projection report. Isn't that . . . ?"

"That's not what I'm talking about and you know it."

"What do you mean?"

"Is this an entrapment?"

"I'm sorry . . ." I frown.

"Is that your plan?"

"I don't understand."

He stands and puts his hands in his suit pockets as if angered. "That's it . . . isn't it?"

"What?" I shake my head, confused.

"Do you really hate me that much that you would stoop that low?"

"What are you talking about?" I frown again.

He screws up his face. "Come off it, Landon. I wasn't born yesterday. It's all making sense now."

"Well." I widen my eyes. "Good, because you can explain it to me. I don't know what you're talking about. What's wrong with this report?"

"I can see it so clearly now . . ." He shakes his head as if having an epiphany. "Of course, that's it," he whispers under his breath.

"Mr. Miles."

"Elliot," he corrects me. "And don't give me your fucking shit." He picks up a remote from his desk and points it to the corner of the ceiling; I glance up and see the green light go off. He just turned the security cameras off.

"So, this is your plan?" he sneers.

"Plan?"

"Turn your stupid boss on, until he cracks and pursues you. Then you have him charged with sexual harassment in the workplace."

My mouth falls open in horror. "What?"

"Oh, please." He screws up his face in disgust. "It's clear as day now—the hot little dress, turning up at that event looking like a walking fucking orgasm and then going home with another man. The sauna, ha." He throws his head back. "The sauna was a good one, what chance do I have seeing you hot and sweaty in a bikini like that?"

I stare at him as my brain misfires.

I turn him on.

"You can cut the shit, right fucking now," he growls.

My temper begins to simmer. "Turn the camera back on for this because I want you to rewatch it later when you're in a strait-jacket." I stand and we come toe to toe. "For your information . . . Mr. Miles," I sneer, "I have just come out of a traumatic period in my life and have just started to refind myself. My new clothes, male friendships, and dresses have nothing to do with you or your inflated ego."

66

He narrows his eyes as we glare at each other.

"This may come as a surprise, but I have only ever treated you as you have treated me, with contempt. Excuse me for not lining up to suck your dick like the rest of the stupid female population."

"You know nothing about me."

"I know that I'm not a bitch. You, however, *are* a fucking asshole . . . and stupidly, for a few moments there, I forgot."

I slam the report folder down on his desk.

"What was the trauma in your life?" he barks.

"None of your business." I turn and walk toward the door.

"Kate."

I turn like the devil himself and point at him. "You don't get to call me that," I growl. "To you, I'm Kathryn." I march out the door and straight through reception, hit the elevator button and bite my lip to hold it in.

I can feel the angry tears coming.

Don't cry . . . don't cry . . . don't you fucking dare let him make you cry.

Entrapment.

What an asshole.

Chapter 4

I storm into the elevator like the Hulk. After the worst day in history I am ready to fight someone . . . anyone.

Come at me, bitches, because I am ready to rumble.

After my meeting with fuck-face Miles this morning, the day started to spiral. Before tea break, we had a computer glitch that appeared for no reason and wouldn't go away. Then when I was on my break, I got an urgent call that the entire network had crashed. I had to rush back from lunch before my food had even arrived and go into damage repair. I ended up having to shut down the entire system and reboot the whole building, then to top off the debacle I got a call from fuck-face to tell me to hurry up about it.

My fury bubbles deep in my stomach. *Hurry up about it.*

I'll give him hurry up about it.

It's now 7 p.m. and I'm just leaving, I'm tired, I'm angry, and worst of all, I'm hangry.

I could eat a horse and chase the rider.

I'm going straight to the nearest bar and having the largest chicken schnitzel and fries, and ten thousand wines.

The elevator doors open and I look out onto the street and roll my eyes. Of course it's fucking raining.

This day is a living hell.

I exhale heavily and walk toward the doors and I hear the elevator ding.

"Kathryn." A deep voice calls from behind me. "Wait up." I turn to see Elliot stepping out of the elevator.

Ugh, seriously?

Just when I think the day can't get any worse, the heavens open up and deliver again.

I want to ignore him and march off, but then I'll look like a petulant child. I stand on the spot as I wait for King Asshole to arrive.

"Hi," he says as he approaches me with a smile. "Bad day?"

I stare at him flatly. Of all the fucking nerve. "You could say that." I turn toward the doors and he falls in to walk beside me.

"What was the problem with the server," he asks.

"You'll have a report about it in the morning."

"Why can't you just tell me now?"

I turn to him. "Because I don't want to."

"Why not?"

"Because my opinion from this morning still stands, you are an asshole and if I talk to you I am apparently trying to"—I hold my fingers up and air-quote—"turn you on and make you crack."

He drops his head to hide his smile. "Still carrying on about that, are you?"

I glare at him as my temper hits a crescendo. "Are you for real?" I whisper through gritted teeth.

"Well." He shrugs casually. "I had a concern and I voiced it." He looks out toward the pouring rain. "We should get a drink to discuss it further."

My face screws up. "What the fuck?" I whisper angrily. "You accuse me of trying to set you up for sexual harassment and then you want to have a drink?"

"It's over to me." He shrugs casually. "And why not get a drink, it's been a bad day. Might be good to let off some steam."

"It's not over for me, nobody can be this stupid?"

"I'm sure we could both do with a glass of wine."

I exhale heavily. This guy is as thick as a brick. "Mr. Miles, as I stated this morning, I have no interest in you. I am highly offended at your accusation this morning, and for your information, I was in the fucking sauna first!"

Amusement flashes across his face. "You're saying 'fuck' a lot today, Kathryn."

I get a vision of myself punching him fair and square in the face.

My nostrils flare as I fight for control. "Good. Bye." I turn and march toward the door and the rain really begins to hammer down. I see the black Bentley and his driver waiting in the drop-off area.

Fuck it . . . now I have to storm off in the rain while he watches from the backseat of his wanker-mobile.

Kill me now!

I open the door.

"Would you like a lift?" he calls.

I ignore him and try to shuffle along as I concentrate on the wet ground. Slipping over now in front of him would be the end of me.

I march around the corner and look for the closest thing under-cover. I don't care where or what it is, just get me out of here.

I see a pharmacy—oh, I have a prescription. I'll get that dispensed now while I'm here and it'll get me out of his sight. I dart inside and turn to see the black Bentley pull out slowly and into the traffic. I let out a sigh of relief; thank God, he's gone.

I dig the prescription out and hand it over the counter to the pharmacist. "Can I get this please?"

"Alright." The kind-looking elderly man smiles as he takes it from me. He reads it over the top of his glasses and then looks back up. "Have you ever taken this medication before, dear?"

"No, I saw a new doctor this week and this is the first time it's been prescribed."

"It's very strong, do you mind me asking what it's for?"

"I have endometriosis and very painful periods. Apparently it should help on day one."

He nods. "Okay, that makes sense. Make sure you take it with food, and no alcohol or operating heavy machinery."

"Alright." I smile. "Thanks."

Thunder rumbles loud from the heavens and we both peer out to see the rain bouncing on the road as it lands. "It's really coming down out there," he says. "It's a good night to be tucked in at home."

"Yes." I smile.

Either that, or getting drunk alone in a bar. I feel myself relax a little for the first time all day.

I'm taking option two.

ELLIOT

Early morning and my door opens. Jameson walks in. "You ready?"

"Yep." I close down my computer and we make our way down to the lobby. We have a meeting this afternoon with the board before Jameson returns to New York in the morning.

We walk out of the lift and see a sexy ass in a skirt in front of us with a group of people. Long legs, sculpted calves, the perfect ass.

Our gazes immediately drop and he raises an eyebrow in a silent *will you look at that?*

I smirk and we keep walking and then the skirt turns as she talks to her friends. It's Kathryn. I'm taken aback.

I nod. "Kathryn."

She smiles politely. "Hello." She smiles at Jay. "Hi."

"Hello." He smiles.

We stand still on the spot and watch her leave the building with her colleagues.

My eyes meet with my brother's. "You should look into that," he says.

I stare after her and then, finally, I snap out of my momentary trance. "Not my type."

Jameson watches her through the front windows as she crosses the road and I feel my hackles rise. "She's everyone's type," he mutters dryly.

Everyone's type.

"Will you shut the fuck up?" I put my hands into my trouser pockets in annoyance. "Are we going or what?"

I send my last email and stretch my arms in the air. It's been a long day . . . week. I get up and go to the bathroom and pick up my briefcase and put it on my desk to pack, and then I remember what day it is.

Thursday.

I glance at my watch: 6:40 p.m.

I wonder if she's . . .

I sit back down at my computer and look around guiltily. This is nothing new. I seem to be always looking around guiltily lately; guilty of watching a certain snarky IT manager as she works.

I've got issues, I know, and I hate to admit it, but her deciding to openly hate me this week after our little episode in my office is a major fucking turn-on.

Hell, I've even been loitering in the sauna after work, hoping for a rematch.

So far, no luck.

I'm never going to do anything about this sick attraction that I seem to have for her, but for some reason I can't stop. I tell myself that this is the last time I'll look at her on the security camera, and sure enough, half an hour later, I find myself doing it again.

Like now, for instance.

I exhale heavily in frustration with myself, click through the security cameras and go to level ten, scroll through until I get to her office . . . it's empty.

I slump in my seat.

Fuck it.

I stare at her office on the screen while I contemplate my next move.

I mean, I could ask her out, but we both know how that's going to end.

I don't even want to go out with her. *She's a raving bitch, remember?*

What the fuck am I doing?

I go to close down my computer and I see a foot coming out of the bottom of the screen. Huh?

I lean closer to get a better look.

It is a foot, wearing a white sneaker. What's she doing on the floor? Is she stretching or something?

I run my finger back and forth over my lips as I watch; she's dead-still.

What's she doing?

A feeling of uneasiness creeps over me.

"Move," I whisper.

I click through the camera angles as I try to see her better. Nothing.

I rest my chin on my hand as I watch for five minutes while she lies dead still.

Ten minutes . . . fifteen.

Fuck.

Something's wrong. I march to the elevator and hit the button for level ten. I watch the dial move slowly as it travels down through the floors. "Hurry up," I mutter. "Hurry the fuck up."

The doors open and I stride out and down the corridor to her office, open the door in a rush to find her passed out on the floor. She's in her red sports dress and sneakers, completely out of it.

"Kathryn." I gasp as I drop to my knees and give her a shake. "Kate, wake up, are you alright?"

Silence.

I shake her again and grab her face in my hands and try and pry her eyes open.

Nothing . . .

"Shit." I grab my phone and dial 999.

"Hello emergency."

"Hi," I stammer. "I need an ambulance to the Miles Media building, level ten immediately."

"What's happened, sir?"

"I've just found one of my employees unconscious on the floor. She's out cold."

"Is she breathing?"

"Hang on, I'll check."

"Put me on speaker, sir, and I can guide you."

I put my phone on speaker and on the floor beside us and I hold her face. "Kate. Can you hear me?"

"Is she breathing?"

I put my ear down to her mouth.

"Check her chest. Is it rising and falling?"

Fuck.

Is she dead?

The room spins as I begin to panic. "Send two ambulances," I bark. "I'm about to have a fucking heart attack myself."

"Check her chest, sir."

I put my hands on her chest and feel it rise and fall. "She's breathing." I sigh in relief.

"Can you feel her pulse?"

I close my eyes. How the hell do I do that again? My mind has gone completely blank; this is why I'm not a fucking doctor, I'm useless in an emergency.

"Put your fingertips on her neck just under her jaw," the operator reminds me.

"Oh, right." I put my fingers on her neck and feel a strong pump. "She's got a pulse."

"Has she fallen? Check her head for an injury."

"What's with the questions? Can you just send a fucking ambulance?" I cry. "She's about to die any second."

"I need to know what's happened, sir, I can't help you without all of the facts."

I look around, and check for blood, but everything seems normal. Her work clothes are in a bag and then I notice something on her desk, a white box of prescription pills.

"There are pills," I stammer as I dive for them. "Prescription."

"What's the name of them?"

I fumble with the box to try and read it out fast and drop it, and I scramble to the floor and under the desk to retrieve them. "Fuck it."

"Calm down, sir."

"Send a fucking ambulance," I yell. "What is your name? I want your fucking name and rank."

This bitch is going down.

Kathryn groans.

"Kate," I whisper, and take her hand in mine. "Wake up."

She frowns as she tries to come to.

"Are you there, sir? What is the name of the medication?"

"Um . . . Hydrocodone slash acetaminophen," I reply.

Kate's eyes flutter open and she looks up at me.

"Are you alright?" I whisper.

"What?" She frowns and tries to sit up and onto her elbow.

"Lie down," I bark.

"How many tablets has she taken?" the operator asks.

"How many tablets have you taken?" I ask Kate.

She frowns. "Huh?" She then flops back to the floor; she appears drunk.

"She's disoriented," I reply.

"She's taken a strong painkiller. Count the tablets, sir. I need to know how many she has had."

"Send a fucking ambulance before I put my hand through this phone and strangle you," I scream.

This bitch is hopeless . . . no wonder people die every day.

"Count. The. Tablets."

My fury bubbles and I count through the blister pack. "There are thirty-eight tablets here."

"How many came in the box?"

I speed-read the directions on the box as I look for the amount. "Pack of forty."

"So, she's had only two?"

I stare at the dazed woman in front of me. "I think she's had more than that."

"Can you look through her belongings and see?"

"What?"

"Just do it."

"Listen here, you motherfucker. I want an ambulance to the Miles Media building right now. If this woman dies I'm having you charged with . . ." I pause as I try and think of an appropriate charge. "Something bad," I splutter. "Murder."

"Just check her bag."

I begin to rattle through Kate's bag, wallet, keys, makeup . . . tampons. I wince and throw them over my shoulder.

"Well?" the operator asks.

"I'm looking, alright? There's a lot of fucking crap in here." Oh, screw this, I tip the handbag upside down onto the carpet and stuff flies everywhere.

"What are you doing?" Kate whispers as she sleepily sits up. "Get out of my bag."

My eyes nearly bulge from their sockets. "Get out of your bag? Are you fucking serious right now?"

"What?" she whispers.

"What's happening, sir?"

I grit my teeth. "The patient is about to get knocked back out. That's what's happening."

"What is your name, dear?"

Kate frowns. "Kate Landon."

"What's happened?"

Kate frowns as she looks around. "I don't know."

"You took some medication?" the operator asks.

"No," she whispers.

I hold the box up and widen my eyes. "Look familiar?"

"Oh." She puts her hand over her forehead as she remembers. "Yes, I took some painkillers."

"What were the painkillers for, dear?"

"Period pain." Kate's eyes flick to me.

I roll my eyes. *Now I've fucking heard it all.*

"How many did you take?" the operator asks.

"Only two."

"Are you sure?"

"Yes."

I pinch the bridge of my nose. "Remind me never to do cocaine with you," I mutter dryly.

"Can you sit up?" the operator asks.

Kate goes to sit up and struggles. I take her hand and pull her up into a seated position.

"I'm dizzy."

"You've had an adverse reaction to the medication, you're drowsy and disoriented. It happens with some people."

"So, is she okay?" I snap.

"She needs to sleep it off."

"I'm bringing her into the hospital, I want her checked out," I reply.

"Sir, you might be waiting for hours in Emergency. If she has only had two tablets I can assure you she needs to sleep it off and nothing more."

My eyes flick to Kate. "How many have you had, really?"

"Two."

I glare at her. "I mean it."

"I promise."

"Fine," I snap.

"Can someone pick you up, dear?"

"I'll drive her home."

Kate goes to stand up. "I'm fine." She slips and stumbles back over.

"Congratulations, sir, you did a great job," the operator says.

Patronizing cow.

"Yes, well, I wish I could say the same for you. It's lucky she isn't dead with your snail pace. There was no urgency whatsoever. Work faster next time. Goodbye." I end the call with force.

Kate looks up at me and then her heavy eyelids close once more.

"Come on, I'll see you home." I sigh.

"I'm fine," she mumbles with her eyes closed. "I'm just going to . . . sleep here tonight."

I begin to pack up her things that are strewn all over the floor. "You need to clean out your handbag, this thing is full of shit." I stuff things back in.

"Like you," she whispers with her eyes still shut.

"Why is this bag so big?" I snap. "This isn't a handbag, this is luggage."

Kate frowns and throws her arm over her face. "Just. Shut. Up," she whispers.

I put her handbag over my shoulder and grab her hand and pull her to her feet; she's still disoriented and staggers to the side. I put my arm around her. "Come on, stand up. Focus."

She looks up at me all sleepy, her hair wild and messed up, and an unwelcome smile crosses my face.

"What?" She frowns.

"Do you know how dopey you look right now, Landon?"

"And I'm . . . in my red netball . . . dress," she slurs.

I smile as I lead her to the elevator. "What a pity."

Chapter 5

I slowly lead her to the elevator and I hit the button. She sways and I put my arm around her to hold her up. "Stay still."

She looks up at me and I smirk as I look down at her.

"Don't," she slurs as she falls to the side.

I pull her back against my body. "Don't what?"

"An"—her eyes flutter—"noy me."

I chuckle. "Impossible." The doors open and I lead her in and we turn and face the front. She puts her head on my shoulder and closes her eyes. I catch sight of us in the reflection on the doors: now that's something I never thought I'd see.

Kathryn Landon, sleepy and calm, under my arm.

The doors open into the lobby and I slowly walk her out; she's so docile.

"Is everything alright, sir?" The security guard comes running.

"She's groggy, had a reaction to some medication."

"Can I do anything?" he splutters as he looks between us.

"No, thank you, I'll see that she gets home safely."

He practically runs for the door and he holds it open for us.

My Bentley is parked in the bay outside, and Andrew gets out and frowns as he sees me nearly carrying Kate. "What's wrong with her?" he asks.

"Just groggy, a reaction to medication, we'll get her home."

He opens the back door in a rush.

"In the car," I say to Kate.

She closes her eyes as her head leans against my chest. "I'm just going to . . . walk."

Fuck's sake.

I put my hand on the top of her head and push her down, maneuver her into the right position, and then with one almighty shove she falls into the backseat.

"Ow." She grimaces.

I shuffle in beside her and close the door. "Where do you live?" I ask as we pull out into the traffic.

She points out of the window. "Over there."

"Over where?"

"Out. There," she snaps as if exasperated.

I roll my eyes; even when drugged this woman is annoying. "Tell me your address or I'm looking through your luggage again."

"It's twenty-four . . ." She frowns and holds her finger up. "No wait, that's my old address . . . ummmm."

"Christ almighty." I drag my hand down my face in frustration.

"I know it," she continues.

"And?"

"It's . . . forty-four/a Kent Road."

"Are you sure?"

"Sshh, stop talking," she whispers as she holds her finger up to her lips in an overexaggerated way. "You're hurting my ears." She points with both hands to her ears.

I smirk at her acting out every word.

"Forty-four Kent Road," I say to Andrew.

"Sure thing, boss." He turns right at the next junction.

Kate's head falls and I pull her back under my arm and hold her close. She closes her eyes and rests against my chest.

We drive for ten minutes in the traffic and then she falls deeper into sleep and puts her hand up on my chest and nestles in tight.

I frown down at her as a weird feeling comes over me.

Hmm . . . interesting.

After a while, Andrew pulls the car into a parking space, then he turns and looks at us. "This is it."

I frown as I peer at the old terraced building. "This is it?"

"Uh-huh."

"Kate," I whisper; she stays asleep and I give her a little shake. "Kate," I whisper again.

"If you're trying to wake her, you don't need to whisper," Andrew mutters.

"Eyes on the road," I snap.

Smart-ass.

He chuckles as he gets out, and opens the back door on my side. I climb out and then lean back in. "Kate," I say loudly. "Wake up, we're home."

Andrew reaches in to help.

"I've got this," I say.

She frowns as she comes to and looks around sleepily. "Huh."

I hold my hand out to her and she takes it and I pull her over toward me, but she slips off the seat and onto the floor of the car. "Oh . . ."

I chuckle as I reach down for her, she's all legs and arms and tangled up. "That red dress a little slippery, old girl?"

Andrew rolls his eyes. "Bloody hell," he mutters under his breath.

I take her hand, pull her out of the car and wrap my arm around her. We slowly walk up the six steps leading to the terrace.

"Walk up the steps," I direct her.

She goes to sit down on the bottom step. "I'll just sleep here."

"Kate," I say in my best authoritative voice. "Concentrate and walk up the steps please."

She goes to sit down again and I glance back at Andrew, who's laughing and leaning on the side of the car as he watches the show.

"Shut up," I mouth.

He smiles with a wink and lights his cigarette.

That's the thing with having the same driver for seven years, they get too fucking comfortable.

"Kate," I snap. "Walk up the stairs and then you can go to sleep."

"Hmm." She smiles with her eyes closed, takes one step.

"That's it."

She takes two more.

"Good girl."

"I sleep here."

I keep pulling her up and we get to the front door, and I ring the bell.

Kate leans on me and closes her eyes; I wrap my arm around her tight.

Two tablets and this is her . . . I would hate to think what would happen if she actually had some hard stuff.

I ring the bell again . . . no answer.

"Kate, is anyone home?"

"Yeah." She smiles goofily up at me. "We are."

"I mean, your flatmates."

She shrugs and goes back to leaning on me.

"Where are your keys?" I ask.

She shrugs once more.

"For fuck's sake." I rattle through her handbag and dig out the keys. "What key is it?"

"Red one."

I get the red key and open the door. "Hello," I call.

No answer.

I look back toward the car and Andrew shrugs.

"Bed for you," I say, walk her in, and close the door behind us.

Once we have negotiated her apartment's front door, I ask, "Where is your bedroom?"

She points up the steep, narrow stairs and I peer up. Oh hell. "Of course it is."

I think for a moment. What do I do now? I can't just leave her here.

"Alright." I bend and lift her over my shoulder.

"Oh . . . don't," she slurs. "Put me down."

"Shut up." I slap her behind. I take one step, then two.

I take another few steps and my thighs begin to burn. My chest tightens.

I stumble back, oh . . . fuck it.

Don't drop her.

Nothing is easy with this damn woman.

I grit my teeth and begin to climb the stairs as fast as I can.

"Put me down," she moans, and I slap her behind again.

"Behave yourself. Breaking my back is the last thing I wanted to do tonight."

We get to the top and I put her back onto her feet as I clutch my chest and gasp for air. Holy hell.

That was hard.

She teeters on her feet and I grab her hand and drag her into her bedroom.

I walk her over to the bed and pull the covers back and lie her down. I take one sneaker off and she kicks her foot as if to get me to stop.

"You know"—I undo the laces on the other shoe—"lots of women would die for me to take their shoes off in bed."

"Desper potatoes," she slurs.

"They are not desperados." I smile as the other shoe comes free. She's wearing pale pink socks, and I tuck her legs in and pull the covers up over her.

She smiles up at me and holds her hand out.

I take it in mine and sit down beside her; her eyelids are heavy and she battles to keep them open. I brush the hair back from her forehead as I look down at her.

Her blonde hair is splayed across her pillow and her big lips are a pouty rose color. Her dark lashes flutter as she tries to keep her eyes open.

She really is quite . . .

I look up at her room, painted cream with a large white timber bed. There is a bookshelf and a dressing table, makeup in baskets, and photo frames; it feels very lived in. Fairy lights are strewn around the ceiling and a large reading chair with an ottoman is in the corner. Looks like a dorm room I would have visited back in the day.

My gaze comes back to Kate and she's sleeping soundly, her hand still holding mine.

I find myself smiling as I watch her. What do I do now? I mean, I can't just leave her here alone. What if something happened?

That would be negligent.

I guess I'll have to wait.

An hour later, I need to go to the bathroom but Kate is still firmly holding my hand. I move it a little and she frowns and grips me tighter. "Don't," she murmurs sleepily.

"I'm coming straight back," I whisper.

"I said no."

Demanding witch. I'm starving fucking hungry and about to piss myself.

Well, tough shit.

I get up and walk into her en-suite bathroom and look around; it's small.

A basket with dirty clothes; pink towels and a matching bath mat. I go to the bathroom and wash my hands and then walk back out into her room. I walk over to her bookshelf and look at all the photos in the frames—one of an older couple, and one of her at a young age with them, they must be her parents. A photo of a dog, a black-and-white border collie. A photo of her and a man who looks around her age, taken a few years ago. I wonder, was this a boyfriend?

She said she didn't have a boyfriend.

I keep looking through her belongings—a few crystals strategically placed.

Don't tell me she's one of those nut jobs who believe in crystal healing.

Hmm.

It's very eclectic in here. So unlike my perfectly styled penthouse.

I look along the spines of the books—what does she read?

Ugh, romance reader.

I would never have guessed that one.

There's a small crystal dish and an array of gold jewelry. I smile as I pick up one of her rings and put it on the end of my pinkie finger.

Tiny hands.

I take it off and put it back and keep looking through her photos. It's like show-and-tell and I'm learning all about her.

And surprisingly, not a cauldron in sight.

I retrieve her phone from her handbag and go back and sit down beside her, and she rolls toward me and puts her hand over my thighs.

My stomach flutters.

Stop it.

I really should be going, I've been here for hours. Where the fuck is that stupid Daniel and his sickly white teeth now?

"Kate." I wake her. "Kate." I hold her phone in front of her. "Unlock your phone for me, I'm going to call someone."

She frowns and nestles closer into my thigh, and I run my fingers through her hair. We sit like this for a while and I'd be lying if I said I didn't like it.

But I'm hungry; it's now nearly 10 p.m.

"Kate." I hold the phone up to her face. "Unlock your phone, please."

"Hmm."

"Kate."

She fumbles around with it with her eyes still closed and passes it back to me.

She nestles back into my thigh and I watch her for a moment.

Okay, I'll admit it.

I like her.

Not like her, like her, I just don't hate her like I thought I did.

I go through the list of contacts as I look for the name Daniel.

Hmm, no Daniel.

I don't know his last name . . . *fuck.*

That guy is fucking useless on all fronts.

Another hour later.

Maybe I'll just go downstairs and get something to eat? Then maybe . . . I'll just sleep here with her?

I mean, I can't leave her alone.

Yeah, I'll do that.

The bedroom door opens and I look up, startled. It's Daniel.

Kate is fast asleep and her hand is in mine.

He frowns when he sees me and looks between Kate and I.

"She's out cold," I offer as an explanation.

"Umm . . . What's going on?" he asks as he walks into the bedroom.

"She had a reaction to some medication and was groggy. I found her passed out in the office and brought her home."

His eyes widen. "We need to take her to the hospital."

"I already called emergency services, and she's okay. Just sleepy, I've checked already. She's conscious, just sleeping."

He stares at her. "Wow."

I stand. "I'll go now that you're here."

He sits on the side of the bed beside her. "Baby?" he says. "Are you okay?"

An unfamiliar feeling swirls in my stomach as I watch him with her.

Don't call her baby.

I clench my jaw as I move toward the door. "I'll leave you to it."

Daniel stands and shakes my hand. "Thank you so much, I really appreciate you caring for her. I'll take it from here."

I stare at him; okay, I don't like this guy.

He's too . . . familiar.

"I'm not sure if I should leave her with you?" I say.

His face falls. "Why not?"

"I mean, how do I know you aren't going to take advantage of her."

"Because I'm her friend . . . and I live with her."

I straighten my tie as I go over my options. "Hmm." I rearrange my cufflinks.

"Look Mr.—" he says.

"Elliot Miles," I interrupt him.

He gives me a stifled smile. "Mr. Miles, thank you for looking after her, but I'm home now. I appreciate all you've done."

"Fine." I take one last look around the room. "I'll be in touch."

I head toward the door and then stop and take the gold business card case from my pocket, handing over my card. "Call me if something is wrong or if anything changes."

He frowns as he takes the card from me. "Okay, I will."

"Goodnight."

I march down the stairs and out the front door, walk over to my Bentley, and get into the backseat.

"Where to, boss?" Andrew asks as we pull out into the traffic.

"Anywhere with food."

KATE

I wake to the deep throb in my stomach and I wince.

Oww, period pain.

I drag my eyes open—I need to go to the bathroom. I sit up and frown as I look down at myself.

Huh?

Why am I wearing this?

I go to step out of bed and tread on a blanket on my floor. "What's that?"

I flick my lamp on and see that Daniel is asleep on top of the couch cushions on the floor beside my bed. "What the hell?" I step over him and go to the bathroom.

It's urgent now.

Damn it, periods are a design fault in the female human body.

I sit on the toilet as I go over last night. Wait . . . what am I doing in my netball dress?

Hang on, I don't even remember playing netball.

I was at the office . . . and then . . . what?

And what's Daniel doing asleep on my floor?

I have a quick shower as I wrack my brain about last night's events. Was I drinking . . .

I'm completely blank, jeez.

I pull my robe on and walk back out into my bedroom to see Daniel awake and leaning up on his elbow. "How are you feeling?"

"Why was I in my netball dress?"

He sits up, surprised. "You don't remember?"

"I . . ." I pause as I try to. "No, I . . . I'm at a loss."

"You passed out at work, apparently had a reaction to some medication or something."

"Are you serious?" I think back. "Yes . . . the pain tablets. Shit."

"Luckily Elliot found you."

My eyes snap back to Daniel. "Who?"

"Elliot Miles brought you home."

My eyes widen. "What?"

"But nobody was here so he stayed with you until I arrived."

My hands go to my head in horror. "What the fuck? He came . . . *here*?"

I begin to pace.

"Looked pretty damn at home too, sitting there holding your hand and all."

I smile in relief. "Oh, fuck off, you nearly had me for a moment. What really happened, did we get drunk?"

"I'm deadly serious." He stands and goes over to my bedside table, picks up a white card and passes it to me.

ELLIOT MILES

0423 009 973

"Nooooooo," I splutter. "Oh no, no, no, no." My heart begins to race. I point to the floor. "He was here. In my bedroom?" I point to the floor again. "Here."

"Yes."

I push my fingers into my eye sockets in horror. "Why did you let him in?" I look around at my bombshell of a bedroom. "This place is a fucking mess."

Daniel shrugs. "He didn't seem to mind."

"Why? What, I mean . . . Why do you say that?"

"He seemed very happy holding your hand."

92

My eyes hit saucer size. "He was actually holding my hand . . . what the fuck was I doing?"

"You were all snuggled into him."

"What!" I screech. I drop my head into my hands. "Oh my God, I'm going to die a thousand deaths."

"You know you should be grateful. He was looking after you."

"Are you kidding me?" I cry, storm into my bathroom, and look around: there's a basket of dirty washing and tampons are on the cabinet next to the sink.

He saw this mess, he saw me asleep . . . I was snuggled into him.

"Kill me now!" I cry. "My life is officially over."

Daniel chuckles as he goes to walk out of the room. "I must say, he's fucking hot though, right?"

I pick up a cushion off my bed and hurl it at him. "Get out."

"Thank you for sleeping on my floor and checking on me all night, Daniel," he says sweetly.

"Thanks for ruining my life and letting him in," I cry.

"I didn't let him in, you let him in."

Oh no.

Another horrible thought enters my brain. "What the fuck did I say to him?"

I begin to pace as I run my hands through my hair in dismay. "What if I told him . . ." I whisper out loud to myself.

"That you think he's hot?" Daniel interrupts my mental breakdown.

My eyes flick up to him. "I do not," I snap.

Daniel smirks. "If you didn't think he was hot, then it wouldn't matter that he saw your dirty panties in the laundry basket and your tampons on the side."

"Ahhhh," I cry as I slap my hands over my eyes. "Get out!"

Daniel whistles as he saunters down the stairs.

I sink into a seated position on the bed as I feel the blood drain from my face.

This is beyond . . . mortifying.

Humiliation, is there a worse emotion?

I take the elevator to the top floor with my tail between my legs.

I inhale with a shaky breath, and I don't know if I've ever been so nervous.

Or horrified.

I've done a lot of stupid shit in my life, and passing out at work in a netball dress is up there. But letting Elliot Miles drive me home while I was high takes the absolute cake.

What kind of fucking idiot invites her bastard boss into her messy bedroom with tampons strewn all over her bathroom and then snuggles up to him?

I pinch the bridge of my nose. This is it, the end of my career. It was nice knowing you, Miles Media. He didn't respect me before, and he sure as hell is going to throw this in my face for all of eternity.

I'll have to find another job? I can't stay here . . . not now.

The elevator doors open at the top floor and I step out. Elliot's PA looks up from her computer and smiles. I wither a little. Does she know? Has he told everyone?

Am I the laughing stock?

"Hello Courtney." I smile awkwardly.

"Go in dear, he's expecting you."

I bet he is.

I fake a smile, trudge up the corridor, and knock on his door. "Come in," his deep voice calls.

I pause and close my eyes, push the door open.

And there he sits, in all his arrogant glory.

Grey suit, white shirt, dark hair, and a jaw that would cut glass. He gives me a slow, sexy smile as he swivels on his chair. "Hello Kate."

I clench my jaw, wanting to correct him that it's Kathryn. "Hi."

"How are you feeling?"

I shrug. "Fine. I'm sorry about last night. I don't know what happened. And I just want you to know that I am mortified and horrified and I'm so sorry you had to look after me and I don't . . ." I look around as I try to find the words. "I am so embarrassed."

He smiles as his eyes hold mine. "Don't be."

I puff air into my cheeks—great, now he's going to get all condescending.

"You scared me," he says as he picks up his pen.

"I apologize." I turn my head and stare out of the window, anything to avoid his gaze.

"Kate."

I focus on the building across the street.

"Kate."

I drag my eyes to his.

"Take the rest of the day off and go and see your doctor please."

I open my mouth to say something.

"And don't give me your smart mouth," he interrupts as he stands. "This is non-negotiable, you scared the hell out of me. I thought you were dead."

My eyes well with tears of shame.

"What's wrong?" he says. His voice is different. Soft, cajoling.

"Don't," I spit.

"This was an accident. It could have happened to anyone, why are you so defensive?" he snaps.

"I'm not. You're the defensive one."

"I'm not defensive."

"Yes. You are, since the second day I met you, you've had an issue with me," I splutter.

He screws up his face in a question. "What?"

"Anyway, I didn't come here to discuss this. I came to say thank you for last night."

His eyes hold mine.

I twist my fingers in front of me. "So . . . thank you." I shrug. "I really appreciate it and I don't know what would have happened if you hadn't found me."

He sits back in his chair and picks up his pen again. "You're welcome." His eyes hold mine.

I shrug again; this is just awkward. I point to the door with my thumb. "I'm going to get going."

"To the doctor."

"Yes."

I turn and head to the door.

"Kate," he calls.

I turn back to him.

"What happened on the second day I met you?"

I stare at him.

"Forgive my rudeness, but I have no idea."

I pause for a moment as I consider if I should elaborate. "I told you that you have the bluest eyes I've ever seen. Not in a sleazy way . . . In a . . ." I shrug. "Observation kind of way." His brow furrows. "And you've despised me ever since."

He purses his lips as if thinking. "I don't remember you saying that to me."

"I know." I force a smile and turn back toward the door.

"Hey," he calls.

I turn back toward him again.

He puts his hands into his pockets. "Vulnerable Kate is quite endearing."

We stare at each other as the air crackles between us.

"Yeah, well . . . she's still high," I whisper.

He smiles softly.

Leave.

Leave now.

I turn and walk from his office as confusion surrounds me.

What was that?

Just like Elliot told me to, I took the day off and went to see the doctor about last night. Turns out it was just a bad reaction, so scratch that medication off my ever-to-do-again list.

It's late at night and I'm tired and have mostly mooched around all day, although that could have a lot to do with my damaged pride.

I can't believe he saw me like that; to have anyone see me like that is a nightmare, but to have him . . . it's unfathomable.

My Messenger pings and I see the name and smile; we've been chatting together all week, me and Edgar Moffatt. I hit open.

Hi Pinkie.

I smile and reply:

Hi Ed.

His reply bounces back.

What you doing?

I type:

In bed, winding down for the day, you?

I hit send.

Same, I'm exhausted. I had the worst night last
night.

I reply:

Oh no, what happened?

I can see the dots as he types, then it stops. Then I see the dots
again as he types, and it stops again. This must be a long message.
I wait for him to finish.

I found one of my co-workers unconscious on
the floor of her office. I called emergency but
thankfully she was okay and I ended up escort-
ing her home.

I stayed with her until her friend arrived but I
couldn't sleep all night for worrying about her.

I sit up. *What?*
Couldn't be . . .
I type:

What happened to her?

The dots bounce again and my heart sits in my throat as I wait.

> She had a reaction to the painkillers for her period pain.

What the fuck?

My hands go over my mouth . . . it can't be him. There is no way in hell that this could happen by coincidence.

Shit . . . my heart is hammering hard in my chest. What will I write?

I think for a moment and eventually I type:

> I hope she's okay. How horrible for you to experience that.

Oh my God, oh my God . . . Oh, my fucking God!

A reply bounces back.

> Not horrible at all, maybe a blessing in disguise.

I leap out of bed and begin to pace as I shake my hands around, adrenaline surging through my bloodstream. "What the hell is going on here?" I whisper.

What do I write?

I type:

> How could that be a blessing in disguise?

A reply bounces straight back.

> I have a bit of a crush on her.

My eyes widen to the size of saucers, and with shaky hands I reply:

What's her name?

The dots appear again.

Kate . . . Kate Landon.

Chapter 6

"What?" I jump from the bed. "No way, no way in fucking hell."
He has to be pulling my chain.

Wait, does he know it's me?

I sit back down at my computer and put my hand over my
mouth as I think.

How could this be happening?

He set it up, yes, that's it.

But then . . . how? I wouldn't even know how to set this up
and I'm the IT specialist.

"Does he know?"

I think for a moment; okay, set a trap to find out for sure.

Yes, that's it.

I sit cross-legged on my bed and pull my hair up into a high
ponytail as I prepare for battle.

If he writes something nice . . . I'll know that he knows it's me
and is attempting to be smooth.

Okay . . . I hold my fingers at the keyboard.

I think for a moment, then I write:

> What kind of crush?

I wait for his reply . . . no answer.

Hmm. I reword it.

> Are you hoping for a grand love affair?

The dots reappear.

> The horizontal kind.

> No grand love affair, she isn't my type.

> I'm a garbologist remember, I have dirty things on my mind.

I smile in relief. Fuck-face . . . you aren't good enough for me, anyway.

I reply:

> And what does this girl do at your garbage depot?

It bounces back.

> She cleans the toilets.

I laugh out loud. You wish, fucker.

> A toilet cleaner isn't dirty enough?

> No.

> What are you looking for—hot, smart, sexy?

I bite my thumbnail as I wait for his reply; why I care about this answer I have no clue.

> I'm looking for extraordinary.

I frown.

> And when I meet her, I will know.

I raise my eyebrow and type again:

> How?

> I believe in love at first sight, when our eyes meet. We will both know.

> And that will be it.

I bite my bottom lip as his words roll around in my head.

> You're a romantic?

His reply bounces back.

> Hopelessly.

I smile softly.

> And Kate, your toilet cleaner . . . what about her?

> Is going to get it good.

I'll ruin her for life.

I laugh out loud as I type:

What does she think about this?

She doesn't know yet, but she's into me, I can
tell.

"Poor bastard." I smirk. "You're so deluded."

How can you tell?

I sip my tea.

Men know these things.

Also, she looked at my dick the other day in
my office.

I choke on my tea and it splatters over the computer screen.
"What? I did not," I whisper. "You're dreaming." Another message comes in from him.

What about you, any luck with those pick-up
lines?

Hmm, I don't want to sound like a loser, so I lie.

Yes, I have a date on Saturday night.

Well, good luck.

I hope it goes well for you.

I stare at his words on the screen. This is so surreal.

Me too.

I'm turning in.

Goodnight, Ed.

A few minutes later a reply comes back.

Goodnight, Pinkie.

Xoxo

"What?" Rebecca frowns. "What do you mean?"

"I mean it's him," I reply. "Edgar Moffatt is Elliot Miles under an alias."

"Oh, bullshit." Daniel frowns too as he snatches my phone from me to read my and Ed's messages. "You mean to tell me that of all the people in the world, you are messaging your boss and he thinks you're someone else?"

"Yes."

I'm out to dinner with Rebecca and Daniel and we are dissecting the latest turn of events.

Daniel reads the messages between Ed and I. "I don't fucking believe this," he whispers.

"I know." I widen my eyes to accentuate my point.

Rebecca holds her hand out for the phone and I take it from Daniel and pass it to her. She reads the messages.

"So," Daniel says as he raises his glass of wine my way, "Elliot Miles has a crush on you."

I roll my eyes.

"The horizontal kind." Rebecca laughs as she gets to that bit.

"And he's not looking for hot," Daniel says.

Rebecca puts her hand over her heart. "Oh . . . he's looking for extraordinary."

"Oh please," I scoff. "He only wants to get his dick wet."

Rebecca winces. "Ewww."

"Well . . . it's true," I spit. "He only wants to have sex with me."

"And . . . the problem is?" says Daniel.

"I'm not into casual sex." I straighten my back to sound more convincing.

"Oh yes you are," Rebecca chimes in. "What about Heath, you two fucked like rabbits for months without a care in the world."

"That was Heath, he doesn't count."

"Why not?"

"Because he had just got out of a relationship, we were rebound fucking." I sip my wine. "That's different."

Daniel screws his face up in disgust. "You would actually rather have blah rebound sex with Heath, than hot and steamy with sex god Elliot Miles?"

"He's my boss," I scoff.

"All the better. Ask for a raise while you're giving him head. Get a two-for-one bonus."

We all giggle.

Rebecca's eyes flick up from my phone as she reads. "Did you really look at his dick?"

"No," I scoff again. "He's dreaming. I've got better things to do at work than look at his stupid trouser snake."

Daniel and Rebecca burst out laughing.

"Where do you come up with these analogies, Kate?"

"Growing up with my brother, Brad." I shrug. "I know every name there is for a dick. Lizard, schlong, rhythm stick," I mutter dryly as I sip my wine. "You name it, I've heard it."

"Hit me with your rhythm stick," Daniel sings. "Isn't that a great song; they need to bring that shit back. Why isn't someone remixing this? I swear I should be a record producer."

"Do they even have record producers anymore?" says Beck. "I mean there are no records, so what's that job called now?"

"Good question," I agree.

"Here you are." The waitress smiles as she arrives with our meals and places them down in front of us.

"Thank you."

She makes her way to the back room and we all begin to eat.

"Oh, and on Saturday night we're going out." Daniel cuts into his steak.

"Where to?" Rebecca asks.

"Club 55 are having an opening at their new venue. I've got four VIP tickets."

"Four tickets? Can I bring Brett?" Beck asks.

"Yeah, sure, why not," Daniel says as he chews his food. "Don't forget we're going work-clothes shopping tomorrow, Kate."

"We just got new stuff on the weekend?" I say.

"Yes, but now the ante has been raised, your hot boss wants to fuck you. We need to make his balls so blue that they fall off . . . until he's begging."

"He's not going to beg."

"Oh yes, he is."

I roll my eyes as I bite the food from my fork. "Great. The way you're spending my money I really do need to earn a bonus."

"Do it on your knees," Daniel says with a raise of his glass. "Earn that dirty money, girlfriend. Tell him you'll swallow for a company car."

"Stop." I laugh. "Will you shut up?"

"Just saying." He shrugs.

I try to hide my smile as I chew my food.

I'd swallow for free.

I sit in the café and stare across the street at the black Bentley parked out front of the Miles Media building. It's just six-thirty, and from the way that the driver is out of the car and leaning on the side as if on standby, I know he must be leaving soon.

I sip my coffee as my mind runs away with itself.

Does he always have a driver?

"Is this seat taken?" somebody asks as they pat the stool next to me.

"Oh, no." I smile. "That's fine, take it."

My attention goes back to the building—I wonder where he lives? I take out my phone and for the first time ever, I type "Elliot Miles" into Google.

> Elliot Miles is the third son of media mogul George Miles and his wife Elizabeth.
>
> Listed along with his three brothers in the USA rich list, he has an estimated wealth of seven hundred million dollars.

"What?" I whisper.

> No stranger to publicity, and true to family tradition, Elliot Miles has been linked to some of the most beautiful women in the world.

Affectionately nicknamed Casanova Miles by the press due to his apparent ability to get women to do anything he wants, he's previously been linked to Emmaline Howser, the renowned pianist, Heather Moretti, the acclaimed art director for US *Vogue*, and more recently, Clarissa Mulholland, the human rights lawyer for the United Nations.

He likes his women intelligent and interesting, beauty a very close but obvious third.

I click on images, and rows and rows of pictures come up with him and women—black-tie events, yachts, nightclubs, opening nights.

He's like a fucking rock star.

I bite my lip and raise an unimpressed eyebrow. Ugh, Casanova Miles . . . give me a fucking break.

Who cares. I click out of images and go back to the main page. I read on.

His art collection is one of the best in the world, estimated to be worth over two hundred million dollars, and is housed in a private gallery in New York. It is understood that his most intimate pieces are kept in his London home.

I screw my face up.

"Private art gallery, you are kidding me?" I mutter under my breath.

I look up at the Bentley, completely rattled.

What the ever-loving fuck?

Elliot's words come back to me from the other night. He isn't looking for hot.

He's looking for extraordinary.

I bite my thumbnail as I think about what that means.

Given all of the beautiful women from around the world that he's dated.

Extraordinary.

Even that choice of word is strange.

And when I meet her, I will know.

I go back over our conversation.

I believe in love at first sight, when our eyes meet. We will both know.

I bite my lip to stifle my smile.

The doors open and I see Elliot stride out, every step purposeful.

Briefcase in hand. Back ramrod-straight. He doesn't have to assert power, it comes naturally. Down to his bones, Elliot Miles is a born leader.

He nods and says something to his driver as he gets into the backseat. The door closes.

The car pulls out into the traffic and I watch as it drives away.

When our eyes meet. We'll both know.

I smile softly.

Elliot Miles still believes in magic.

And I know it's not me that he's waiting to meet.

I'm not extraordinary.

We didn't have that breathtaking eye-lock moment and we most definitely don't get along.

This isn't a grand love story.

I'm just an ordinary girl and his crush is horizontal.

I lean my chin on my hand as I stare out of the window.

But that's okay.

One day a man is going to walk in here and sweep me off my feet and we'll ride off into the sunset and live happily ever after.

I smile wistfully. I guess Elliot Miles and I do have one thing in common.

I believe in magic too.

We climb out of the car as cameras flash, and Daniel grabs my hand and pulls me in through the fancy black doors. "See." He smiles proudly. "This is why you have to look good at all times. The paps are here."

I tip my head back and laugh out loud at his delusion. "They aren't here to get us, you idiot, they're here to snap the actual celebrities. And please don't say the word paps, you sound ridiculous."

It's Saturday night and we are at the opening of some swanky club.

Daniel flashes a broad smile as he adjusts the straps on my dress. "Hey, we *are* on the guest list."

"*You're* on the guest list, I'm just the slummy sidekick."

"And don't you look fabulous."

I smile nervously as I run my hands down my thighs. "Are you sure this isn't too much?"

He links my arm through his as we progress in the line. "Darling, there's no such thing as too much."

I giggle as I glance down at myself: I'm wearing a hot pink, fitted minidress with little capped sleeves and nude strappy stilettos. My hair is out and tucked strategically behind one ear, and for the first time ever, I'm wearing pink lipstick. It kind of looks like I just stepped out of a high-fashion sixties magazine, and I hate to admit it, but I do look good.

We arrive at the front of the line and Daniel hands over our tickets. "Pity Rebecca didn't come."

"I know, she's in such a rut lately. She won't go anywhere," I reply.

Daniel scrunches his nose up. "This is why I'm not falling in love any time soon." He leads me into the club.

"Why, because you're not boring?" I ask.

"Precisely." He chuckles.

My eyes widen as I look around. "Oh wow."

The ceilings are so high that I can't even see the roof; it's dark and glamorous, with staircases around the edges that lead to the upper levels.

"Now this. Is a club." Daniel smiles. "Let's go for a walk and check it out."

Hand in hand we walk around the bottom level. There's a dance floor and tables and chairs. Huge leather couches are placed around a fireplace area. We walk up to the next level to find a swanky cocktail bar where the music is demure, and just wow at the people there.

"Everyone is so beautiful," I whisper, feeling very out of place.

"I know," Daniel replies. "I don't know who to look at first, I'm going cross-eyed, it's like a fucking smorgasbord."

I giggle as we walk up the stairs to the next level, which has a completely different feel. This has a whisky bar and an outdoor terrace with large, comfy chairs and fairy lights. "Oh, this is my favorite floor." I smile as I look out at the terrace. "Can we sit there?"

"Yes, let's check out the top level and we'll come back down to have a cocktail here."

"Okay."

He leads me up the crowded stairs, and when we get to the top I am completely flabbergasted.

A huge dance floor, filled with beautiful women in hardly any clothes.

"This must be the model floor." Daniel smirks as he watches them.

I tug the hem of my dress down, suddenly feeling self-conscious. *Jeez.*

"Okay, back downstairs," I say.

Daniel's eyes stay fixed to the girls. "Can we not stay here for a while?"

"I'm not drunk enough for this floor." I grab his hand and lead him back down the stairs.

"We're coming back here as soon as possible."

"Fine. Cocktails first though."

The stairs are busy and a group of men are coming up, and I lock eyes with Elliot and flick Daniel's hand away like a hot potato.

"Kate." He tries to hide his smile and fails miserably. "What are you doing here?"

"Cooking lessons," I reply, to try and be witty.

His eyes drop down to my toes and then back up to my face. "And I can see that you've got that stove smoking hot."

Oh . . .

My eyes go to Daniel and he smiles broadly. "I would say on fire."

Elliot's eyes flick back to Daniel. "What was your name again?"

"Daniel."

"Daniel who?"

Daniel smiles. "Daniel who lives with Kate, that's all you need to know."

Elliot stares at Daniel; his face is emotionless but he's clearly unimpressed with that answer.

I look from one to the other. Oh . . . jeez, *awkward.*

"Um, we should go. It was nice seeing you." I smile as we continue walking down the stairs.

"Goodbye," Elliot says as he continues walking up.

"Oh my God," I whisper. "Daniel who lives with Kate . . . what the hell was that?"

"He wants to google me."

I screw up my face in confusion. "Why would he want to do that?"

"To see if I'm a threat."

"What?"

"I'm telling you this guy has got it for you. The other night when you were out of it, he nearly didn't leave." We approach the bar on level three. "Can I have two margaritas please?" he asks.

"Sure thing." The waitress turns to make them.

I stare at Daniel. "Why?"

"Said that he didn't know if he should leave because I might take advantage of you."

"Elliot?" I frown.

"Yes."

"He actually said that?"

"Uh-huh."

"He didn't want to leave you with me. Why not?"

"Here you go." The waitress hands over our drinks.

"Thanks." We clink glasses.

"Obviously he doesn't like his stuff being touched."

I square my shoulders. "Well, that's ridiculous, I'm not his stuff."

Daniel chuckles. "Baby, I think we both know that he's circling. I mean . . . he told you so himself."

"That was Edgar. He didn't know that was me and maybe he'll never do anything about his horizontal crush. Thinking it, and actually doing it, are two completely different things."

Daniel's eyes hold mine. "Have you ever known Elliot Miles not to go after what he wants?"

My eyes hold his.

"Prepare for his onslaught baby, we both know it's coming. I can feel it in my waters."

I sip my drink as nerves flutter deep in my stomach. I hate to admit it but so can I.

Fuck.

Four hours later, Daniel throws his head back and laughs out loud and I smile into my drink: he's sitting opposite me on one of the couches out on the terrace. He's in the middle of a couple, a guy and a girl, and the three of them are talking, and the thing is, I have no idea which one he is actually flirting with.

But I think both.

They are bouncing off each other and the chemistry between the three of them is palpable.

What happens in these kinds of situations? Does he go home with them and the guy watches while he fucks his wife, or does he fuck the guy too?

God . . . I'm so vanilla.

"I've been looking for you," a deep voice says.

I turn to see Elliot sit down beside me. He hands me a red fancy-looking cocktail.

He's here.

Act. Cool.

"Oh, hi." I smile as I take the drink from him. "What's this?" I gesture to the drink.

"Ring My Bell. Recently become a personal favorite."

I smile and take a sip. "Oh . . . it's strong."

He watches me wince. "I like things to taste strong."

The hairs on the back of my neck stand to attention: the way he said that was decidedly sexual. I swallow the lump in my throat.

"We're going to dance," Daniel says, interrupting my thoughts.

"Okay," I stammer.

Shit . . . don't leave me with him. My eyes turn back to Elliot.

"Tell me." He sips his drink and his finger traces a circle on my shoulder. "How have you been moonlighting as a boring IT specialist for seven years?"

I smile. "I'm still a boring IT specialist."

"You're like Clark fucking Kent."

I giggle at his analogy; the feeling of his finger on my skin is doing things to me. "And what are you under the disguise?" I whisper.

His dark eyes hold mine. "Hungry."

The air crackles between us.

He picks up my necklace and straightens it around my neck, and puts the pendant to the front.

He tucks a piece of hair behind my ear as he stares at me.

I can't breathe.

He leans down and puts his lips to my ear. "I want you, Kate." He softly bites my ear and goosebumps scatter up my arm.

"I want you underneath me."

Chapter 7

Elliot

My teeth graze her ear and all of my senses are heightened.

I run my hand up her arm to feel goosebumps.

Fuck.

She's hot.

It's dark and I take her face in my hands and kiss her softly; she smiles against me and kisses me back.

Arousal begins to pump hard through my body and my cock hardens in my pants.

Her tongue dances with mine and I frown. Fucking hell . . .

She's really fucking hot.

Yes.

Yes.

Our tongues dance seductively as I begin to lose control. I lean into her.

My grip on her face tightens as my body begins to throb. She pulls back from me and licks her lips as she stares at me.

I reach for her and she holds her hand up as if to stop me.

"What are you doing?" I pant.

"I've had enough." She sits up and takes her lipstick from her purse, totally unaffected.

My eyebrows rise in surprise. Huh?

She opens a compact mirror and begins to put her bright pink lipstick on.

I lean in and nibble her neck and goosebumps scatter up her arms once more. She smiles.

"Don't bother with the lipstick; it will rub off on my dick," I breathe into her ear.

She turns her head and seductively licks my lips; I almost blow on the spot.

"I'm going," she whispers.

I smile darkly as I sit up to leave. "Yes . . . we are."

She rolls her lipstick on. "Sit down, you're not coming."

"What?"

"Sorry." She shrugs. "I guess I'm just not that into you."

What does she mean?

She puts her mouth to my ear. "And for the record, *you* would be underneath *me*."

I smirk. I like this game.

She bites my ear hard and I grab her head and hold it to mine.

For a moment, we stay close, bathing in the electricity between us.

And holy fuck, there's a lot of it.

"What am I supposed to do about this?" I take her hand and place it over my hard cock.

Her eyes darken and she leans forward and kisses me again. "Go upstairs and fuck a model," she breathes into my mouth.

I jerk back from her, unimpressed with her tone. "Careful," I warn her.

She stands, steps over me, and with her long legs straight and on either side of mine, she leans down to me one more time. "Elliot," she whispers.

I run my hands up her long legs. "Fuck off, we're going home now." I sit forward and she pushes me back in my chair. "My cock won't go down," I whisper up at her.

She kisses me as she reaches for something on the table and then I feel her hand at my crotch.

Hell . . . what must we look like?

Who fucking cares?

She kisses me once more and I smile against her lips as she undoes my fly.

Is she just going to jerk me off, right here? Fuck . . . she's an animal.

Yes . . . yes . . . yes.

I feel a burn on my balls and my eyes snap open.

Cold, ice fucking cold.

"That better, baby?" she whispers as she stands, runs her hand down my stubble.

I look down to see that she has put a handful of ice down my briefs. "What the fuck?" I growl.

She laughs, blows me a kiss, turns, and I watch as her sexy hot ass sashays through the crowd.

I dig the ice out of my pants and throw it under the table. I look around to see if anyone just saw what happened. I try to catch my breath as I drag my hand down my face. "What the hell was that shit?" I murmur.

I sit back and stretch my arms out along the back of the chair.

Testosterone is thrumming through my body, the primal urge to fuck is hard and real.

Her words come back to me: *I guess I'm just not that into you . . .*

Liar.

Nothing's easy with this woman. I want to go to her house and drag her into bed.

But of course, I won't.

Lesson number one, don't play with a player.

I smirk into my glass.

Kate Landon is going to get it.

Hard.

KATE

"Taxi," I call as I hold my arm up.

One pulls up and I dive into the backseat. "Quick, drive," I say to the driver.

"Okay lady, calm down," he says as he pulls out into the traffic. "What's wrong with you?"

"Just getting away from a bad date," I lie. I turn and look out the rear window and watch the club disappear into the distance.

I turn back to face the front as relief fills me. I can't believe I just did that.

I get a vision of Elliot in the club right now with ice down his pants, and I smile goofily.

Wow . . . *who am I?*

I think this is my favorite moment of all time.

I giggle to myself—go me.

Three hours later, the problem with playing hard to get is that you don't get it.

I lie in the dark and twist my mother's ring around my finger as I think. It's late—4 a.m.

I haven't heard from Elliot; I thought he would have messaged me, if only to give me a mouthful. And after sitting at my computer for an hour when I got home, Edgar hasn't answered my message either.

Which leads me to believe one thing: Elliot did in fact go back upstairs and fuck a model.

Just like I told him to . . . I throw the back of my arm over my face in disgust.

Ugh, you idiot.

Why did I say that?

I keep going over and over the way he kissed me, the way his broad shoulders felt under my hands.

And can we just take a minute to appreciate that humungous hard dick in his pants?

It's ridiculous, nobody can be that blessed.

He's like a porn star or something, or maybe it's just been a really long time for me and I've forgotten what erections feel like.

Hot and smooth, thick veins . . . hmmm.

A deep ache thumps in between my legs, my body pissed that I didn't deliver the goods.

Hell, I'm pissed.

A good fucking would have been just what I needed tonight, but the reality is a different story. I have my period.

And if I ever did fall into bed with the elusive Elliot Miles, he's going to have to work a lot harder than that . . . even if I am just a horizontal crush.

I mean, I don't want anything more than that anyway, but I'm not easy.

Especially not for domineering assholes who kiss like the devil.

My inner ho reappears and I wonder what it would be like to be underneath him . . .

Stop it.

I roll onto my side and nestle in, trying to find a comfortable position.

Just go to sleep.

I feel his breath on my neck and his teeth on my ear and I smile into the darkness.

For the first time in years, I feel alive.

Monday morning, I walk into the Miles Media building like a rock star.

Wearing a tight black dress and my hair in a high ponytail, I'm ready to take on the world.

I'm over my confidence crisis now. It doesn't matter if Elliot did fuck a model.

He's nothing to me.

Nope, nope, nope. I am not falling for his little seduction . . . Well, I now know it's not so little, but whatever.

And Edgar is in the shit too, where has that asshole been all weekend?

He's got no excuse not to reply to my messages, I'm just his platonic penpal friend.

Anyway, poof to men.

They all suck.

I arrive at my desk, and half an hour later I glance up through the glass wall to see Elliot standing at one of the desks talking to someone. He's wearing his navy suit, a white shirt, and he looks even more orgasmic today if that's humanly possible. I snap my gaze away.

Okay.

He's coming.

I sit up and rearrange my boobs in my bra. *I'm ready for you, big boy . . . bring it.*

For ten minutes I pretend to look at my computer screen.

What's he doing?

I keep my head to the front but I move my eyes in his direction. Stalker style.

He's talking and laughing with two girls.

What's so funny, asshole, and since when do you chat with people?

I raise my eyebrows. Ugh . . . typical.

I keep pretending to work, and then he walks past my office as he talks to Henry.

Here he comes.

He casually knocks on my window as a greeting and keeps walking, totally unfazed. He keeps chatting and they both get into the elevator, and disappear out of sight.

I stare at the closed doors and blink.

What?

A knock.

That's it?

That's not what he was supposed to do.

He was supposed to march in here and get all caveman and demand I have sex with him on this desk right now . . . and I just may have worn sexy panties by chance to rise to the occasion.

My blood boils . . . now he's going to pretend that nothing happened.

He wants to make me sweat . . . well, I'm not!

Typical Elliot fucking Miles style.

Screw you, asshole.

Jeez, maybe nothing did happen and I was just high on his aftershave. I mean, it's totally possible; he does smell really good.

"What do you mean he said nothing?" Rebecca huffs as we walk along.

"Just what I said, nothing. Not one word," I reply.

Daniel powers up in front and he turns back toward us. "Hurry up, this is supposed to be exercise."

Beck and I walk as fast as we can across the road to try and catch up.

"You know, if I'm going to walk with you girls, you have to step it up. I want to elevate my heart rate," he says.

"What's stopping you?" I roll my eyes. "Off you go then."

"Then what?" Beck continues.

"Nothing. I saw him numerous times in passing and he hasn't acted strange at all. Not one bit." I spread my hands out. "Completely normal."

She frowns as we walk.

"He's playing games," Daniel chimes in. "It's blatantly obvious."

"I doubt it," I pant. "And what happened to you on Saturday night, you didn't come home?"

Daniel shrugs as he walks on. "A bit of this and a bit of that."

"What does that mean?" Rebecca puffs. "Can we slow down? I'm about to go into cardiac arrest."

"Did you go home with that couple?" I ask.

He shrugs. "Maybe."

"Did you sleep with the guy or the girl?" Rebecca asks.

"A gentleman never tells."

Rebecca and I exchange exasperated looks. "We need details," I huff.

"Well, you're not getting them," Daniel fires back. "I had a wonderful night, is all you need to know."

"So, you slept with them both," I improvise.

"Who was better?" Rebecca says.

"Shut the hell up, I am not having this conversation," he fires back to Rebecca. "Talk to your friend about grabbing her boss's boner in a club and dousing it with ice."

I put my hands over my eyes. I can't actually believe I did that. "Stop talking about it!"

"Seriously, goals for sure," Rebecca says, and we walk for a while. "So what are you going to do now?"

"I don't know." I shrug. "We only have one week left of work before Christmas shutdown."

"That's bad timing," he replies.

"Why?"

"Well, the heat will die down, won't it? He will have slept with someone else by the new year for sure."

"If he hasn't already." I sigh.

"True," Rebecca agrees.

"Like I care, anyway." I continue to walk along as my mind begins to wander . . . Oh well. It was fun while it lasted.

It's late and I hear a notification ping; I smile and get out of bed.
Edgar.

> Hi Pinkie,
>
> Sorry, I didn't see your message until just now,
> I was working all weekend.

I roll my eyes. Liar.

> That's okay, I thought you must have had a hot
> and heavy weekend with your crush. How are
> you?

I see the dots as he types.

> No hot and heavy this end. How was your date?

I frown. No hot and heavy . . . at all? Or no hot and heavy with your crush? I'm going to lie about my date.

> Date was great, I'm a little smitten.

I smile as I wait for his reply.

Lucky you.

I frown and write:

So, you didn't see your crush at all?

I did, we kissed.

I smile goofily, and reply:

And?

And nothing, she wants to play games and I'm not into it. I've lost interest.

My mouth falls open in horror. What the fuck?
I type:

Attention span of a goldfish!

I delete.

You scuzzbucket . . .

I delete.
I exhale heavily. God, this is stupid. I sit back, deflated.
I eventually reply.

How was your kiss?

I see the dots as he types.

Incredible. I've thought of nothing else since.

I smile softly. *Me too.*

Well maybe you should ask her out on a date
or something?

Maybe . . .

How was your day?

Okay. I worked and then had a PT session.
Looking forward to going home for Christmas.

I frown. I already know where his home is but I'll play along
as if I don't.

Where's home?

Where I grew up, near my parents.

I smile sadly; it must be hard to live away from everyone.
Another message bounces in.

Are you going home for Christmas?

My shoulders slump. I write:

It's just me and my brother and sister now.

Christmas is a sad time of the year for me.

I'm sorry.

Me too.

Well, if it makes you feel any better, my mother makes me and my brothers wear knitted sweaters with reindeers on them.

I giggle as I imagine the big powerful Miles brothers in knitted Christmas sweaters to please their mum. I type a smiley face.

☺

I exhale as I wait for his next message.

Why are you smitten?

Maybe I'm smitten with the idea of being smitten.

Aren't we all?

He's so swoony in messages. Too bad he's an asshole player who loses interest really fucking quickly in real life. I type:

Maybe you'll meet your extraordinary girl over Christmas?

Maybe. Or maybe I'll spend my life having meaningless sex with people?

I frown and type:

Is that a bad thing?

No.

But what?

I want more.

More of what?

If I knew I would have found it.

I lie down in bed—I should tell him it's me. He's starting to tell me personal stuff and he's going to be pissed if he ever finds out that he's confiding in me. But for some reason I feel like he's flat and I want to comfort him.

You'll know when you meet her.

Will I?

I smile sadly.

Of course you will.

Will you?

I don't think I even want to love anyone. It hurts
too much when you lose them.

Silence for a few minutes. Eventually a reply bounces in.

Who hurt you?

My parents.

How?

They died.

I unexpectedly tear up and I quickly sign off so I can get offline
before he replies. I don't want to get into this; I don't know why I
even brought it up.

I'm tired,

Goodnight Ed,

Xoxo

I put my head back against the wall as the sweat runs down between
my breasts.

I'm in the sauna at the work gym, it's 8 p.m. on Wednesday
night.

This week has been long and I just want it to be Friday already.
I'm not even going to the stupid Christmas party tomorrow night—
not feeling very jolly.

This time of year is always shitty. Christmas is the climax that reminds me of what I don't have. But I get solace knowing that I'll wake up the day after Christmas Day and the weight of the world will be gone and I'll feel myself again; I always do. I just wish I could blink and be at that day.

The door opens and Elliot walks in wearing only a towel. "Hey." He takes a seat opposite me.

Shit.

"Hi."

He stays silent and I feel the air around me begin to circle with energy.

There's a sexual chemistry between us that I can't deny.

He inhales and puts his head back against the wall, and from my peripheral vision his muscles begin to taunt me.

Shit.

For fifteen minutes we sit in silence.

He's acting completely cool and normal, as if we didn't have those kisses in the club.

As if he's forgotten all about the things he said to me. Did it even happen or did I dream the entire thing?

With every minute that passes, my anger rises inside of me, until I can't stand it anymore. My inner rubber band snaps in a spectacular fashion.

"What is your problem?" I spit.

He gives me a slow, sexy smile . . . Damn it.

He won.

"You know, I don't care if you win this stupid fucking game," I whisper.

He watches me intently.

"And I don't care if you slept with ten models on Saturday night."

Amusement flashes across his face.

132

"Because I certainly don't want to sleep with you."

He raises an eyebrow.

"And what is that look? Don't give me that look, Elliot, because I know what you're doing."

He smiles and puts his head back against the wall as he closes his eyes. He's completely unfazed and I internally kick myself.

"What am I doing, Kathryn?" he asks.

Kathryn . . . I'm Kathryn again.

"You're trying to fuck with my head," I snap.

"Your head has nothing to do with it. I want to fuck your body."

My mouth falls open in horror. "Do you have to be so crass?" I whisper angrily.

He shrugs casually. "It's who I am. If you're looking for romance, move along."

I stare at him—where's the dreamy guy from online? Is it even the same person?

I like Ed a lot fucking better.

"I *am* moving along," I say as I tighten my towel.

"Why?"

"Why?" I scoff. "How is that even a question?"

"I have something you want, you have something I want. We could help each other."

"You mean, be each other's booty call."

He smiles as he closes his eyes again. "No."

"No what?"

"Well, a booty call is coming quick after a night out."

"Oh, please." I roll my eyes.

He sits forward and puts his hands on my thighs and spreads my legs. "I'm talking about spreading you out and eating you up."

I swallow the lump in my throat.

133

"And riding you so hard for hours that you won't remember anyone before me."

Our eyes are locked.

"And you'll be wet, and full of me." He grabs a handful of my hair and drags my face down to him. He puts his mouth to my ear. "And I'll be full of you." He whispers as his tongue darts out to lick my face. My eyes flutter closed at the feeling of his thick tongue.

Dear God.

Goosebumps scatter up my arms.

He releases me and sits up as if completely detached. "Take your time and think about it. I know this isn't everyone's cup of tea and a lot of women can't handle it."

"Think about what?" I ask.

"I don't do things in halves, I don't do relationships, and I most definitely don't share."

"What *do* you do?" I whisper.

"I can fuck you like nobody has before."

The air crackles between us.

"Make up your mind, because if we do this, we do it hard." He drops to his knees between my legs and licks up the length of my inner thigh. I watch him, transfixed.

Fucking hell . . .

He flicks his tongue up my thigh as his eyes hold mine and I glance at the door. What if someone comes in and sees him on his knees doing this?

"You want sex with no strings?" I whisper.

"Yes." With one last open-mouthed kiss on my bikini bottoms over my sex, he stands. "I want a consensual arrangement."

My insides begin to melt.

"Will we see other people?" I ask.

"No."

"Why would I do that?"

His eyes hold mine. "Because it's the only way you can have me."

Damn it, how does he know?

He leans down, cups my face in his hand and kisses me softly, with just the right amount of suction. "You know how to reach me."

He walks out of the door and doesn't look back, and the door closes behind him.

I close my eyes as I try to control my breathing.

Holy fucking fuck.

Chapter 8

I push the food around my plate with my fork.

"I said, don't you like it?" Rebecca says as if repeating herself.

"Huh?" I look up in a daze. "I'm sorry, I didn't hear you." I quickly shovel a mouthful in. "Of course I like it. This is my favorite."

Daniel watches me. "What's wrong with you tonight?"

"Nothing, why?"

"Because you've hardly said two words since you got home."

"Tired, I guess." I shrug, not wanting to tell them the news that Elliot Miles licked my thigh in the sauna and wants sex with no strings and I'm not allowed to see anyone else and he has a big dick and this whole month is turning into a fucking disaster.

"Have you heard from Elliot?" Rebecca asks.

I shake my head. "No," I lie. I'm embarrassed about his indecent proposal. I don't want to have to explain the situation because, quite frankly, I don't understand it myself.

"What about your online crush, Edgar?" Daniel asks.

"No." I chew my food. "I haven't spoken to him either."

I'm lying up a storm here tonight.

Why wouldn't I? When Edgar told me that it wasn't a grand love affair and that it was just a horizontal crush—boy, he wasn't lying. It's not even a steamy affair . . . it's a business transaction of seminal fluid.

"He's an ass," Daniel replies. "This is why you're down."

"I'm not down," I huff. "Elliot Miles is nothing to me."

Okay, maybe a little down.

When Elliot told me he wanted me, for a moment there it was exciting and new and a way to get myself out of this rut. Hell, putting ice down his pants was the highlight of my year. But now that I know that he sees me as a walking vagina . . . his crush has lost its shine.

And what's worse, I'm actually considering it. I know it's stupid, I know that he's going to turn out to be an asshole and that I'm probably going to get fired, or hurt.

Worse still, both.

I remember back to the sauna, with him on his knees between my legs, and I get a flutter in my stomach, but he's just so . . .

He makes me feel something, and even if it's bad, it's still a feeling.

I now realize I've been numb for years and that if I want to come back to being myself, maybe Elliot is a good stepping stone to get there.

I continue to eat in silence as Daniel and Beck talk about some new Pilates app they have downloaded.

My mind wanders off on a tangent again . . . I like Edgar. He's sweet and intelligent and swoony but then I remember who he really is.

I don't need a complication like Elliot Miles in my life. Far from it, I'm not a young girl blinded by lust with doe-in-the-headlight eyes. I don't need my boss going down on me in the work sauna to feel alive.

I know better.

But . . . *my boss going down on me in the work sauna* . . . even that statement turns me on.

I've got fucking issues.

I'm finally just getting my shit together . . . I'll be going backwards by falling into bed with someone as gorgeous and dominant as him.

It's a disaster waiting to happen.

"You like him, don't you?" Rebecca says as she directs the conversation back to me.

"Who?" I act dumb.

They both roll their eyes. "Elliot Miles."

"I don't know him, and why are you two going on about this all night?"

"Sorry." Rebecca widens her eyes.

We continue eating.

"You've got your work Christmas party tomorrow night, haven't you?" Beck asks to change the subject.

"Just drinks in the office. What have you guys got on?"

"I'm sleeping at Brett's," Rebecca answers.

"I'm going home to see my folks for a few days," Daniel says. "My mum is a bit down."

"Is she okay?" I ask.

"She had cancer this year and it's taken its toll. I'm going home to help her wrap and prepare for Christmas Day. My father is useless."

I smile as I put my hand over Daniel's on the table. "You're a good man, you know that?"

"Well, there's only me this year—my sister's deployed and won't be home until February."

"She's in the navy, right?" I ask.

He nods proudly. "She's a badass. Could totally kick my butt."

We chuckle.

"You're having Christmas Day lunch here for your brother and sister, right?"

I nod. "It sounded like a good idea at the time."

"Not so much now?" Daniel asks.

"Ugh, I haven't even thought about what I'm cooking. It's all just too hard."

"Well, I'm only going away for two days and then I'll come back and help you prepare the food. I don't leave to go home until Christmas Eve, and we could have most of it done before I go."

"You don't have to do that." I smile.

"Babe, what else am I going to do? Being at home for more than two days drives me crazy and tomorrow is my last day at work. We can work out a few recipes over good wine."

I smile, grateful for my new friend, and turn my attention to Rebecca. "What are you doing for Christmas Day again Beck?"

"I'll be refereeing fights with my dysfunctional family." She sighs.

We smile as she continues.

"You know, you would think that when your parents get divorced the shit show stops. But no . . . they get new fuckwit partners and you get to have a double shit show with whipped cream and extra topping."

We all chuckle.

Daniel raises his glass and we both touch it with ours. "To Christmas, the ultimate shit show."

"To Christmas."

It's just gone 11 a.m. and I sit down at my desk with a cup of coffee. My email pings.

Elliot Miles.

Hello Kathryn,

I'd like a meeting with the ITM team please.

All of you in my office in thirty minutes.

Elliot.

"Shoot." I get up and walk into the office next to mine. "Bob, did you just get the email from Elliot?"

Bob looks up from his computer. "I haven't checked, hang on." He opens his email and scrunches up his nose. "Yep." His eyes come back to me. "You think it's about the internet crash last week?"

"Of course it is." I roll my eyes. "I'm not in the mood for this today."

Bob exhales heavily and then Joel pops his head around the doorjamb. "Did you two get the email?"

"Yep."

We all stare at each other for a moment. When you get a private email invitation to Elliot Miles's office, it isn't for a tea party and cake.

You are about to get in deep shit.

"If he starts on me today, I'm telling him to stick it," Bob snaps.

"Stick what, exactly," Joel teases.

"His stupid fucking job up his stupid fucking ass," Bob replies.

"Yeah, yeah, tough guy," Joel replies. "You know the drill, just let Kate do the talking."

Bob nods in agreement.

Wimps.

Great . . . just what I need.

Half an hour later we arrive at the top floor. "Hello." Courtney smiles. "Just go in, he's expecting you."

Bob, Joel, and I exchange glances.

"Great." I fake a smile, we walk through, and I drop my shoulders and steel myself for his onslaught.

Elliot Miles is a lot of things; weak is not one of those.

Bob knocks on the door. "Come in," the deep voice calls.

"Fuck this," Joel whispers.

I smile—it's actually hilarious how scared the boys are of him.

We walk in to find Elliot sitting behind his desk. He sits back and raises his chin to the sky and I instantly know that stance.

He's not mad, he's raging fucking angry.

"You wanted to see us," I ask.

He points to the conference table with his pen. "Let's sit over there."

I exhale.

I hate that fucking table.

He stands and undoes his suit jacket with one hand—he's wearing a navy suit and a fitted crisp white shirt—takes his jacket off and throws it over the back of his chair, his tight behind on display. As he stands I can see the muscles flex in his shoulder as he pulls his chair out.

Great, just what I need to see—suit porn.

His dark hair is hanging over his forehead and his eyes are a brilliant blue. It would really help my cause if he got a little uglier.

"I want to talk to you about the internet outage last week." He slaps the printed report on the table in front of us. I'm instantly pulled out of my daydream.

Focus.

"I thought you might," I mutter under my breath.

"Explain it to me," he says.

I open my mouth to speak.

"Not you. Joel," he interrupts.

Joel and Bob exchange nervous glances.

"Well, we had to upload a new system into our admin site and to do this we needed to add a new WAP code."

Elliot picks up his pen and holds it in his hand as he listens.

"What we didn't realize was, that when we added the new WAP code it was going to completely override the system for the entire building."

"Why didn't you realize that?" Elliot stares at him blankly.

Joel shrugs.

"Isn't it what I pay you for? An IT expert to stop an impending disaster before it comes to fruition."

Joel goes to open his mouth and then shuts it again; his eyes flick to me for reassurance and I give him a stifled smile.

"Don't look at Kathryn, look at me. Who specifically out of you three uploaded the system?"

"I approved it," I reply.

"That's not what I asked," Elliot replies sharply. "Who uploaded this system?"

Fuck's sake.

"I did," Bob whispers.

Elliot sits back in his chair, and glares at Bob. "Tell me . . . Bob." He sneers. "How many Miles Media employees are in this building?"

Bob swallows the lump in his throat. "Around two thousand, sir."

"Two thousand, one hundred and seventy-one," Elliot barks. "And what do you estimate the hourly wages are for that many people, Bob?"

Bob begins to perspire.

"Mr. Miles, with all due respect . . ." I say.

"Do. Not. Interrupt. Me. Kathryn," he bellows.

We all wither in our seats.

"The hourly wages for this building alone are seventy-four thousand, nine hundred pounds."

We all sit still. Fuck . . . get me out of here.

"Let's multiply that by the three hours that I didn't have any goddamn internet," he growls.

Bob drops his head.

"That's two hundred and twenty-four thousand and seven hundred pounds your incompetence has cost me."

I exhale. Oh hell.

"Would you like me to deduct that from your salary?" He looks at the three of us.

We stay silent.

"Answer me!" he bellows.

"No sir," we all reply.

He stands and leans on the desk with both hands as he glares at us. "And yet, you have deducted it from mine," he growls. "Tell me why I shouldn't terminate your contracts on the spot."

He's such an asshole.

I sit back, angered. "That's fine with me, terminate my contract."

Elliot narrows his eyes, his temper seconds away from an impending explosion. "Oh, you'd like that, wouldn't you? Run away from your incompetence instead of facing the music. I don't know why I would expect better."

I roll my eyes.

"Do not roll your eyes at me," he yells, making us all jump.

The door opens. Christopher pokes his head in and looks between us and fakes a smile. "Elliot, can I see you for a moment, please?"

"I'm busy," he snaps.

"Now." He widens his eyes.

Elliot marches from the room and the door clicks closed behind him. Bob and Joel slump in their seats.

"Don't you dare resign," Joel whispers.

"I agree," Bob says.

"Screw this," I whisper back. "I'm sick of his shit, he's a fucking asshole. I'm out of here."

"Calm down, he's been like this for years. Why is it suddenly bothering you now?" Joel whispers.

Because I didn't want to sleep with him then.

"I don't know why he's going on and on," Bob whispers. "He makes two hundred thousand pounds every ten minutes."

The door reopens and Elliot walks in, takes his seat, his composure completely restored.

Christopher Xanax Miles: he's the only one who can calm Elliot and his temper.

I've seen it many times.

Elliot picks up his pen and sits back as he looks between us. "This is not to happen again, do I make myself clear?"

"Yes," the three of us reply.

"I'm disappointed. When I pay for the best, I expect the best." He exhales heavily as he looks between us and tosses his pen onto the desk as if giving up. "You may return to your offices."

We all stand.

"Kathryn, you stay back. I need to see you as regards to the prospectus you sent through."

My anger bubbles and I sit back down, biting the inside of my cheek to stop myself from saying something snarky like *Fuck you and fuck right off.*

The door closes behind Joel and Bob and his eyes come to me.

We stare at each other for a moment until I can't stand it anymore and I raise my eyebrow.

"What do you want to discuss about the prospectus?"

144

He gets up and comes around the desk and leans his behind on the back of it. He crosses his legs in front of him at the ankle and grips the desk behind him with two hands.

"Don't threaten me, I don't like it," he says calmly.

"It wasn't a threat."

"I keep my professional and private lives separate, I thought you could too."

"I do." I straighten my back. "I mean, I am."

His eyes hold mine. "That's a lie. You've never threatened to leave before. In fact, you have stayed to spite me. Suddenly today, you want to resign?"

"Nobody gets to speak to me like that, whether I'm sleeping with them or not."

"We haven't slept together . . . *yet*." He accentuates the yet. "Although, I'm rectifying that situation very soon."

You wish.

I stay silent, unsure what to say that won't sound melodramatic. He's right, I've never contemplated leaving before today; maybe I can't separate the two.

"I leave for New York in the morning," he says.

I nod.

His eyes hold mine and then he raises an impatient eyebrow. "And?"

"And what?" I reply.

"Am I going to see you tonight?"

"I'm going to be at the Christmas party like everyone else in the building." I shrug casually. "So, I guess that means yes."

He narrows his eyes. "What's with the attitude?"

I stand. "You know, for an intelligent man, you're pretty stupid. If you think you roasting me and my work colleagues over an honest mistake is a turn-on, you've got another thing coming."

He puts his jacket back on and his hands in the pockets. "I'm a professional, Kathryn. I wouldn't be who I am if I wasn't. Incompetents won't be tolerated, I don't care what my relationship with them is."

I squirm and look out of the window to evade his glare.

"Do you want preferential treatment—is that what you're saying?"

"No, of course not," I snap.

"Then look at it from my angle, do you want to be treated the same at work or don't you?"

I clench my jaw . . . fucker has got me.

"I can separate the two," he continues. "The Kathryn I work with and the Kate that I want."

He puts his finger under my chin and brings my face up to meet his; his eyes drop to my lips. "Now let's talk about Kate," he murmurs. "I like her."

His eyes are so blue . . . and I feel myself lean toward him.

Just one kiss . . .

I snap out of my trance. "Let's not." I turn and march from the office. I hit the elevator button with such force I'm surprised I don't break it. I storm into the elevator and take it to the ground floor. I need to go for a walk in the fresh air to try and clear my head.

Everything is just so confusing at the moment. My life is a head-fuck . . . and not in the good way.

Music is piping through the gym and the sound of laughter can be heard throughout the space. Trays of champagne and beer are being walked around by waiters and there are balloons and Christmas decorations.

I'm at the work Christmas party and this isn't how it was supposed to be. Miles Media was to be going away for a mini break overnight just outside of London, but the country club we were having it at burned down last month.

I stand at the back of the crowd with my team and sip my champagne as I people-watch.

Christmas parties always bring out the worst in people; you see your colleagues in a completely different way. Last year, Little Miss Innocent Prim and Proper from level two spent the night in one of the married managers' rooms. She was the talk of the office for weeks. Marcus and Neil, who are both married, were caught kissing each other in the photo booth, and Mandy from level nine took her top off and danced in her bra because she was hot. I smile as I remember it—it really was a funny night.

My mind comes back to the present and to Elliot's indecent proposal.

As much as I'm attracted to him, and I am, I can't deny it—and after today, I don't even know why—I don't want to be the workplace fool.

He's told me straight up: no strings, no relationship or feelings, and no other people.

So, why would I even consider doing it?

I mean, isn't the point of seeing someone about having fun, going to places, and getting to know each other? If I'm not going to be seeing anyone else, don't I want to be with someone who's proud to be with me?

I really wish I'd never messaged Edgar Moffatt now. It's given me an inside insight into Elliot Miles that I shouldn't have seen and I feel closer to him than I actually am . . . and I shouldn't.

I know he's a cold bastard and that he would never be satisfied with just me . . . I could never be that incredible woman he's searching for, no matter how hard I tried.

Actually, let me rephrase that: I wish I had met Edgar instead of Elliot. He does have everything I'm looking for.

Elliot Miles and he couldn't be more different, which is ridiculous because I know that they are the same person.

But then I remember that he's looking for extraordinary and he still believes in fairy tales and I know there's more to him than meets the eye.

Ugh . . . I'm going around and around in circles with this.

One minute I'm excited, because this is new and interesting and hot and we could have amazing unbridled sex.

The next moment, I imagine Bob and Joel finding out about me sleeping with him and what they and the rest of the office would think of me, and I'm mortified.

I know what I have to do, as tempting as it is to be carefree and alive.

I'm going to decline.

And already I hate the thought of it . . . so what's that saying about the hold he has on me already?

Damn it . . . we've only made out.

I get a vision of us from the other night at the club and the way he kissed me.

The way he held my face in his hands, the way his eyes were closed.

He's just so . . . *gah.*

I look across the room to see him arrive with Christopher, talking with the rest of the top-floor management staff.

He's in his perfectly cut suit and has a Corona beer in his hand, and I can see his eyes scanning the place as he talks.

He's looking for me.

Enough.

This isn't happening.

I dig my phone out from my bag and pretend to answer it. "Oh really, I'll be right there." I hang up and turn to Joel. "I have to go. My sister's car has broken down and she's stranded on the motorway."

"Oh." His face falls. "Okay." He kisses me on the cheek. "Have a great Christmas break."

"You too." I turn and kiss Bob on the cheek. "See you next year, Bob. Merry Christmas."

"You too, darling."

"Don't tell anyone I slipped out," I whisper.

"Sure thing."

I look across the room and lock eyes with Elliot. He gives me a slow, sexy smile and sips his beer. His eyes are dark and hungry and I feel them all the way to my toes.

Fuck.

I drain my glass and walk toward the restroom. I need to throw him off.

I walk in, look at myself and turn around, walk straight back out and dart to the corridor and into the elevator.

With my heart hammering in my chest I ride the elevator down to the ground floor.

Don't let him follow me . . . please don't follow me.

I need some distance.

He goes away for two weeks tomorrow, which will give me some breathing space.

The doors open and I walk out through the lobby and onto the street to a taxicab stand, and I dive into the back of one.

"Hello."

The driver smiles and looks back at me. "Where to, love?"

"Home, take me home . . ."

The snowflake drifts from side to side until it eventually finds its place on the ground. So insignificant on its own, but together with its friends it creates a magical ice blanket.

The moonlight is reflecting off the street below and, in my pajamas, I sit curled and crossed-legged in the window seat of my bedroom, staring out at the world . . . it seems so still and peaceful.

It's 11:30 p.m. and I can't even think about going to bed. I'm still wound up.

My mind is ticking at a million miles per minute.

I watch as a car appears around the corner, two headlights light up the road and they come to a stop outside my house. I peer down: it's a black Bentley.

The back door opens and Elliot climbs out and walks up to my front door.

Shit . . . he's here.

Chapter 9

Knock, knock, knock echoes from downstairs.

It's not a gentle *are you home* knock, it's an *I'm here and I'm pissed* knock.

Knock, knock, knock sounds again.

What is he doing? It's 11:30 p.m., what if the others were home? I storm downstairs and open the door in a rush.

And there he stands, in all his overbearing gorgeousness.

"Yes?" I say.

"Why did you leave?"

"I was tired."

He raises an eyebrow as his eyes hold mine; he knows that's a lie.

"What do you want, Elliot?"

"Are you inviting me in?"

"No."

"Why not?"

Honestly, this man is infuriating.

"Because it's late and like I told you, I'm tired."

"We have things to discuss."

"No, we don't. I've already said my piece."

"Like hell." He barges past me and walks upstairs to my bedroom. I exhale as I'm left standing in the hall. "Please, come in." I close the door and walk up the stairs to find him pacing back and forth in my room, preparing for battle.

"What do you want, Elliot?" I ask as I close the door.

His eyes find mine. "You know what I want."

"No, I actually don't." I walk over to the window and stare out over the street.

I don't know what to say without sounding needy or whiny, perhaps just plain bitchy . . . damn it, I don't even know what I am.

"The thing is . . ." he says.

I turn and sink down to sit on the floor, up against the wall.

He stops what he's saying mid-sentence and we stare at each other, and after a while he comes and sits down on the floor beside me, his back against the wall like mine.

We sit in silence and stare straight ahead. It's like he doesn't know what to say either.

A first for Elliot Miles.

"What did I say?" he asks softly.

"When?"

"On the second day that we met and you told me that I had blue eyes, what did I say?"

"I don't remember," I lie.

"I've been thinking about this. There's a reason why you've hated me for all these years."

I stay silent.

"Just tell me."

"You told me that you didn't appreciate women being inappropriate in the workplace."

He frowns.

"And I . . ." My voice trails off as I stop myself.

"You what?"

I shrug.

He continues to stare straight ahead and we sit in silence for a while. "Kate . . . at the risk of sounding conceited . . ."

"*You* . . . sounding conceited?"

He smirks.

"Go on." I smile.

"I get hit on by women a lot . . . and it's not because they like me."

I listen.

"It's my surname and bank balance that women find attractive."

My heart drops.

"I deflect flirting all day long, I don't even notice that I do it. My brothers are the same."

I frown.

"So, when you told me that I have big blue eyes all those years ago—not that I remember you doing it, by the way—I obviously took it that you were hitting on me . . . and I put a stop to it before it carried on."

I bite my lip as I listen intently.

"Is that why you've been a bitch to me for all these years? To show me that you weren't flirting?"

"I've been a bitch to you because you're an asshole."

He drops his head and chuckles.

I find myself smiling too. "Well, it's true."

He picks up my hand and links his fingers through mine. "What are your reservations about doing this with me?"

"Well." I glance over at him. "Don't you think it's weird that you're suddenly attracted to me?"

"Yeah." He nods. "I do, I can't explain it."

I frown again; that's not what I was expecting him to say.

"I don't know why this happened but it was instantaneous. I saw you dancing in your red netball dress and I got hard."

"What?"

"I have a confession."

"Such as?"

"I might . . ." He pauses as if choosing his words carefully. "Watch the footage of you dancing in the photocopying room from a month or so ago . . . on repeat."

"Huh?"

He picks up my hand and kisses the back of it. "Let's just say, you rang my bell."

My mouth falls open in surprise as I put the pieces of the puzzle together. "Are you serious?"

He bites his lip to stifle his smile.

"Elliot." I gasp in surprise.

"I couldn't help it, you're just so fucking hot."

I smirk.

"Do you know how many times I've jerked off to that footage?"

I burst out laughing. "What?"

He falls serious once more. "What else, what are the other issues?"

"Well." I think for a moment. "Why don't you do relationships?"

"Because I've learned not to want more."

"Why?"

"Because as soon as I openly date someone, it's all over the tabloids and whoever I'm seeing gets hounded by the press over the impending nuptials. Everything we do is scrutinized and splashed over every headline."

I listen.

"Do you know how much pressure that puts on a relationship?" he asks.

"I can't imagine."

"If I sound cold and detached . . . it's because I am."

"Elliot," I whisper sadly.

He shrugs casually, as if he's totally at peace with being cold and detached. "I decided about six years ago that I was only going to see people in private and not openly date anyone. That way,

154

there's no gossip, there's no paparazzi stories, it's easier for me this way. And I know that it's selfish, but it is what it is."

"What happens when you meet the right girl?"

"I guess I'll work that out with her when the time comes."

I smile softly and I bump him with my shoulder. "That's a good answer."

"I know." He bumps me back. "Can we have sex now?"

I giggle in surprise. "No."

He smiles and puts his head back against the wall. "You know, I was coming over here to seduce you . . . having a heart-to-heart wasn't on my agenda."

"I needed to have this conversation." His answer makes sense and maybe I could deal with this. "Can we just . . . I don't know, take it slow?"

He turns his head to look at me and lets out a deep exhale. "Not exactly my strong point."

"Please." I lean over and kiss him softly. "For me?"

Our kiss deepens and he takes my face in his hands. His tongue swipes through my open lips. We kiss again and again and oh . . . I just love how he kisses me.

He grabs me and pulls me over to straddle him. My hands are in his hair as we kiss, it's soft and tender and with every lash of his tongue my temperature rises.

I feel his erection as I rock against him.

Oh . . .

I pull back to stare at him. "Slow . . . remember?"

He curls his lip. "You've got to be fucking joking me."

I smile with a wince. "Please."

"But I'm away for two weeks."

I have to stop now if I want to be able to, so I stand and pull him up by the hand. "I know."

He takes me into his arms and kisses me softly. "Remember our deal."

I smile up at him. "Remind me."

"No other people."

"That goes for you too, you know?"

"I know."

"What are you going to do in New York?"

"Jerk off to your netball dress movie, no doubt."

I giggle and brush the hair back from his forehead as I stare up at him. "Thanks for coming over."

He hugs me and we stay in each other's arms for a moment and he's so different to what I thought.

"I'm really fucking horny," he murmurs into my hair.

"Two weeks." I laugh.

I take his hand and lead him down the stairs and open the front door. He turns to kiss me.

"Two weeks," I remind him. He loses control and slams me up against the wall and he kisses me.

Our kiss turns desperate. His hands are on my behind and his erection is digging into my hip; my insides begin to melt.

"Slow," I pant against his lips.

He pulls back from me and we lean against each other with our foreheads touching.

Energy is swirling between us and I'm so close to caving and dragging him back up to my room.

"You've got two weeks." He kisses me softly. "And then you're mine."

I nod, as I control my erratic breathing.

One last look. "Goodbye," he says.

The door shuts and I lean on the back of it as I try to pull myself together.

Did that really just happen?

Excitement bubbles deep in my stomach.

Two weeks to lose weight, wax everything, and somehow get hot.

I smile goofily. Piece of cake.

Hi Pinkie,

What's happening?

How was your day?

I smile and type my reply. It's been three days since I saw Elliot, but Edgar has messaged me nonstop.

With every message I get from Edgar, my guilt toward Elliot grows; he's confiding in me and I'm just blatantly lying to him. I want to tell him that it's me, but it never feels like the right moment. I just love talking to Edgar and I love this insight I have into Elliot. It's like I have a secret identity, one that reveals his deepest, darkest secrets.

I'm going to tell him, I have to. I'm just waiting for the right moment, and soon—this can't go on.

It's the weirdest thing. I know they are the same person, but it doesn't feel like the same person. Elliot is strong, stubborn, and sexy, and on the other end of the spectrum, Edgar is deep, emotional, and sweet. Elliot hasn't contacted me at all.

And it's not flirty messaging, we really are just chatting.

Hi Ed.

My day was good. I went to the gym and then did some Christmas shopping and managed to

get it nearly finished. I just have my brother to
buy for now. What did you do?

I thought about Kate all day.

I smile as my heart does a somersault in my chest.

You've got it bad for this girl.

It seems so . . .

I bite my lip as I think what to write. I type:

What do you like about her?

I don't know, but I can't wait to find out.

I lean on my hand and smile dreamily at my computer.
I can't wait to find out either.
Eleven days to go.

Michael Bublé's swoony voice echoes through the house as the
sound of Christmas carols surrounds us.

"I think that's nearly it, darling," Daniel says as he fills his glass.
"Presents are wrapped, food is prepared, and don't forget you have
to put the trifle together in the morning."

I hold my glass up and he touches it with his. "Thank you." I
smile. "I couldn't have got all this done without you."

"It's a pleasure. Are you sure you won't come to my folks' for
tonight?"

"No, I'm fine here, honestly."

"I don't like the sound of you spending Christmas Eve alone."

"I'm going to the gym and then I'm going to get an early night. Being the host on Christmas Day is hell."

The doorbell chimes and Daniel's eyes meet mine. "You expecting someone?"

"No."

I open the front door to find a delivery man holding the biggest basket of beautiful pink flowers that I have ever seen.

"Kate Landon?"

"Yes."

"I have a delivery for you."

"Oh."

"Sign here please." He directs me where to sign and I take the huge basket from him.

"Thank you." I close the door as I struggle with the basket and put it down on the dining table. "What in the world?" There must be three hundred flowers here, pinks and whites in every shade. I touch the precious petals. "So beautiful," I whisper.

"Who are they from?" Daniel snaps.

"I have no idea." I take the small, white envelope and open it.

Kate,

Merry Christmas,

Elliot

x

"Oh." My mouth falls open in surprise. "A kiss at the end." I hold the card to my heart.

"Who's it from?" Daniel urges.

I pass him the card, he reads it, and then his eyes rise to meet mine. "Elliot . . . Miles?"

I smile.

His eyes widen. "Elliot Miles is sending you flowers?"

I snatch the card from him. "He's just being nice, that's all."

"Are you kidding me?" He gasps. "What's going on?"

"Nothing." I carry the flowers up the stairs with Daniel hot on my heels.

"Has something happened between you?" he asks.

"No."

"Bullshit, something has to have happened."

"He told me he liked me, that's all."

"And you didn't think to mention it?"

"I didn't know if he was serious." I place the flowers on my dressing table and smile as I reposition them.

"Well . . . I'm thinking he was serious, Kate. Call him, go over there right now, and thank him in the flesh."

I burst out laughing. "He's in New York, you idiot."

"He's in New York and is sending you flowers back home?" he shrieks. "Oh . . . he's got it bad." He snatches the card from me and reads it out loud.

Kate,

Merry Christmas,

Elliot

x

"Oh, merry fucking Christmas to you too, hot stuff," he says. "He could have at least written 'love' on the card, don't you think? It's very generic."

I snatch the card back from him. Excitement bubbles in my stomach as I stare at the flowers. I imagine Elliot ordering what to write on the card. "I need to call him and say thank you."

"Yes." Daniel smiles as he grabs my shoulders and turns me toward the door. "Yes, do it now. Come downstairs so I can listen."

"No." I laugh. "I'm doing it in private tonight after you leave."

Daniel puts his arm around me as we walk toward the stairs and he kisses my temple. "Seems Elliot Miles has some taste after all."

I pace back and forth with my phone in my hand. It's 8 p.m. on Christmas Eve and I have to call him.

I'm nervous as hell and my heart is beating hard and fast in my chest.

He called me years ago at a conference looking for a report, and I saved his number so I knew not to answer if he ever called me again. Never in a million years did I think I would be calling to thank him for flowers.

What do I say?

Thank you for the flowers, they're beautiful . . . then what? Hopefully he will lead the conversation from there.

I close my eyes as I steel myself.

I have to call, it's rude not to thank him.

Right.

Just do it.

Oh hell. I put my hand over my stomach to try and calm myself. I feel like I'm about to throw up.

My finger hovers over his name . . . shit. I close my eyes and press call.

I pace back and forth as it rings. Maybe he's busy. I mean, it's Christmas Eve, of course he's busy.

"Hello," his deep voice answers.

Oh fuck.

"Elliot, hi. It's Kate."

"Hello Kate." There is chatter in the background. "Let me go somewhere quiet so I can hear you." I hear him walk and then a door close. "That's better."

I screw up my face. "Thank you for the flowers, they're beautiful."

"Like you."

I smile goofily. "Are you always so smooth?"

He chuckles. "I do my best."

We fall silent.

"What are you up to?" he asks.

"Nothing much, just wrapping presents. You?"

"I'm at a cocktail party at my parents' house."

I imagine the rich and famous people that he would mix with; his life and mine are complete opposites.

"I won't keep you, I'll let you get back to the party," I whisper.

"No rush, I'd rather talk to you. These people are dull."

I smile as I pace back and forth, so nervous that I can't stand still.

"What are you doing for Christmas Day tomorrow?" he asks.

"My brother and sister are coming over, what about you?"

"Just at my parents' house in the Hamptons. Tristan cooks."

"Really?"

"Yeah, he fancies himself as a bit of a chef. He's done it since he was about eighteen; the meals have thankfully gotten a lot better since then."

I smile as I imagine the gorgeous Tristan Miles in an apron.

"Ten days until I see you," he whispers.

What?

My heart somersaults in my chest. "I can't wait," I whisper back.

We fall silent again.

"Go back to your party." I smile.

"I don't want to."

Oh . . . he's just so . . .

"You've made my day," I whisper. "Thank you."

"You're most welcome."

"I'll see you soon."

"Not soon enough."

I close my eyes as excitement thrums through my body.

Is this really happening?

"Merry Christmas, Kate Landon," he whispers in his deep, sexy voice.

I smile broadly. "Merry Christmas, Mr. Miles."

We hang on the line for longer than we should, neither of us wanting to hang up.

Eventually the phone clicks as he ends the call and I throw it onto the bed and twirl on the spot in glee.

Holy fucking shit.

We sit around the Christmas table and eat in silence.

The food is delicious, the carols are on in the background.

But it's hard—there are two people who should be here. Every year I hope this is the last bad one; every year I'm sadly disappointed.

It's all I can do not to run up to my room and cry on my bed. I don't want to do Christmas if it makes me feel this empty.

It just isn't fair.

Elanor, my sister, and Brad, my brother, eat in silence too—I know we all share the same feelings on this one.

We are all so different. Elanor is classically beautiful, she's sophisticated and smart and wears only designer clothes. She mixes with the elite crowd and has a swanky job in imports, always traveling the world with some new exotic boyfriend. My eyes roam over her: every man who has ever laid eyes on Elanor has fallen hopelessly in love with her.

My dad used to say that she was blessed by the gods. Even her birthmark is perfect, a small, pink love heart just below her ear high up on her neck. How is it possible that a birthmark is sexy?

Brad is more like me and appreciates the simple things in life. He's a physiotherapist and has just opened his own practice here in London. He had a girlfriend for six years but they recently broke up. He said that they became best friends and the fire just fizzled out between them. I thought they were going to be together forever; the thought of fires fizzling out between two people so in love scares the crap out of me. If it could happen to them, it could happen to anyone.

"This is beautiful, Kate." Brad gestures to his food. "It really is."

"Thanks." I try to make conversation. "The potato is Grandma's recipe."

Brad nods, too welled up with emotion to reply.

We usually hang out with our extended family, aunts and uncles and cousins. But three years ago, we decided to be on our own at Christmas, so if we wanted to be sad, we could. There is nothing worse than pretending to be happy when you're dying a little inside.

"I've found a buyer for Mum and Dad's house," Elanor announces.

I frown. "We aren't anywhere near selling, it's going to take six months to clean out everything."

"I've done it."

"Done what?" Brad replies.

"Cleaned out Mum and Dad's house."

"What?" I frown again. "What do you mean?"

"It's been six years, someone had to do it."

"We told you we wanted to do it together."

"Well, you two have been fucking around for forever."

"Because we weren't ready," I stammer. "Where is their stuff?"

"Gave most of it to charity."

I fall back in shock as my eyes well with tears. If she hit me with an axe it would hurt less. "Tell me you're lying."

"What good is it to us? I donated it all."

"What?" I cry as I jump from the table. "How could you?"

"You better be fucking lying," Brad growls. "We told you not to touch their house."

"Somebody had to do it. I'm sick of waiting for you two."

"Where are their things?" I cry.

"I told you, I donated a lot of it."

I get a vision of all Mum and Dad's precious belongings sitting in a charity shop. "Where?" I begin to cry uncontrollably.

"Calm down," she huffs. "I kept the photos."

"What about my things in the attic?" I ask.

"Gone." She shrugs casually without a care in the world.

I think of all Mum's cross-stitch and crockery, her clothes and all the things I wanted to pass down to my children one day, and I cry harder.

How could she?

"I cannot believe you would do this to us . . . Actually, I can," Brad yells. "You think of nobody but yourself. You're the most selfish person I've ever met. You know damn well Kate wanted those things."

My chest is wracked with tears and I just need to get away from her.

I run upstairs to my bedroom and slam the door.

I can hear Elanor and Brad having the screaming match of all screaming matches and I put my pillow over my head to try and block out the sound of fighting.

It's not supposed to be like this.

Merry fucking Christmas.

Hi Pinkie,

Merry Christmas,

How was your day?

I can hardly read his message through my swollen eyes. I'm not going to drag him down.

It was great.

How was yours?

I screw up my face in tears as I wait for his reply.

When I talk to him, I feel better.

Edgar Moffatt, my sweet distraction.

The only problem is our friendship isn't even real.

Elliot only wants me for sex and I have to lie to Edgar for him to even talk to me.

I angrily swipe the tears away so I can read his messages.

I know it's bad; my life is a mess.

My phone rings and the name Elliot lights up the screen, and my heart somersaults in my chest.

"Hello." I smile as I answer it. I haven't spoken to him since I called him to say thank you for my flowers a few days ago.

"Hi," his deep, sexy voice replies.

"How are you?" I ask. It feels good to hear his voice. I mean, I message Edgar every day but he doesn't know it's me.

"I'm back in London."

I frown. "I thought you were getting back next week."

"I couldn't wait to see you."

My mouth drops open in surprise. "Really?"

"Yes, really. I'll pick you up at seven tonight?"

I smile. "Okay."

"See you then."

He hangs up and I put my hands over my mouth.

Holy shit . . . *he couldn't wait to see me.*

I stare at myself in the full-length mirror in awe. I'm pimped up to the nines and I like what I see.

Daniel has had a field day picking out my clothes for tonight— we shopped up a storm today. I'm wearing a black fitted dress with spaghetti straps and nude stilettos; my blonde hair is out and full and I have natural makeup on.

I may have also had a little spray tan and I hope he doesn't notice. I don't want to appear like I'm trying too hard.

It's just turned seven when the headlights pull up out the front, and I put on my long black coat and make my way downstairs.

Daniel's door opens and I point to him in a warning. "Don't come out here."

"Have fun."

I blow him a kiss and he waves, before closing his bedroom door again. I asked them to stay in their rooms while Elliot picked me up, just for tonight. It's awkward enough without adding other people to the mix.

He knocks at the door and I close my eyes—*here we go.*

I open the door in a rush and there he stands: black jeans, grey shirt, and a blazer.

His dark hair is messed to perfection and his big, blue eyes smile as he sees me.

"Hi," I breathe.

He steps forward and takes me firmly into his arms and kisses me, no hello, no warning.

Just lips, and suction, and oh hell . . . I've had a good night already.

Chapter 10

He stands back and with my hand in his, he holds it up while his gaze drops to my toes and back up to my face. "You look beautiful," he whispers.

I smile softly.

He kisses me again. "Let's go, before I eat my dessert before dinner."

He leads me out to the Bentley and opens the rear door and I slide in.

The driver nods in a greeting, and Elliot slides into the seat beside me.

"Andrew, this is Kate."

"Hello."

"Hi."

Andrew pulls out into the traffic and Elliot holds my hand on his lap; his thumb dusts back and forth over it as if he's deep in thought.

"How was New York?" I whisper. Can Andrew hear what we are saying? This is weird, having someone listen to our conversation.

Elliot gives me a slow, sexy smile and leans down and takes my lips in his. "It didn't hold me there, put it that way," he murmurs against my lips; his thumb rubs back and forth over my cheekbone as he stares down at me.

Oh . . .

Good grief, this man wrote the book on seduction.

I already want my dessert too.

I smile bashfully as I feel my cheeks heat.

He's so intense.

He pulls back and licks his lips, tasting my lipstick. "In a moment, Andrew is going to drop you at the restaurant. We will circle the block and you will go in and say you are a guest of Mr. Miles—they will take you to a private dining room."

My face falls.

"I'll join you in two minutes. We'll have privacy this way." He lifts my hand and kisses the back of it as if to soften the blow; he can sense my disappointment. "You'll get used to it, sweetheart," he says softly. "This is how I am."

I fake a smile and turn my attention out of the window; he doesn't want to be photographed with me.

Stop it.

"Maybe I should do a runner before you get there," I murmur.

He chuckles. "Try it and see what happens to you." He lifts my hand to his lips once more. "I would track you down."

"I can run fast," I tease.

"I run faster."

We stare at each other and I get the feeling that on some level I've just been warned.

He likes control.

"We don't have to go to a restaurant if you don't want to," I offer. "Seems like a lot of hassle."

"No, I've booked already. It's my favorite, the food and cocktails are to die for. You'll like it, I promise."

I nod and he holds my hand on his lap.

Moments later the car pulls up outside an Italian restaurant. I can see a few photographers seated on crates just up the road.

"I'll let you out around the corner, Kate," Andrew says casually.

"Okay."

The car turns the corner and pulls over. "Just go into the foyer of Bella Donna and tell them you're a guest of Mr. Miles, they're expecting you," Elliot reminds me.

I nod. "Okay." I go to get out of the car and he pulls me back into the seat and kisses me once more. My nervous eyes flick to Andrew in the front seat as he stares straight ahead: how many times has he seen this scenario?

This is weird.

I pull out of his kiss and open the car door in a rush.

I walk around the corner and into the restaurant.

The hostess smiles. "Hello."

"Hi, I'm a guest of Mr. Miles."

The woman fakes a smile and looks me up and down. "Of course, this way please."

I follow her through the restaurant and she opens a large door and we walk down a corridor; she opens another double door and there's a room with its own fireplace and a table set for two. It's lit with candles and the room is ultra-romantic.

She pulls out a chair and takes my coat. "Can I get you a drink while you wait for Mr. Miles?"

I stare at her, she knows the drill; how many women does he bring to this room?

"Yes, I'll have a margarita and a tequila shot, please."

She smirks.

"Actually, make that two shots."

"Okay." She goes to walk off.

"Can you hurry with the shots please?" I all but beg.

She smiles broadly. "One of those nights?"

"You could say that."

"Sure thing." She disappears out and I look around the room. Wow. It really is out of this world, looks like I'm in a fancy ski lodge in Switzerland or something . . . not that I've ever been to a fancy ski lodge in Switzerland, but this is what I imagine it would look like.

The door opens and Elliot appears, smiles, bends, and kisses me before taking a seat. "Hello."

He's very kissy.

I force a nervous smile and the waitress arrives with a silver tray.

Oh no, you were supposed to bring that before he got here, fool.

"Here you are, one margarita and two tequila shots." She places them down in front of me; my eyes flick up to Elliot and he smirks, clearly amused.

"Thanks."

"Thirsty?" he asks.

I nod, pick up my margarita and take a sip, wishing I could drain the whole damn glass.

"I'll have a bottle of Barbaresco 1996," Elliot tells the waitress.

"Of course, sir." She disappears again.

With a shaky hand I sip my margarita and Elliot leans his face on his hand as he watches me. His pointer finger runs up his temple, and he seems completely relaxed. "Are you nervous?"

"Little bit." I take a bigger gulp of my drink.

"Is there anything I can do to help?"

"You can pass me that tequila."

He raises an eyebrow and passes me a shot glass.

Oh hell, I look like the world's biggest loser, but it's either skull this or be a nervous nutcase all night. I tip my head back and drain the glass.

"You swallow well."

I glance up.

172

His eyes are dark and we both know he's not talking about the tequila.

Okay, it's official, Elliot Miles has plans to break my vagina tonight.

I can already tell.

"Umm . . ." I hold my hand out for the other glass, not drunk enough for this conversation.

He passes the other shot glass over and I knock it back, just as the waitress arrives with the fancy bottle of wine. "Here you are, sir." She pours a little into a glass for Elliot to taste.

He swishes it around his mouth. "That's fine, thank you. We'd like privacy please. I'll call for you when I want something."

I can see her smirk under her serious facade.

"Yes, sir." She disappears back into the kitchen and I know that she knows exactly why I'm slugging tequila like a sailor. I want to go back to the kitchen, discuss this messed-up situation, and drink with her.

Elliot reaches under the table and, with a sharp movement, pulls my chair around closer to his. "That's better." He puts his large hand over my thigh. "I want to touch you."

The heat of the tequila begins to warm my blood. "You're very touchy," I whisper.

"You're very touchable." His eyes drop to my lips and he reaches down and cups my face. "What did you do while I was away?"

"Nothing much . . ." My voice trails off; how am I supposed to string a sentence together when he's looking at me like that?

He puts his mouth to my ear. "Did you touch yourself?" he whispers. His breath tickles my skin and goosebumps scatter up my arms.

"Did you?" I ask.

His lips dust mine. "Every day. Coming is my favorite pastime."

I get a vision of him pulling himself and my insides begin to melt into a puddle.

How is he so hot?

"You come every day?" I whisper.

"Yes." He sits back. "Don't you?"

I shake my head.

"Well." He takes my hand and puts it over his crotch; he's rock-hard underneath his jeans. "We'll have to do something about that." He flexes his dick beneath my hand. "Won't we?"

I stare at him as my brain begins to melt down.

There is just no mincing words, he's full-on sexual. I know Elliot, I know he's an aggressive man, and when he sees something that he wants, he gets it.

I don't know why I'm surprised that he's like this . . . but on some level, I am.

"You're going to make me come . . . every day?" I whisper.

He chuckles and grabs a handful of my hair and drags me to him. "Baby, I'm going to make you come until you pass out."

Fucking, fuck, fuck.

No need to even get me naked, I'm about to pass out now.

I smile as my tequila bravery begins to kick in. "We'll see."

"We will." He pats his lap. "Over here."

"What?"

"Spread those pretty little thighs and sit on me."

"Here?" I squeak.

His grip on my hair tightens and he kisses me, long, deep, and slow, and I begin to lose control.

"Kate," he demands. "When I ask you to do something, you do it. No questions asked."

My heart begins to hammer in my chest.

"Now," he repeats.

I blink in surprise. What have I got to lose, I'm going straight to hell already for sneaking around with a bad man. I stand up and he lifts one of my legs and puts it over him, and then he pulls my dress up so I can spread my legs as he pulls me down so I'm sitting on his lap.

We come face to face, our bodies snug up against each other. "That's better." He kisses my chest and nips my breast with his teeth.

We are in a restaurant.

This is like nothing I've ever done before—so unexpected. Wrong, but holy hell, so hot.

He stares up at me. "Make yourself come, angel."

"What?" I whisper.

"Rub yourself over my cock, I want you to come before dinner."

"Elliot," I breathe, "are you crazy?"

He smiles up at me as his lips take mine. "My pleasure comes from watching your pleasure."

He grabs my hips and circles them as he kisses me, my clitoris strategically placed over his erection. Teasing, taunting me to want more.

And I do.

He's so hard beneath me, and his dick is rubbing in all the right places. "Elliot," I breathe into his mouth.

"That's it, baby, can you feel me? Feel what I've got for you?" He kisses me deeply. "I'm so full." He murmurs into my mouth, "I need to come, it's yours. Take it."

Oh . . . fuck.

The sound of his familiar deep voice saying such dirty things fries my brain and I shudder as I begin to lose control.

"You want to come, too?" He circles me deeper. "I can feel how bad you need it." His lips go to my ear. "Are you swollen and wet for me?"

175

I close my eyes as my body begins to rock of its own accord; it has an agenda now and I couldn't stop it if I tried.

"Maybe I should spread you out on this table and lick you out . . . right here." He bites my ear. "You don't know how badly I need to taste you. It's all I can think about." He bites my neck hard and I jump, teetering on the edge of pain.

What the ever-loving fuck—Elliot Miles is the king of dirty talking . . . and we haven't even made it home yet.

I shudder again and his grip on my behind tightens to near painful.

His eyes are dark, his big, beautiful lips are hungry. "Give me some cream, baby, you fuck that cock of mine."

I convulse as I tip over the edge, the orgasm so strong that I whimper into his mouth; he smiles triumphantly as he kisses me as I come back to earth.

He leans back and watches me; he tenderly tucks a piece of my hair behind my ear.

"Now . . . we can eat."

Chapter 11

I stare at my reflection in the bathroom mirror of the restaurant. My face is flushed with a satisfied glow.

Who are you and what have you done with Kate?

What the hell just happened?

One minute I was nervous, next minute I was dry-humping him on his chair before we even ate . . . ugh, what came over me?

I acted like a sex-deprived teenager.

How embarrassing. Way to play it cool, you idiot.

The cruel words from my Google search come back to taunt me: *Affectionately nicknamed Casanova Miles by the press due to his apparent ability to get women to do anything he wants.*

Damn straight he can.

Oh hell, now I'm one of those women . . . kill me now!

I take my time washing my hands and I fix my hair a little, and to be honest, I just want to run away, this man makes me want to do things that I never imagined.

I walk back into the private dining room and take a seat.

Elliot is leaning back in his chair, wineglass in his hand, and his eyes assess me. "Everything alright?" he asks.

"Yes." I pick up my margarita.

"You've gone quiet."

"Oh." I shrug shyly. "A little embarrassed."

A frown flashes across his face. "About what?"

"Forget it, it's nothing." I sip my drink—what did I say that for?

"Kate," he warns.

"I just . . . can't believe I did that before."

"Did what?"

I stare at him: he's completely clueless, this must be normal behavior for him.

"Within two minutes of sitting down, I was dry-humping you in your chair."

He stares at me. "What are you embarrassed by?"

"Forget it." I put my drink down sharply. "You ready to go?"

"No." His eyes hold mine. "Explain to me what you just said."

"Elliot."

"Don't *Elliot* me, what did you mean by that?" he snaps.

I stay silent, unsure what to say.

He sits forward in his seat. "There is no one here but you and I, Kate. And what happens between us . . . is nobody's business," he says softly. "And if sexually pleasing me makes you embarrassed, then . . ." He shrugs.

"Then what?"

"Then what are we doing here?"

I frown. "Why do you insist on making me feel like an errant teenager?"

"Because you're acting like one?" He picks up his glass and swirls it around. "I'm adventurous, Kate. I like sex, I like it hard, and I like my women to come . . . often." He lifts his glass to his lips and takes a sip; I watch as his tongue darts out and swipes over his bottom lip. "If you want vanilla, I'm not the man to deliver it."

"I never said that—"

"Are you going to be embarrassed every time I make you come?" he cuts me off.

"Keep your voice down," I whisper angrily as I look around.

"We are alone in a room, just the two of us."

I stare at him.

"And we will always be alone, just the two of us. Nobody else is in our bed." He leans over and cups my face in his hand and dusts his thumb over my lip. "Don't punish yourself for feeling something new, angel," he whispers, then he leans down and kisses me tenderly and I melt against him.

"I will push you . . . but it will only ever be what you need." His tongue gently dances against mine, and I smile softly as I wrap my arms around his broad shoulders.

Oh . . . this man.

"Stop judging yourself," he murmurs against my lips, "or this is never going to work between us."

I nod and pull back from him. He's too . . . much. We lean against each other with our foreheads touching. He gently kisses my cheek as we stay close.

There's an intimacy running between us that shouldn't be there.

Every word that leaves his mouth is sacred, it's like he's coaching me into a role that he designed. Training me up to be what he needs.

Whatever that is.

But this plaything has a heart, and I fear she's in danger because we haven't even scratched the surface yet and if tonight has taught me anything it's that you can't hide from Elliot Miles.

If he wanted to, he could bring me to my knees. I can already feel my defenses slipping, and yet I don't want to get off the ride.

He stands and holds out my coat for me and I slide into it, then he turns me in his arms and kisses me as if we have all the time in the world. It's slow, erotic, and tender, and I smile softly against his lips.

His kiss is like a drug.

I can hear warning sirens screaming in the distance . . .

Let the games begin.

The black-metal garage doors rise slowly. My hand is in Elliot's on his lap in the backseat of the Bentley, Andrew is behind the wheel.

We drive in slowly and pass an array of swanky cars lined up in their bays; there are security guards walking around and this place looks more like a high-end car dealership than an underground parking lot. Andrew pulls the car up at the glass doors that lead into an elevator. He gets out, opens the car door for me, and I climb out. "Thank you."

Elliot puts his arm around me and ushers me into the elevator, pushes the button, and we begin the ride up. He stares straight ahead with this trace of amusement on his face.

"What is that look?" I smirk.

"Nothing." He kisses my temple. "Not every day I get to take *the* Kate Landon home," he replies casually.

"We're having coffee, Elliot," I say. "Don't get ahead of yourself."

"I wouldn't dare."

"Good." I square my shoulders as I try to hold my smile; I like this game.

He steps forward and I step back, his hands above my head on the wall behind me. "You know, I could just hit the stop button . . . deliver your coffee right here."

My eyes widen. "You wouldn't dare."

He chuckles as his lips take mine. "Oh, but I would."

"Elliot," I whisper.

The elevator dings as we reach our floor.

He smiles against my lips as the doors open. "Saved by the bell." He bites my bottom lip and then takes me by the hand. We've arrived in what looks like a private reception area. A large, round table with a floral arrangement on it sits in the middle; a huge, abstract painting in reds and black is hanging on the wall. Elliot puts his hand over a scanner and the door clicks as the lock releases.

We walk in and my breath is instantly stolen. Glass from ceiling to floor, showcasing a magical city view, bright city lights twinkling in the distance. The ceiling is so high and I look up in awe; I see a grand staircase in the middle. "Your apartment is two levels."

"Uh-huh," he replies casually as he leads me into the kitchen, takes my coat, and sits me up on the countertop, then stands between my legs.

The kitchen is white and modern and I look around. "Wow . . . This is beautiful."

"Who cares about my house, let's talk about the coffee." He bends and bites my bare shoulder.

I giggle. "Okay . . . we could do that."

His eyes rise to mine. "How do you like it?" His hair is messed up and his eyes are wild.

"My coffee?"

"Yeah." He smiles and drops his lips to my breast and nips me through my dress.

"Ow . . ." I giggle.

"Cappuccino, long white, short black . . ." He whispers as he goes through the options.

"Straight up sounds pretty good."

He drags my hips toward him in one sharp movement, spreads my legs a little further, and slides his hands up my bare thighs. "Risky," he murmurs as his eyes follow his hands.

"Risky?" I whisper as his thumbs dust my sex through my panties.

His eyes darken. "Easy to get injured with a straight up."

We stare at each other as the air crackles between us. "Well, what do you suggest . . . to lessen the risk."

His fingers move in a circle. "Sugar."

"Sugar," I whisper as his fingers slip under the leg of my panties; he circles them through my wet lips and my insides begin to quiver.

"Sugar always helps with a straight up." He slides a finger in deep and we both inhale sharply as we stare at each other, his jaw ticking as he clenches it. "Especially if the cup is so tight and small." He slides another finger in and we let out a collective gasp.

His lips take mine as he kisses me. My legs are wide and his strong fingers begin to work me.

With every lash of his tongue, his fingers get stronger and I can hardly keep my eyes open. The sound of my arousal sucking him in echoes around the room. "This is excellent coffee," I whisper, my hands in his hair.

He smiles. "This is sugar . . . coffee . . ." His eyes flutter closed as he temporarily loses control. "Fuck. Coffee is close."

"Percolated," I breathe.

"Plunger," he hisses. He adds another strong finger at piston pace with a twist at the end, and I begin to shudder.

Yessss . . . this is good.

It's embarrassing how quickly this man can make me come.

I grab his head in my hands and kiss him with everything that I have. "You better deliver that coffee right now, before I spill it on the floor."

"Fucking hold it," he whispers against my lips. "This cup, I'm drinking."

I struggle to control my breathing, my arousal at fever pitch.

He scoops me off the countertop and carries me up the stairs; he's so strong, and I cling to him for dear life. He marches down the hall and kicks open the door, and in one sharp movement he takes my dress off over my head.

I stand before him in my black strapless bra and panties, and he smiles as his eyes drop down to my toes. When they rise to meet mine, they're blazing with desire.

He undoes my bra and throws it to the side, and then slides my panties down my legs and kisses my sex before he rises.

"Get on my bed and spread your legs for me," he whispers darkly, his fists clenched at his sides.

I've never been with such a sexual creature. Never wanted to please someone so much.

I lie on the bed and, feeling brave, I spread my legs.

His eyes roam over me and I feel the heat of his gaze as it sears my skin, then he tears his shirt over his head and in slow motion undoes his jeans and pulls them to the ground.

The air leaves my lungs. Holy fuck.

His skin is olive, his chest is broad with a scattering of dark hair, his stomach is lean and ripped. My eyes drop lower.

He's big . . . really big.

This is the best fucking coffee shop that I ever saw.

I swallow the lump in my throat as my nerves begin to thump.

Our eyes meet and his face breaks into a breathtakingly beautiful smile. "Hi," he whispers softly.

My heart somersaults in my chest. "Hi."

"I'm naked with Kate Landon."

I laugh out loud, this is crazy. "What's happening?"

He smiles darkly and drops his head to between my legs, as he lies down and makes himself comfortable. "I don't know, but I like it." His thick tongue swipes through my sex and I nearly jump from the bed. He holds my thighs open as he licks me and his eyes close in pleasure. "So good," he murmurs to himself.

I watch him, in a detached state, somewhere between heaven and hell. My hands go to his hair and I run my fingers through it: it's thick and feels curly to the touch.

He gets rougher and his two-day growth begins to tingle my skin; he licks deeper and deeper and then he's all in, his whole face rubbing me.

My back begins to arch from the bed. "Ell . . . Oh God." I throw my head back in pleasure. "Get up here. Get up here. Get up here," I begin to chant. "Now." I sit up and pull his face by the hair up to meet me. "Elliot, now!"

We stare at each other, my arousal glistening on his big, beautiful lips.

Just like I used to imagine.

Without a word he pushes me back to the mattress and spreads my legs, rolls a condom on, and kneels over me. He lifts my foot up and kisses it and then puts it over his shoulder. He kisses my other foot and puts it over his other shoulder.

In this position, I'm completely at his mercy.

We stare at each other and then he drags his tip through the lips of my sex, back and forth, back and forth.

I can't breathe as I wait for him.

He walks over me on his hands, my legs still up, and he pushes in a little.

I cling to him, and he kisses me softly. He pushes forward again and I tense.

Ouch.

That smarts.

His grip on my calf muscles tightens and I put my hands on his shoulders, "Ell, careful," I whisper.

His forehead furrows. "Nobody's ever called me that before."

"That's a lie," I whisper. "I just did."

"Smart-ass." He smiles as he pushes in further.

"Ouch," I whimper. I cling to him, my fingers digging into his back.

"Nearly there, baby. Nearly there," he whispers softly.

I screw up my face, oh God . . . he's . . . "Stop, stop, stop," I whimper. "Give me a minute."

He drops and kisses me, his tongue dancing with mine, and I hold him close in my arms. We kiss for a long time and it's then, with tenderness between us, that my body opens up and lets him completely in.

He circles his hips, first one way and then the other as he stretches me out.

Desperation builds between us and our kiss gets rougher.

He spreads his knees and pulls out, he slides back in, he does it again and again, until finally I'm loose and then he lets me have it.

With his hard and thick pumps, the bed begins to hit the wall with force. His jaw hangs slack and with his dark hair falling over his perspiration-clad face, I don't think I've ever seen something so perfect.

Elliot Miles fucks like he does business, hard and unapologetic.

I knew he'd be something else, I just didn't know it would be everything.

His teeth are on my neck, his hands are on my ass, his cock filling every last inch of my body. But it's the moans that are coming out of him, the moans of sheer pleasure . . .

My eyes roll back in my head.

The possession, the burn . . .

Oh . . .

The absolute best sex of my life.

My toes begin to curl and I shudder hard as I clench around him.

"Fuck, fuck, fuck," he growls as he hits the sweet spot. "Yessss." He holds himself deep and I cry out as I come hard. I feel the telling jerk as he tips his head back and I smile up at him in awe.

Our eyes are locked and then, with unexpected tenderness, he bends and kisses me.

It's soft and raw and intimate and everything that this isn't supposed to be. I feel the last of my defenses slip from my reach.

"You're incredible, Kate Landon," he whispers.

"I know, right?" I tease as I hold him tight.

He smiles into my neck. "I better check again though, just to make sure." He flips me over. "This time I'm going to be thorough."

ELLIOT

I lie on my side, propped up on my elbow, and watch her as she sleeps. The sun is peeping through the sides of the drapes and as the time passes, with more light, I can see her more. Her honey hair is splayed across the pillow, her big lips are pouty, and her eyelashes flutter sporadically as if she's dreaming.

She rolls onto her back and for the first time I see her exposed neck.

Fuck.

Teeth marks all over it. The bruising only faint, but still there. With trepidation I peel down the blankets to look over the rest of her body.

Her full breasts rise and fall as she breathes and it's all I can do not to lean over and suck them. She definitely delivers in that department.

Who am I kidding? She delivers in every department.

My eyes roam down over her stomach and I frown when I get to her hips: four distinct bruises. I sit up so I can see her other hip and am appalled to find the same.

Finger marks.

I get a vision of us toward the end of last night, her on her knees on the bed with me standing behind her. The grip I had on her hips, the way she rode my cock . . . I feel the slow tantric beat of blood pumping through my body as I harden again.

She stretches as she sleeps and her legs fall open and the air leaves my lungs.

Fuck it.

Beard rash, all over her pretty lips. Red and prickly, it looks tender and sore.

I lie back down in disgust with myself. I completely lost my head. She's covered in fucking bruises.

It's been a long time since I had a night like that . . . if ever.

For someone so tight, she sure knows how to ride cock—I've never had sex so good.

Every inch of me was on fire.

My cock begins to throb; just the memory of last night incites arousal.

Cut it out, no sex for you.

She stirs, her eyes flutter open, and she gives me a big, beautiful smile. "Hi," she whispers.

I smile, lean over, and kiss her softly. "Hey." I brush the hair back from her forehead as I stare at her beautiful face.

Why am I so kissy?

She takes me into her arms and holds me tight and I smile into her hug, which doesn't feel awkward, or weird. Quite the opposite—it's nice. Familiar.

She pulls back and brushes the hair away from my forehead. "Last night was incredible," she whispers, her voice husky.

"You're incredible." I pull her closer.

She smiles as she closes her eyes. "Does that thing ever go down?"

"Oh." I pull back from her, realizing that she thinks I want sex again. "Sorry."

She grabs my hip and pulls me back toward her. "Don't be sorry, I'm not complaining."

"You will be when you see your neck." I widen my eyes in jest.

Her fingers go to her neck. "What's wrong with my neck?"

"There's about fifty bite marks on it," I mutter.

She smirks. "You're a fucking animal, my entire body is throbbing. I feel like I've been hit by a truck."

Unable to help it, I lean down and bite her breast and she jumps. "I'm sorry, I was hard on you last night," I apologize.

"Are you kidding? That was the best sex of my life."

I stare at her as my brain misfires. *The best sex of her life.* "You're so different from what I thought you would be."

"Why?" She smiles up at me with an honesty I don't know if I've ever seen.

My stomach rolls.

"I thought you'd be playing hard to get."

She leans over and kisses me; her lips linger over mine. "And I thought you'd be cold, but you're the opposite. Warm and tender . . . delicious."

I blink, surprised. *Tender . . .* when have I ever been described as tender?

Okay, this is getting fucking weird now.

I straighten my back and slide away from her a little.

"No, you don't," she whispers, and pulls me back toward her without missing a beat. She snuggles her head into my chest. "You stay close to me."

I put my arm around her. I can feel her heart beating against mine and I frown as I hold her.

This. Is. Fucking. Weird.

Too comfortable, as if we know each other already.

She leans up onto her elbow and smiles as she watches me. "So, if you came home six days early only to see me"—she kisses my chest—"does that mean I get you to myself for the next week, because technically, nobody else knows you're back?"

I smile as I cup her face in my hand, dust my thumb over her bottom lip. "And what would you do with me for a week if you had me to yourself?"

She kisses down my stomach and I inhale sharply as I spread my legs.

Woman's insatiable.

She licks up my length. "Run away with you."

She takes me fully into her mouth, and I lie back and put my hands into her hair. "Why don't we go away?"

She looks up, surprised. "Huh?"

I push her head back down. "Don't stop. Multitask. Suck and listen."

She giggles and goes back to her job.

Yeah . . . why couldn't we go away?

That's actually a good idea.

If we stay in London for the week we can only be at my place or hers. But if we went away . . . the jet is here. I could organize something . . . I mean it would be short notice, but . . .

"I'm taking you away for the week," I announce.

She looks up and frowns. "What?" she mouths around me.

I smile. Fuck she's adorable. "Don't talk with your mouth full."

She pulls off. "We can't go away. I have to prepare and then there's the—"

"Kate." I pull her up and she lies on top of me. "If we stay here, we can't leave this apartment."

She looks down at me and I can see her brain processing.

"It's one week."

"Well, where would we go?"

"Somewhere with sun and cocktails." I see a trace of a smile cross her face. "My treat." I try to sweeten the deal.

She kisses her way back down my body. "Is this my company bonus, sir?" she teases.

I chuckle and spread my legs again. "Yes, so depending how well you suck me will determine where we go."

"You can't afford a resort that good." She sucks me deep along with a long stroke of her hand, and my eyes roll back in my head.

I shudder as my balls contract. "You could be right."

I turn into Kate's street and pull up across the road. "I'll pick you up in a few hours."

"Are you sure about this?" She frowns.

I lean over and kiss her. "Positive."

It's one week, don't get excited.

"Okay." She smiles. "What will I pack?"

"Nothing, we won't be wearing any clothes."

She giggles and we look over to see that guy she lives with come out the front door. He's dressed up and walks down the stairs and gets into the Audi that's parked out the front—he's good-looking and dressed well. We watch as the car pulls out and drives away. "What's his name?" I ask.

"Daniel?"

"You know who I'm talking about, don't be cute."

"What is your problem with him?" She frowns. "He's lovely."

"I bet he is."

He wants her.

"What does that mean?"

"Nothing, he's very touchy with you, that's all."

"That's just his personality."

"I don't like it."

Kate rolls her eyes. "He's a friend, Elliot." She opens the car door. "I'll see you in a few hours."

"Okay." I nod and hold my tongue about her touchy-feely, fuckwit roommate.

I'll deal with him later.

My phone rings and the name Tristan lights up.

"See you soon." She kisses me quickly and jumps out of the car.

"Hey." I answer my phone on speaker.

Kate turns and waves and I sit and watch her walk inside.

"Can you talk?" Tristan asks.

"Uh-huh."

The front door closes behind Kate and I pull out into the street.

"How was last night?" Tristan asks.

"Good." I smirk.

Incredible.

"And?"

"And what?"

"Well, it must have been fucking good to make you leave New York a week early. Anyone I know?"

I smirk again. You could say that. "Nope."

"Are you seeing her again?"

"I'm going away with her today for a week, actually."

"What? Didn't you say last night was the first date?"

"It was."

"Your second date is a week away?" He gasps. "Fuck me dead, it must have been some fucking date."

I smile as I turn the corner. "Don't get excited, she's not Mrs. Miles."

He laughs. "Famous last words."

"It's just a week, I don't have to worry about paps then."

"Fair enough. Where are you taking her?"

"No clue, any ideas?"

"What are you after?"

"Something private, hot, and beachy. Cocktails and restaurants."

"Hmm, St. Barts?"

"No, I'll run into someone I know there at this time of year. Under the radar if possible."

"I'll have a look now."

"Okay. Thanks." My phone beeps as another call comes in. "I've got another call, I'll call you back. Elliot Miles," I answer.

"Hello Mr. Miles. It's Peter from Strathborn Investigations."

"Ah." I've been waiting for them to get back to me. "How are you?"

"Very well. I have some good news."

"Great."

"We finally have a lead on your artist, Harriet Boucher."

"What is it?"

"We think we've located where she is."

I listen intently. I've been searching for this woman for over a year.

"And?"

"If it's the right woman, and we think that it is, she's currently in the South of France."

I frown as I listen. "Are you certain it's her?"

"I'll have confirmation this week. She flies completely under the radar."

"When you have confirmation, I'll book a flight. I want to meet her in person."

"Mr. Miles, do you mind me asking what your business is with this woman?" he asks.

"It's of a personal nature," I reply curtly.

"Okay, I'll be in touch."

"Thank you." I hang up and turn the corner. I don't know what my fascination with Harriet Boucher is . . . but I need to find out.

She's calling to me through her paintings . . . and I don't know why.

But I keep coming back to her, I can't drop this.

One word describes her.

Extraordinary.

Chapter 12

KATE

I bounce up the stairs and turn and give Elliot a wave; he smiles and gives me a playful salute.

I smile and push the door open. "Hey," I call to Rebecca.

She comes rushing out of her room. "Oh my God, what happened?" She looks at her watch. "You're only getting home now? Holy crap, I need all the details."

"Well . . ." I give her a coy smile and shrug. "It went well . . . I think."

"What happened?" She lies along the back of the couch.

"We went to dinner and ate in a private dining room."

"Private dining?"

"Then we went back to his house and it's a wonder that I can walk."

Her eyes widen. "You had sex? You never fuck on first dates."

"I know, but damn it, I should. Because I had the best night ever."

She smiles dreamily. "Are you seeing him again?"

"Uh-huh."

"When?"

"He's picking me up in three hours, actually."

"Ooh, date the next day, he is keen."

"We're going away for a week."

"What?" She sits up so fast that she overbalances and falls over the back of the couch, lands spectacularly on the ground, and smashes her elbow. "Oww."

"Oh my God, are you okay?" I rush to her side and help her up. She rubs her elbow. "That fucking hurt."

I chuckle as I help her to her feet. "Pretty funny, but."

"You're going away with him?" she asks, horrified.

"Yeah, what's that look for?"

"You don't even know him."

"So?"

"Are you staying in the same room? What happens when you need to take a crap?"

I open my mouth to speak but no words come out.

"What happens if you fart, or snore . . . or . . ." She throws her hands up in dismay. "Dribble in your sleep? This is a logistical nightmare, Kate. You can't impress a man with a week-long stayover."

I stare at her as the horrifying scenarios play in slow motion through my mind. "I didn't think of that."

"What happened to playing hard to get?"

"Oh, who cares." I throw my hands up in surrender. "He made me come at dinner, I'm pretty sure there is no playing hard to get."

Her eyes widen to saucer size. "You orgasmed at dinner?"

I wince. "Kind of."

"How did you kind of come?"

I puff air into my cheeks as I realize how this is going to sound. "Dry-humped him while he sat on his chair."

Rebecca's eyes pop from her head and she slaps her hand over her mouth as I burst out laughing. "Look, I know how this sounds."

"Do you? But do you really? You're going to fall in love with him and he'll lose interest because he hasn't had to chase you . . . *at all*. And then you'll be brokenhearted."

I laugh. She's so damn dramatic. "Or . . . we could just be having fun and using each other for sex, while spending time on a beach in the sun with some cocktails."

She raises her eyebrows.

"Look, we've had the talk, I know exactly where I stand with him. He's not looking for a relationship and neither am I," I reply. "I just . . . I want to enjoy myself for a while without worrying about the future."

"Since when? Last time I knew, you were searching for Mr. Right to be the father of your children."

"Will you stop?" I snap in exasperation. "Don't read into this, I'm not. It's a week in the sun." I march over to the door and open it in a rush, gesture out the front at the blizzard conditions. "Snowy London isn't that appealing over the Christmas holiday, Rebecca. I have a week off left, and look." I point out at the snow. "What the hell am I going to do here in this?"

She stares at me.

"It's one week and I'm not stupid." I march up the stairs. "It's Elliot Miles, for fuck's sake, as if he could break my heart."

"You're delusional," she calls after me.

"And you're a drama queen," I call back with a roll of my eyes. I flop onto my bed. Fuck's sake.

I lie for a moment and feel sorry for myself—hate that she isn't excited for me.

A broad smile crosses my face . . . To hell with her, because I am.

Right. I stare at the open suitcase on my bed: what else do I need for a romantic getaway with a sex god?

Hmm. I go through my list.

Passport   *check.*

Bikinis	*check.*
Sunscreen	*check.*
Date dresses	*check.*
Lingerie	*check.*
Shoes	*check.*
Books	*check.*
Laptop	*check.*
Sweater	*check.*
Toiletry bag	*check.*
Phone charger	*check.*

Contraceptive pills   check.

*Lubricant   check, check, and double check. I'm
so fucking sore that it's a joke.*

The man's an animal. I smile—not that I'm complaining. It's definitely a hurt-so-good scenario.

I stare at the suitcase for a moment while I think what else I could possibly need.

I smile and go to my closet.

Red netball dress   touchdown.

An hour later, my email pings and I smile. It's Ed—I have his notification as a different sound.

> Hi Pinkie,
>
> How are you?
>
> What's new?

I smile and reply:

> I'm great, how was your date with the toilet cleaner?

Nerves swirl in my stomach as I see the dots. He's typing.

> Incredible.

My eyes widen and I put my hands over my mouth in surprise. What?

I smile broadly and can hardly contain my excitement to write back.

> Incredible is a strong word.
>
> What was so good about it?

I see the dots and do a little dance on the spot. I knew he felt it too.

It's not just me.

> Her, she is . . .

There are no words for how hot this woman is.

Let's just say it was a great night.

I'm taking her away today for a week, so I may
not have internet service to email you.

I giggle out loud in excitement. Oh wow, for the first time I
feel optimistic about us. Perhaps this trip will bring out more of
my Edgar in Elliot.
God, I hope so.

Taking her away?

Wow.

What brought that on?

I hold my breath as I wait for his reply.

I want her to myself for a while.

I smile as I close my eyes. *I want you to myself too.*
I pace as I think. What will I write?
Umm . . .

She's a lucky girl.

Have a great time, check in if you can.

oxo

Okay, speak soon.

Xoxoxo

A text sounds on my phone.

I'm out the front.

x

I smile through the window of my bedroom and see the black Bentley pull up to the curb.

A kiss at the end of his message really shouldn't excite me as much as it does.

I take one last look around my bedroom and get the distinct feeling that I'm forgetting something, but God knows what it is.

I bounce downstairs. "Beck, I'm going," I call.

She appears from her room and smiles as she holds her arms out. "Be safe."

I hug her. "I will."

"Have a great time."

"Okay."

"And just come home any time you want. If you aren't getting on, bail instantly."

I widen my eyes. "Yes, Mum. I wish Daniel was home, I wanted to see him before I go."

"He's out for the day."

"Tell him I said goodbye."

"Okay." She opens the door and I brush past her in a rush. I feel like I'm Scarlett O'Hara escaping Alcatraz or something. I know I shouldn't be this excited, but holy hell I am. Andrew is at the door and takes my suitcase from me.

"Thank you." I smile.

I try to walk calmly to the car and Elliot gets out and opens the door for me. "Hello," he says.

He's so tall and towers above me; I go up onto my tippy toes and kiss him. "Hi."

His hand goes to my behind as he smiles down at me. "Hello," he repeats.

"Long time, no see," I whisper up at him.

He chuckles and moves out of the way so I can get into the car. I glance up to see Rebecca standing in the open door watching our interaction.

Yes, I know I'm kissy . . . but he secretly thinks I'm incredible and you need to mind your own business already.

I get into the car and Elliot slides in beside me.

Andrew gets into the front seat after placing my bag in the trunk.

"Thank you, Andrew." I smile.

He dips his head in the front seat as he pulls out onto the road. "Hello Kate, nice to see you again."

Elliot sits back in his seat as he watches me, wearing blue jeans and a white T-shirt and runners, with a navy bomber jacket on the seat. His big blue eyes look especially piercing today . . . or that could just be my *incredible* rose-colored glasses.

I reach over and put my hand on his thigh and take his hand in mine. His quads are thick and muscular and I get a thrill that I can touch him like this.

He picks my hand up and kisses my fingertips and I smile goofily over at him.

"What is that look, Kathryn?" He smirks.

My eyes flick to Andrew in the front seat—I can't say it out loud for heaven's sake.

He raises his eyebrow in question.

"Just excited," I whisper.

He gives me a slow, sexy smile. "Well, that makes two of us."

My eyes flick to Andrew in the rearview mirror. Can he hear us?

I lean into Elliot. "Where are we going?" I whisper.

He smiles as he puts his arm around me and pulls me close. "It's a surprise."

"Does that mean you don't know yet?"

He chuckles and kisses my temple. "Yes."

I glance up to see Andrew's eyes flick back to the road—he just saw that.

I snuggle in close; Elliot's chest is broad and his strong arm is around me. His aftershave is out of this world, how does he smell so good?

"I feel like I forgot something?" I whisper.

"All you need is your birth control pills." He smirks.

My eyes widen and flick to Andrew.

"Stop it," Elliot mouths.

"He can hear us?" I mouth back.

"So?" Elliot raises his eyebrow. "Forget he's there."

Jeez, this is awkward. How do you forget someone is there listening to everything you say?

I wonder what he's heard before . . . what I wouldn't give to put him on the lie-detector machine for an hour. I bet that would make for some interesting listening.

My phone rings in my handbag and I dig it out. The name Daniel lights up the screen. I glance up to see that Elliot has read his name, and I go to put it back.

"Answer it," he says.

"No, I'll get it later."

"Answer it," he repeats with more force as he takes his arm off my shoulders.

Oh fuck, it's going to look obvious if I don't answer it now.

"Hi," I answer with an awkward smile.

"What are you doing?" Daniel snaps.

"Ha-ha, oh hi, Daniel." I fake a laugh. Oh crap, Elliot can hear this conversation. "I'm on my way to the airport."

"You're going away with him?" he barks.

I push the phone nearly halfway through my skull to try and block it so that Elliot can't hear. "Yes, just for a few days."

"Are you crazy?" Daniel blurts out. "That's fucking stupid."

Elliot's eyes narrow as they hold mine.

I swallow the lump in my throat. "Um, crazy excited. I have to go, now is not a good time." I fake-laugh again, oh hell on a cracker. Why are my flatmates such wet blankets?

"Don't go, this is a bad idea," Daniel barks.

I see the Adam's apple in Elliot's neck swallow as if he is clenching his jaw.

"One night with him and you're already doing what he says. No dick is that good, Kate."

Oh hell, I feel the blood drain from my face.

There goes the neighborhood.

Elliot glares at me and I can feel his contempt from here.

"Goodbye Daniel."

"You can call me—"

I hang up, cutting him off.

I awkwardly stuff my phone back into my bag. Why wasn't my phone on silent?

Well, that was just fucking great.

"Ah." I shrug, embarrassed. "Daniel's a bit protective."

"And has a death wish," Elliot mutters dryly. His attention goes to out the window.

We sit in silence as we drive along for a while. Elliot's thoughts are on God knows what and I'm plotting ways to cut out Daniel's tongue.

God . . . what next?

Elliot had already told me this morning that he didn't like Daniel touching me.

Imagine what's going to happen next time they see each other . . . And they obviously will, I live with one and am sleeping with the other.

And where the heck is this coming from? Daniel was excited for me when Elliot was chasing me. Now it's suddenly a bad idea?

Ugh, this is a fucking disaster.

We arrive at Heathrow Airport but instead of going to the main entrance, we continue to a side street and are stopped at a checkpoint barrier.

Andrew passes out some kind of paperwork to the security guard through the window and the guard takes it back to his little station and checks it.

Elliot is silent and broody and I know Daniel has pissed him off.

It's not my fault.

If it's any consolation, Daniel pissed me off too.

I don't want to say anything that Andrew might hear so I remain silent. We are ushered through the barrier and moments later are driving along a road that seems to connect to a tarmac.

I want to ask what we're doing, but I don't want to sound stupid. The car drives for what seems like miles and then we pull up next to a fancy-looking plane.

The car stops and Andrew gets out.

My eyes widen as I stare at the plane: it's big and lush and looks like a jet. "This is your plane?"

"This is a Miles plane, yes."

"How many planes do you have?"

"Three."

"Oh . . ." I feel my stomach flutter with nerves; what do you even say to that?

It's easy to forget that my sweet garbologist Ed is a Miles.

I mean, I know it is . . . but . . . he really doesn't seem like the same person.

Fear runs through me—what if he isn't?

My thoughts are interrupted as Elliot opens the car door and holds his hand out for me. "Come."

I take his hand and climb out of the car; it's windy and my hair blows up in the air.

The plane's engine is noisy. Elliot leads me to the stairs and a fancy-looking stewardess and a pilot in full uniform are standing at the top.

"Good to see you, Mr. Miles," the pilot says.

Elliot shakes both of their hands. "Thank you."

The stewardess smiles and her eyes hold Elliot's a little longer than needed . . . He puts his arm around my waist in a clear signal.

Hmm . . . who's she?

He leads me through and past them . . . so no introduction of me?

I wither a little, feeling insignificant.

It's a weird setup, no aisle. Cream leather seats in sets of two and a large room at the back—the doors are closed so I can't see what's in there.

One huge television is on display in a lounge area.

He opens the overhead. "You can put your handbag up here."

"Okay." I reach up to put it in and his hands drop to my hips as he takes it from me and places it above.

"Thanks," I whisper.

He gestures to a seat by the window and I sink into it; he sits in the one beside me.

I feel awkward; I just got on a plane where the pilot and stewardess addressed him by name, and yet he didn't introduce me to them.

Weird . . . *and annoying.*

I stare out of the window so I don't say something.

I remind myself that nobody is supposed to know about us, and that he's just protecting his privacy.

So why didn't he give them a fake name for me . . . hell, call me fucking Pussy Galore for all I care.

Ugh, this shouldn't bother me; I annoy myself.

"Can I get you anything?" the beautiful stewardess asks as her eyes linger on Elliot's face.

"Yes." He smiles as he sits back in his seat. "Two champagnes please."

His eyes flick over to me. "Would you like anything else?"

"No thanks." I fake a smile: don't talk to me, I'm not in the mood to talk to rude people.

"That will be all, thank you," he says.

She smiles and disappears into the little room at the front.

Elliot slides his hand up my thigh and I twist my lips—don't say it . . . don't say it.

He brushes his fingers between my legs as he leans over and looks out of the window.

I flick his hand off. "Stop," I whisper.

"What's wrong with you?"

"Nothing, but seeing as I don't have a name it doesn't matter anyway, does it?"

Amusement flashes across his face. "You're annoyed I didn't introduce you?"

"Nope." I cross my arms and look out of the window again.

Damn straight, I'm fucking annoyed.

"I have my reasons," he whispers.

"Clearly." I smile sweetly. "I love being at a whim to your *reasons*."

He chuckles and leans his head back against his seat as he looks at me.

"What?" I ask dryly.

"I wondered how long until Kathryn showed up."

I tilt my chin to the sky as I stare out of the window. "Kathryn doesn't put up with your shit, Elliot."

"No, but she sucks my cock so well . . . so, I can forgive her."

"Sshhh," I whisper angrily as I look around for the stewardess. "Will you shut up?"

He leans over and nuzzles into my neck.

"Stop it," I say. He bites me, holding my head to his, and I smile as I try to subtly get away from him.

"Promise me something," he whispers.

"What's that?"

"Promise me that we can have angry sex soon. I need to fuck you when you're raging fucking angry with me."

I laugh out loud in surprise; the man's an idiot. "With your annoying personality, I don't think that will be a problem, Elliot." I take off my cardigan.

"Where's my cute nickname from last night?" he whispers.

I twist my lips as I try to act serious. "What?"

"Ell," he whispers.

"I have no idea what you're talking about?"

"Although, I think it went like . . . oh Ellllllllllllll." He moans as he simulates me having sex. "Fuck me harder, Ell, oh God yeah . . . just like that." His eyes roll back in his head and I whip him with my cardigan.

"Shut. Up," I whisper as I try to hold my smile. "You can talk, you moan like a fucking cow."

He laughs out loud and pulls my head to him and kisses me. "It's actually a prize-winning bull, get it right, Landon." I smile against his lips and our kiss turns deeper, and then I remember the pressing point and I pull out of his grip. "Stop kissing your way out of the shit."

"I wouldn't dare." He leans back again. "Although, for the record, I won that argument."

My mouth falls open. "You did not."

"Here you are, two glasses of champagne." The stewardess passes them over to us; we both jerk back from each other guiltily. She puts down a tray of chocolate-coated strawberries on the table in front of us.

"Thank you." We both smile.

"Can I get you anything else?" she asks.

"Not at this stage. Maybe a top-up after we take off," Elliot replies as he takes my hand in my lap.

The stewardess smiles and goes back to her little room at the front.

Elliot holds his champagne in the air.

"What are we toasting?" I smile.

"The Canary Islands."

My eyes widen. "We're going to the Canary Islands?"

He smiles as he sips his champagne.

"Where to?" I whisper in awe as I sip my drink.

"There's a sex club down there," he replies casually.

I frown . . . *what?* Oh, hell on a cracker . . . I didn't think this through.

"Go on," I mutter dryly.

"Masked men tie you up and you get to watch me have sex with copious other hot women."

I choke on my drink and cough out loud. "What?"

He slaps me on the back. "But don't worry, if you behave, I'll let you clean me up when I'm finished with them."

"Are you serious?" I laugh. Thank God he's joking. "And how will I clean you up?"

"With your tongue, of course." He sips his drink with a mischievous smile.

I lean closer to him. "But what you failed to read on the brochure, dear Ell, was that while you were having boring sex with mediocre women"—I sip my champagne—"I'm getting tag-teamed by the huge masked men, who, I may add, are allowed to"—I pause as I think of the right wording—"do their business inside of me . . . and it is you who gets to clean up their mess . . . with *your* tongue." I smile and clink my glass to his.

He winces as if getting a vivid visual and then his lip curls in disgust.

The plane begins to hurtle down the runway and I grip the armrests and close my eyes.

"You're a dirty girl, Landon," he whispers as the plane lifts off the ground.

"I try my best," I reply as I hang on for dear life.

"How come they get to come inside of you and I don't?"

"Because they're a fantasy," I whisper with my eyes closed. "And you're a real-life player who has probably had sex with ten million women."

"It's nine and a half million, don't get carried away."

I laugh out loud and so does he. Our eyes hold each other's and he picks up my hand and kisses it with an unsaid affection. It's not forced and it doesn't feel wrong.

Elliot Miles is fun.

I like this game we're playing . . . although I have no idea what it's called or whether it has any rules.

All I know is that the playing field is in the Canary Islands and I'm going to have a good week. Probably the best.

I smile as I look out of the window, but sadly, I get the feeling Elliot is going to give me the hangover of all hangovers.

The high will be worth the fallout . . . I think.

"Would you like a top-up, sir?" the stewardess asks. I never did get her name. Although I must admit, with every glass of champagne her pining eyes over Elliot get a little more annoying.

He's taken, bitch.

Okay, he's not taken. But he is today and . . . for the next week, so back off already.

"No thank you, Clarise. We are going to retire," he replies casually.

"Oh." She nods as if taken aback. "Yes, of course." She turns. "Call me if I can be of any service." She walks into her room and closes the door behind her.

"I will." His eyes return to me as amusement flashes across his face.

"Not funny," I reply, deadpan. She will never be of any service; how dare he even joke about that.

He stands and holds his hand out for me.

I frown. "What are you doing?"

"Retiring."

"From what?"

"Here." He drags me to my feet and pulls me to the back of the plane, and opens the double door that reveals a luxurious bedroom with a huge bed.

A bed . . . a bed . . . what's a fucking bed doing here?

My eyes meet his and he winks.

Horror dawns.

"No," I whisper.

He pushes me in and closes the door behind us, and then he crash-tackles me onto the bed and crawls over me. He lifts his T-shirt off over his head and throws it to the side.

His playful smile arrests me and, for a moment, I forget where I am.

Then I remember.

"What are you doing?" I whisper in a panic as I try to escape. "Stop it, get off me," I snap. "They're just out there."

His lips drop to my neck and I feel his erection as it hardens up against my stomach.

"Are you fucking crazy?" I whisper. "Elliot." I buck to try and get him off me. "You are a bona fide sex maniac," I stammer.

He smiles sexily and stands and tears his jeans off. He throws them and they hit the back of the door; the button makes a clanging sound and I slap my hands over my eyes. "Oh. My. God . . . What the actual fuck are you doing?" I whisper.

"Giving you a membership." He smiles as he undoes my jeans and wrestles to pull them down.

"To what?"

"The Miles High Club." He pulls my jeans completely off.

I laugh out loud and then slap my hand over my mouth. I hold my finger to my mouth in a *sshh* signal.

"You're the one making all the noise." He pulls my shirt off over my head, twirls it around over his head like a lasso, and bucks the bed as if riding a fake bull.

I burst out laughing as I bounce beneath him. "What the fuck are you doing?"

"Getting ready to moan like a bull." He smiles as he drops and kisses me and pulls my panties off. He inhales them deeply and then hurls them at the wall. They hit the back of the door and fall on the floor, and his lips find mine again.

I imagine the snooty stewardess walking in and finding us in a compromising position. "Elliot." My eyes widen in horror. "We can't have sex, they're just out there," I whisper in a panic. "They can hear us, and you're fucking loud, you know?"

He puts his hand over my mouth, his mouth drops, and he sucks on my nipple. "Shut up and fuck me, Landon."

I laugh through his fingers; my eyes are wide. "Elliot." He bites my nipple and I buck as hard as I can as arousal begins to pump through me. I can feel the heat as it warms my blood. His tongue flutters at just the right tempo. My fear of getting caught mixed with his couldn't-care-less factor is a heady combination.

Naughty meets nice.

He nudges my legs apart with his knees, and then, as if remembering something, he bounces off me and goes to his jeans, shuffles around in the pocket, and produces a small bottle of lube and two condoms. He holds them up and wiggles his eyebrows as if he just won the lottery.

I laugh, I can't help it. He's fucking adorable like this.

"Who are you and what have you done with grumpy Elliot Miles," I whisper.

He lies back over the top of me and then in some kind of practiced move he flips us so that I am on top of him. My legs are straddled wide over his hips and he pours some lube onto his fingers and glides it between my legs.

My hands are on his broad chest as I hold myself up, his fingers exploring as he looks up at me. "He's right here," he whispers.

And isn't he beautiful.

As we stare at each other, the feeling of his fingers on me, the shared arousal between us, something changes. I don't know what it is, but it brings a flutter to my chest.

"Don't," he whispers. He grabs my hips and eases me down onto his hard body, slides my open lips up the length of his shaft.

"Don't what?" I shudder. Oh . . . that feels good.

"Look at me like that."

"Like what?"

"Like . . ." He slides into me again and his eyes roll back in his head.

I want to cut him off; I don't want to hear what he has to say.

I know damn well how I was looking at him.

With ownership.

"Like I'm about to fuck your brains out?" I ask as I lift from his dick and slide it in deep as a distraction.

His knees rise as he takes me, overwhelmed by the sensation of our bodies locking together.

"Don't open your mouth to say anything other than how hard you're going to fuck me," I whisper.

He chuckles and grabs my hip bones. "Yes ma'am."

I smile down at him.

"What?" he grinds out.

"You sound so American when you say 'yes ma'am.'"

"Funny that, seeing as I am a fucking American." He lifts me up and slams me back down and I scrunch my face up to stop myself from crying out.

Oh God . . . *that's so good* . . . too good.

"No." I bend down and bite his lip. "I'm the one fucking an American."

He chuckles and slaps my behind, with a crack as his hand connects. "Do it harder."

We fall into a rhythm, and every now and then he lifts me too high and our skin slaps out loud.

"Sshh," I whisper as I glance at the door. I grind down hard again, it's quieter this way.

The feeling builds until it gets to fever pitch and I close my eyes to block him out. I can't look down at him when I feel like this.

"Open," he whispers.

I ignore him.

He grabs a handful of my hair and pulls me down to his face. "Open your fucking eyes and look at me while you come."

I drag my eyes open, only millimeters from his face, and we stare at each other.

Frantic, animalistic, depraved.

He's moving at piston pace, my body wet and open for him. He reaches up and bites my lip as he jerks violently inside of me. "Oww," I whimper.

His hands hold me close and I shudder as I come hard.

He moves back from me and he licks his lips as if still hungry, his gaze dark and dangerous.

So different from the carefree man who brought me into this room.

Uneasiness creeps over me. Dear God, who am I sleeping with?

There are two versions of Elliot Miles.

Chapter 13

My chest rises and falls as I struggle for air and I fall onto Elliot's chest. He tucks me safely under his arm and kisses my temple, and we lie in comfortable silence for a while.

I look up at him. "How many people have you slept with?"

"I don't know." He drags his hand down his face. "A lot." His eyes meet mine. "Why? How many have you slept with?" he asks.

I trail my finger in a circle on his chest; why did I ask? Now this is probably going to make me sound lame. "Seven."

A frown crosses his face. "Seven?"

I nod.

"Including me?"

I nod.

"Oh . . ." He pulls me close and I feel his smile as he kisses my forehead.

"What does 'oh' mean?" I ask.

"Nothing." He shrugs. "Surprising, that's all."

"Why is it surprising?"

"I think I was at seven while I was in my teens."

"That's 'cause you're a man whore."

He chuckles. "Could have something to do with it."

I lean up on my elbow so I can see his face. "How old are you?"

"Thirty-four." He gives me a breathtaking smile as he reaches up and twists a piece of my hair as it curls. "How old are you?"

"Twenty-seven."

He frowns.

"What?" I ask.

"So . . . you're seven years younger than me, I'm the seventh person you slept with, and you're twenty-seven?"

I smile goofily as he does the math.

"When is your birthday?" he asks.

"Seventeenth of July."

"What?" He sits up against the headboard. "Bullshit."

"I swear."

"The seventeenth of the seventh?"

I laugh. "Aha."

He stares at me and I watch as his frown turns into a slow, sexy smile.

"What?"

"Your number is seven."

"What does that mean?"

"Seven is the number of the gods, it's magical."

"What, since when?" I smile. "How do you know that?"

"Numerology. Google it."

I lie down on my back. "Well, I don't feel very magical."

He rolls over on top of me and holds my hands over my head. "I'll be the judge of that." His lips drop to my neck and he begins to nibble his way down my body.

"Numerology doesn't refer to my vagina, Elliot." I giggle softly.

He takes my nipple between his teeth. "Yes it does."

The hired car pulls into the driveway and I peer out of the window at the house before us. It's white and traditional, with a large wrap-around veranda and beautiful well-kept gardens. The driver stops the car and gets out to unload the luggage from the trunk.

Elliot dips his head to look in. "It seems okay."

"You've never been here before?" I ask.

"No, but a friend of Tristan's has, he said it was nice."

I smile and hunch my shoulders in excitement. "Anywhere will do. I don't care if we go camping. Maybe next time we can?"

"Yeah, okay." He chuckles as he opens the door. "My brother has told me all about camping, I'll meet you there."

I smile: that's code for *I'm never going camping*.

We get out of the car and Elliot tips the driver, and then he wheels our two suitcases up the path to the house.

The front door opens and a man comes into view. He's wearing a white uniform that looks like scrubs. He's elderly, perhaps in his sixties. "Hello Mr. Miles." He speaks in a strong accent. His hair is dark and he's quite handsome for his age.

"Hello." Elliot shakes his hand. "Nice to meet you."

"My name is Henley and I'm the caretaker of Brogana. Welcome."

Elliot gestures to me. "This is Kathryn."

"Hello." I smile and I shake his hand.

"Come in, come in." He gestures to the house as he walks in; we follow him inside and my breath is stolen.

"Wow," I whisper in awe.

Elliot's face breaks into a broad smile as he looks around. Everything is white and the furnishings are a dark timber, in the antique style. There are huge rugs in bold colors and abstract art is hung. The entire back wall is glass bi-fold doors with a breathtaking view over the beach and sea. A huge deep-blue infinity pool is by the deck. This place is out of this world.

"There's a private track through that gate that leads down to the beach," Henley says as he gestures to an antique-looking gate to the left. "The bedrooms, bathrooms, and gymnasium are down the corridor and you have twenty-four-hour room service—there are staff in the quarters on the property that are at your beck and call. If there is anything that you need, please just ring the bell." He hands a remote to Elliot. "I hope the property is to your standard, sir."

Elliot nods. "It's lovely, thank you."

Henley smiles and nods with a bow. "I will leave you alone, sir."

"Thank you." I smile as excitement fills me.

"Henley," Elliot says, "can you tell me a good restaurant to eat at tonight?"

He smiles kindly. "Of course, sir, what do you feel like eating?"

Elliot's eyes come to me. "What do you want, sweetheart?"

My stomach flips; I love it when he calls me that. "You pick, Henley, surprise us." I smile. "I like everything."

Henley nods. "Very well, Kathryn, what time?"

"Um . . ." I look between them.

Elliot glances at his watch. "Perhaps in an hour and a half."

"Of course, sir. I'll notify you of the booking once I've made it." Henley walks out and closes the door behind him.

Elliot takes me into his arms. "Seven days here." He smiles down at me.

"I know." I stand on my toes to kiss his big, beautiful lips. "I'm not sure I can cope with such torture."

"Well," Elliot replies. "I hope you like eating goat's testicles for dinner."

My face falls in horror. "He wouldn't."

"Rule number one in traveling, Kate." He kisses me again. "Never say you like every food." He taps me on the nose. "Because trust me, you don't." He turns and wheels our suitcases up the hallway toward our room and I smile after him.

"I like your balls," I call. "And you're a bit of a goat."

He laughs out loud and it's deep and happy and it rumbles deep in my psyche. I smile goofily as he reappears and sees my face. "What's that look for?"

"You have a beautiful laugh."

He raises his eyebrow. "For a goat, you mean?"

"Yes." I giggle. "For a goat."

The fairy lights twinkle overhead and I smile across the table at my dreamy date.

Thankfully we are eating seafood, not a goat's ball in sight.

The conversation is smooth and witty and never seems to run dry; it's so weird, Elliot and I really do get along very well. We laugh and talk and everything feels very organic between us. There's a lot more to us than steaming hot sex . . . even though there does seem to be a lot of that.

Not that I'm complaining.

It's a clear night in a beautiful outdoor terrace restaurant.

"You know, I think this would be one of the hardest jobs on earth," I say as I crack open a crab claw.

"What would be?" Elliot says as he concentrates on the task at hand.

"Being a fisherman. Out in the elements, sun and wind. Never knowing what kind of catch or day it would be." I put some shells into the dish provided.

"You've got to be kidding, sounds like the best job in the world to me. No suit, no pressure." He pops some crab into his mouth. "No office assholes."

I stop eating as I stare at him. "You know, you really are a surprise. You're nothing like I thought you'd be."

Amusement flashes across his face as he sips his wine. "Don't be deluded, Kate, I'm everything that you thought."

"But you're not."

"I'm in holiday mode and it's seven days." His eyes hold mine.

"What does that mean?"

"It means that I can't give you more than seven days."

Why the fuck would he say that?

I stare at him for a moment and then I continue to crack my crab claw with my pliers. It feels like he's giving me a warning.

"When was your last girlfriend?"

"Years ago."

"How come?"

He shrugs. "I don't know, me and relationships don't mix."

I stay silent, unsure what to say to that.

"When was your last relationship?" he asks.

"Serious relationship, six years ago." I sip my wine. "I thought he was the one."

"And he wasn't?" He keeps his eyes on his task.

"Obviously not."

"What happened?"

"A lot of things, can we talk about something else?"

His eyes rise to hold mine and he raises an eyebrow, unimpressed with my short answer.

"Look, I get it. You don't want anything for more than a week and that's fine with me."

He picks up his drink and sips it, clearly annoyed.

"I'm sure that you have every woman in the Western world in love with you, Elliot, but I can assure you that I won't be one of them. You are not the type of man I would fall for long-term."

"Good."

"Good," I snap.

We eat in silence for a while.

"I should have fed you goat's balls," he mutters dryly.

"You already did," I say. "On the plane."

He smirks and then, unable to hold it, breaks into a broad smile. "And you loved them."

I cut up my food as I try to keep a straight face. "They were tolerable . . . I guess."

We stare at each other as the air crackles between us.

"I might feed you them again tonight," he whispers darkly.

"No." I bite my food off my fork.

"No?"

"You can show me your culinary skills tonight . . . seeing as you only have six days to impress me," I reply flatly as I act bored. "You're running out of days, Miles."

He smiles, clearly amused.

"Seven including tonight, and I'll impress you, Miss Landon . . . don't you worry about that."

I try to keep a straight face; I like this game.

"We'll see."

My back arches off the bed and I scrunch the sheets up in my hands beneath me, wet with perspiration.

He's gone down on me, we fucked, I came, then he's back down there with his tongue. Again, and again.

He's flipping me around like a rag doll and holy fucking hell . . . *I'm impressed.*

I've come three times and still he won't stop.

He's proving without a doubt that he holds the sexual power between us and I can't argue, there's no contest. When we are both naked, *he owns me.*

221

I shudder hard and I grab a handful of his hair to try and pull him back from my sex.

"Enough," I whimper. "Please, El," I beg.

He smiles into me, his eyes flickering with satisfaction. "I'll tell you when you've had enough." In one movement, he rises and flips me over onto my stomach and pulls me up by the hips to my knees, then he slowly eases himself into me and I close my eyes at the sound of his deep guttural moan.

Fuck . . .

The man's a god.

He slowly pulls out and then pushes back in, and the sound of my wet body echoes throughout the room. "Do you know how fucking hot that sounds?" he whispers. "Your body sucking me in."

He pulls out and slams in hard.

"She wants it," he says darkly. "She wants to be fucked hard." He slaps my behind and the crack echoes all around us.

I slip into some kind of out-of-body experience, a sub space.

So lost in a deep arousal that I can't even speak.

Then he's riding me, deep, punishing pumps, and I can do nothing but try and keep upright on my knees.

"Watch," he growls.

He grabs a handful of my hair and pulls my face back to face the mirror on the wall.

His dark eyes meet mine in our reflection and he begins to slowly pump me; I can see every muscle in his torso, every perspiration droplet on his sheened skin.

My breasts are swinging as he pounds me and he tips his head back to the skies as he deals with the pleasure.

There's no mistaking our bodies are on fire together—this is pure, unadulterated lust.

Something I've only ever heard about, I thought it didn't exist in real life, but hell . . . I've been missing out . . . big time.

He lifts his foot to rest it on the bed as he rides me, and the change in position tips me over the edge. I scream into the mattress and he pushes my body down so that my behind is sitting up. Completely open for his onslaught.

Our bodies begin to slap and I can feel every inch of his beautiful cock.

So deep . . . so good . . .

His moans get deeper, louder, his grip on my hip bones is nearly painful, and I smile as I feel his oncoming orgasm overtake his control.

This is how I love him, unfiltered and, just for the moment, mine.

He holds himself and cries out as he comes deep and we both gasp for air. The pumps slow as he completely empties himself, and then he leans down and takes my face in his hands and gifts me with a kiss.

It's sweet and tender, so different to the love that we just made.

He lies down beside me and we take our time with our kissing; we both know this is going nowhere, but damn it, he makes me wish it was.

He brushes my hair back from my forehead as he stares at me and my heart constricts.

Does he feel it too?

"You're very good at that," he whispers softly.

I smile shyly, overwhelmed with emotion.

As if sensing my fragility, he pulls me close and holds me tight, kisses my forehead. "Sleep, baby," he whispers.

I close my eyes as I rest my head on his chest. It's warm and safe here. If I could pick anything in the world to do tonight, it would be being here with him, doing this.

I know that six days with this man isn't enough . . . I already want more.

He traces his finger in a circle over my bare shoulder. "Do you know how beautiful you are to me, Kate Landon?" he whispers.

I close my eyes in regret.

Elliot Miles is a heartbreak waiting to happen.

Chapter 14

I turn the tap off and get out of the shower, and wrap the towel around me.

I watch as Elliot slowly pulls the razor down his cheek while looking in the mirror. "Does that hurt?" I ask.

"Nope." He rinses the razor under the hot water; he has a white towel around his waist and looks completely edible.

"I hate the grating sound." Fascinated, I lean on the bathroom vanity as I watch him.

"You get used to it, I've been shaving for . . ." He pauses as he thinks. "Twenty-one years now."

I sit on the cabinet in front of him. "You're so old."

"Thanks." He taps his razor on the sink. "Although, you're only as old as the woman you feel." He raises his eyebrows. "That makes me . . . twenty-seven."

I take the razor from him. "Can I have a go?"

"I'm not a ride, Kathryn."

I giggle as I hold the razor to his face. "Could have fooled me." I concentrate. "I rode you pretty hard last night."

He chuckles as he pulls my hips toward him on the counter. "And fucking loved it."

I hold the razor up and bite my bottom lip as I focus.

He closes his eyes. "This isn't a good idea."

I slowly glide the razor down his cheek. "What isn't?"

"A woman having a razor in the vicinity of my throat, can't end well."

I giggle. "I'm actually good at this."

"I'll be the judge of that."

"Why are you shaving on holiday, anyway?"

"Because I want to kiss you and my stubble is sharp as fuck."

"Aww . . . your first sacrifice for me." I pause and smile as I run my hand through his messed-up hair. "You're so sweet . . . Pooky bear," I say in a baby voice.

He rolls his eyes. "Hurry up." He stretches his face out. "And don't call me Pooky bear, it's emasculating."

"Oh please, Mr. Miles, you do know that you're going to be my bitch by the end of the week . . . right?" I tease.

He smiles and takes the razor from me. "I wouldn't count on it."

"What are we doing today?" I ask.

"Whatever you want."

"Oh . . . what shall we do? The possibilities are endless." I smile dreamily.

He washes the razor out under the tap and then picks up my toiletry bag; he takes out my contraceptive pill pack and studies it. He pops out today's pill and holds it on the end of his finger for me. I take it from him and swallow it down.

"When was your last STD test?" he asks.

"Why?"

"Interest's sake."

"Why?"

"I don't want to use condoms while we're on this trip."

I frown. "Why?"

He shrugs as he leans in to kiss me. "I just don't want to."

"No." I pull back from him.

"Why not?" He seems surprised. "I've never had sex without a condom before."

I stare at him as my brain malfunctions. "Never?"

"No."

"So why would you want to do it with me?"

"I don't know, I just do."

"Well, you're going to have to wait a bit longer." I jump down from the cabinet and walk into the bedroom, go to the walk-in closet, and begin to look for something to wear.

He follows me. "Why?"

"Because it's too intimate for me, that's something you share with a partner."

"We're partners."

"For the week, Elliot. That doesn't count."

"No, we'll see each other at home. We made a deal, remember? Exclusive casual."

I try to hide my smile; this is the first time he's mentioned anything long-term.

"Well . . ." He puts his hands on his hips as if outraged. "Have you done it with anyone else?"

"Yes, of course I have. That's what boyfriends are for."

"Well, I'm your boyfriend . . . for the week."

I roll my eyes as I get my clothes out and lay them on the bed.

"That counts for something," he says.

"Not really." I drop my towel and pull my bikini bottoms on.

He takes me into his arms as he tries to sweeten the deal. "I'll make it worth your while." His lips drop to my neck.

"No. Discussion over." I pull out of his arms and put my bikini top on. "Get dressed, we're going out."

"Where to?"

"Anywhere away from a bed." I smile as he bites my neck.

"That won't save you, I don't need a bed." He pushes me up against the wall. "I'm an all-surface kind of man."

I laugh out loud. "Shut up, you fool. It's not happening."

The Canary Islands are everything I ever dreamed of. Sun, sand, and sea, all with such a beautiful backdrop. We've eaten at the most beautiful restaurants, laid on the beach for hours and sipped cocktails at quaint little ocean-side bars until late into the night.

This place is heaven, with old colorful buildings perched high on the cliffs overlooking the ocean; I've never been somewhere so utterly perfect.

Three days.

Three magical days is all it's taken to transform me into an Elliot Miles disciple.

We've talked for hours, laughed, eaten all the beautiful food, and made love in every possible way.

It's not awkward or foreign, it's organic and beautiful . . . the kind of feeling that I have always searched for.

His dark eyelashes flutter, his big lips slightly parted, and I watch as his chest rises and falls as he sleeps, the white sheet pooled around his hips.

Elliot Miles is a force to be reckoned with. It's not who he is.

It's what he is.

For the first time in my life, I feel heard.

And I know that sounds ridiculous, even to me . . . because, of all the things I know about Elliot Miles, being a good listener isn't one of them.

I lie on my side, propped up on my elbow as I watch him—I've been doing it for over an hour. I need to go to the bathroom but I don't want to get up and disturb my uninterrupted view.

My eyes roam down over his broad chest and down to his navel and the small trail of dark hair that disappears under the sheet. His skin is olive, his hair dark.

Physically, he's a beautiful man.

But I know a secret about Elliot Miles: it could start wars, end dreams, and light up a city from space.

His heart is his strength, and maybe it's not mine to keep.

But I'll cherish this week that I had it in my hands, forever.

His eyes flutter open and he frowns as he focuses on my face, then breaks into a slow, sexy smile. The one I've become addicted to.

"What are you looking at?" he whispers as he pulls me onto his chest, holds me tight, and kisses my forehead.

"Just your goat face."

He chuckles and it's deep and husky and surrounds my senses. "Bahahaha," he says.

I laugh out loud. "Goats don't bahahaha."

"What sounds do goats make?" He smiles.

"I don't know, but I know they don't bahahaha."

He rolls me onto my back and comes over me, and his lips softly take mine. "Well, if I don't bahahaha, you better make me moan." He puts his knee between my legs to spread them.

I smile up at him. *Oh, this man.* "You mean like a cow?"

He chuckles. "I'm a fucking bull, Kate. I told you before."

ELLIOT

I follow the hot little ass up the trail—black leggings, a white midriff tank top, and a blonde ponytail swinging as she walks.

What a view to behold.

Kate and I are climbing a mountain, and it's steep. She turns and looks out behind me. "Oh El, look at that."

We turn and stare over at the view.

She smiles wistfully into the wind and I stare at her. "It's so beautiful," she whispers.

"She is." I smile.

Her eyes find mine and she gives me a shy smile. "I'm talking about the view."

I take her hand in mine and kiss her fingertips. "I know."

She smiles softly. "Can I take a photo of us?"

"If you want."

She takes her phone out and puts her face to mine, and with the backdrop in the background, she takes a shot. She looks at it with a huge smile. "I want to see what you looked like on film before you piggyback me up to the top."

I laugh. "Angel, if you want to fall spectacularly down this mountain and die, let me carry you."

She turns and begins to walk up the trail again. "I could carry you," she replies casually.

"I have no doubt," I huff as I climb. "Horses can do that."

She laughs. "You know I haven't gone hiking in such a long time . . . since my parents died, actually."

I frown; this is the first time she's told me this. "Your parents both passed?"

She continues to walk in front of me. "Yeah, they were killed in a car accident six years ago."

Shit.

"I'm sorry."

"Me too."

We keep walking.

"What were they like?" I ask.

She turns. "My mother was like me."

"A sex maniac, then."

She laughs out loud. "And my father was the sweetest man on earth."

I keep climbing as I listen.

"We used to have this thing that we would do together on special occasions."

I puff as I climb. Fuck, this hill is steep. "What was that?"

"Eat Cornetto ice creams."

I smile as I listen.

"Watching a movie, Cornetto ice cream. Something was celebrated, a Cornetto ice cream. When I got my first job, he picked me up with a Cornetto ice cream."

"I haven't had one of those ice creams in years," I say.

"Me neither . . . not since he died."

We walk for a while. "What are your parents like?" she asks.

I think for a moment. "Busy."

She turns and frowns, as if surprised by my answer. "And that bothers you?"

"Not necessarily." I walk for a bit. "I just never had that time as a kid to hang around and be bored."

She listens.

"I went to boarding school from the age of seven. Holidays were always rush, rush, from one exotic resort to another." I shrug. "I don't know . . ." My voice trails off.

"Will you send your kids to boarding school?"

"Not on your life."

She turns as if surprised. "What would you do differently—I mean, to the way you were brought up."

"Give them my time."

She stops and turns. "You didn't get time with your parents?"

"Still don't."

She stares at me for a moment. "What about your brothers?"

"My brothers." I smile. "They take up too much time, I love those fucks."

She giggles and continues walking.

"We only ever had each other growing up. They mean the world to me."

We walk for a while.

"Our formative years were spent preparing us to take over Miles Media. We all sometimes resent that we never got to choose our own path."

She keeps walking in front and I don't know why I feel the urge to tell her all of this.

"I should probably shut up now." I pant. "This hill is getting steeper."

"Yeah, time to piggyback me, Miles. Impress me with your power."

I laugh and we keep climbing.

"You know, I wish you were a plumber," she says casually.

I frown. "Why?"

She turns. "Because then I wouldn't have to share you."

We stare at each other.

"And you could be a normal boring guy and fall for me."

That would be the easiest thing in the world to do.

I smile softly. "That's the nicest thing anyone has ever said to me."

"If that's the nicest thing you've ever heard"—she laughs and turns back to climbing—"you must know some real assholes."

"True, I do . . . I'm very good at cleaning out pipes though. So, I am a plumber . . . of sorts."

She laughs out loud. "I know. A damn good one too."

I lie on the deckchair and sip my cocktail.

The afternoon sun is just going down over the water and the sound of the gentle waves lapping on the shoreline fills my senses.

Kate is playing volleyball with some kids by the water's edge. I watch as she laughs and talks with them as if they are long-lost friends.

She's animated and laughing loudly, so carefree and happy.

She's in a white bikini and I don't think I've ever seen something so beautiful and flawless.

Calm.

That's what she is . . . she brings me a sense of calm that I don't ever remember feeling before.

I don't have to try to be something I'm not, I can just be myself.

She doesn't care about my name or my money, or how cool she looks.

She hasn't worn makeup or styled her hair for our entire trip and I don't think either of us have looked in a mirror once.

It's liberating not trying to impress each other. She's seen me at my absolute worst . . . and I've seen hers; and yet somehow, we just work.

I take out my phone and open my messages, smile when I see Pinkie's name.

I've missed her.

Hi Ed,

I hope your holiday is going well?

Things are going well for me, my new boyfriend is turning out to be lovely.

It's cold here, wishing I was in the sun somewhere . . . next year I hope to be away.

Enjoy your trip, in no time you will be back
to being a garbologist.

Pinkie

Xoxo

I smile. Kate's laughter echoes and my eyes rise to watch
the volleyball game.

This is the weirdest friendship I've ever had. Pinkie Leroo is
the absolute opposite of the kind of women I date, but she gets
me, and I somehow get her.

I like our friendship.

What will I reply?

We walk home along the water's edge holding hands. "I got you
something."

"What's that?" She smiles up at me.

God, this could go either way . . .

I put my hand in my pocket and pull out two Cornettos.

Kate stares at them in my hand and her eyes immediately well with tears.

Fuck.

"I mean . . . I just thought," I splutter. "It's our last night and all . . ."

Her eyes search mine and she smiles softly and goes up onto her tiptoes to kiss me. "Thank you," she whispers as she takes one from me. "You're so thoughtful."

I've been called a lot of things in my life, but never that.

She drops to sit on the sand and taps the ground beside her, and we both open our ice creams.

She stares at hers. I watch as a lone tear rolls down her cheek and I don't know if this was the right thing to do.

I put my arm around her and we both eat our ice creams, me in silence, her through tears.

I can feel the memories and love swimming around in her psyche as they overtake her.

She makes me wish I was a plumber too.

The moonlight streams through the window and I slowly peel off Kate's dress.

Something's different with her; something changed between us when I bought her that ice cream.

Her walls came down and I see a new vulnerability in her.

It's overpowering, intoxicating, and I want her more than ever if that's humanly possible.

Our lips are locked as we kiss tenderly, our hands undressing each other as fast as we can.

Naked . . . I want to be naked.

She pulls my shorts down and my cock springs free, and I lie her down on the bed.

235

"Do you have any idea how beautiful you are to me?" I whisper.

She smiles up at me and my heart constricts.

"Hang on." I go to retrieve my condoms.

"El . . . don't," she whispers.

"Don't what?"

"Put on a condom. I want all of you tonight."

We stare at each other and . . . Fuck me.

This woman . . .

I lie down over her, the urge to be close so overbearing that I couldn't control it even if I wanted to.

We kiss and hold each other and, with an intimacy I've never known, she takes me.

And holds me.

And ruins me forever.

KATE

The plane pulls to a halt on the tarmac and I want to just throw myself onto the floor and kick and scream.

I'm not getting off this plane, you can't make me.

Elliot lets out a deep sigh as he stares straight ahead. He looks over at me as he leans against the headrest. "We're home," he says.

"Yep." I fake a big, fat smile. "Yay."

He chuckles and leans over and kisses me. "I know."

The stewardess—what the hell is her name, anyway? I still haven't caught it—comes from her little room, retrieves our luggage, and takes it to the door, and then the two captains come out and disengage the door. "Lovely to fly with you." Elliot smiles, and shakes their hands. "Thank you."

"Thank you, have a good night," one of them replies.

A bag attendant boards the plane and takes our bags. "Just these three?" he asks.

"Yes please," Elliot replies.

He disappears back down the stairs.

"Thank you." I smile as I make my way out of the door; I'm hit with an icy wall of snow. Everything is white and miserable.

Fucking freezing London . . . ugh . . . why do I come from here?

Elliot walks out behind me and winces. "Fuck," he mutters under his breath.

"Why aren't I Spanish?" I say.

"Because you're English," Elliot says as he takes my hand. "Careful," he warns. "The stairs are slippery." He slowly leads me down and into the car that's waiting, a black Audi, not the Bentley.

The driver is female and she smiles and opens the back door. Huh . . . who's she?

"Hello," Elliot says as he gestures for me to get into the car first. He climbs in behind me and closes the door.

The driver gets in and turns. "VIP parking on level 1A?"

"Yes, thank you," Elliot says as he takes my hand and brings it over to his lap.

I frown in confusion and he kisses my fingertips. "I got Andrew to bring my car. I wanted to drive you home myself."

"Oh." Maybe he's going to stay over?

I inwardly deflate. It's probably so that Andrew doesn't have to see my sad face when I get out of the car. "Great," I lie.

Five minutes later the driver pulls up in an underground parking lot and, sure enough, there, parked in pole position, is Elliot's black Mercedes sports car.

I wonder who brought Andrew home after he dropped the car here—did he catch a bus or did someone pick him up? What happens in these situations, is there a driver for the driver?

Elliot puts my things into the trunk and ten minutes later we're on the road to my place.

He's quiet and pensive, with both hands firmly on the wheel, and I'm staring through the windshield, internally wondering if I can tie him up and throw him in the trunk, perhaps hijack his plane and force them at gunpoint to take us back.

I feel a distance creeping between us already: he isn't my playful El here in London, he's Elliot Miles . . . the hard-ass CEO of Miles Media.

And the reality is, we don't really know each other.

Which is crap; if he wanted casual and didn't want anything from our relationship, why did he have to be so damn sweet and affectionate? Is he even aware that he did it?

Talk about mixed messages.

It didn't matter in the Canary Islands because we both knew the small amount of time that we had together was finite. Tied in a nice little bow, a week's escape from reality.

No strings attached.

But now that we're back, I feel uncertain already.

I already know that I'm not ready to let him go yet, and maybe there is hope for us because damn it, we're so good together. I just hope he feels the same.

The car pulls up outside the front of my house and Elliot turns the engine off, leans his arm on the steering wheel, and looks over at me.

"Thanks," I whisper.

He nods as his eyes hold mine.

"I had an incredible time."

He breaks into a breathtaking smile. "Me too."

"Do . . ." I shrug. I shouldn't be saying this but I can't stop the words coming out of my mouth. "Do you want to come in?"

"I can't." His gaze goes to out the front windshield. "I have a million emails to go through before work tomorrow. I haven't opened my computer up once in a week and I can't work late tomorrow night because I have a function on. If I don't tackle them tonight the entire week will be a write-off."

"Ah . . ." I nod as the busy picture is painted.

His hand runs up my thigh. "You're a bad influence on me, Landon. I've never not worked on vacation."

I smile. "Well . . . you're pretty fun to distract."

His eyes hold mine and there's something hanging in the air between us.

It feels a lot like . . . regret.

"Okay." I fake a smile.

"Okay . . ." he replies.

We stare at each other for a moment and I don't know if he's waiting for me to say something or . . . is he going to say something?

When are we seeing each other again?

Don't ask, *just be cool.*

I open the car door. "I'll let you go."

"Alright." He gets out of the car and opens the trunk.

He has to ask to see *me*, I'm not pushing for something. He is the one who told me we're just fucking after all, even though I know we aren't. So, if he changed his mind, he has to pursue me.

"Do you want me to carry your suitcase up to the front door for you?" he asks.

"No." I take it from him. "I've got it. Thanks anyway."

We stare at each other and it's there again, the swirl in the air of unspoken words.

"Goodbye Kate." He leans down and kisses me softly, and my heart constricts.

There's no passion, no forbidden element, no promise of slamming me up against the car and taking me here; his kiss feels sad and full of regret. Or is that just me feeling clingy?

Whatever it is, it sucks.

I step back from him, the change in his demeanor something I don't like. "Bye." I turn and walk up the front steps and turn and give him a wave; he waves back and then, without hesitation, gets in his car and drives away before I've even put my key in the door.

Deflation fills me. He's gone.

I watch the car as it disappears up the street, and I push the door open and walk in.

Fuck's sake.

"I'm home," I call.

Daniel comes rushing from his bedroom. "Hello darling." He laughs as he pulls me into a hug, holds me by my arms, and looks me up and down. "You look fabulous, darling—that suntan, though. How was it?"

"Great." I smile. "I had a wonderful time."

His face falls. "What does that mean?"

"Nothing, I had a great time," I reply. "How could I have a bad time on holiday?"

"And?" He raises his eyebrow.

"Elliot was . . ." I pause as I think of the right wording. "Amazing." I look around and fall onto the couch, and he falls down beside me.

"I thought you were going to come back all in love and he would break your heart and I would have to hire a hitman."

"No." I smile sadly. "Although, it would be very easy to fall in love with him."

"What happened?"

"Nothing, he's just fucking amazing and, like he said, it was just a week. He didn't give me any false promises and I'm not reading into it, but I'd dearly love to see where it goes."

He nods as he processes my words. "Well, if he has half a brain he'll come knocking the door down and will never let you go."

I smile, feeling grateful for his kind words. It's not so bad to be back in my safe place. "Yeah . . . that's what I was thinking."

"Have you eaten?" he asks.

"I ate on the plane. Have you?"

"No, didn't want to cook."

"I'll come with you if you want to go out somewhere."

"Yeah?" He smiles as he puts his arm around me.

I put my head on his shoulder.

"Do you feel like going to a Thai restaurant to watch me eat?" he asks.

I smile. "Sure, I do."

Monday morning, I walk into the elevator like a rock star and I push the button to my floor with conviction.

I've got this; whatever happens, happens.

Elliot didn't call me to say goodnight last night. I don't know why I thought he would. Ed didn't message me online either and it really doesn't matter. I hardly noticed at all.

I'm fine, fine, totally fine.

I had the best holiday ever . . . let's leave it at that.

I'm faking it till I make it here, but whatever. It's making me feel better.

At least I now know that my heart still beats.

I'm still in there somewhere, albeit a little damaged and broken, but I didn't die with my parents after all, and there is happiness in my future, I just know there is.

I smile as I step into the office; it was fun while it lasted.

I'm hoping for more, but for the first time in a long time, I know I'll be okay if there isn't.

It is what it is.

Eleven a.m.

Knock, knock, sounds at my office door. "Kathryn," the familiar voice says.

I glance up, it's Elliot. A smile overtakes my face. "Hi." I beam. I missed him last night.

"Do you have that report on search engine usage that I asked for?" he snaps.

I frown, taken aback by his greeting, or should I say, lack of it. "No, I can generate it now if you like."

"Thank you. Make it fast please, I need it in an hour."

He's cold and detached—the Elliot Miles that I remember.

My eyes search his.

"For God's sake don't look at me like that, I'm not in the fucking mood," he snaps before walking out.

I stare after him . . . *Huh?*

I sit in the cafeteria and the world is a blur.

How was I looking at him?

Was I all doe-in-the-headlights? Was my heart beating through my chest—could he see it?

Probably . . . God.

Back to reality with a thud.

"Did you see Elliot Miles this morning?" one of the girls at the table says.

"Fuck yes, with a suntan he's even more lethal."

The hackles on my back rise as I eavesdrop.

"He probably spent the break on a yacht in Ibiza with a supermodel or some shit. Who knows, he probably got married," another girl replies.

"He wouldn't marry a supermodel," an older woman comments. "Elliot Miles wouldn't settle for that."

My eyes flick up. "What do you mean?"

"Elliot will marry an artist, or an author or something philanthropic."

"Why do you say that?"

"He's very deep. Haven't you noticed where his interests lie?"

"No, where do his interests lie?"

"In the art world. He will marry someone super-unique. That's why he guards his private life so fiercely, so that all these little flings he has with bimbos along the way won't hurt his chances when he meets the one that he wants."

My heart drops. "I guess."

I sip my tea . . . am I one of the said bimbos now? His words from earlier come back to me and I feel sick.

For God's sake don't look at me like that, I'm not in the fucking mood.

"Kate, wake up," Daniel says as he sits on the bed.

I try to pry my eyes open. I hardly slept a wink last night worrying about Elliot all night long.

He didn't call me, I didn't hear from him, and I have no fucking idea what's going on between us, but it's not okay how he spoke to me yesterday.

"Look at this," Daniel snaps.

He holds a folded newspaper up in front of my face.

"What?" I frown.

"Fucking look at it."

I screw up my face as I focus my eyes and read the headline.

Elliot Miles leaves gala night with Varuscka Vermont.

Huh?

I sit up and snatch the paper from him.

My eyes read the headline again and I look at the picture.

Elliot is in black tie, and he and a dark-haired beautiful woman are in the back of his Bentley . . . Andrew is driving.

"When was this photo taken?" I ask.

"Last night."

My horrified eyes meet Daniel's. "What the fuck?"

Chapter 15

I storm up the road like a monster, my inner rage at an all-time high.

How dare he?

How fucking dare he?

Okay, so he didn't want anything more . . . man up and tell me, you fucking spineless dipshit.

Last time I checked, when you spend most of a week inside someone's body, you at least owe them a simple conversation.

Ugh, I'm furious. I can feel my blood boiling under my skin.

I guess this is the mission accomplished, given that I dated Elliot to try and feel something.

And I feel something for sure: thermonuclear atomic rage.

I march into my building.

"Good morning, nice day." The doorman smiles.

Is it?

I fake a smile and keep walking. I can't even make myself lie and agree with him.

Stay out of my way world, I want blood.

At 1 p.m., my email pings.

Kate,

I would like to see you in my office immediately.

Elliot.

Ha, I bet you would . . . *you stupid fuck.*
I reply:

Elliot,

Sorry, I am too busy.

Please email me your request and I will attend
to it as soon as possible.

Kate.

A reply bounces straight back.

Kate,

Whatever you're doing can wait.

Get up here now!

Now . . . exclamation mark . . . What?
How dare he?
My eyes nearly pop from their sockets.
I hit the keyboard so hard I almost break the damn thing.

Elliot Miles.

Go fuck yourself!

No, I sound like a child. I delete my message and I try again.

Elliot.

Are you so incredibly stupid that you can't see
out of your . . .

No, I delete.

Don't give him the satisfaction of stooping to his level. I close
my eyes and inhale deeply as I try to calm myself down. Don't let
him get to you . . .

Just ignore the stupid email.

I get back to work and half an hour later my email pings again.

Kate.

Are you on your way?

I'm waiting.

My pressure cooker boils to the breaking point. I write back.

I'm not coming.

As I told you, I'm busy. Please forward your
request via email.

Stop wasting my time with unreasonable
demands.

I hit send.

I don't know who this guy thinks he is?

How dumb can a human being be?

I get up and walk to my filing cabinet and I slam it open, put the file in, and slam it shut.

"Stupid asshole twat-head," I mutter under my breath. I sit back down and hit my computer keys. "Stop turning off, fucker."

I exhale heavily, calm . . . calm . . . calm. Keep fucking calm.

My stomach is churning and, honestly, I haven't felt this out of control and unstable for a long time. I can't do this to myself, I already know that this isn't a healthy relationship for me. I can't let myself be pulled back down into darkness by a toxic man.

My office door opens and clicks closed and I glance up: Elliot stands before me. Perfectly fitted grey suit, square jaw, and dark hair. His presence instantly takes over the small space. Damn him for being so attractive. It really is infuriating. I drag my eyes back to my computer screen.

"What are you doing?" he snaps.

Don't give him the satisfaction of reacting.

"Working," I reply calmly as I keep my eyes to the front.

"I asked to see you." From my peripheral vision I see his hands go into his trouser pockets as he waits for my reply.

"And I said, email me your request. Now if you don't mind, I'm very busy, Elliot. Please close the door on your way out."

"I gave her a lift, nothing more."

My eyes rise to his.

"She had a fight with her date and was waiting for a cab, I simply offered her a lift."

I stare at him . . . *is that true?*

I turn back to my computer. "I've no idea what you're talking about."

248

He stays silent for a while as if assessing the situation. "What's with the attitude?"

Fury bubbles dangerously close to the surface and I turn back to him. "It's called work ethic, Elliot, and there *is* no attitude."

"Good." He tilts his chin to the sky in approval. "I'll have Andrew pick you up tonight, around seven."

A frown crosses my brow. *Give me strength.* I turn back to my computer and print out a spreadsheet. "I can't tonight, sorry. I have something on."

"Like what?"

Ignoring him, I stand and open the top drawer of my filing cabinet, and he swiftly puts his hand over mine and closes it, causing it to slam. "Like what?" he growls.

"Washing my hair," I snap as I lose the last of my patience.

"So, you *are* angry?"

I sit down in a rush and twist back to my computer screen.

"What was I supposed to do, leave her on the street?" he replies.

"I don't know what you're talking about?"

"This is why relationships and me don't work. There is always fucking drama. It was a lift."

"We are not in a relationship. You have already made that crystal clear and I really don't care if you want to take Varuscka Vermont on your stupid Miles jet. This has nothing to do with giving someone a lift home. Get out."

"So?" Amusement flashes across his face. "You did see the story."

"Elliot, I'm not interested in this game. I'm tired of it already."

He puts his hands on his hips. "What's that supposed to mean?"

"It means . . ." My voice trails off.

"We had a deal."

I roll my eyes. "Do you mean the deal about you not being seen or photographed with me but it's perfectly fine for you to be seen leaving with another woman, or do you mean your deal of nobody knowing about us and you speaking to me like a piece of crap whenever you feel like it? Newsflash, it isn't that appealing, Elliot, excuse me if I want to pass."

"I had a stressful day on Monday," he barks.

"I'm having one now," I growl back.

His eyes hold mine. "What are you saying?"

"I'm saying you may as well go out with Varuscka. This arrangement isn't going to work between us."

"What?" he explodes.

My door opens without warning. "Do you want a coffee?" Kellie asks.

"Knock before you enter an office," Elliot snaps.

Kellie's eyes widen as she looks at us. "Sorry," she whispers as she swiftly closes the door.

Elliot glares at me, his nostrils flaring as he grapples for control. "Are we done here?" he sneers. I can feel his anger as it radiates out of him.

"Stop being a drama queen." I keep staring at my computer; I don't want to look at him.

"Kathryn," he bellows.

"Do not speak to me like that and then barge in here with demands. I'm unsure how things work for you with other women, but I can assure you, it doesn't cut it with me."

I can almost feel the atomic bomb as it goes off. Tangible fury radiates out of him.

Without another word he storms from my office and slams the door. The windows rattle from the bang.

Beep, beep.

The horn sounds out on the street. I peer out of my bedroom window and smile and wave when I see the small truck.

Excitement fills me: I get my brother to myself for a whole twenty-four hours. I've taken some leave. We're going back to Mum and Dad's to pick up what's left of our things—Elanor has put them into a storage unit for us. Brad has hired a removals truck and I've booked us a hotel to stay at tonight.

We're going to go out for dinner and chill and hang out. Spend some much-needed family time together.

After the shitty week I've had, this weekend is a welcome distraction. Elliot Miles is the epitome of cold. He hasn't looked at me since that day in my office, let alone made eye contact, not once.

And it's not that he hasn't had the chance; he's walked by me in the corridor without any acknowledgment and even caught the same elevator as me this morning, and still not a word.

It's like I imagined the whole damn thing, and maybe I did?

I don't know, but I'm sick to death of myself overanalyzing it. If he can move on so easily, I really did do the right thing.

Not that it hurts my feelings or ego any less.

I grab my things and make my way downstairs. "Bye, I'm going," I call.

Daniel comes out of his room. "Have fun, darling." He kisses my cheek. "And forget all about Douchebag Miles."

I smile up at him as I flick the hair out of his eyes. "Who's that?"

He taps my nose. "That's the spirit."

"Where's Beck?" I ask.

"In the shower."

"Okay." I head toward the door. "Say goodbye to her for me."

"I will . . . oh, and I'll be here to help you unload tomorrow if you need me."

"It should be okay, Brad will help. Have a good night," I call as I head out of the door. I'm hit with the icy conditions and I wrap my jacket around me tighter. "Fuck off, snow," I mutter under my breath.

I run across the road and climb into the truck. Brad is wearing a trucker cap and he flexes his arm muscle. "Gangster as fuck, in the truck."

I giggle as I put my seat belt on. "You're ridiculous."

He chuckles and pulls out into the street. "Let's go get our shit."

"I'm here to collect the belongings from storage unit 405 please?" I smile at the receptionist.

"Of course, we've been expecting you." She turns and goes to the key cupboard and produces a set of keys with a little yellow tag. "Go down aisle five and then turn at the last right. Your unit is the last on the left."

"Okay, thanks."

I walk back out and Brad links his arm with mine. This is a hard day, one I never thought in a million years I'd be doing. With trepidation we follow the girl's directions and get to the storage unit, and Brad puts the key in the lock and slowly pulls up the garage door.

Ten lonely boxes sit at the back of the practically empty locker.

We both blink in surprise; we were expecting a lot more.

"Where's the rest of it?" I whisper.

Brad shrugs.

Panic sets in—my parents' whole entire life does not fit into ten boxes. "Where's the rest of it?" I stammer. "She said she kept everything important."

Brad takes out his phone and dials Elanor's number. "Hey. Are we at the right unit? There are only ten boxes here."

I can hear her talking fast in reply, and my heart begins to hammer hard in my chest. She does that when she's guilty.

Brad's haunted eyes meet mine and I know that it's all gone.

252

"Are you fucking kidding me?" Brad growls. "You knew that we wanted everything, how fucking dare you do this to Kate? I personally had more than ten boxes of things kept at Mum's and Kate did too." He marches off as he screams at her and I screw up my face in tears as I look around the virtually empty unit, my heartbeat banging hard in my ears. The thought of losing all their beloved possessions and all of our childhood memories is like losing them all over again.

No . . . she couldn't do this.

She wouldn't.

Nobody is that heartless.

"Tell me." He listens for a moment. "What fucking charity shop, Elanor?" I hear him cry from up the aisle.

I drop to my knees in despair; she donated almost everything. Even Brad's and my personal belongings. We had so much there, the attic was full of memories.

Mum's Christmas decorations . . . Her china from Grandma, her tapestries. Dad's tools. All my hobbies . . . gone?

Oh, this hurts.

I put my hand over my stomach as the air leaves my lungs.

Brad's big arms come around me and he pulls me into an embrace and he holds me as I cry. "I'm so sorry, Kate. I'm so sorry."

We sit at dinner, both staring into space, the mood somber and sad.

We are feeling a deep sense of loss all over again.

"I just don't get it," Brad says softly. "How the hell is she genetically related to us?"

I stare at his sad face, he's as torn up about this as I am.

"Elanor looks after Elanor." Brad sighs. "She needed the sale money and wasn't prepared to wait for us to sort it."

"You know, if she was going to do this, why wouldn't she just tell us?"

"Because she knew we'd say no."

We sit in silence for a while.

"Did she say where she was?"

"She was on a business trip."

"To where?"

"I don't know, probably Ibiza partying with some rich guy. You know how she operates, they fall at her feet, I don't know how she gets them."

"She's beautiful, that's how." I sigh.

"Nobody is this fucking beautiful."

"What is it with her and money anyway? Why does she like it so much? We aren't like that and we were brought up in the same house."

Brad shrugs. "You know, she's after your boss."

I frown. "What?"

"Yeah, we had breakfast together a few months ago and she was reading out the rich list that had just been released in the paper. Told me she was going to snag herself that Miles chap."

The air leaves my lungs. "Which one?"

"The head one."

"Jameson in New York?"

"No, the English head one."

"Elliot." My heart begins to beat fast in my chest.

"Yeah, that's him. She brought him up on her phone and showed me a picture of him and everything."

My eyes widen in horror. "You've got to be joking." I frantically search for a picture of Elliot and I hold my phone out for Brad. "Is this him?"

"Yeah, that's the one. Reckons she already had things underway." He rolls his eyes in disgust. "Stupid witch."

My stomach drops; Elanor is way more suited to Elliot than I am.

I know how she operates, I know her appeal to men, they have no resistance against her.

If she really wanted him, she could have him.

Elanor is extraordinary. Dread fills my every cell.

I get a vision of her turning up at a family event with him and I feel my chest tighten. I know that one day I'm going to have to watch him with someone else.

But please . . . not her.

Anyone but her.

Its 11 p.m. on Thursday night and I sit alone in the darkness.

I type:

> Dear Ed,
>
> How are you? I'm sorry, I only just saw your message from last week. I've been really busy.
>
> We haven't spoken in a long time, just checking to see if you're okay.
>
> Pinkie.
>
> ox

I haven't spoken to Ed since Elliot and I had words last Tuesday. He messaged me that night and I haven't got back to him.

What would be the point? It would only make me feel more crap than I already do.

I mean, how much could I actually mean to him if he's chasing a conversation with Pinkie, and yet being an asshole to me, the actual woman who he's sleeping with?

It's blatantly clear that I am last on Elliot Miles's list, and I can't pretend it doesn't sting, because it does. More than it should. I knew the rules of this game before I started playing and yet stupidly, I jumped in anyway.

Hindsight, what a slap in the face you are.

This week has been taxing. I'm stressed out and being haunted by the prospect of getting an invite to my evil sister's wedding to my dream man.

I mean, he isn't really my dream man, but . . . he was mine first and this is my fantasy, bitch.

Back off.

Elanor told Brad that she had things underway with Elliot—what does that even mean? Is that code for she's hooked up with him already in the past?

My stomach rolls at the thought.

Please no.

I see the dots, and my heart skips a beat. He's replying.

Hi Pinkie,

I missed you.

All good here, nothing new to report. How is everything at your end?

How is your romance going?

Ed.

I exhale heavily. I can't even tell him the truth, I can't even let on who I am. I'm too deep in this lie now, but I guess there's no reason to fess up right now, he's not going to be seeing Kate in the future anyway. This isn't good for me though and I do need to cut off from him completely, this can't go on. I don't want to hear about his future conquests . . . or fucking Elanor.

Ugh, kill me now . . . Imagine?

I lie.

Romance is great, he's perfect.

I go to hit send and then I pause . . . and add:

How's Kate?

I hold my breath as I wait for his reply. I know it's going to be hurtful.

That was a stupid thing to ask.

Kate and I are over.

I close my eyes in regret and I type:

Why, what happened?

I was too attached to her.

I sit up in shock. What?

My heart beats hard in my chest.

What makes you say that?

On the first day back at work I hadn't seen her for twenty-four hours and I missed her.

I didn't like it.

My eyes widen . . . what the fuck?

Did you tell her?

No, I was angry that she had me like this after a
week so I snapped at her . . . two days running,
and I haven't heard from her since.

I jump from my chair. What the hell?
Is that how he saw it? What will I write?
I begin to pace back and forth, wave my hands around as I try
to think.
Umm . . .

Maybe she liked you too much.

Perhaps she was scared of getting hurt?

No, I'm sure that's not it. I'm not wasting my
time on someone who walks away over something so trivial. She wouldn't even have a conversation about it.

It obviously meant very little to her, I don't have
time for stupid drama.

I'm done.

My heart drops and I slump back in my chair . . . Fuck it.
Damn it . . . you idiot, Kate.

He's right, why wouldn't I at least talk to him?

Fuck's sake . . .

What the hell do I write now? Damn it, I hate how I can't tell him who I am.

This is one colossal fuckup that has to stop.

I write:

> That's a shame, what have you got planned for the weekend?

> Busy weekend planned. Moving into my new house tomorrow and then going to an art auction tomorrow night. I guess, unpacking all weekend.

> What about you?

I puff air into my cheeks. I want to write . . . *pining over you all weekend*, but I refrain.

> Nothing much, quiet one here.

> Okay, I'm turning into bed, great to finally be in touch.

> I missed you.

> Goodnight.

> Ed

> Ox

I read through our messages again.

I was too attached to her.

I flop onto my bed.

He was too attached to me . . . Did I read that right?

I get up and read it again and again. No, I didn't dream it.

It's written right there in black and white.

He was scared . . . and maybe I was too?

A goofy smile crosses my face.

There is hope for us yet.

ELLIOT

I smile as I drive up the tree-lined country road. It's green and tranquil with rolling hills. "It's beautiful, isn't it?"

Christopher nods. "It is." He frowns as he looks around. "What the hell are you going to do out here?"

I shrug happily. "Raise my kids—you know I don't want my kids to grow up in a city."

"You don't even have a girlfriend," he mutters dryly.

"She's close." I smile. "I can feel her near."

Christopher drags his hand down his face in disgust. "You know, she's not a ship in the night who's nearby. You simply decide that you're ready to settle down and pick someone to do it with."

I screw up my face. "That's not how it works."

"It is."

"Well, not for me." I drive in silence for a few moments. "You don't just pick someone and hope for the best. You follow the signs."

Christopher rolls his eyes. "Oh please, you and your stupid signs. What do you think is going to happen? You're going to meet a girl and a neon sign is going to appear over her head saying *this is her, I'm the one.*"

I chuckle. "Basically."

"What if you already know her?" he replies casually as he looks out of the car window.

"I don't think I already know her."

"Oh, that's right, because you're going to have this big romantic moment when you see her . . . you'll know." He shakes his head. "How are we even fucking related?"

"I am getting that moment, sue me for believing in destiny. When I meet her, I will one hundred percent know."

"What happened with that girl you went away with?"

Kate.

I grip the steering wheel tighter as anger rolls around my stomach; it pisses me off that I'm pining over her. She's got me by the balls, not that I'll ever admit it. "Didn't work out."

"Is that why you've been a moody prick since you got back?"

"I have not," I snap.

"Oh bullshit, you've been a fucking nightmare to be around. A bear with a sore head."

"Shut the fuck up."

We drive for a while in silence.

"Doesn't Julian Masters live out here somewhere?" he says.

"Yeah, like ten minutes away. That's how I first found this area, I came to his house for his son's christening. It took me eighteen months to finally find the house I wanted. Well, the land I wanted, the house may go completely yet. But the property is beautiful, three hundred acres."

"What's the plan?"

"I'm going to move in here as it is for three months or so, find out what I like about the current house and what I don't. Then remodel or rebuild. It's huge, has ten bedrooms and five living areas as well as what used to be servants' quarters; it used to be a big country estate back in the day. The house is a couple of hundred years old so it needs a lot of work."

Christopher's eyes flick over to me. "It's probably fucking haunted."

"Shut up."

I glance over at him and he holds his hands up in a spooky gesture. "Ohhhhhhhhh." He makes a ghost sound. "You're not going to be scared out here all alone, in this big old haunted house . . . where nobody can hear you scream?"

"Shut the fuck up," I snap, as I imagine being terrified all alone.

"I wonder how many people died in it."

"That's it." I stop the car. "Get out."

He bursts out laughing.

"I mean it, get out. I brought you here to look at my new house, not so you can scare the fuck out of me."

"So, you admit it, you are scared? At least now I know what I'm getting you for a housewarming present."

"What's that?"

"Ghostbusters' voucher."

"I'm going to punch you."

I continue driving and we pull into a driveway. The stone sign next to the gate reads:

Enchanted

"What does that mean?" Christopher frowns.

"It's the name of the house." I widen my eyes. "You can't be that stupid."

He raises his eyebrows. "You've got to change that though, right?"

"No."

"Oh God, this just keeps getting worse. You want to live in the enchanted castle with your princess?" He curls his lip.

"Something like that." I smile and keep going up the long, tree-lined driveway for around three miles.

"This is all your land?" Christopher asks as he looks around the rolling green hills—it's picture perfect.

I smile proudly. "Yep."

"Wow, impressive."

"That's me, fucking impressive."

He chuckles and we drive around the lake and arrive at the house. The real estate agent is parked and she gets out of her car. I give her a wave and pull up.

Christopher peers through the windshield at the old sandstone house. "Yep. She's fucking haunted, alright. It's even got a moat."

"It's a lake, dickhead," I whisper as I get out of the car.

"Elliot." Brianna smiles, shakes my hand. "Welcome to your new home."

"Thank you." I feel Christopher walk up behind us. "This is my brother Christopher." I introduce him. "This is Brianna."

"Hello." She smiles shyly, her eyes lingering on his face, and I have to try and stop my eyes from rolling. How this woman sells any houses with the amount of flirting she does is beyond me, although it does explain the amount of listings she has.

"Welcome to your new home." She hands the keys over; a red bow is tied onto the keyring. "When do your things arrive?" she asks.

A vehicle sounds in the distance and we all turn to see the moving truck slowly coming up the driveway. "That'll be them."

"There is an envelope in the top drawer in the kitchen with all the instructions for everything."

"Thank you."

"I'll leave you to it then. Congratulations, I'm sure you're going to be very happy here."

I shake her hand. "Thank you."

"And remember, if there is anything I can do. *Anything*," she accentuates. "You have my number."

I fake a smile. "I do, thank you. You've been very helpful."

She smiles as if waiting for me to say something more.

I look over to Christopher and he raises his eyebrows. I have zero attraction to this woman.

Awkward.

"Okay, bye." I march up to the front door and with a sad wave she gets into her car.

I put a key into the lock, it doesn't turn.

"Did you fuck her?" Christopher asks as he watches her car drive away.

"No." I wince as I struggle with another key. "As if."

"She's very—"

"Weird." I cut him off as I try another key.

"Yeah, anyway. Open the door."

"What do you think I'm trying to do here?" I jiggle the lock.

The truck pulls up and four movers all get out. "Hey there."

"Hello," I call. "Won't be a moment." I struggle with yet another key. "Fuck it," I whisper. "Why didn't she tell me what damn key it was?"

"Maybe you're supposed to just walk right through the door?"

I inhale deeply. "Christopher, so help me fucking God." The key finally turns and the door pushes open with a deep, long creak.

Christopher and I peer in and then look at each other, and then go back to peering in.

It's gigantic, and grand, with incredibly high ceilings and fancy cornicing. Dated and otherworldly.

It's like a step back in time.

Utterly beautiful.

"Wow," Christopher whispers in awe.

I smile broadly as I imagine how cool I can make this place.

"I know how it got its name," he whispers again.

"Me too. I'm enchanted already."

KATE

I lie on the couch while eating Nutella out of the jar with a spoon.

"You know that shit gives you a fat ass, right?" Daniel says as he puts his laundry away.

"Nobody is going to see my ass anyway." I sigh.

"Oh, except Elliot Miles. What's happening there anyway, you haven't mentioned him all week. Is that what's wrong with you?"

"This has nothing to do with Elliot Miles," I lie.

Maybe a little.

"What then?"

"The fact that my sister is a bitch. I just want a sweet sister who cares, you know? Sisters are supposed to be built-in best friends."

He smiles and sits at my feet, picks them up and puts them on his lap. "That's it, I'm dragging your ass out tonight."

"I'm not going out." I sigh.

"Come on, it'll be fun."

I raise my eyebrow. "You always say that."

"And it always is."

"Where are you going?"

"An art auction."

"What?" I sit up. "Where at?"

"Here in London. Do you want to come?" He smiles sweetly.

"Actually." I bite my lip as an idea rolls around in my head. "Maybe I do." I stand with purpose. "But first you need to make me look insanely hot."

Daniel chuckles. "Mission accepted."

It's nine when we walk into the Halifax function room, a ballroom at the Conservatory of Music. The venue for the art auction.

I'm wearing a deep-blue fitted dress with long sleeves and a low back, sky-high stilettos, and my hair is down and full. I'm totally dressed up in designer samples and I look good.

At least I hope I do.

To the left of the room is a bar and everyone is mingling; canapés and champagne are being walked around on silver trays. To the right of the room an auction is going on, and you can hear the auctioneer calling. The crowd is eclectic and the sound of jovial chatter is loud as it echoes around the high ceiling.

I look around: Where is he? Is this even the right auction?

"Let's go and look at the auction," I whisper.

Daniel puts his arm around me and we walk over to that part of the room. There is a huge painting on an easel and about fifteen people are gathered around it.

"One point one," I hear the familiar voice snap. Elliot is standing front and center, bidding.

I pull Daniel back so we can watch unhindered.

"I hope his dick is as big as his wallet?" Daniel whispers.

It is.

I giggle.

"Be nice," I whisper back.

I watch as Elliot bids on the painting, completely focused on his task. He's wearing black jeans and a black knitted sweater; his dark hair is messed to perfection. His words come back to me.

I was too attached.

I smile to myself as the bidding war continues. We stand at the back and watch the proceedings; I don't know whether I'm appalled or impressed at his drive to own the painting. It's obvious for all to see that he won't back down, that painting is as good as his.

It's unsettling to watch him like this, cold and detached to achieve his desired outcome. His words come back to me: *I'm looking for extraordinary.* Is this what he would be like to achieve that goal? Emotionless and hard; is that why he pushed me to the side . . . to make way for his extraordinary woman?

"Sold," the auctioneer yells as he slams the hammer down. "Mr. Miles, congratulations."

The crowd all clap in awe.

"Honestly, he has more money than sense, the painting isn't even that great," I say.

"Do you see that handbag?" Daniel leans in and whispers. He gestures to a woman.

"Yes."

"Fifteen thousand pounds."

My eyes nearly pop from their sockets. "What the hell?" I whisper.

Daniel laughs and pulls me closer with his arm around me as we chat.

I glance up to see the glare of Elliot, the fury emanating from him is thermonuclear.

Huh?

He marches over. "Get your fucking hands off her," he growls.

My eyes widen in horror.

What?

Daniel's grip around my waist tightens. "Go to hell."

Chapter 16

"Elliot," I stammer. "What are you doing?"

"I said. Get. Your. Fucking. Hands. Off. Her," Elliot sneers through gritted teeth.

Daniel smiles sarcastically, totally unruffled; he raises an eyebrow. "What's your fucking problem?"

"You are."

Holy crap. I pull out of Daniel's grip, this is a nightmare. I glance around to see that people are noticing the commotion.

Elliot steps forward until they come face to face.

I step between them, my back to Daniel. "Will you stop it?" I whisper.

"Get out of my way, Kathryn," Elliot whispers angrily.

"Go home, pretty boy, she's here with me," Daniel whispers.

Elliot's nostrils flare as he teeters on the edge of a complete meltdown.

"Will you two stop it?" I whisper. "Elliot, I want to talk to you . . . outside."

His eyes stay glued to Daniel, like a cobra ready to strike.

What the hell?

"Now, Elliot." I grab his hand and pull him back from Daniel. "We need to talk."

He ignores me.

"Now." I drag him through the crowd and out of the back doors and onto the terrace. I pull him over into the corner. His hands are clenched by his sides. Fury is oozing out of him like a volcano.

"What the hell are you doing?" I whisper angrily.

"What the fuck are you doing?" he growls. "You ended it with me . . . for him?"

"No. Who said we were ended?"

"I'm not fucking stupid, Kate, he's all over you like a rash." He drags his hand through his hair as he grapples for control.

"We're just friends," I whisper.

"With benefits."

"No." I throw my hands up in disgust. "Me and you are friends with benefits."

"You left out the dramatics part."

"What? You spoke to me like crap," I snap. "And for your information, you're the one that wanted casual."

"With no other fucking people," he interrupts.

"Oh, you can go home with Varuscka but I can't live with him?"

"It was a fucking lift and nothing more."

I roll my eyes. "The jury is still out on that one."

"Does he sneak upstairs whenever he's horny?" He nods as if picturing something. "I'm getting the full picture now. Of course, that's it."

"Listen." I poke him hard in the chest. "If you want to spend time with me, act like a grownup and not a fucking petulant child."

"What?" he explodes loudly; people around us all turn to see what the commotion is.

"Keep your voice down," I whisper angrily. "Where's the swoony guy who took me out?"

He holds his hands out wide. "I'm right fucking here, Kate."

"No. You're not. You're being Elliot Miles on me, the power-hungry control freak, and I don't like him. I've never liked him."

"I can't change who I am."

"I'm not asking for a marriage proposal, Elliot. I'm not even asking for a full-on relationship."

"What are you asking for?"

I stare at him for a moment as I collect my thoughts. I know I can get hurt here, it's a real possibility, but I'm sick of being scared of feeling something . . . anything. And even if this ends badly, I won't have the what-if regrets that I already do.

Fuck it, I'm going to try.

I have to.

"I want you to give us a chance, and not be an asshole every time you get scared," I whisper softly. I need to cool this situation down.

"I'm not scared," he spits.

"Bullshit." I take his hand in mine. "Stop trying to hide from me, Elliot. I can see straight through you."

He snaps his eyes away from me, infuriated. "I don't want him touching you."

"Okay."

His eyes meet mine.

"Elliot . . . I don't want to end this . . . whatever *this* is," I whisper. "I'd like to see where it goes, but I don't want you making me feel like shit every time you're having a bad day."

A frown crosses his brow.

"Can we just see how it goes, and you not be an asshole for two minutes?" I ask.

"I told you, I can't change who I am."

I think he may just be the world's worst communicator. Empathy fills me and I stand up on my tippy toes and softly kiss him; he frowns against me as if surprised.

"I'm not a plumber, Kate," he murmurs as he puts his hands on my hips.

"But you are very good with my pipes."

"Well . . ." He gives me a slow, sexy smile and I know that for the moment, my tiger has been tamed. "They are great pipes to work with."

"Can we go home?" I whisper.

"What about your date?" he replies flatly.

"Daniel?" I shrug. "I'll handle him. He just needs someone to walk into a venue with, he'll pick up a gorgeous woman in about ten minutes flat. You don't need to worry about Daniel, Elliot, he is the last of your worries with me. I've seen him pick up women a million times. I promise you, we really are just friends."

A trace of a smile crosses his face and I know he liked that answer. "If he baits me again, it's on."

"Okay." I smile up at the mercurial man before me. "I'll talk to him."

"I just moved house today." He shrugs. "I'm not sorted yet; my house is full of boxes."

"That's fine." I smile. "I don't care if we sleep on the floor."

"Who said anything about sleep?" he says as he raises an eyebrow.

I smile up at him and he takes me into his arms and hugs me, and it's tight and tender and full of unexpected emotion.

Maybe we really do have something here?

"Meet me out the front in ten minutes?" I ask. "I just need to go and say goodbye."

He pulls back and keeps my hand tightly gripped in his.

"I'm coming out in ten minutes, tops," I reassure him.

He exhales heavily, and I know he doesn't want me to go back inside to Daniel.

"Elliot."

"Fine. You have five minutes."

I kiss him quickly and make my way back into the auction room. Daniel has moved and I look around. Where is he?

I find him talking to a group of women in the corner, and I smile. I wasn't lying before to Elliot, he really does very well in the hook-up department. He glances up, sees me, and excuses himself.

"Hi."

"Thank God you got rid of that fuckwit," he whispers.

"Um . . ." I frown. "About that."

He rolls his eyes. "Don't tell me."

"We just need to talk."

"With body fluid? Come on, Kate."

"Stop it, I want to see where this goes."

"Why?"

"Because he makes me forget who I am, Daniel, and when I'm with him, I'm not sad Kathryn any more. For the first time in years, I feel like my old self. I need you to be my friend and support me in this."

"For God's sake," he mutters under his breath. "He's a psycho."

"Maybe." I shrug. "Are you okay if I go?"

"Fine," he snaps. "Fuck off then."

I smile.

He kisses me on the cheek. "Bye."

"Are you sure?"

He widens his eyes. "Positive."

"See you at home?"

"Yeah." Daniel turns back to his conversation with the girls, fully distracted. I let out a sigh of relief and, with nerves swirling around in my stomach, I turn toward the door.

I walk out of the front door and look around, see the black Mercedes double-parked. I cross the road and go around to the passenger side, the lock clicks open, and I get in, and because of his close proximity my mood instantly changes from anxious to excited in two seconds flat. "Hi," I whisper.

He stares over at me and the air crackles between us.

"You piss me off," he says.

I smile softly. There's the bossy man I know.

"And I'm not taking your crap, Elliot, don't ask me to. It won't fly with me."

He goes to say something and I cut him off.

"Shut up and kiss me."

He grabs my face and pulls me to him; his tongue takes no prisoners as it swipes through my open lips. His grip is dominant and hot and . . . oh . . . "You pissed me off," he repeats.

"What are you going to do about it," I murmur against his lips.

His grip on my face tightens, his teeth graze my bottom lip. "You'll see." He pulls out into the traffic and revs the car hard as he takes off at speed. I look between him and the road as I swallow the lump in my throat.

Fuck.

I think I'm in for one hell of a night.

What seems like a long time later we are somewhere in the country. "This is where your new house is?" I frown.

"Uh-huh." He nods, his eyes staying glued to the road.

"When did you move here?" He told me about buying a new place but I never asked where it was.

"Today."

"So, this is your first night here?"

"Yep."

"Oh." I try to hide my goofy smile; I like that I get to spend his first night here with him. He turns off the main road and we see a stone sign, although I can't make out what it says. "Is this your road?"

"This is my driveway."

"Your driveway?" I gasp. "All this land is yours? Holy hell, Elliot."

A trace of a smile crosses his face as we wind up the hill on the small road. I can't see much because it's so dark, but there are loads of trees in the headlights.

"This is only temporary," he says, his eyes still on the road.

"What do you mean?"

"I'm going to live in the house for a few months as it is, work out what works and what doesn't, and then renovate or rebuild. It's very"—he pauses as if searching for the right word—"original, in its current state."

"I like original."

"I like you," he fires back as his eyes flick over.

I smile. "I like you too."

He reaches over and runs his hand up my thigh. "You can show me just how much in a minute." He slides his hand under my dress and rubs the backs of his fingers over my sex.

And there he is, the bona fide sex maniac that I know so well. "If you behave," I whisper.

He lets out a deep chuckle and I look out of the windshield, and my eyes widen in shock. "This is your new house?"

"Yes." He pulls the car into a large circular parking area and turns the car off.

"Holy shit, Elliot."

He leans over and kisses me. "Come." He gets out and opens my door, and takes my hand and leads me up to the veranda of the grand house.

It's huge and like something out of a movie, and it's pitch-black inside.

"Put your phone light on for me."

I fumble with my phone and put the flashlight on and shine it on the door.

He takes a set of keys out of his pocket and, in the distance, I hear the sounds of animals in the fields that surround us. I look out into the deserted darkness. It's a little bit scary out here, if I'm honest.

He puts one key in and it doesn't turn, so he tries another. "Fucking keys," he whispers.

I smile as I watch him struggle; so unlike him to not know how to do something.

"Do you want me to try?" I ask.

"No," he snaps. "I'm perfectly capable of working a lock, Kathryn."

"But are you?"

He glances up, unimpressed.

I giggle and hold my hands up playfully. "Okay. Sorry, boss."

He struggles with the key and I run my hand down his back and over his tight ass. "That's more like it," he mutters as he keeps trying. "Keep doing that." He fumbles some more. "Why are there so many fucking keys on this ring?" He jiggles the huge door with force.

"You must have a lot of doors."

"That are about to be kicked in," he snaps in frustration. The door finally gives way, and he pushes it open. It lets out a long, slow creak as it swings and I shine my phone light inside.

"Where are the light switches?" I ask.

"Who knows?" He takes my hand and leads me inside. "Shine the flashlight on the walls."

I giggle as I do as I'm told. This is so unexpected. "There they are. Next to the door, imagine that?"

Elliot flicks them on and the room is brought into the light. I look around at the grandeur and my mouth falls open.

"Elliot," I gasp.

"You like?" He smiles softly as he looks around.

"Oh my God, I love." I look around in awe. "This is incredible."

I turn back to see Elliot staring at me intently, and my heart constricts. I wasn't lying before, I don't know what this is between us.

But it makes me feel *everything*.

The good, the bad, and the ugly . . . but mostly, alive.

I twist my fingers in front of me. "Thank you for inviting me to stay here on your first night . . . it means a lot."

"Well." He shrugs casually. "I need someone to use as a shield, on account of the ghosts."

I giggle and step toward him and he takes me into his arms, and we kiss.

Ever so gently, he melts toward me. The emotion bounces between us like an echo.

And I know it shouldn't, but *this feels real.*

A frown crosses his brow, and he pushes the hair back from my forehead as he looks down at me. He presses his lips together as if stopping himself from saying something out loud.

Why does he do that?

"Do you need to eat . . . or?"

"I don't know what I need anymore," he whispers as he stares at me.

"I do." I take his hand and lead him toward the stairs. "Where is your bedroom?" I ask.

"Upstairs somewhere, I have no fucking clue."

I giggle and he pulls me back by the hand and I slam into his body, and he kisses me.

Hard and urgent and the emotion behind it tears my heart wide open.

He leads me up the grand double-width staircase, and when we get to the top, it falls into pitch-black darkness again. "Are there really ghosts here?" I whisper.

"Relax, nothing's as scary as you."

I scare him . . . *I knew it.*

I'm not imagining it, there is something here between us.

"I think my room is this way."

"You really don't know where your room is?" I laugh.

"The removalists put my bed up for me while I went to the art auction. I was only here for half an hour before I had to go."

I giggle and we turn right and walk down to the end of the hall. He flicks the light on and a huge bedroom comes into view. It has ornate ceilings and beautiful original chandeliers, bay windows with window seats and so much character I could die. There is a large timber four-poster bed in the middle. This place looks as if it's straight out of a romance movie.

"It's a little dated," he murmurs, and it's apparent he's uncomfortable with it the way that it is. He's used to having the best of everything at his fingertips.

I gasp. "Are you kidding, it's incredible."

He walks me backward to the bed, and lifts my dress over my shoulders and throws it to the side. Silence falls between us as his eyes drift down my body. I can feel the heat as his gaze sears my skin.

I stand before him in my underwear, vulnerable and at his disposal, and when his eyes rise to mine, they are blazing with desire.

"Did you miss me?" I ask.

He takes my face in his hands and kisses me deeply, uninhibited and wild.

We kiss again and again and I feel his hard length as it pushes up against my stomach.

He can hide his emotions from me all he wants . . . but his body doesn't lie.

It can't, he has nowhere to hide.

Literally.

As we kiss, he takes my bra off and then slides down my panties, his hands roaming all over me as his kiss deepens. He grabs my behind and lifts me to rub me over his hard cock.

His breathing becomes labored, and *holy hell* . . . how this man makes me feel.

I don't know if I've ever been with a man who physically affects me this way.

I take his shirt off over his head and then undo his jeans, and our tongues dance together.

The arousal between us is at fever pitch.

I slide his pants down and his cock springs free. He smiles against my lips and I give an excited giggle as he picks me up and my legs go around his waist.

We fall down onto the bed as we keep kissing, his body cradled in between my legs, and he slides his length through my wet flesh.

He stares down at me and I smile up at him in awe.

The tip of him slowly slides in and my breath catches as I lift my legs.

He closes his eyes and pulls out.

"What are you doing?" I stammer.

"Condom."

"No, El."

"Stop," he snaps as he climbs off me.

He's lost trust in me.

Back to square one, *fuck*.

He fumbles through his wallet and pulls out two condoms and I watch as he rolls one on, and when he turns back to me his demeanor has changed. My sweet El isn't here anymore.

Elliot Miles, the hard-ass fucking machine has arrived.

Not that I'm complaining, I love him too.

He lies over me, and instead of the intimacy we shared only moments ago, he lifts my legs so that my knees are up near his shoulders. With dark eyes he rubs the tip of his cock back and forth through my wet lips.

"You want this?" he whispers.

I nod, unable to answer.

"Answer me," he barks.

"Yes," I whimper.

Satisfaction flickers in his eyes and he pushes himself in. Hard and unapologetic, my body struggles to take him. He pushes harder. Pinning me to the mattress.

I whimper again and he turns and kisses my knee, his tongue softly lapping at me. "Open," he commands in a whisper against my skin.

"I'm trying." I wince.

He pushes forward again and rotates his hips. "Try harder."

A flutter of arousal shimmers through the sting and I smile softly. "That's it."

He rotates his hips again and my back arches off the bed in approval.

"Yes . . ." I pant. He pulls out and pushes back in and I moan. "Oh God."

My body floods with moisture, allowing him to go deep, and he smiles darkly. "That's it, baby, open up. Let me in." He rearranges my legs over his shoulders and turns and softly kisses my foot.

Watching the intimate act brings a flutter to my heart.

He's right here with me, I know he is.

He pulls out and slides back in deep, my body sucks him in, she's ready to go.

He rotates his hips and I shudder deep inside.

Nobody fucks like Elliot Miles, he was born to do this.

The master.

He begins to ride me hard and deep and I close my eyes as I run my hands up and down his muscular back; I can feel every ripple on his torso.

His lips are on my neck, at my ear. His breath makes goose-bumps scatter up my spine. The burn of his possession is sending shockwaves through my blood, and he pulls out and moves down my body, his thick tongue swiping through my wet flesh.

Oh fuck.

I've never been with a man who does this before: he goes down on me in the middle of sex, he loves it.

I love it.

It drives me fucking wild.

He holds me open and licks me up like I'm his last meal, and the look of pure ecstasy on his face brings a smile to my face.

Elliot Miles doesn't go down on a woman for her pleasure.

He does it for his, and I've never seen or felt something so fucking hot in my life.

He lifts my legs and really begins to eat me, my body convulsing at the burn of his stubble.

My back arches off the bed and I slam hard into a freight train of an orgasm, my entire body convulsing, and in one sharp movement he's flipped me onto my stomach and dragged me up onto my knees.

He slides in deep and then . . . he lets me have it with both barrels.

Hard, thick pumps, the sound of our skin slapping together is loud and echoing throughout the room. His grip on my hip bones is almost painful, the burn of his cock working at piston pace is out-of-this-world good.

Fuck . . . this is what sex is supposed to be like.

Hot, hard, and sweaty.

Where the rules are: there are no rules.

He pushes my shoulders down onto the mattress, changing my position, and then he begins to moan. Deep, low, and guttural.

He's lost control now, his body taking on its own agenda to feed.

Taking what it needs from my body.

Thick and hard . . . Elliot Miles is a hell of a lot to take.

"Fuck me," he growls. "Fuck me harder."

I clench as hard as I can and his knees nearly go from underneath him, and he cries out as he holds himself deep. I feel the jerk of his cock deep inside of me.

I face-plant into the mattress as I come again, and he slowly moves to completely empty his body into mine.

We come back to earth and he falls over me, our bodies wet with perspiration. I can feel his heart as it hammers alongside mine.

"The bed works," he pants.

I smile sleepily, completely spent. "I'll say."

I wake to the feeling of the bed dipping as Elliot gets out of bed, and smile as I stretch.

Wow, what a night.

I hear Elliot go to the bathroom and I doze for a few minutes. I hear him going through an overnight bag and I sit up onto my elbows. "What are you doing?"

"I'm fucking starving," he mutters as he digs through his bag. "We didn't eat last night."

"Well. We did."

"I mean food, Kate."

I sit up. "I'll make us breakfast."

"There's no food to cook."

"Shit."

He grabs my hand and pulls me out of bed. "Come on, we'll go get something."

"Okay." I go to the bathroom and come out to find that he has gone downstairs. I throw on his button-up shirt and make my way down.

"What is that?" I hear him mutter as he opens the curtains in the living room.

I can hear a strange sound, like hail hitting a window or something.

I frown as I try to focus. "What's that noise?"

He looks around. "I don't know."

We walk through the house, opening the curtains as we go from room to room. "Is something in the walls?"

His eyes widen in horror. "Like what?"

"I don't know, rats?"

"What?" he barks. "Surely fucking not."

As we walk toward the back of the house it gets louder and louder.

Elliot's holding his hands out as if pre-empting an attack of some sort and I smile as we get closer to a huge curtain, which must be covering a sliding door.

"What the hell is out there?" he whispers, wide-eyed.

"I don't know."

He peers through the crack in the curtain and then stands up as if disgusted.

"What is it?"

"Ducks."

"Huh?"

He flicks open the curtain and I see a group of ducks all pecking at the glass like maniacs. They appear frantic and are jumping over each other to get to us.

"What are they doing?" I frown.

Elliot opens the door in a rush. "Fuck off, ducks," he snaps.

They jump over his feet and run inside.

"What the hell?" he cries.

They run through the house with their wings up in the air, squawking loudly.

"What are you doing?" Elliot screams.

I burst out laughing.

"Get out of my house!" he yells as they all jump up at him. "What the fuck are they doing?"

They are so loud and making such a commotion.

It's him they want, they're all jumping up at him, and he storms outside and they all run after him. "Fuck off," he cries as he tries to get away from them. "Call somebody."

I tip my head back and laugh loud. "Who do I call?"

The sight of Elliot Miles running down the pathway with a bunch of ducks chasing him is simply too much and I nearly fall over as I laugh hard.

"This isn't fucking funny, Kathryn," he yells, and he kicks out to try and move them and they squawk louder. "Fuck off, ducks!"

Chapter 17

"Hello Brianna," Elliot barks as he paces back and forth. "We have a problem."

I listen as I sit on a stool at the kitchen countertop.

"Ducks. That's what." He listens. "Well, they attacked me." He listens for a moment. "Feral ducks."

My face breaks into a broad smile. After fifteen minutes of running around like a maniac, Elliot closed the doors and the ducks have retreated back to their lake.

Elliot frowns as he listens. "No. What clause, I never agreed to any such clause." His horrified eyes meet mine.

"What?" I mouth.

He shakes his head. "Well . . . I don't want them."

He listens again.

"Since when would the sale of a house have animals in the contract? That's preposterous." He walks to the window and peers out over the field. "A goat?" he snaps. His eyes meet mine and I bite my bottom lip to stop myself from smiling. "A fucking what?" he explodes. "A pony and a pig? No way. Not on your life. Come and take them away. Right. Now."

He shakes his head in disgust.

"Who the hell do I sell them to?" he fires back. "This isn't Jack and the Beanstalk, Brianna, you don't go to fucking market to sell a pig."

I burst out laughing, Elliot glares at me, and I slap my hand over my mouth.

"What do you mean?" He paces again, looks out the window and down at the paddock, then his eyes meet mine. "Well . . . you better find out." He listens intently. "Fine." He hangs up.

"What happened?" I ask.

"Apparently the woman who I bought the house off was eighty-eight and has a menagerie of animals. It was a condition of sale that the new purchaser keeps them on because she's gone to a retirement community."

My eyes widen. "Oh."

"She's finding out what I can do with them."

My face falls. "Why?"

"I don't want farm animals, Kathryn, I'm not Old McFucking Donald."

"It's a settling-in period, they'll calm down."

"Absolutely not."

I walk to the back door and look out over the paddocks. The ducks are pecking away at the ground next to the lake. "They're probably just hungry."

"For human blood?" He grabs his keys. "I'm telling you now, it won't be mine. We need to go and find breakfast before I faint." He takes my hand in his. "Let's go."

Two hours later we pull up outside the front of my house. "Thanks." I smile.

Elliot rolls his lips as he looks at my house, and I know he's not happy about me going inside to Daniel. "What are you going to do all weekend?" I ask.

"Unpack a million boxes."

I can help . . . No, play it cool.

286

"Okay, well, have fun with that." I smile.

"What are you doing?" he asks as he slides his hand up my thigh; I lean over and kiss his shoulder.

"This afternoon I'm cleaning my house and then tonight I'm having dinner with my brother."

"Okay. Have fun."

We stare at each other and I smile shyly. Elliot Miles makes me feel like a schoolgirl; the earth spins fast and I'm giddy.

"I'll give you a call?" he says.

"Okay." I lean over and kiss him and his lips linger over mine. I hate saying goodbye to this man.

Our kiss deepens and he smiles against my lips. "Stop it or I'll drag you back to my place to play Old McDonald."

I giggle and open the car door, get out, and lean in the open window. "Good luck with your ducks."

He rolls his eyes. "Don't remind me."

"What are you going to do?"

He shrugs. "Wait for the damn real estate agent to call me back."

"Okay, good luck." I give him a wave. "Bye."

With a smile and a wave, he pulls out and drives away.

ELLIOT

I pull up at the valet area in the underground parking lot and get out of my car.

"Nice to see you, Mr. Miles."

"Hello Raymond." I smile. "Is my brother in?"

"I believe so."

I hand my car keys over and take the elevator to his floor, get out at the private reception area, and ring the bell. I hear it let out an internal buzz and I wait, noticing a new painting which I inspect closely. "Hmm, average," I mutter under my breath.

The door opens and a disheveled-looking Christopher comes into view, wearing only boxer shorts. He frowns. "Hey."

I smile and rock up onto my toes. "Hi."

"What are you doing here?"

"Picking you up, get dressed."

"Now isn't a good time—"

I cut him off as I barge past him into his apartment, and come face to face with a beautiful brunette lying on the couch in only a T-shirt. "Oh." I wince and turn to Christopher. "Sorry to . . . interrupt."

Christopher widens his eyes in a subtle *fuck off* gesture. "That's fine. Elliot, meet Siena."

I nod. "Hello."

"Hi." She beams.

I hear a sound coming up the hall to see a drop-dead gorgeous redhead . . . also scantily clad in one of Christopher's

T-shirts. "Ah . . ." I smile. Two of them . . . I really *am* interrupting. "Hello."

"Meet Chantel," Christopher interrupts me.

"Hi," she purrs as she hungrily looks me up and down.

She's familiar, I've seen her on the circuit. With looks like hers she's easy to remember.

My eyes go back to my brother's and he twists his lips in a further *fuck off, right now* gesture.

"I'm sorry for the interruption, ladies, but I need to steal my brother for a few hours."

"Oh no . . ." Siena frowns.

"Ah, duty calls," Christopher replies casually as he walks into the kitchen. "Party's over, girls. Until next time."

"Aww," they both complain.

I smile and follow my brother. I remember these days well. So many women, so little time.

Christopher turns on his coffee machine and makes two cups. "What the fuck are you doing here at this ungodly hour?"

I glance at my watch. "It's ten thirty and we have a major issue."

"What's that?" he mutters dryly as he sips his coffee.

"There are killer ducks roaming around my new house."

"What?" He frowns.

"Ducks, at least a dozen. They attacked me this morning, chased me, wanting my blood."

His eyes widen. "Like, duck ducks?"

"Yes, Christopher," I snap. "What other kind of ducks are there?"

"Well, what do you want me to do? I know nothing about fucking ducks."

"Get dressed."

"Why?'

"You're helping me catch them."

"We can't do that?" he splutters. "Call somebody."

"No."

"Why not?"

"I'm not calling someone every single time something goes wrong in this house. I want to do it myself."

"Listen," he mutters into his coffee. "If you must do this little-man-versus-the-wild experiment in enchanted land, can you at least leave me out of it? I'm a city man, haunted castles with wild animals are completely out of my realm."

"No." I stand. "Hurry up."

"Fuck's sake."

The girls appear in the kitchen. "We're going."

Christopher stands. "Frederick will drive you home." He kisses Siena and then turns to the redhead; his hand drops to her behind as he kisses her and I know from his body language that she's his favorite.

They turn to me. "Nice to meet you."

"Likewise." I fake a smile. Fuck off already. I want to go. Christopher walks them to the door and I hear the soft giggles of the girls as they say their goodbyes.

Not so long ago, this was me: how did this life ever captivate me for so long?

I'm way past stupid women; womanizing just doesn't excite me anymore.

I know it was fun at the time, but looking back it's all a blur. Not one of them ever stood out.

Not like her.

I get a vision of Kate last night on top of me, the way she looked down at me as she rode me . . . the sheen on her skin, the arousal in her eyes . . . a tingle runs through my body at the mere memory.

"What's that look?" Christopher mutters as he walks back into the room.

I look up, my fantasy interrupted. "What?"

"What are you thinking about?"

"I'm thinking you're taking too long. Hurry the fuck up."

I bring the car to a stop outside the front of my house. Christopher and I peer out the window. "I don't see any ducks," he says.

All seems silent.

"Hmm." I open the car door slowly.

"Be careful they don't peck your old fella off," Christopher says as he climbs out of the car.

I look around, the coast seems clear. "My old fella would win a fight with a duck, hands down."

Christopher and I stand on the edge of the gravel driveway. We go around the side of the house and look down toward the lake. "So where are they, then?" he asks.

My eyes roam around the lake, and over the paddocks. "I don't know . . ." We both turn in a full circle as we search.

Completely peaceful.

"I don't see any ducks," he repeats.

With hands on his hips he looks over the valley. "Umm . . . EJ?" he calls.

"Yeah," I call back.

"Is that your land over there too?"

I look back to see that he is looking over paddocks to the right of the house. "Yeah."

He narrows his eyes as he focuses on something in the distance. "What's it doing?"

I walk over and look to where his gaze is. "What is what . . . ?" I fall silent.

There's a huge, black sheep, but it's a different kind of sheep, with curly, round horns. We watch as it walks backward, takes a hard run-up and then head-butts the fence post as hard as it can.

We hear the bang as it connects; the sound echoes for miles.

"What the fuck is that?" I whisper.

"I don't know." Christopher frowns as he watches it run back and smash its head as hard as it can. "Some kind of psychotic sheep."

Our eyes meet. "What is this godforsaken place?" I whisper.

Suddenly we hear squawks from behind us, and we turn to see the ducks running toward us up the hill, full throttle. Their wings are in the air, beaks open and ready to attack.

"Run," I cry as I take off in the direction of the house.

"Ahh, fuck," Christopher cries.

I grab the keys from my pocket, the sound of angry ducks coming up close.

I look down at the keys on the overcrowded keyring. "Oh no."

"What?" Christopher cries as he runs alongside me.

"I don't know what key it is."

"How can you not know what fucking key it is?" he cries.

"The car. Run for the car."

We dive into the car and jump in and slam the doors behind us. The ducks all squawk as they circle us.

"You weren't kidding." Christopher pants as he holds his chest, looking down at our attackers. "What do we do now?"

I start the car. "We get the hell out of here."

We eat lunch, drink some beer, and devise a plan. Two hours later we head back up the driveway. I glance over to see the trusty shovel we bought sitting perfectly on the backseat.

I park the car and hand the house keys to Chris. He frowns as he looks through the keys. "Do you know which one it is at all?"

"I think it's one of the copper smaller ones, though I can't be sure."

He nods. "The coast seems clear."

"Hopefully they all drowned in the lake," I mutter as I look around.

"What's the plan?" he asks.

"I'll guard you with the shovel, while you get the door open."

"Okay." He goes to get out of the car and then turns back. "Don't slam the door."

"Good thinking," I whisper.

We all but tiptoe up to the porch, and Christopher quietly begins to try the keys, while I stand with my back to him, shovel in hand. Waiting for the attack.

"Hurry up."

"What are you going to do if they come?" he whispers as he fiddles with the lock.

I grip my shovel hard. "I'm going to show them who's boss around here."

He chuckles. "Yes, you certainly look like the master of this domain."

"Fuck off."

The lock finally gives way and he opens the door. We go in, and I slam the door behind me. "This is ridiculous," I snap as I march to the kitchen. "I didn't sign up for this shit." I begin to open the drawers in a rush. "Where is that envelope?" I open and shut all the drawers and finally locate it. I speed-read the letter and I get to point three:

> *The ducks will need to be fed their pellets each morning and will become aggressive if hungry.*
>
> *The pellets are kept in the stables.*

Huh?

"What does it say?"

I look up at Christopher in shock. "They're hungry."

He frowns.

"We were supposed to feed them."

"Well, what do they eat?'

"It says here, pellets."

"Where are they?"

"Stables."

His eyes widen and he points at me. "If you think I'm going near that psychotic sheep you've got another thing coming."

I pick up my keys. "Come on, we're going back into town."

"What for?"

"To buy fucking duck food, what do you think?"

I sit by the open fire and sip my Scotch; red shadows dance across the wall. It's dark, the room lit only by the lamps and the glowing embers, and a sense of achievement is running thick through my veins. Not only did I unpack a lot of my things today, I sorted the ducks.

Poor bastards were starving . . . actually, they're girls, so . . .

I smile as the golden fluid warms my throat. Either way, they were happy to receive their stupid pellets.

I look around at my surroundings and pride fills me. I love this house; there's so much to do and it doesn't feel like home yet, but I know it will as soon as I hang Harriet's paintings on the walls.

I've had her art close to me for years, not seeing it is weird.

I pick up my phone and glance at the time: 9:30 p.m.

Should I call Kate?

No.

She's out with her brother, leave her be.

I want to hear her voice.

I only saw her last night, calm down.

I get up and refill my glass, walk back through the house as I look at my surroundings. I love this house, I love everything about it . . . maybe not the ducks, but everything else is perfect.

I might message Pinkie instead . . . no, I want to speak to my girl.

Just a quick call to say goodnight.

My finger hovers over the name Kate. I shouldn't.

But I will.

I press call and I listen as it rings.

"Hi there," she purrs.

The sound of her voice brings a smile to my face. "Hi."

"Hi," she repeats, and I can tell she's smiling too.

"I called to say goodnight."

"Did you now?"

Excitement rolls around my stomach.

"What are you doing?" she asks.

"Wondering how I can possibly last the night without you."

"No need to wonder, come and get me."

I smile. "I've had a few glasses of wine, I'm unable to drive."

"Oh."

"I can send Andrew to collect you."

"Really?"

"Where are you?"

"I'm just leaving the restaurant now; can he pick me up from my place in say, half an hour?"

"Okay."

She waits on the line.

"Oh, and Kate."

"Yes."

"Pack yourself a bag, that way you can stay for the weekend."

I hesitate; *slow down.*

"Still in need of a human shield, you see," I add.

She giggles. "How are your ducks?"

"All in a row."

"I'll be the judge of that."

I chuckle.

"Okay, see you soon."

"Goodbye." I drain my glass and march upstairs. I need to shower and I need to . . .

I need to last longer tonight. She turns me into a schoolboy; she only has to look my way and my dick begins to weep.

I turn the shower on and take out the lube from my bathroom cabinet, squirt it into my hand and smear it on my already hard cock.

I run my hand up over my length and then back to the base . . . hmm, that feels good.

The room begins to fill with steam as I work myself, sliding my fingers up under my balls and cupping them hard as I imagine it's her hand touching me . . . satisfying me now so that I can give her more later.

I don't know if I've ever jerked off so much since I became besotted with Kate Landon.

She's the ultimate taboo.

The employee I can't date, the one I shouldn't want.

The woman I can't get out of my fucking head.

At this moment in time, my dick lives and breathes to be inside of her.

Nothing else matters.

My chest rises and falls as I begin to perspire, my strokes getting harder and harder. My need skyrocketing by the second.

I close my eyes and I see her naked on my bed, her legs spread, her pink, wet flesh open for me. She slowly slides her finger deep inside her sex, warming herself up for me. She spreads her pink lips open in a come-here signal. "Elliot," she whispers.

I grunt as my hand works at piston pace. Fuck yeah.

Already . . . what the hell?

I tip my head back and aim up onto my body, and my cock jerks hard. White, thick semen glistens over my chest.

I pant as I come down from my high, and I step under the hot shower, aim my face up to the water. It runs down over my head and I put my hand on the tiles to hold myself up.

She doesn't even have to be here to make me come hard.

The memory of her is enough.

I need to get a hold of myself. That was only one minute. *Fuck.*

An hour later I sit on the couch by the fire. I've left the door slightly ajar.

The car has just pulled up and I know Kate isn't far away.

I've given myself a few rounds, whatever it takes to keep the monster at bay.

I need to last longer . . . fuck it.

The door opens and Kate comes into view. It takes a few moments for her to see me sitting in the semi-dark.

"Hi." She smiles.

I sip my Scotch. "Hi."

She's wearing a black, long jacket and high stilettos. She walks over to stand in front of me and slowly undoes her jacket and drops it to the floor.

My breath catches: she's wearing a black silk corset and suspender belt, with tiny black lace panties.

The light flickers as it dances on her skin.

I inhale sharply and she drops to her knees between my legs and pushes them open with force.

Yes.

With dark eyes she takes me into her mouth, her tongue flicking over my end, and I put my hands in her hair as I watch her.

Fuck.

This woman will be the death of me.

For ten minutes I watch her, feel her. Want her with every fucking fiber of my being. Until I can't stand it, and I drag her up to me. We kiss violently, our teeth clashing with desire, and she straddles me over my lap. I pull her panties to the side and slide in to the hilt in one deep movement.

We fall still and stare at each other, the air electric as it zaps between us.

A tantric force that I have no control over.

"Can you feel how deep inside of me you are?" she murmurs.

I swallow the lump in my throat as I stare up at her. I nod. Unable to speak.

She brings herself to a squatting position, and I can feel every muscle inside her perfect body.

"Fuck me . . . Mr. Miles," she whispers darkly, her eyelashes hooded, her voice husky and filled with desire.

My grip on her hip bones tightens, my control close to its end.

She puts her lips to my ear and licks it. "I've been waiting for your beautiful cock all day," she whispers before kissing me deeply.

My eyes close as our tongues dance. I can't . . .

I grab her hip bones and slam her down hard. "And so you shall have it."

Chapter 18

Kate

I smile softly, my eyes still closed as I feel the soft fingertips trail up my arm and over my shoulder. My hair is carefully pushed back from my face and a soft kiss dusts my neck, then another, and another.

He holds me tight and takes my hand in his, his body snuggled up behind mine.

Waking up in Elliot Miles's arms will never grow old.

It's as if the anger of his world disappears while he sleeps and he wakes a demure, more tender version of himself.

"Good morning," I whisper.

He kisses my cheek. "Good morning, sweetheart."

I smile—I love it when he calls me that. I roll onto my back to face him. "How did you sleep?"

"Like a log."

I cuddle up to him. "And what a handsome sleepy log you are."

He kisses me softly. "Of course, it could do with the fact that you are fucking me into unconsciousness."

I giggle and then I remember something and look over to him. "What happened with your ducks?"

"Ah." He smiles and rolls out of bed. "Apparently . . . they were just hungry."

"What?" I smile as I look up at him.

"I would go as far as to say fucking starving, actually." He stands, completely comfortable with his nudity. My eyes roam down his body, over his broad, thick chest and olive skin. He has hardly any body fat, revealing every last sinew. Muscular and fit, with thick quad muscles and a defined abdomen. His arms are strong, with rope-like veins running down his forearms.

My eyes drop lower, to the well-kept, dark pubic hair and large family jewels.

There's no denying that Elliot Miles is the epitome of male perfection, but there's a lot more to him than meets the eye. Just what that is, I've yet to discover.

But unlike most men I've met in the past, the more I get to know him, the more I like about him. He's like an onion, slowly being peeled back layer by layer before my eyes.

He gives himself a slow stroke and my eyes rise to meet his and he shrugs. "If you're going to look at me like that, I may as well give you something to look at."

"Like what?" I smile.

"Like you're going to eat me."

I burst out laughing. "I was not."

He picks his T-shirt up and whips me with it. "Don't deny it." He throws his T-shirt over his head and pulls his boxer shorts on.

"What are you doing?"

"I've got to feed the ducks before they go postal."

"What?" I sit up on my elbows.

"True story."

"Are you really knocking back sex . . . to feed your ducks?" I laugh.

He climbs over me and holds my hands over my head. "Hold that thought, I'll be back." He kisses me and I smile against his lips.

"If they chase you again, I'm filming it."

"Come on." He pulls me up by the hand. "Rise and grind."

"What?"

"Rise and grind," he says as he rakes through his closet and throws me his robe.

"Is that what you do every day?" I ask. "Rise and grind?"

"Nope." His eyes dance with mischief as they hold mine. "Only the days that you're here."

"Ha, nice save."

He takes me in his arms roughly and bites my neck, then we make our way downstairs and into the kitchen and I watch as he carefully pours pellets into a container. "How did you find out they were hungry?"

"A letter was left." He gestures to the letter on the countertop and I pick it up.

Dearest Mr. Miles,

Congratulations on your new home.

I trust our beloved Enchanted Estate will bring you much joy.

My late husband and I were lucky enough to spend the last sixty years here and they were the happiest days of our lives.

As you know, at the tender age of eighty-eight and with pressing health conditions, the time has come for me to move into a retirement home.

Thank you so much for agreeing to take on our beloved animals.

They are all fourth or fifth generations born on the estate and have known no other life.

The thought of them being evicted broke my heart. It made me so happy when I found that I could leave them in your loving care.

I have listed below some simple care instructions for them. Please call if you need any help with anything.

I can be reached on 0434358922

The local veterinarian   Max Manalo
99952132

Rosie the Shetland pony is found in the bottom paddock. She has a lovely temperament and thrives on human company. She has chaff feed kept in the stable at the bottom of the property and is mostly self-sufficient.

Billy the goat is kept in the far paddock. He is a little rebellious but a nice goat all the same. He eats mostly natural feed but has a bag of feed, also in the stable. It is marked clearly with his name.

The ducks.

Our lovely ladies are a source of many hours of pleasure. However, they do get anxious when they haven't been fed.

There isn't enough natural food for them in the lake and they will need to be given their pellets each morning. Adhere to their regular feeding schedule and all will be easy with them.

Humphrey the ram.

Now, Humphrey was my husband's and is an acquired taste.

He doesn't like people, and will become violent if confronted.

He is completely self-sufficient and it is best not to toy with him.

Call the veterinarian if you need any assistance on his welfare, do not attempt to tend to it yourself.

The only person he ever took to was my beloved husband and I'm afraid he hasn't been the same since he passed.

Thank you so much, Mr. Miles.

You have no idea what a relief it is to know that they are to be cared for.

Yours sincerely,

Frances Melania

I look up at Elliot in surprise.

"Can you believe that shit?" he asks.

My eyes skim the letter again. "So . . . you're a fully fledged farmer now?"

"No." He takes the container of pellets to the back door and peers around the side of the curtain. "It's just temporary until I get something sorted."

"No, Elliot. You gave her your word, or at least your solicitor did. They have to stay."

He gives a disgusted shake of his head and opens the door in a rush. The ducks catch sight of him and begin to run toward him with their wings in the air, squawking loudly.

He runs down the lawn and throws the pellets in the air in their direction, and then he bolts back to the house. He rushes in and slams the door behind him as if a wild animal has just chased him. "There," he announces proudly. "See . . . I know what I'm doing." He dusts his hands together as if he's just fought a dragon and won.

I smile broadly; the poor bastard is scared for his life. "I'm very impressed, Mr. Miles."

Elliot takes my hand in his. "Come on, we have to get back. It's going to be dark soon."

Hand in hand we begin to walk up the hill toward the house. It's been the best day. We've spent it walking around the property and checking things out. It really is beautiful and there is so much to see.

"When did you buy this place?"

"Last year, in June."

"Over six months ago?" I ask in surprise.

"Yes. She wanted to stay as long as she could after I completed on the property. So, I waited."

I smile as we make our way back up the hill. "It was worth every second, it's breathtaking."

Elliot's eyes roam over the rolling hills before us. "From the moment I saw it, I knew that it would be mine."

I smile at his dreamy stance. "Have you always wanted to live out here?"

"No. For a long time I resented having to live in the UK. I just wanted to go back to New York."

I frown as I listen. "You couldn't go back?"

"I could, but not if I wanted the job that I have now. It could only be here. Jameson is the CEO in the States."

I nod as a clearer picture comes through. "What changed?" I ask. "To make you want to . . ."

"I don't know," he says as he walks. "A few years ago, I went home to New York and I was sitting in a bar with a big group of friends that in the past I had always missed."

I listen intently.

"And not one of them had one thing to say that interested me."

I frown.

"It was like a lightbulb went off, and I had an epiphany, one that for some reason had previously eluded me. I realized that my only connection with America and New York was my family, and I see them all the time wherever I am. I decided that day, then and there, that I would make my life here."

I smile.

"And besides"—he picks up my hand and kisses the back of it—"I have a thing for English girls."

I smirk. "Plural, Elliot," I remind him.

"Girl," he mouths.

We walk for a while. "And the art thing?" I ask.

"Ah." He smiles, as if he's been waiting for me to ask. "I've collected art since I was old enough for pocket money."

306

"Why?"

He raises his eyebrows as if searching for an answer. "It calls to me."

"How?"

"I don't know." His gaze goes over to the paddocks as he contemplates his answer. "It's like I feel the artists' emotions as they painted." He bends down and picks a flower and passes it to me.

I feel my heart constrict.

"There's this one artist, for instance. Harriet Boucher. I am totally and utterly besotted with her."

I giggle. "Should I be worried?"

He picks up my hand and kisses my fingertips. "She's old."

"How old?"

"I don't know, I think in her nineties. I've been searching for her because I know my time to find her is running out."

"What do you mean?"

"I own all but three of her paintings that are out in public. But there are more that I don't own, and they're probably all in storage somewhere. I want to find her before she passes so that I can make her an offer and ensure that they aren't lost."

I frown. "What's so good about these paintings?"

"Everything." He smiles. "I know it sounds ridiculous but I have an affection for them that I can't explain. I stare at them for hours and still I need more. It's like they speak to me in an other-worldly way."

I smile as I listen.

"I have a connection to the artist." He shrugs as if embarrassed, bends and picks another little pink field flower and passes it to me.

"Thanks." I take it from him.

"I don't know what it is. Perhaps we knew each other in another life."

Goosebumps scatter up my arms as I stare at him and, unexpectedly, I well up, and blink to try and hide my tears.

"What's wrong?" He frowns.

I shrug, embarrassed. "Nothing." I give a subtle shake of my head. "That's just . . . probably, the most beautiful thing I've ever heard anyone say. You need to find this old woman so you can tell her in person." I smile dreamily. "I can't imagine how happy you will make her heart."

"Most people think I'm crazy."

"I think it's . . ." I pause as I search for the right word. "Magical."

He smiles shyly. "I don't know about that, it could be one big wild goose chase."

"Well, you were chased by ducks." I widen my eyes to accentuate my point. "Kind of the same thing . . ."

He goes to grab me and I pull out of his grip and take off up the hill. He lets out a roar and chases me and I laugh out loud.

It's been a great day, the best.

Whoever named this estate was right on the money. I am totally enchanted.

Monday morning, 11 a.m.

I sit in the boardroom along with my colleagues, waiting for Elliot for our monthly meeting. After the most incredible weekend in history, I'm floating on cloud nine.

Elliot walks in, back ramrod-straight and in a perfectly fitted blue suit. His dark hair is messed up to a perfect just-fucked look and his eyes find mine across the room. "Morning," he says as he closes the door behind him.

His presence instantly takes over the room, power personified.

My stomach flutters. Good grief, I'm totally fan-girling over this man.

In my defense though, there's a damn lot to fan over. I've never met anyone quite like him.

"Good morning." I concentrate on keeping a straight face and acting normal.

He puts his computer down on the large boardroom table. "How was everyone's weekend?" he asks as he looks around.

"Good thanks." They all start to answer and chat.

"How was yours?" I ask.

His eyes find mine and he gives me the best come-fuck-me look I have ever seen. "Exceptional."

My heart skips a beat.

I bite the inside of my lip to stop myself from openly swooning at his feet.

Get a hold of yourself Kate, *slow it down.*

He begins to read through the meeting notes from last month and my stomach contracts with a sharp pain.

Oh no.

My period.

I close my eyes. Damn it. Not now.

The meeting continues as pain throbs through me, and perspiration wets my skin.

Elliot is standing at a whiteboard talking with a marker in his hand.

My stomach twists hard and I drop my head.

Oh . . . this hurts.

His eyes come to me and a trace of a frown crosses his face as he talks.

He continues but I feel the hot release and stand in a rush. "I'm sorry, I have to leave," I whisper through pain.

"Is everything alright?" He frowns.

"I'm unwell." I rush for the door. "I'm sorry, I'll catch up in the notes."

I make it down to my floor, grab my handbag, and practically run to the bathroom.

I don't have time for this crap.

Elliot

I dial Kate's office; it rings out. Where is she?

I exhale heavily and get back to my report, something is wrong. I dial her floor manager. "Hello Peter, can you put me through to Kathryn, please."

"She's gone home sick, sir."

I frown. "Ahh, okay." I hang on the line as I roll my pen underneath my fingers on my desk. "Did she mention what was wrong?"

"Stomach problems."

"Thank you." I hang up.

I dial her cell phone. "Hi El," she answers softly.

"Are you alright?"

"Yeah, sorry to leave early."

"What's wrong?"

"Just my period, I'll be okay."

"Do you have something that you can take?"

"I'll be fine, Elliot, don't worry," she whispers, and it's obvious she wants to get off the phone in a rush. "I'll see you tomorrow, okay?"

I frown. *Tomorrow* . . . oh. "Are you at home yet?"

"Yeah, I caught a cab," she whispers.

"Okay."

"Goodbye."

"Call me if you—"

She hangs up before I can finish my sentence.

Oh.

I sit back in my chair . . . Hmmm. I inhale and get back to work.

Two minutes later . . .

What if she takes one of those tablets again and falls down the stairs?

No, she said she wasn't taking them anymore.

I remember how out of control she was last time, and I imagine her lifeless body at the bottom of the stairs. She wouldn't be that stupid.

Would she?

I keep trying to work, but twenty minutes later I press my intercom. "Courtney."

"Yes sir."

"I'm leaving for the day."

"But . . . you have meetings all afternoon, sir."

"Reschedule them."

"Is everything alright, sir?"

"Everything's fine," I snap. I stand and put my suit jacket on. "I just need to go."

I march into Christopher's office. "I need your car."

He glances up from his computer. "What for?"

"I've got to check on something."

"Like what?"

I stare at him as I try to think of something. "There's an emergency with the ducks."

Fuck . . . I'm a bad liar.

Christopher's eyes widen. "What happened?"

I shrug. "Um, they attacked the postman."

He gasps. "They what?"

"Attacked the postman and he fell off his motorbike. It's a terrible mess."

He tips his head back and bursts out laughing. Loud and deep. "Oh my fuck, wait until the boys hear this."

He hits speed-dial on his desk phone.

"Hey." I hear Jameson's voice.

Great, a conference call, just what I need.

"What's doing??" I hear Tristan's voice.

I hold my hand out. "Give me the fucking keys."

"It gets better." Christopher laughs. "His ducks attacked the postman and he fell off his motorbike."

Tristan roars with laughter and I punch Christopher's chest. "Give me the keys, prick."

"Oh hell." I hear Jameson sigh. "Get him a fucking gun already."

I hold my hand out. "Keys."

"I need my car tonight, I have a date," Christopher snaps.

"You have four cars."

"No."

"I'll have Andrew pick you up after work."

"Why don't you get Andrew to come now?"

"Because he will take too long. Keys," I demand as I get to the last of my patience.

"Fine." He hands them over. "Fuck off, I hope the postman sues you."

"I can see the headline now," Tristan says. "Death by duck."

They all roar with laughter and I storm from the office.

Fuckers.

Twenty minutes later I knock on Kate's door.

No answer.

I knock harder.

No answer.

I call her cell phone, it rings out.

"Fuck's sake," I mutter. I call her again.

"Hello," she says sleepily.

"Open the door."

"What?"

"I'm at your front door, can you walk down the stairs?"

"I told you, I'm fine."

"You are not fine, Kate. Open the fucking door."

"Ugh." She hangs up and moments later the door opens and she comes into view. "What are you doing here?"

Relieved, I take her into my arms. "I came to check on you."

"I'm fine." She turns to walk up the stairs and I follow her like a puppy. She climbs into her bed and pulls the blankets over herself.

I sit on the edge of the bed, unsure what to say.

"I just need to sleep."

"Well." I look around her room. "I'm not leaving you here alone."

"Be careful, Elliot." She smiles with her eyes closed. "You're sounding very boyfriend-like."

That's ridiculous. I frown and stand; she stays still and I sit back down.

Fuck.

What do I do now?

For ten minutes I sit on the side of the bed as she sleeps.

Screw this.

"Kate." I shake her. "What do you need? I'm packing you a bag."

"Why?"

"I'm taking you home."

"I'm fine."

"You are not fucking fine, Kathryn. Now shut up and tell me what you need," I snap.

She pulls the blankets over her head. "Go. Away."

"Fine, I'll pack your bag then, myself."

I go into her bathroom and grab her toiletry bag, I put her toothbrush and toothpaste inside. I grab her sanitary pads and tampons, and a packet of tablets. I look around her bathroom to see what else I need. There are two books on the side table. Is she reading this? I pick the top one up and see the flower that I picked her yesterday pressed between it and the other book.

She kept it.

I pick it up and stare at it in my hand. So many telling emotions rolled up into a flattened pink flower.

"What are you doing in there?" she calls.

"Cringing at the hair in your razor."

The sound of her laugh makes me smile.

I carefully place her flower back where it was and make my way out. She lies on her back, looking up at me. "I'm packing you a bag and I'm taking you home."

"This *is* my home."

Is it?

You feel more at home at my home . . . or maybe it's me that feels at home when you're there. I swallow the lump in my throat, unable to answer her.

I go to her dresser and open the top drawer. "Should I be packing all of these granny knickers?"

She bursts out laughing. "Look at you . . . being all English and shit."

I smile.

"I'll convert you yet, gov'nor," she says in a strong cockney accent.

I chuckle. "Are you high?"

She makes a pinch with her fingers. "Little bit."

I smile as I pull her up by the hand. "Come on, let's go home."

Chapter 19

KATE

I wake to the sound of a bird cry in the distance, and judging by the shadows on the wall, it's just dusk. From the corner of my eye I glance over to see Elliot sitting at a small table near the window, his laptop open, fully engrossed in work. He types at a furious speed and then hits send.

I can tell by the way he's angrily hitting the keys that he's emailing someone who has annoyed him and he's telling them just how much.

I smile; some things never change. I sit up on my elbows. "Hi."

He glances up and his face instantly softens. "Hello."

I tap the bed, he walks over and sits beside me. "How are you feeling?"

"Good."

He pushes the hair back from my forehead. "You have tomorrow off too, I've already called it in."

"I don't—"

"It's not up for negotiation," he interrupts me.

He stares at me and it's obvious he has something on his mind. "I've made you an appointment with a decent doctor."

I frown. "By decent, you mean expensive?"

He rolls his eyes.

"Why?"

"Because this isn't normal."

"It is for me."

He exhales and stands. "I'm not having this discussion, Kathryn. I've already made the appointment, you'll see the specialist tomorrow at two. I'm coming."

"You are *not* coming," I scoff as I flick the blankets back, not in the mood for this shit.

He tilts his chin to the sky. "Why not?"

"Because." I pause as I think of the right thing to say. "We're not even . . ."

"Not what?"

"Officially going out together." I walk into the bathroom.

"What?" He marches in behind me.

I pick up a sanitary pad.

"If we're not together, what are you doing here?" he barks.

"You brought me here, when I was half dying."

"To look after you."

Guilt fills me—he's right, I'm being a bitch. I force a lopsided smile. "And I appreciate it, thank you."

"And we *are* together. Just because nobody knows about us doesn't make our relationship any less important." He crosses his arms angrily. "I have every right to know what's going on with your body."

I roll my eyes. "Look, thank you for your concern, but I just need to take care of this stuff myself . . . okay?"

He stares at me flatly.

I hold up my pad. "Do you mind?"

He keeps staring at me.

"Elliot, give me a minute."

He storms back into the bedroom.

I sort myself out and wash my hands as I stare at my reflection in the mirror.

What's going on here?

He told me he doesn't do relationships and yet here he is, acting like the possessive boyfriend.

Perhaps he's changed his mind and he does want more? Not once this weekend did he act like this is a casual, sex-only thing.

Excitement fills me. *Don't get carried away*, I remind myself.

The only problem is that it's been so long since I had a boyfriend I think I've forgotten what to do . . . or what to let him do.

I know if I want this to work between us, I have to try harder to let him in.

I walk back out to see him sitting at his little table, his laptop open in front of him. He doesn't look up and it's clear that he's annoyed.

"Thank you for making the appointment," I say softly. "I'll go."

His eyes rise to meet mine.

"This is new to me, having someone . . ." I cut myself off, unsure what to say next.

He nods but stays silent.

"I just don't want you hearing about all of my faults."

His face softens, and he presses his lips together as if stopping himself from speaking.

I twist my fingers in front of me nervously. "I don't want to wreck this, you know?"

He stands and comes to me, his hand cups my face and he stares down at me. "And there she is," he whispers.

My eyes search his.

"The vulnerable Kate that I adore."

I inhale deeply as I feel emotion overwhelm me. "I wouldn't be nice to me this week if I were you, not unless you want me to cry like a baby. I'm completely unstable."

"Alright." A trace of a smile crosses his face. "Would you like to suck my dick before or after you eat your dinner, you filthy wench?"

I giggle, grateful to him for making light of the situation. "Careful, my mood could go either way, it's a very fine line. Who knows what's going to come out of my mouth?"

He bends and kisses me, his tongue tenderly swiping against mine. He smiles against me as if having a thought. "It's what's going into it that I care about."

I ride the escalator down to the ladies' department in Harrods. After my doctor's appointment this afternoon I've decided to have a little retail therapy before I go home.

My phone rings, the name Elliot lights up the screen, and I smile broadly. "Hello."

"How did my girl go at the doctor's?" Thankfully he didn't come. "Good."

"What did he say?"

"Not a lot that I didn't know." I begin to walk through the racks of women's clothes as I talk.

"Such as?"

"You really want all the gory details, Mr. Miles?"

"No, I'm asking as a dare, what do you fucking think?"

I smile, I love that he cares. "Basically, I have to go in for surgery at some point soon for an endometriosis clean-up, but other than that I'm doing everything right."

"Well . . . what kind of surgery, is it dangerous?"

"No, I've had it a few times before. Keyhole."

"Oh, okay." I can hear the relief in his voice. "What about the pain?"

"It's normal. I'm fine, El, you don't need to worry."

"Well . . . I do."

I smile and look up. Over in the lingerie department I see a familiar figure, and pause on the spot. Navy suit, ramrod-straight back, phone to his ear. He picks up a two-piece black lace bra and G-string set and eyes it, then he puts it back and riffles through the sizes and then throws one over his arm. "Where are you?" I ask.

"Running errands."

I duck behind a column and smile as I watch him. Completely focused on his task, he moves on to white, silk nightdresses and flicks through the rack.

"What kind of errands?"

"I'm at the post office," he lies.

"Don't you have a personal secretary for that?"

"This parcel is of a personal nature," he replies casually as he walks through the rows of expensive lingerie.

"Did you order me a big dildo?"

His face breaks into a breathtaking smile and I feel it all the way to my toes. "Most definitely not."

"Why not?" I tease.

He picks up a pretty pink camisole. "If you think I'm sharing your orgasms with a battery-operated device, you're deluded, Kathryn."

"Maybe I need more," I tease.

He stops mid-step, and a slow, sexy smile crosses his face; he likes this game. "We haven't even begun your training yet, angel," he whispers darkly.

"Training?"

"We can start tonight, if you like?" He throws a camisole over his arm.

I bite my lip to stifle my smile; I like this game too. "Why haven't we begun yet?"

"I've been on my best behavior so far; my depraved tastes aren't for everyone and I need your trust before we start. I didn't want to scare you off before we get there."

I frown, what's he talking about? I trawl my brain for a logical answer.

Anal . . . oh fuck.

"If I haven't run away yet, El . . ." I whisper as I act brave. I've never done anything anal before and he knows it. "The more I get to know you, the more I want you."

His face softens and butterflies flutter in my stomach.

Watching his face light up as he speaks to me really is something, as if my heart isn't already freefalling out of my chest.

"Well, Miss Landon." He stops walking. "The feeling is completely mutual." His voice is soft, cajoling. So different to the voice that used to bellow at me.

I smile as I watch him. "I should let you go."

"Okay, sweetheart, I'll pick you up about seven?"

"Can't wait. See you then."

He holds his phone to his ear and pauses as if waiting to hear something, and I do the same as I watch him.

There are unspoken words between us.

And I know we're not there yet, but this . . . *whatever this is,* feels a lot like—or at least the beginning of—love.

"Bye El," I whisper.

"Goodbye." I watch as he hangs up and stuffs his phone into his expensive suit pocket. He continues to shop and, for a long time, I stand and watch him.

Elliot Miles, walking through a lingerie section, shopping . . . for me.

I smile—or maybe it's for him.

Either way, it's fucking perfect.

Just on seven I watch the headlights of the black Bentley come around the corner. *He's here.*

I grab my bag and bounce down the stairs. Rebecca and Daniel aren't home; it seems like I've hardly seen them in the last few weeks.

I've spent nearly every night with Elliot since we started seeing each other and I know I really should be playing hard to get or something, but what's the point? I want to see him and I'm sick of games.

And he seems pretty set on seeing me too.

I make my way out of the front door and Elliot climbs out of the back of the car, looks up and sees me, and breaks into a breathtaking smile.

Oh . . . that smile.

I feel myself swoon as I cross the road toward him. "Hello," he says as he leans down and kisses me softly.

"Hi." I beam.

He stares down at me with a goofy smile and I smile right back up at him; it's like a long-lost hello after not seeing each other for forever, but the truth is we saw each other only ten hours ago.

Okay . . . we're a little pathetic . . . not that I'm complaining.

He stands back so I can get into the car and I dive in. "Hello Andrew." I smile as I scooch across the seat.

"Hello Kate." He gives me a kind smile in the rearview mirror.

Elliot slides in after me and takes my hand in his lap, and I lean over and kiss his cheek as the car pulls out into the traffic.

Okay . . . I need to chill. Seeing him buying that lingerie today has set off some kind of hopeless love bug and I'm completely forgetting how to be hard to get.

"How was your day?" he asks.

"Good, now. How was yours?"

He gives me a smile. "I bought you a present today."

"You did?" I act surprised. "What is it?"

"I'll show you when we get home."

Home.

My stomach flutters. "Is it what I think it is?" I tease.

"What's that?"

"You know." I widen my eyes, as Andrew can hear.

He frowns in a question.

I put my mouth to his ear. "The big dildo."

"Andrew, pull the car over, please. Kathryn's getting out, she can walk home from here," he says as he pretends to be angry.

"Don't, Andrew." I giggle.

Andrew's amused eyes flick up to me in the mirror and he keeps driving.

Did he hear what I said?

Half an hour later, we pull into the enchanted driveway. It's pitch-black as we motor up the windy road. "Did I tell you I love your house?" I ask.

He gives me a sexy wink as he tucks a piece of my hair behind my ear. "Once or twice."

We stare at each other as the air crackles between us.

The car pulling up in front of the house interrupts our moment, and Andrew climbs out and opens my door. "Have a good night, Kathryn," he says.

"Thank you, you too."

Elliot climbs out and goes to the trunk. He takes out about ten shopping bags and I can hardly contain my excitement. "Oh . . . you have been busy," I say as I act cool.

"Not as busy as you're going to be wearing them," he mutters as he walks up the steps. "Thank you, Andrew, see you in the morning."

"Goodnight Mr. Miles." He gets back into the car and starts the engine.

Elliot opens the door and we walk in and turn the lights on. I look up into the hall and smile. "Oh Elliot, this place is so beautiful that it takes my breath away."

"I know," he agrees. "Me too. I've decided I'm not knocking the house down, I'm going to renovate. The house has too much character to get rid of it completely."

"I agree." I smile.

He passes me the shopping bags. "Now, I've been looking forward to this all day. I'm going to cook us dinner . . . and you"—he kisses me softly—"are going to give me a fashion parade."

I bite my bottom lip as I peer into the bags: expensive tissue paper, lace, and silk is all I see.

"Ummmm." I frown.

He raises his eyebrow. "Um what?"

"You remember that it's that time of the month for me . . . right?"

He looks at me flatly. "What does that mean?"

"Well." I shrug. Do I have to say it out loud? "I can't have sex tonight."

"And . . . your point is?"

I stare at him.

"If I only wanted you for sex, Kathryn, I'm pretty sure we wouldn't have got past the first date."

My mouth falls open. "What?"

"I mean . . ." He gives a subtle shake of his head as he corrects himself. "That came out wrong."

I give him a smile as I cup him through his trousers. I rub my thumb back and forth over his tip, and feel it enlarge beneath my touch. "What am I here for?"

"So that I can fuck your hot little ass."

I burst out laughing and he turns me toward the stairs and slaps me hard on the behind. "Go. Before you get yourself into trouble."

With the bags in my hands, I take the stairs two at a time in excitement.

Hell on a cracker, this night is turning out amazing.

He's amazing, I knew it all along.

There's hope for us yet.

Elliot takes a shower and walks into the bedroom in only a towel; he drops it before me and I feel myself flutter. No matter whatever goes on between us, his sexuality or my body's reaction to it is never in question.

He turns off the light and crawls in behind me, takes me into his arms and kisses my cheek.

I smile softly at his touch.

He puts his big, warm hand over my tender stomach and we meld into each other's bodies. The air between us is alive with intimacy and comfort. We both lie in silence and I know he's not going to sleep; I can almost hear his brain ticking away in the darkness.

"We aren't just fucking, Elliot," I whisper.

"I know."

"What are we?" I whisper again.

"Too tired for this conversation."

I frown.

"Go to sleep, baby," he murmurs, then kisses my cheek and holds me close.

Questions roll around in my psyche and yet, here in his arms, I feel safe.

Too tired for this conversation . . . What does that even mean?

It's like I'm swimming out to sea with no sight of land. I know it's dangerous, but I can't get out of the rip tide as I get swept along. Perhaps I wouldn't, even if I could.

The water is dark, but it's too late. I'm too far from the shore to turn back.

* * *

My dearest Pinkie,

Tell me something interesting, my day is dull.

Ed

X

I smirk and look guiltily around my office. I really shouldn't be speaking to Ed while I'm working, but my day is pretty dull too. We've got into the habit of speaking numerous times a day. Completely platonic of course, but fun nevertheless. If it wasn't for the sarky sense of humor, I couldn't reconcile that he and Elliot are the same person at all.

Dearest Ed,

There are two body parts on a human that never stop growing.

The nose and the ears.

Pinkie

X

A reply bounces straight back.

Pinkie,

I must say, I'm let down with your so-called interesting fact. Another mundane piece of information I didn't need to hear.

Thankfully I'm blessed with perfection. Unfortunately I know that I can't say the same for you.

Perhaps you should update your profile picture from a cat to an elephant now to evade catfishing more poor unsuspecting suitors.

I giggle. "You idiot."
I type:

My dearest Pinocchio,

I am a very busy woman, doing a very important job.

Stop annoying me and go and tend to your garbage.

I smile and click out of my email. Edgar Moffatt, my sweet distraction.

Saturday night, Andrew drives through London; Elliot and I in the backseat.

"Do we really have to go?" I sigh. "I hate the thought of walking into this thing alone." I'm dressed in a long, black, fitted evening gown, my hair is curled, and my makeup is natural. Elliot approves—I had to fight him off before we even left home.

"I told you already"—Elliot picks up my hand and kisses the back of it—"Miles Media have made a very generous donation and I have to be there for the presentation."

"I guess." I exhale heavily as I stare out of the window.

"I've arranged for us to be seated at the same table and we can leave as soon as the speeches are over." He leans over and kisses me just below my ear to try and sweeten the blow. "Then we can go to your favorite restaurant."

"You mean, your favorite restaurant," I whisper. We've been to the private dining room twice, and each time I've ended up giving Casanova Miles a lap dance with a happy ending. Something about that place makes me putty in his hands.

Elliot gives me a slow, sexy smile. "Well, you do seem to enjoy yourself there."

My eyes flick to Andrew—can he hear us?

I slide my hand up Elliot's thick quad and dust my fingers over his crotch. His eyes hold mine and I feel a twinge beneath my touch as he flexes his dick.

"Why can't we walk in together?" I whisper.

"You know why." He kisses me softly.

"How long is this going to go on for?" I murmur into his mouth.

"You don't want the attention that comes from dating me, Kathryn. Trust me on this." He tucks a piece of my hair behind my ear. "When it's just me and you, nobody else can fuck this up," he whispers.

I smile; he's right. I nod, feeling a little better.

"Let me out here, Andrew, and drop Kathryn at the door please."

"Yes sir." The car pulls up to the curb.

Elliot takes a ticket out of the inside pocket of his suit jacket and passes it to me. "Go inside, check the seating, and I'll meet you at our table."

I nod, my nerves beginning to thump. "Okay." He kisses me quickly and gets out of the car and Andrew pulls back out into the traffic; we go around the corner and up the street and he pulls into a large circular driveway. He turns and smiles. "Here you go, Kate."

"Thank you." I get out of the car and walk up the oversized sandstone steps, hand my ticket to the doorman, and walk through the large archway. The ballroom is huge and extravagant, with big, round, candlelit tables and beautiful fresh flowers in arrangements. I walk through to the seating map and make my way to the table.

The table is already full except for three seats. "Hello." I smile as I sit down beside a kind-looking couple.

"Hello," everyone replies happily, and they all introduce themselves one by one. The waiter walks past with a silver tray full of glasses of champagne. I take one—hell . . . just leave the entire tray, please.

"Hi." A man across the table smiles at me. He's around thirty, with fair hair, very good-looking, actually. "Are you alone?" he asks.

"Yes." I clutch my purse with white-knuckle force on my lap. Damn Elliot, this is the first and last time I'm doing this.

"Me too." Without a word the man gets up and swaps his name tag with Elliot's.

He slinks into the seat beside me. "That's better." He holds out his hand. "I'm Charles."

I smile and shake it. "Kathryn."

He picks up my hand and kisses the back of it. "Lovely to meet you, Kathryn."

I feel him before I see him. Elliot slinks into the chair opposite, his eyes find mine and I pull my hand from Charles's lips.

Crap.

"Mr. Miles," someone from the side splutters. "How lovely to see you again."

Elliot turns and fakes a smile. "Hello." He does the honors and shakes everyone's hands at the table.

"Charles." The man reaches over to shake Elliot's hand.

Elliot raises an eyebrow in a silent *you're in my seat* signal. "Elliot Miles."

"I know who you are." Charles smiles broadly. "Doesn't everyone."

Elliot rolls his lips as he stares at him flatly, clearly unimpressed.

Awkward.

I tip my head back and take a gulp of champagne.

"I switched seats with you," Charles jokes. "I saw beautiful Kathryn here and simply had to sit next to her. You snooze, you lose, old boy."

Elliot's eyes hold his and I bite my bottom lip to hide my smile—oh, this is priceless.

Charles turns his attention back to me. "So, Kathryn, we were meant to meet tonight. I feel like the gods have shone down on me—tell me all about you."

Good grief.

My eyes flick to Elliot, who raises an eyebrow as he takes a sip of his champagne.

What's going through that control-freak head of his?

I tip my head back and skull again.

Help.

Oh what hell it is to ride on a charity ball tonight.

At first I thought teasing Elliot with Charles was a little fun, harmless flirting, but as the night goes on . . . not so much.

Charles is now openly flirting with me and I don't want to be rude, but with Elliot in earshot it's my worst nightmare. Elliot is talking to other people at the table, but I know he's listening to my and Charles's every word.

I'm deflecting compliments and sidestepping his flirting, but with every new tactic he tries, and he's fucking trying them all, my blood pressure rises a little more.

At any moment I'm expecting Elliot to go bat-shit crazy, and dive across the table and punch Charles straight in the nose, because that's who he is.

But to my surprise, he's being calm and collected, his public persona firmly in place.

It's very unsettling.

His eyes hold mine as he lifts his Scotch to his lips and takes a sip, emotionless and cold.

He's fucking pissed.

Out-of-control Elliot Miles is manageable. Cold and calculating Elliot Miles is a completely different story. This situation is a ticking time bomb waiting to explode.

"Elliot." We hear a sexy voice with a German accent, and I look up to see a drop-dead gorgeous woman in an ice-pink, strapless evening gown. She has long, dark hair and a body to die for.

Elliot glances up and then says something to her in another language. I can tell by the look on his face, it's flirty . . . I know that look all too well.

She laughs on cue.

Huh?

What did he just say?

She replies in . . . I think it's German.

He gives her a sexy smile and stands and holds his hand out for her. He says something else to her in German and she throws her head back and laughs out loud.

What the fuck?

"Who is this?" Charles asks.

Excellent question, Charles . . . *you giant dickhead.*

"This is Varuscka." Elliot replies as he looks at her all adoringly. "And we're dancing." He leads her by the hand to the dance floor and takes her in his arms. I glare after them as my blood begins to boil. Varuscka Vermont, the woman he gave a lift home.

Seeing him and her together now . . . maybe there *was* more to it.

What the actual fucking fuck?

I pick up my glass and drain it, then refill my glass so fast that it sloshes over the side.

"Steady on." Charles laughs. "Don't want to get drunk and disorderly, do we?"

I glare at him, shut up, shut up. This is all your fault, you fucking idiot.

He's playing games . . .

He just wants to pay me back for talking to Charles all night, it's obvious.

Calm, calm . . . keep fucking calm.

With a shaky hand I lift my glass to my lips and I glance over to the dance floor. Elliot is holding her close in his arms, his back to me. Tall, dark, and handsome in a black dinner suit, he looks orgasmic, a standout in the crowded room. He's talking in her ear and by the look on her face it looks like he's telling her how many ways he could lick her to heaven.

My eyes begin to glow red as adrenaline pumps through my bloodstream.

Are you kidding me?

He brings me here, makes me pretend I'm alone because he can't be seen with me, then gets pissed when someone hits on me . . . then flirts in German with God's gift to men to pay me back.

Asshole.

The song finishes and they dance again, she's laughing and chatting, looking up at him all adoringly. Her eyes are all love-heart shaped with a rose-colored blush on her face.

I know that look, I've seen it in the mirror many a time.

Have they slept together? Is she one of the nine and a half million women that he's slept with?

Casanova fucking Miles.

Charles is still rattling on and I've filled my glass three times. Will you shut the hell up, Charles! I am not in the mood to hear your fucking crap. I've got enough of my own crap to deal with here.

The song finishes but, instead of coming back to the table, Elliot goes to the bar with Varuscka.

What?

My blood boils and the last of my sanity snaps.

That's it . . . it's go time.

You want a fight, fucker? You just got one.

He gets two drinks at the bar, one for Varuscka and one for him, and he stands facing me in among the crowd as they talk.

I glare at him and he glares right back, raises his glass of Scotch to me in a silent salute.

I throw my napkin on the table and push my seat out. Fuck this, I'm out.

How dare he?

"I'm going," I say to the table.

"Oh, so soon," Charles cries. "The night is young."

"I have to work in the morning," I lie with a fake smile.

"I'll walk you out."

"Not necessary." I smile through gritted teeth. "Nice to meet you all." I grab my clutch and give the table a weak wave and walk toward the door.

"Nonsense," I hear Charles call from behind me.

I burst through the doors and out into the lobby. Damn it, my coat is in the cloakroom. I don't want to wait but the coat is my favorite, so I dig out my ticket and stand in line.

Charles runs as he catches up, puts his hands in his pockets as he waits beside me. I stare at him and, funnily enough, in any normal circumstances I would have thought this guy was gorgeous. I mean, he is.

He's just not him.

Ugh, I'm infuriated. Why do I have such shit taste in men?

"Let's go and get a drink somewhere," Charles says. "I want to get out of here, too."

"The only place you'll be going is to the fucking morgue," Elliot growls from behind us.

Charles turns. "Mr. Miles," he stammers.

Elliot glares at him. "Get out of my fucking sight."

Charles eyes widen as he looks at us in turn. "I mean—"

"Now!" Elliot barks. "And don't you dare contact her again."

Oh, hell.

"Next," the coat girl calls. I step forward in a rush and hand over my ticket, so angry I can hardly see straight, and in my peripheral vision I see Charles practically run back into the ballroom.

Wimp.

I get my coat and march to the door, Elliot hot on my heels. "Go away," I whisper angrily.

"Fuck off," he snaps as he follows me.

My eyes nearly bulge from their sockets. I barge through the doors and see the black Bentley parked and waiting for us.

"Get in," Elliot barks.

"Go to hell." I begin to march along the pavement.

"Get. The. Fuck. In. The. Car." He opens the back door.

I look up to see people are stopping and staring, I don't want a scene. Fuck's sake.

I get in the back of the car and he gets in behind me.

"Hello." Andrew smiles as he pulls out into the traffic.

"Take me home."

"My house," Elliot growls.

334

"Let me out of the car." I lose control and I don't give a damn any more. "You fucking asshole," I scream.

Andrew's eyes flick up to me in the mirror.

"Drive to my house," Elliot demands, punching the seat in front of us. "You do not play fucking games with me. Do you hear me, Kathryn?" he screams.

"Oh, but you can flirt in German?" I yell. "Do me a favor and go back inside to her, you self-centered fucking asshole."

Andrew grips the steering wheel; I can tell he's unsure where to drive to.

"Do not fucking tempt me," Elliot yells as the car slows at the traffic lights.

What the actual fuck . . . he didn't just say that.

My anger hits a crescendo, I go to open the car door to get out and it's locked. "Open the door," I yell.

"Do not open the door," Elliot orders.

Andrew's nervous eyes flick up to the backseat. He's unsure what to do.

"So help me God, Andrew, drive me to my house or I'm having you charged with kidnapping," I scream.

Andrew's eyes widen and he makes an instant U-turn.

Elliot punches the seat in front of him again.

The car pulls up at my house and the door lock releases. I get out and slam the door.

Elliot does too, and he follows me up the steps to my house. "Get the fuck away from me," I snap. "How dare you."

"How dare I what?" He holds his hands out wide as if shocked. "You're the one that's carrying on."

"Don't tempt you to go back to her? Be my fucking guest, Elliot. I dare you," I spit.

He narrows his eyes.

"*You're* the one who doesn't want to be seen with me."

335

"That's not it and you know it," he yells. "I don't want drama, cut your shit."

"Well, I don't want to be your unpaid fucking prostitute any longer. If you're ashamed to be seen with me in public, don't see me in private." I unlock the front door and push it open with force. Thank God nobody's home, we're screaming the house down here.

"Don't fucking threaten me, Kathryn," he growls.

"It's not a threat." I slam the door in his face. "It's a promise," I scream through it.

He punches the door and it rattles the front of the house.

"Leave!" I yell.

He punches it again and it echoes through the whole house.

"You are going to break the fucking door, Elliot. I mean it. Go. Away!" I put the deadlock on, and march up the stairs.

I peer out of the window and see him pacing on the pavement. Andrew is out of the car talking to him, obviously trying to calm him down.

My heart is pounding as I wait for his next move. Angry Elliot Miles is a beast to behold, and damn it, I don't want to deal with him tonight.

Please . . . just go.

Ten minutes later, I hear his door slam, peer through the crack in the curtains, and watch the car slowly pull away. Relief fills me and I drop onto my bed. "Ugh," I fume. "What a fucking asshole."

Chapter 20

Elliot

I sit in the bar and sip my Scotch. I went to work this morning, but left early.

Not in the mood for work today. Not in the mood for anything, really.

I have a lead ball in my stomach, one that isn't going away. I screwed up on Saturday night . . . bad.

But in my defense, she's fucking infuriating. Did she really think I would sit there all night and watch someone come on to her without consequence?

I glance at my watch, it's 2 p.m. I haven't heard from her and I know that I'm not going to.

Typical fucking Kathryn Landon, stubborn as all hell.

I go over my options: there aren't any. I either have to grovel or kiss her goodbye. I know she isn't going to come looking for me anytime soon.

I exhale heavily and scroll through my phone, find the number I'm looking for and give a disgusted shake of my head. This is a first, I've never done this before. I'm usually glad when they leave. Sucking up to a woman is a new kind of uncharted-territory hell.

"Hello, Park Avenue Florist," the girl answers.

"Can I send some flowers as a matter of urgency please?"

"Sure. We can deliver that in an hour, where to?"

"Kathryn Landon, Miles Media building, level ten."

"What would you like to send?"

"Ummmm." I think for a moment. "What would you suggest for . . . to get out of . . ."

"An apology?"

"Yes."

"Well, how big an apology do you need?"

"Pretty big." I roll my eyes. "The biggest you've got."

"Okay, so red roses?"

"I guess."

"A dozen."

I frown. "Umm . . . stubborn kind of woman."

"Four dozen?"

"Yeah, maybe."

"Okay, and what do you want the card to say."

"Hmm." I think for a moment. "Maybe just, 'I'm sorry.'"

That's so lame.

"Okay." I can hear her typing. "Four dozen red roses and 'I'm sorry' on the card."

"Yes."

"Name?"

I frown as I think; I really should come up with something witty but I can't think straight when she's angry with me. "'Love, Elliot.'"

Damn her.

She's got me by the balls, and she fucking knows it.

"So, 'I'm sorry, love Elliot'?" she asks as she checks the details.

"Yes. Can you call me as soon as they've been delivered, please?"

"Of course, sir." I pay her with my credit card and I hang up and wait.

An hour and four glasses of Scotch later, my phone rings. "Yes."

"The roses have been delivered, sir."

"Did she receive them?"

"Yes, signed for them herself."

"Thank you." I hang up and roll my lips; this could go either way. I dial Kate's number.

"Yes," she answers.

I clench my jaw at the sound of her voice. She wants to fight. "Hello Kathryn."

"What do you want, Elliot?"

"I . . ." I hesitate as I think what to say. "I wanted to see if you got your roses."

"I did, thank you. However, there aren't enough roses on earth to make up for your behavior."

I roll my eyes. *Did she even read the fucking card?* "I'm sorry."

She stays silent.

"I acted appallingly and I regret it."

She stays silent.

"But in my defense, this could have been easily avoided. Why didn't you just tell him that you had a boyfriend?"

"I don't have a boyfriend, Elliot, you have made that quite clear."

"Well, maybe you do," I spit.

I scrunch up my face. *Shit.*

"Well, maybe my boyfriend is a fucking idiot."

339

"It's possible."

"And maybe he better get his act together or else he's getting dumped."

I smirk. "Maybe you should be quiet now?"

"Don't shush me, Elliot, and so help me God if you fucking ever flirt with someone in another language in front of me again—"

I cut her off. "You know I was only doing it to make you jealous."

"It didn't work."

I can tell she's smiling, I've nearly got her. "Maybe a little."

"Elliot," she snaps. "I swear to God, if you ever pull a stunt like that again . . ."

"Did you miss me last night?" I ask. "Because I missed you."

"No, and I'm very busy."

"Doing what?"

"Putting your roses through the shredder."

I chuckle, I wouldn't put it past her. "I have an art auction tonight, I'll come over after."

"No, that's fine. I'll just see you tomorrow night."

I sip my Scotch. I don't want to get off the phone, this damn woman has me like a puppy. "Am I forgiven?" I ask.

"Don't count your chickens before they hatch, Elliot. I'll think about it."

I smile and I know that I am.

I hear someone talk to her in her office. "Who are they from?"

"My boyfriend," she replies.

I wince . . . fuck . . . *boyfriend*, how did that happen? Slipped that one in under the radar, didn't she?

"Call me later." She sighs.

"Okay." I hang on the line.

"Goodbye Elliot." She hangs up and I smile into my glass. Mission accomplished.

I stare at the painting on the easel in front of me.

Immortal

"Isn't it the most beautiful thing you've ever seen?" I say to Christopher as he stands beside me.

He scrunches up his nose, unimpressed. "Hmm . . . I don't even know what you see in this artist. It's just a painting to me."

"Harriet Boucher is not just an artist, Christopher. She's a genius."

He rolls his eyes. "If you say so." He glances at his watch. "How long is this going to take, I'm fucking starving."

"The auction starts in twenty minutes."

I look up across the crowd and I see the ballerina. My heart skips a beat.

She's blonde and beautiful, a frequent visitor at art auctions, but she has always eluded me.

I have no idea if she's an actual ballerina, but seeing as we don't have a name for her, we've nicknamed her that.

What is it about this woman?

I've always gotten the feeling that I should know her, that she is somehow connected to something, although just what that is, I just don't know.

Our eyes are locked across the crowded room, the air between us swirls with electricity.

Tonight, she seems different, her big eyes hold mine.

She's not running, she's not trying to escape; if anything, she's trying to silently will me over.

I inhale a steady breath and drop my head.

Fuck . . . perfect timing.

On any normal day I'd be over there, pursuing her and persuading her to have dinner with me. Making myself known to her and wanting to know all about her.

I've always seen her across the room in the heat of an auction battle, but never once gotten to speak to her. She always disappears before I can find her. I've wanted her for so long. But it's different now.

Kate.

My beautiful Kate is at home waiting for me and I am not going to fuck this up, so I drag my eyes from the ballerina and focus on the painting.

I can feel her looking at me.

"Holy fuck, look who's here," Christopher whispers. "It's her."

I swallow the lump in my throat and try not to look.

"Oh my God, she's fucking perfect," he whispers.

My eyes flick up to her, and he's right, she is perfect.

I clench my jaw and drag my eyes away again.

"What are you doing, get the fuck over there," he whispers. "This is your chance, she's not running tonight."

"I can't."

"Why not?"

"I'm not interested."

"What?" He frowns. "Since when?"

"Shut the fuck up," I whisper angrily as I pinch the bridge of my nose.

Why now, of all the times in the world she could want to talk to me . . . it has to be now, doesn't it?

342

"What's wrong with you?" frowns Christopher. "You've wanted her for years. Go fucking get her."

"Shut. Up."

I don't need this shit.

The auctioneer walks into the room and I am momentarily distracted. I look back over to the ballerina and she's gone. This time, instead of disappointment, I'm relieved.

Good . . . fuck off back to wherever you came from, I don't need temptation. Even if it is from someone that I've wanted for a long time.

I think of my girl at home and my heart swells.

I'm with Kate.

KATE

My phone buzzing on the bedside table wakes me and I scramble to answer it. "Hello."

"I'm out the front," Elliot's deep voice says.

"I thought I wasn't seeing you tonight."

"You thought wrong, open the door."

I make my way downstairs and open the door and there he stands. Sexy suit, gorgeous smile, and enough charisma to light up space. He takes me into his arms and kisses me. "Hi there."

"What happened to seeing me tomorrow?" I ask.

"One night without you was bad, two nights is intolerable."

I smile against his lips and take his hand and lead him up the stairs. If the truth be told, I missed him too.

I get back into bed and he sits on the side and stares down at me with a soft smile.

He's different.

"What?"

"Do you know how beautiful you are?" he asks softly.

I smile. "We're not having sex tonight, just so you know."

He chuckles as he leans in to kiss me, and his lips take mine with such tenderness that I feel all my defenses fly out of the window.

He kisses me deep and slow and oh . . . maybe we should fight more often. "I'm going to take a quick shower, sweetheart."

"Okay."

He kisses me again as he holds my face and I nearly lift out of the bed.

He's just so . . .

He has a shower and ten minutes later he walks out in a white towel, his perfect body on display in the moonlit room. He drops his towel and I swallow the lump in my throat. No matter how many times I see him naked, it always floors me to see how gorgeous he is.

He pulls back the covers and climbs in beside me. He lies up on his elbow and kisses me, long and slow and oh God . . .

His big, powerful body is snug up against mine, his teeth graze my neck and his hard length rubs up against my panties in just the right spot.

For a long time, we kiss in the darkness, as if we have all the time in the world, and something about him making the boyfriend commitment has amped up my arousal tenfold.

His large body rolls over mine and I pant as he writhes between my legs, grinding me into the mattress. My hands roam all over his muscular back as he stares down at me.

He's hot, hard, and ready to fuck.

And good God, I come just from the way he's looking at me.

His breath quivers on the inhale and I know he's close to the edge of control. I wrap my legs around his thick body and he pushes forward, his hard dick running over my clitoris, adding more heat to the already burning inferno.

"I need you." He breathes against my neck; his hands knead my breasts with force.

He pushes forward, his cock coming dangerously close to breaking through the material of my panties.

"Elliot."

"Fuck. Kathryn," he whispers as if in pain. "You want me to beg? I'll fucking beg."

I stare up at him.

"I need it," he moans as his lips take mine. "Please." His eyes close as we kiss and I know he's right here with me.

345

I need this intimacy too.

We stare at each other and, without a further word, he takes my panties off and he slides in deep.

Our eyes are locked in the darkness, his body deep inside of mine. His eyes flutter shut as he loses control; he tenderly moves inside of me, with care, so much tenderness and sheer adoration . . . I slip into the abyss.

"El," I whimper.

"I know, baby." He kisses me with his eyes closed. The emotion between us is palpable. A tangible force that we no longer control.

This is special. *He* is special.

Elliot Miles is everything I never knew I needed, and regardless of our differences I can't deny it.

I am utterly and irrevocably in love with him.

ELLIOT

I lean on my elbow as I watch her sleep.

Her hair is splayed across the pillow as she lies on her side facing me, her bare breasts falling across her chest. I lean in and kiss her temple softly, the need to be closer to her almost primal.

We crossed a boundary tonight, broke through some kind of invisible barrier.

My heart is freefalling from my chest and I have no way of stopping it. Nor would I want to.

What's happening?

I've never felt like this before.

There's no border between us; the separation of the two of us is blurred. She's like an extension of my body . . . only, in a better way.

She stirs and puts her hand out for me. "El," she whispers.

"I'm here, baby," I whisper as I snuggle in closer, put my head on her chest.

She smiles softly with her eyes closed and falls back to sleep.

In the darkness, in her arms, I listen to her heartbeat.

And I lose sight of mine.

"Good morning, girls," I say as I walk through reception.

They look up from their tasks. "Good morning, Mr. Miles."

Christopher is standing at his office door. "Hey."

"Lovely day, isn't it?" I smile.

He frowns. "Not really."

"Oh." I look out of the window and shrug. "Ah, but it's not snowing, is it?"

"Who are you and what have you done with my grumpy prick of a brother?" Christopher replies dryly. "It's like the fucking *Sound of Music* around here."

The girls laugh and I walk into my office and unpack my computer as amusement fills me.

"What's going on?" I look up to see Christopher watching me as he leans on the doorjamb.

"Nothing, why?"

"Well, you're up, you're down, furious, then quiet, you're like a one-man fucking circus."

I log into my computer. "A good night's sleep is all we needed. I mean me," I correct myself. "I slept well."

He walks in, suddenly interested. "No, you said 'we.'"

"I meant me."

"No, you didn't." He sits on the side of my desk. "You're seeing someone aren't you?"

I type in my email login.

"Who is she?"

"None of your business. Get out."

Knock, knock: I glance up to see Kate standing at the door. *Shit.*

"Morning, Kathryn," I say, my eyes roaming down to her toes and back up to her face. Her fair hair is down and tucked behind one ear and her smile instantly lights up the room. She's wearing a black, fitted pencil skirt and a cream, silk blouse; her top button is undone with just a hint of what's underneath—perfection.

I feel the blood as it rushes around my body.

Was she always this hot . . . or do I see it more clearly now that I know what she does with those killer curves?

I get a vision of her on top of me naked and I bite my bottom lip to push the pornographic thought away.

"Is now a bad time, Mr. Miles?" she asks. "I have the report you've been waiting for."

"No." Christopher smiles. "Come in, Kate. You can help me pry information out of him."

"Information?" She looks between us.

"He seems to be in a very uncharacteristic good mood lately. I want to know what's responsible." He crosses his arms in front of him. "Or who?"

"Oh." A trace of a smile crosses her face. "I don't think you have to worry, in no time he'll return to his ogre self. Let's enjoy the peace while we can."

"Fair call," he agrees.

"Just give me the report and get out, both of you." I sigh as I throw a manila folder onto my desk.

"Ah, there he is. Crisis averted." Kathryn smiles. "Give it three minutes and he'll be screaming the office down."

"Keep going and I will be," I snap.

Kathryn's eyes dance with mischief as her eyes hold mine. My cock throbs . . . *stop it.*

What is it about this woman? She turns me into a horny schoolboy. "Are you staying for this meeting?" I ask Christopher.

"No, I got my own shit to do." He gets up and ambles out. "Do you want the door closed?"

"Yes." My eyes hold Kate's. "Thank you."

Christopher leaves and I stand and walk to the door, flick the lock.

Kate's eyes widen. "Elliot, no," she whispers.

I walk toward her. "Telling me no is the ultimate aphrodisiac, Landon." I grab her roughly on the behind and pull her

349

toward me. I bite her bottom lip and drag her over my hard cock.

"Stop," she murmurs against my lips.

"Do you really want me to stop?" I grab her hair aggressively and pull her face back to mine. "Or do you want me to take you into my bathroom and pump you full of come. Like the naughty employee you are." I knead her breast with force as I bite her hard on the neck, and she throws her head back, granting me full access.

Fuck I love these tits; her body was built for sin.

My sin.

"Elliot," she murmurs, her eyes fluttering closed, and I know that look.

She wants it.

I take her hand and drag her into the bathroom and close the door, fall onto the chair in the corner and in one quick movement, I unzip my fly and pull her skirt up. I pull her panties to the side and position myself at her entrance.

I put my hands on her shoulders and slam her down onto me, stretching her tight body to the hilt.

We fall silent as we stare at each other.

"You're a bad man, Mr. Miles," she whispers.

A slow smile crosses my face. "And you're a dirty girl. Get those fucking legs up, Landon, and work my cock." I bite her neck with force, the need to bruise her overwhelming.

With dark eyes she brings her legs up and puts her feet on the chair, bringing her into a squatting position. She's only just learned how to take me like this; my size was an issue and we had to work up to it.

I feel every one of her muscles as they ripple around me, and it's all I can do not to blow.

We're in my office for Pete's sake . . . this isn't good, but there's no way in hell I can stop. My addiction to Kathryn Landon isn't slowing down. Like a forest fire in a wind storm, I'm completely out of control.

She fucks me.

Hard, unbridled, and wet.

Like animals, we feed from each other's bodies . . . and I love every fucking second of it.

KATE

I walk down the street on the way to meet Elanor for lunch. She's in London for a rare week, and I'm trying to patch things up between us. I don't know what's going on with her lately, but I do know she needs my compassion, not my anger.

My phone rings and I dig it out of my bag; the name Elliot lights up the screen.

"Hi."

"How's my girl?"

I smile at the sound of his deep, sexy voice. "Good."

"I have to go to New York next week."

I frown. "Oh . . . Okay."

"I want you to come with me."

I stop on the spot. "Why?"

"Because I can't go seven days without seeing you."

I smile goofily down the phone, and I know it's true. We've spent almost every night together for weeks. We're so besotted that it's just assumed we will spend each night together, it's not even a question. I can't go seven days without seeing him either.

"I can show you my New York home and take you to my gallery. And besides, I want to have you to myself for a week," he says as he tries to talk me into it.

Excitement fills me, I don't need convincing. *It sounds like heaven.*

"I'll have to work through the days of course, but I can arrange a meeting so that you have an excuse to be there—"

"No," I cut him off. "I'll take leave, I have lots owing. I don't want anyone from work knowing about us."

"Okay."

"I mean—" That came out wrong. "You know what I mean."

"I do. Where are you?" he asks.

"On my way to meet my sister for lunch."

"I keep forgetting that you have a sister, what's her name again?"

"Elanor." I pause for a moment. "Actually, do you know her? Elanor Landon."

"I don't think so, how would I know her?"

"She goes out with the kind of men you mix with, perhaps you've seen her around?"

"Hmm, the name isn't familiar, who knows? Maybe I've seen her before, I'll know when I meet her, I guess."

I smile as hope blooms in my chest. He's planning on meeting my family . . . Oh, this is going too good to be true, and not at all as I expected.

"So, you'll come to New York?" he asks.

"If I can get time off work."

"I'm pretty sure that your boss would insist on it." I can tell that he's smiling.

"Well, my boss *is* a sex maniac." I smirk.

"Happily so," he says in his deep, swoony voice.

Well, that makes two of us.

"Goodbye, Kathryn."

I smile; not that long ago I hated it when he called me Kathryn, but now it's a term of endearment.

"Bye, El." I hang up and practically float to the restaurant. I'm going out with God's gift to women *and* he's taking me to New York *and* he thinks I'm fucking fantastic.

Life is good.

I walk into the restaurant and look around. Elanor is sitting at the back and she smiles and waves as she sees me. I smile and wave and make my way to her.

"Hi." She stands and kisses me on the cheek, holds me by the arms and looks me up and down. "You look fantastic."

"Thanks." I smile proudly—that would be all the orgasms. "So do you."

I'm not lying, she really does. She's wearing a fitted, cream woolen dress and knee-high boots. Elanor is a lot of things, but her beauty is unmatched.

"Sit down, sit down," she says as she ushers me into my seat. "I ordered some wine."

"I'm at work today."

"One glass won't hurt, darling." She rolls her eyes as if I'm an idiot.

I fake a smile, ugh . . . here we go, Elanor and her condescending eye rolls.

She pours us both a glass of wine. "So . . ." She looks me up and down. "Why do you look so amazing, are you seeing someone?"

I beam with happiness. "I am, actually."

"Hmm." She sips her wine. "Well, happiness suits you. Anyone I know?"

I open my mouth to tell her who it is and then I shut it again. What if she blurts it out to the world? I'm sure she would know the same people that Elliot knows. But he did say he was my boyfriend?

Hmm, but he hasn't announced anything yet. I guess I'll wait to tell her until I've spoken to him first. "Nobody you would know, just a guy from work," I reply. Technically that *is* true. "What about you, are you seeing anyone?"

"No, I broke up with Frederick."

I frown. "What happened to Alexander?"

"Oh." She screws up her face. "I broke up with him months ago, he got so boring. When we had sex he would come in two minutes flat. I have needs that I'm not compromising on."

Poor Alexander. I wonder if he knows she's telling the world about his performance. Seriously . . . what a cold bitch. I take a big gulp of wine. Jeez. I guess I shouldn't be surprised.

Don't say it.

"Tell me, how's that boss of yours doing. Elliot Miles, the gorgeous specimen."

I cough as I choke. "What?" I wince.

"I'm in London for a few days, I might look him up."

Horror runs through me. "Do you know him?"

"We've seen each other before, but no formal introduction. Although I'm making sure that changes."

"He's getting married," I lie.

"And?"

"Well, he's taken," I scoff.

"Darling." She smiles as if I'm stupid. "If I want Elliot Miles, I will take him from whoever I have to."

I clench my jaw as fury runs through me. "You would actually stoop so low as to break up a happy relationship?"

"Of course, why not? I've done it before and I can do it again." She casually sips her wine. "Where does he go out to? What clubs? What do you know?"

My angry heartbeat echoes through my ears. "I'm not sure." I tip my head back and drain my glass.

She stares into space as she thinks. "Maybe I can come and see you at work, accidently knock on his office door."

My eyes widen in horror. "No. You won't do that," I snap. "I forbid you to try and see him, Elanor. This is my job, don't ruin it for me."

"Oh hush." She rolls her eyes again. "Always so dramatic. You're acting like you have a crush on him or something."

"Maybe I do," I blurt out.

She gives me a smile and raises her glass in the air as a silent salute. "Well then."

"Well then, what?"

"Nothing." She shrugs casually as if she has a secret.

"What, Elanor?" I snap.

"You've worked for him for years and you haven't snagged him, it's obviously not going to happen. Is it?" She sips her wine. "And besides, you're seeing someone else."

Damn it, why did I lie?

"What makes you think he would fall at your feet anyway?" I snap.

She flicks her hair over her shoulders. "Because he will."

I sit at the table and push my food around my plate with my fork.

"What's wrong?" Elliot asks as he watches me. "You've been quiet all night."

I exhale heavily. I know this is going to make me sound insecure and pathetic but I can't help it, I have to say it.

"My sister told me today that she is making a play for you."

He frowns.

"And she's beautiful, Elliot, and she gets whatever man she wants."

His tongue swipes over his bottom lip as he tries to hide his smile. "And there she is. My beautiful, vulnerable Kate." He takes my hand over the table.

I roll my eyes, knowing how pathetic I sound. "Don't."

"Well, did you tell her that I'm taken?"

"Yes."

"And what did she say?"

"She told me she could get you to leave any woman."

He picks up my hand and kisses my fingertips, clearly amused by my insecurity. "I'm with you. Your sister . . . or any other woman for that matter, doesn't stand a chance."

My eyes search his.

"You have my word," he promises.

I give him a stifled smile. "I just know—"

"She's not you, Kate," he cuts me off, leans over, and takes my face into his hands and kisses me tenderly. "There is only one Landon sister that I want, and she's right here." He puts the palm of my hand over his chest.

I smile against his lips, feeling a little better.

"And just so you know, if one of my brothers made a play for you? They wouldn't survive it."

My heart swells, and just when I think I can't care for this man more than I already do . . .

He proves me wrong again.

I wake alone and stretch in the dawn light as it streams through the window. Where is my man? I make my way downstairs; the house is empty. Where is he?

I look out the back and catch sight of him in the gardens.

Elliot has his back to me and is looking out over the lake, fully dressed in his suit with his coffee in his hand, the steam from his cup rising in the cold air. The ducks are around his feet, happily pecking at the ground. He walks along, totally entranced by his surroundings as they all follow him like long-lost friends. Every now and then a duck gets too close and he kicks his leg out to clear himself some space.

I lift my phone and take a few photos of him. He really does love this place and I can't say I blame him. I love seeing him so happy here.

A loud sound comes up the drive and I look out of the window to see a utility truck pull up.

I watch through the window as Elliot walks over and talks to the man in the truck. They shake hands as they introduce themselves.

Who's that?

I go out to the front just in time to see the man unload Billy the goat from the back of his truck.

"My apologies," Elliot says as he takes the rope tied around Billy's neck. "I don't know how he got out?"

"This is the fourth time in two weeks," the man says.

Elliot notices me. "Alan, meet Kathryn, Kathryn, this is Alan. He owns the property next door."

"Hello." I smile. "What's happened?"

"Your goat keeps getting out. I found him on the road."

"Oh."

"I'm worried he's going to cause a car accident and someone will be killed."

"Yes." Elliot frowns as if imagining the scenario. "Thank you for bringing him back. I'll make sure he doesn't get out again," he says.

"Nice to meet you." Alan smiles as he gets back into his truck. We give him a wave and he drives away.

"What did you do?" Elliot snaps at his goat.

The goat looks up at him, totally clueless.

"Bahahaha," Billy bleats loudly.

"You want to run away? That's fine with me." He pulls the rope and the goat follows him on the leash. "Just don't do it on the fucking road." He keeps walking over toward the paddock.

"Bahahaha."

"Go inland, fuck off to bumfuck nowhere and don't come back. But don't do it on the fucking road."

"Bahahaha."

I roll my lips as I follow them to stop myself from laughing out loud.

Elliot opens the gate to the top paddock and leads him in. "You are now grounded to the top paddock."

"Bahahaha," Billy bleats.

"Seeing that you can't be trusted."

Oh my lord, this is priceless.

Tough guy Elliot Miles grounding his goat.

He undoes the rope around Billy's neck. "I'm watching you, fucker. One wrong move and it's off to . . ." He pauses as he thinks of the right wording. "The knackers."

"Bahahaha."

"Do you know what they do to naughty goats there?" he asks.

I burst out laughing.

"Go inside," Elliot snaps.

I turn and walk inside as I continue to laugh.

"Bahahaha," Billy bleats.

"Stop making that noise, too," Elliot barks.

I giggle as I walk up the stairs. My life is officially complete.

I've heard it all.

"Bahahaha." The loud noise echoes through the silence.

I glance at the clock: 1 a.m.

"Bahahaha."

"Fuck this," Elliot whispers as he throws the blankets back.

I scrunch up my face to stop myself laughing; this is comical. Billy hasn't stopped crying all night.

Elliot opens the window in a rush. "Shut. The. Fuck. Up," he yells, the sound of his voice echoing around the valley. He slams the window shut so hard it nearly breaks.

He gets back into bed and rustles around.

"Bahahaha."

I smile into my pillow.

"Dumb fucking goat," Elliot whispers under his breath.

"Bahahaha," the loud bleat echoes.

This really *is* bad.

How the hell are we supposed to sleep at all?

"Bahahaha."

"That's it," Elliot explodes, and he jumps up and storms downstairs like the Hulk.

I hear the front door open in a rush and I run to the window and open it to watch what he does.

He marches out to the paddock. "What?" Elliot cries with his arms wide. "What the fuck do you want?"

Billy looks at him blankly.

"You have food, you have water. You have the whole fucking paddock to yourself. Is that not good enough for you, you spoilt fucking goat?"

"Bahahaha," Billy bleats.

Elliot turns and kicks a bucket as hard as he can; it goes flying into the air and crashes spectacularly to the ground. "See that?" he yells at Billy. "There's more of that coming your way if you don't shut up."

I laugh out loud.

Elliot marches back inside and I hear the front door slam. He stomps up the stairs and picks up his phone and sits on the window seat.

"What are you doing?" I ask.

"Googling how to kill a goat, what do you fucking think?"

I laugh.

"This isn't funny, Kathryn," he growls.

"It is." I get up and walk over to him and sit on his lap. Oh my God, he really is googling how to kill a goat. I take his phone from him and throw it on the floor, kiss him softly. "Maybe there's something wrong with him," I whisper.

"There is—impending death."

"No, I mean maybe he's sick."

He stares at me.

"Put some earplugs in, take a sleeping pill or something, and tomorrow we'll call the vet. He will know what to do."

Elliot lets out a shaky breath as he tries to calm down.

I smile up at my man and push the hair back from his forehead. "He's just a little goat."

"Who's ruining my fucking life."

I stare up at him in the darkness. I always knew he was a hot-head, but I thought it was only me who annoyed him to boiling point. Every day a little more of the Elliot Miles puzzle falls into place. And every day, he becomes a little more endearing.

"Come on. Bed." I pull him by the hand.

"How?" he snaps. "This is intolerable."

"Oh . . . boohoo." I roll my eyes as I climb into bed.

He cuddles my back and pumps me with his hips. "I'll give you fucking boohoo."

I wake alone, and exhausted.

The last time I looked at the clock it was 4:38 a.m.—we've hardly slept at all. I throw on some clothes, go to the bathroom, and make my way downstairs. "Elliot," I call. No answer. I walk to the sliding glass door and look out to see a car as it comes up the driveway. Who is it now?

Elliot meets the car and a man gets out; they fall into a deep discussion and head toward the paddock.

Oh no, who's that?

I quickly walk out of the house. "Hello."

The man turns to me. "Hello. I'm Mathew, the vet."

"Oh." Relief fills me.

A trace of a smile crosses Elliot's face; he knows who I thought it was, a hired goat hitman. "This is Kathryn."

"Hello."

"He's this way." Elliot gestures to Billy's paddock.

For fifteen minutes we both watch in silence as the vet checks Billy all over.

"Well," Mathew says. "You have nothing to worry about, he's perfectly healthy."

Elliot sighs. "What's wrong with him then? He keeps running away, he's crying all the time."

"He's looking for a mate," Mathew says. "It's normal for a goat of around this age to want . . ."

"He's horny?" Elliot fumes.

"Figuratively speaking. Yes."

Elliot glares at Billy and gives a subtle shake of his head. "How old is he?"

"Around three years, at a guess."

"And how long do goats live?"

"Approximately fifteen years."

Elliot exhales heavily. "I'm sorry to have wasted your time, please send me the bill."

"No problem at all." They shake hands. "Goodbye, Kathryn."

I smile. "Thank you."

He drives off and Elliot marches back down to Billy. "Are you fucking kidding me? You kept me up all night because you're horny?" he whispers angrily. "Just what I need, a sex maniac goat." He storms back up to the house.

"What do you expect?" I call as I pat Billy's head. "He is your son . . . after all."

"Shut up," Elliot calls as he walks. "I'm not in the mood for your shit today, either."

I walk down the street with Daniel, who's come to have lunch with me; it feels like forever since I've seen him. "Can we have Thai?"

"No." I sigh.

"Why not?"

"Because then I'll have to eat an entire kilogram of rice and I'll be tired as fuck all afternoon."

"Hmm, the dreaded carbohydrate coma." He exhales as if exasperated and I feel guilty.

"Fine." I sigh. "Thai. I'll have you know I'm tired as fuck today. Elliot's goat kept us up all night."

"What?" He screws up his face. "Elliot Miles has a goat?"

"Yep. And ducks, and a weird sheep . . . -like thing."

He widens his eyes as if surprised. "Who knew?"

I giggle.

"When are you going to invite me over?"

"Soon." I shrug. "It's only early days, you know."

"Oh my God, look who's coming." He looks up ahead.

"Who?"

"It's Rande Gerber."

"Who?"

"Cindy Crawford's husband."

I screw up my face as I peer down the street.

"He's gone now." He cranes his neck to look. "I swear it was him."

"Let me ask you this, if you got a chance to sleep with Cindy or her husband, who would you choose?"

"Hmm." He thinks for a moment. "That's an excellent question." He twists his lips as if really thinking hard. "Probably Rande."

"Okay." I smile as I think of another. "If you had the chance to sleep with me or Elliot Miles, who would you choose?"

He chuckles and throws his arm around me. "No contest." He kisses me on the forehead. "You."

I smile. "Why?"

"Well, because you are totally fucking hot."

"And?"

"I'm pretty sure Elliot Miles isn't going to take it, which means I would have to, and to be honest I think he's a little too much man meat than I could handle. I'm not entirely sure I would survive it."

I burst out laughing. "You're right, he is a whole lot of man meat. Even for me."

At 7 p.m. the Bentley pulls into the driveway at Enchanted, behind a truck. We're just getting home from work and are exhausted.

No sleep last night has really taken its toll.

Andrew parks the car and it's then I see the herd of goats in a pen behind the truck. "What's going on?"

Elliot gets out and smiles at the men. "Thank you for coming," he says. "I'll go get him."

Huh?

Elliot disappears, and a few minutes later returns with Billy on a rope leash.

"As you requested, Mr. Miles, these are the three-year-old females that we have."

What in the world?

Elliot lets Billy into the pen with the goats. "Pick one," he instructs him.

Billy's little tail begins to wag and he sniffs all of the goats.

Oh my God . . . Elliot had female goats brought here so that Billy could choose his own mate.

My heart constricts as another piece of the Elliot Miles puzzle clicks into place.

The rest of the world has their opinion of my man—hell, I know it well, I used to share it. But now, I really can see him. Here he is, the epitome of power, in his ten-thousand-dollar suit . . . worrying about his farm animal's feelings.

With a lot of bleats and sniffing, Billy stays close to one goat. She's a pale color and has a pretty face. She seems to like him too.

Elliot stands back, his arms folded, and eventually he speaks. "We'll take that one." He ties the rope around her neck and leads her into the paddock and Billy runs after them.

He turns to the men in the truck. "Thank you, I appreciate it. Send me the bill."

The men begin to herd the goats back onto the truck.

That just may be the sweetest thing I ever saw.

I get out of the car and move to go inside, and as I walk up the stairs I glance back to see Elliot and his two goats in the distance, and a smile crosses my face.

Casanova Miles, goat-matchmaker extraordinaire.

"Do you have everything?"

"Uh-huh."

Elliot wheels my suitcase out of the front door.

"Oh, I forgot my computer." I take the stairs two at a time. "I won't be a moment."

"Hurry up. Why do you always forget something?" he calls as he disappears to join Andrew.

We leave for New York today and I'm excited and nervous and wound up and I hardly slept last night for overthinking every little thing. I know I shouldn't be nervous, but I can't help it, I am.

New York is Miles Media territory and I really feel like this is a make-or-break week for us.

I take one last look in the mirror and swallow the lump in my throat.

May the gods be with me.

Twelve hours later, the doorman opens the door to Elliot's apartment in New York and the air leaves my lungs.

Wall-to-wall glass with the most spectacular view of a city I have ever seen.

It's huge, grand, and super modern, and I'm instantly reminded who I'm with.

A Miles Media mogul.

Son to one of the most powerful men in the world.

It's easy to forget who I'm with when he's screaming at goats in his underpants.

But here . . .

The power that emanates out of him, the way the staff downstairs were scrambling when they saw him, this apartment.

His life.

It makes the time we spend together seem so insignificant, or maybe it's just me that feels insignificant.

I knew coming here with him would throw me, to take a peek at the life he lives.

The life he left.

I walk through his apartment with my heart in my throat; he stays silent as he watches me.

"It's beautiful," I whisper nervously.

I have never felt so out of place as I do here.

He presses his lips together as if stopping himself from saying something.

"Would you like a drink, sweetheart?"

I nod.

"Wine?"

"Tequila."

He chuckles, clearly amused. "Tequila, coming right up."

The vibration of Elliot's phone buzzing on the bedside table wakes us and he frowns.

"Elliot," I whisper. "Your phone."

"Go away," he mutters.

"Something might be wrong at home."

"Huh?" He jumps up and answers it.

"Happy birthday," I hear a voice say as clear as day.

I sit up. What? It's his birthday?

"Fuck off, Tris, it's too early for this shit," he grumbles sleepily as he rubs his eyes.

"What are you doing?" I hear the voice ask.

"You woke me up."

"Are you alone?"

He rolls his eyes. "Yes. I'm alone." He reaches over and tweaks my nipple hard and I buckle to get away from him.

"Hurry up and come into the office, Mom and Dad are coming to see you at nine."

"Yeah, yeah." He hangs up.

"It's your birthday?" I whisper, wide-eyed.

"So?"

"And when were you going to tell me this?"

He smiles and crawls over me and holds my hands over my head. "Why do you think I brought you here?"

"Why?"

"Well, it wouldn't be a happy day for me"—his lips touch mine—"if I didn't get to see you."

I smile up at my beautiful man. I didn't get him a present, I want to do something special for him. "I'm making you breakfast."

"Happy to eat you."

I giggle as I crawl out from under him. "No, tonight. You have to go."

I have to get him a present today . . . Fuck. What the hell do you buy a man who has everything?

I get out of bed and pull my boxer shorts on and throw on his T-shirt from last night. "Is there food here?" I ask.

"Yes, it would have been stocked. You don't need to cook, we can eat out."

"We can be seen together here?" I frown in surprise.

"This is New York, I have a lot more privacy here through the day."

"How come?"

"There are much more exciting celebrities for the paparazzi to chase. Nighttime is a different story, but daylight is good. London is like a fishbowl with nowhere to hide."

"Oh." I walk toward the door. "I'm going to make you the best damn breakfast you ever did see."

He jumps up, fully naked, and picks me up and wraps my legs around his waist. His lips take mine and he opens the bedroom door. "But first." He walks out of the bedroom as he holds me up. "I am going to fuck you on every hard surface of this apartment."

I giggle as we kiss.

We hear a woman's gasp. "Elliot."

We turn to see Jameson, Tristan, Christopher, and Mr. and Mrs. Miles just standing there. Mrs. Miles has a Happy Birthday balloon in her hand, and her eyes are wide.

"Mom," Elliot gasps.

Everyone's mouth is open in horror.

"Surprise." Jameson smirks as he raises an eyebrow.

Oh fuck. The blood drains from my face.

Tristan throws back his head and laughs hard.

My worst nightmare just came true.

Chapter 21

Elliot runs into the bedroom and slams the door.

I stare at his family in horror.

Christopher's eyes are as wide as saucers. "Kathryn Landon," he whispers in shock.

The bedroom door opens back up in a rush, and Elliot grabs my arm and drags me in and slams the door behind us.

I put my hands over my eyes. "No, no, no, no," I whisper. "That did not happen. Tell me that didn't happen."

Elliot is pacing, his hands are in his hair. "Tristan is a fucking dead man," he fumes.

I slap him with both hands on the chest like a drum as I lose control and spiral into a panic. "Oh my God, Elliot. They'll think I'm a ho. They'll think I'm a ho."

"You think you've got fucking problems," he whispers angrily as he points to his dick: it looks hard and angry. "Not exactly what I want to show my mother before breakfast, Kathryn."

"Elliot," Tristan calls through the door.

"Prepare to die, fucker," Elliot hisses.

"Should . . . we go?"

"Yes. No. I want Mom and Dad to meet Kate," he calls.

I put my head in my hands. "They already met me, being a fucking whore bag," I whisper in despair.

Elliot's eyes widen. "Just a minute," he calls loudly. "Get dressed," he whispers as he marches into the closet.

I run after him like a child. "What will I say to them?"

He stares at me as if completely lost for words and then shrugs. "That you like my dick."

The situation overwhelms me and I put my hands over my mouth and burst out laughing. "Will you be serious?" I whisper.

"Listen, I don't know what you should say." He digs around in my suitcase. "I've got my own worries. I just showed my mother my hairy helmet."

I laugh hard, trying to keep quiet. "What the hell is a hairy helmet?"

"A colossal troublemaker." He throws a dress at me. "Get. Fucking. Dressed."

Elliot pulls up his jeans commando-style and throws a T-shirt over his head. He looks down at his crotch. "Now you decide to go down, after you've already ruined my fucking life," he whispers angrily.

I smile as I throw my dress over my shoulders and pull it down, run into the bathroom and smooth out my dress and quickly wash my face.

Elliot goes to the door and holds his hand out for me. "Come."

I close my eyes, dread filling my every cell.

"It's fine, don't worry."

My eyes search his. "Is it really fine?"

"Not in the least, it's abysmal." He opens the door and pulls me out of the bedroom. We find his family all sitting in the living room.

Christopher, Jameson, and Tristan are all wearing goofy grins, as if this is the best thing to ever happen. His mum and dad are pensive and on the other couch.

"Mom and Dad." Elliot holds his hand out. "This is Kathryn. Kathryn, this is Elizabeth and George, my parents."

His mother fakes a smile and stands. "Lovely to meet you."

"I'm so sorry," I whisper as I shake her hand. "To meet you like this is my worst nightmare."

George stands. "Could have been worse, dear, you could have been on one of those hard surfaces."

The boys all burst out laughing, and my cheeks heat with a blazing fire. I've never been so embarrassed in my entire life.

"That's impossible. I'm a virgin, Dad," Elliot mutters as he kisses his mother's cheek. "Sorry, Mom."

She smiles adoringly up at her son. "That's okay, dear, sorry to interrupt."

She turns her attention back to me. "So . . . Kathryn."

"Kate," Elliot corrects her.

My heart hammers so hard in my chest that I can hear it in my ears.

"Kathryn—you work for us, don't you?" George asks.

"Yes sir." I cringe. Kill me now.

"She's the head of IT in London." Elliot smiles proudly. "Damn good at her job, too."

Elizabeth smiles softly as she stares at me. I can feel her gaze as she assesses every inch.

"Who wants coffee?" Tristan stands.

"Me," I answer way too fast.

"Me, yes please. Yes, me too," they all answer.

Tristan looks at Jameson and Christopher. "Come help," he says. The boys both stand and Tristan knocks twice on the table as he walks past it. "Now, *that* is a hard surface."

Jameson chuckles as he walks past a cabinet and knocks twice on it too. "Rock hard," he says. They disappear into the kitchen and we hear another two loud knocks on the wall.

"Found another one," Christopher calls.

Elliot pinches the bridge of his nose and George smiles. "Don't mind them, dear, small things amuse small minds." He walks in after them.

"So, this is the girl you brought home for me to meet?" Elizabeth says.

"This is her, Mom," Elliot replies.

Nerves simmer.

"Don't mind this morning, my dear, I'm well equipped. I have brought up four very unruly boys, you must remember."

I nod, grateful for her kindness.

"What are you doing today, Kate?" she smiles. "I'd like to take you to lunch."

Elliot frowns, uncomfortable with her suggestion. "That's not necessary, Mom—"

"Nonsense, Elliot," she cuts him off. "When you called ahead and told me you had someone you wanted me to meet, I assumed she was from New York."

My eyes flick to Elliot: *you rang ahead?*

"But now that I know I only have limited time to get to know her, I'm taking Kate to lunch." Her eyes flick to me. "That's if she wants to, of course."

This is the last thing on earth I want to do. "That would be lovely," I lie.

Elliot looks like he just swallowed a fly.

She smiles. "I'll have Henderson pick you up at one."

I nod. *Please earth, swallow me up into a sinkhole, never to be recovered.* "Great."

She stands. "George," she calls. "We're leaving."

"I didn't have my coffee yet."

"We'll get one at breakfast." It's blatantly obvious who's the boss around here. She turns to me. "I'll see you at one?"

I nod.

"And we have a family dinner tonight at Tristan's. You can meet all of my beautiful grandchildren."

I fake a smile and nod. I wanted to move to the next level but this is going way too fast. "Fantastic." I wish I would swallow a fly, a poisonous one that would put me in hospital for a week.

George appears and shakes my hand. "See you tonight, honey."

She and George leave, and the door closes behind them.

"You are all fucking dead," Elliot yells. "Why the hell would you bring them here? What kind of fucking stitch-up is that?"

His brothers burst out laughing in the kitchen.

Tristan comes around the corner with two cups of coffee. "That was the best thing I've ever seen." He passes the cup of coffee to me. "Here you go."

"Thank you." I smile as I take it from him.

I sit down on the edge of the couch and sip it; ugh, it's so strong it tastes like petrol.

This is the literal day from hell.

Jameson takes a sip. "Fuck, you make shit coffee." He grimaces.

Christopher stares at me with a sarcastic smirk. "Kathryn Landon, what the hell are you doing here? You *hate* him."

"Perhaps it's the hard surfaces that she likes," Tristan says with a cheeky wink.

Jameson raises his coffee in the air in a cheers gesture.

I feel my cheeks heat with embarrassment again and a dutiful smile crosses my face.

Kill me now.

"Will you just all fuck off," Elliot snaps. "I've got gray hair after this morning." He stands and looks at his hair in the mirror.

"Your face though when Mom said happy birthday," Jameson says, and the boys all laugh as if picturing it once more. They break into chatter and Elliot's eyes find mine across the room and he smiles softly.

I love seeing him with his brothers like this; they aren't at all as I imagined.

Fun, carefree, and full of banter.

Surprisingly normal.

I glance at my watch: 12:45 p.m. Mrs. Miles will be here soon.

Fuck.

I'm so nervous I could die.

My phone rings and the name Elliot lights up the screen. "Hello Mr. Miles." I smile.

"Hi. You ready for your lunch date?"

"Nope." I sigh. "What do I say?"

"Everything except anything."

"What?"

"My mother wants to get you alone so she can dig for information."

"Like what?"

"She's nosy."

"What will I tell her?"

"Nothing. Tell her nothing."

My eyes widen. "What if she asks me questions?"

"Oh, she will. Don't you worry about that."

"How will I answer them?"

"Just be evasive."

I close my eyes. "This day is a nightmare, Elliot," I whisper.

He chuckles.

"Did you really bring me here to meet your mother?"

"Maybe."

"Why?"

"I told you already, I didn't want to go a week without seeing you."

My heart swells.

"What if she doesn't like me?"

"It doesn't matter, I like you."

I smile as I run my finger along the countertop.

"Does that count for something?" he asks.

"It does."

"After you finish lunch with her, come and see me at work."

"Really?" I sigh. God, so much pressure in one day. I've been running around all morning looking for the perfect gift. "I'll just see you tonight."

"Kate, it's my birthday."

I roll my eyes. "Fine."

"Don't drink too much at lunch," he reminds me.

I giggle.

"I mean it, she hates drunks."

"Oh." He's serious. "Okay."

"And don't tell her anything about us."

I shrug. What could I possibly tell her—I don't even know what's going on. "Okay."

"And—"

"Elliot," I cut him off. "You're making me more nervous than I already am," I splutter.

"Sorry." He exhales.

"I'll see you this afternoon?"

"Alright. Bye babe."

I hang up and rush to the bathroom to check how I look one last time. I'm wearing a black, long-sleeved dress that Daniel made me buy, and nude high heels with a matching clutch. My hair is styled and I have minimal makeup on.

I'm going for sensible-classy, not sure if I've achieved it, but whatever, this is all I've got.

The door buzzer sounds and I run out and push the intercom. "Hello."

"Your car is here, Miss Landon," a male voice replies.

"I'll be right down."

I stare at my reflection in the mirror and I let out a shaky deep breath, putting my hand over my stomach to try and calm the butterflies. What was I thinking, agreeing to this?

I make my way down and walk out to find a black limousine parked at the curb, and my nerves hit an all-time high.

Fuck.

The doorman opens the back door. "Miss Landon." He nods.

"Thank you."

I climb in to find Elizabeth sitting in the backseat; she smiles warmly. "Hello Kate."

She's immaculately dressed in designer labels and looks like a beautiful fashion model.

The look of money oozes out of her and I'm quite sure that Daniel would bow at her feet. Imagine the designers that would swarm around her.

"Hi." The door shuts behind me; is it too late to run?

"I've booked us into my favorite restaurant." She smiles. "I hope you like it."

"I'm sure I will." I clasp my hands in my lap so tightly that I nearly cut off the circulation.

Fifteen minutes later we pull up outside a swanky-looking restaurant and I follow her in. "Mrs. Miles." The waiters all smile. "How lovely to see you."

"Hello."

"Your table is this way."

We are shown to our table and the waitress asks, "Can I get you anything to drink?"

"Yes." Elizabeth smiles. "Would you like some wine, Kathryn?"

"No, thank you, I don't drink that often," I lie. "Just a mineral water for me, please."

"Oh." A trace of a smile crosses her face. "I'll have the same."

Her eyes hold mine and she links her fingers under her chin. "I can see why Elliot is so swept away with you, you're lovely."

I smile bashfully. "Ah . . ."

Our mineral water arrives and she pours us both a glass. "Has Elliot warned you not to elaborate on anything to me?"

Oh hell.

I smile shyly. "Maybe."

"He's a very private person."

"Yes." I nod. "I know."

She opens her menu. "I'm afraid that out of all my children, growing up in the spotlight has had the biggest effect on Elliot."

I frown as I listen.

"He guards his privacy with his life and I'm quite sure that some days he despises his surname."

"I don't think—"

"Now, now." She cuts me off. "There's no need to make excuses, my dear. I understand where he's coming from."

"Where is he coming from?" I whisper.

"Elliot is a dreamer," she continues. "He lives in a world where he is forced to be a realist, but in his heart, he is a romantic."

I smile; I already knew this from my interaction with Ed. "Yes, I know."

"When he called me last week and told me that he was bringing a plus-one to his birthday dinner, I knew that you must be special to him."

"Why is that?"

"Darling." She takes my hand over the table. "You're the first woman he's ever brought home to us."

My face falls as I stare at her. "He's a very confusing man," I whisper.

She gives me a knowing smile. "Hang in there, my dear." She sips her drink. "Once Elliot commits to a woman, she would be his entire world."

I drop my head. I know he told me not to tell her anything, but if there's one woman who knows him better than anyone, it's her. "It's only early days, he doesn't even want anyone to know that we're seeing each other."

"It has nothing to do with you," she replies. "Elliot hates press, he hates the invasion of his privacy. When they nicknamed him Casanova Miles he was mortified; he believes that once something becomes the property of the gossip pages, that it's no longer special, or belongs to him."

I frown.

"He's watched Jameson go through very public battles with the media and the ramifications it has caused in his private life."

I listen intently; this isn't how I was expecting our conversation to go.

"He doesn't want that for himself or his partner. In his own way, he is protecting you."

"Who would ever have thought that a media family would hate the press so much?" I say.

"The irony." She smiles. "Christopher has filled me in on your and Elliot's history, you haven't always liked each other or gotten along?"

"No."

She smiles as she watches me. "Why is that?"

Fuck.

I stare at her, lost for words.

She reminds me what it was like to have a mother figure pry for information: it feels nice. Familiar.

She takes my hand in hers once more. "I hold honesty in the highest regard, Kate."

Shit, that was code for . . . *lie to me bitch, and you're done.* Oh hell, I brace myself to tell her the truth. Here goes nothing.

"I thought he was a self-absorbed, self-righteous womanizer."

She chuckles in surprise. "Elliot is *all* of those things."

I smile too.

"But if you get underneath all that, and not many people get the chance to, he is kind and warm and generous."

I well up; she's completely right. "I know." I sip my drink. "Don't take this the wrong way, Mrs. Miles," I whisper. "But I wish Elliot was a plumber."

"Why?"

"Because then we would come from the same world and I wouldn't have to share him. And he could just be whoever he wanted to be."

She puts her hand under her chin as she stares at me.

Shit . . . I shouldn't have said that. I crossed the line.

"I'm sorry, I shouldn't have—"

"That's okay, dear," she cuts me off. "Can I ask you a question, Kate?"

I nod.

"What don't you like about Elliot?"

"Um." I pause. Fuck . . . he told me not to go there with her and here I am having a deep and meaningful. I've fallen for her trap. *You idiot, Kate.*

"Umm . . ." I pause again.

"Be honest with me. What don't you like about Elliot?"

"His arrogance, his money, his temper . . ." I pause as I try to articulate my words. "He's closed off and cold, reserved, and can be mean—"

"What do you like about him?" she interrupts.

I think for a moment. "His kind heart."

Her eyes hold mine and eventually, she smiles softly. "It's lovely to meet you, Kathryn," she whispers.

"I'm so sorry about this morning," I whisper back. "You can't imagine how horrified I am that we met that way."

"Oh, don't worry about that." She laughs. "I know what my son is like, I'm not delusional. He's definitely no angel and his nickname was well earned."

She seems happy and I'm not sure, but I think I answered her questions right.

"I can't wait for you to meet Emily and Claire tonight."

I put my hand over my stomach. "It makes me so nervous."

"Don't be." She smiles. "We've been waiting for you."

I arrive at the top floor of the Miles Media building and the elevator doors open into a huge swanky space.

It's all white and complete luxury, with a floor-to-ceiling glass wall and view over New York.

"Kathryn?" The receptionist smiles as she stands.

"Yes."

She shakes my hand. "I'm Sammia." She turns to her colleague. "And this is Lindsey, from HR."

"Hello." I smile as I shake their hands; well, this is awkward. Elliot failed to mention that the female employees here are shit-hot.

"Elliot is expecting you, his office is the last on the right."

"Thank you." I walk down the long corridor over the white marble and knock on the last door on the right.

"Come in," his strong voice calls.

I open the door tentatively and he raises his chin as if defiant. "Miss Landon," he snaps. "Do you have that report I'm waiting on?"

I roll my lips to hide my smile; he's playing pretend. "Yes sir."

"Come in," he barks.

I walk in and close the door behind me.

"Lock the door." He stands.

I frown and slowly turn the lock.

"I've worked out what I want for my birthday, Miss Landon," he says as he walks around his desk. "I've been wanting it for about seven years now. The time has come for you to deliver."

I swallow the lump in my throat, what's he talking about?

He knocks hard, twice, on his desk and my eyes widen.

Oh no, a hard surface.

His dark eyes dance with arousal and he pushes everything off his desk.

"Elliot," I whisper.

Then he is on me. He pushes me up against the back of the door and kisses me hard.

"Elliot."

He bites my neck as his hands slide up my dress and down the front of my panties.

"They're just outside," I whisper.

"I didn't give you permission to speak, Miss Landon," he growls in a whisper.

His fingers circle the lips of my sex, he slides in one finger, and my eyes flutter closed.

"Elliot," I whimper as he slides in another.

His eyes hold mine as he begins to work me hard, thick pumps of his fingers as he pins me against the wall. "Open your fucking legs, Landon," he hisses.

His harsh words bring a rush of arousal and he smiles as he bites my ear. "I want it wet, swollen." He adds another finger and I throw my head back against the wall.

Oh hell.

The sound of my wet body sucking him in echoes around his office.

"What if someone walks in?" I whimper.

"Then they'll have to wait their turn." He grabs a handful of my hair and drags my face to him. "You're going to bend over my desk. You're going to open up that pretty little pussy for me." He jerks me hard, his grip on my hair is almost painful. "And you're going to take my cock and then get on your knees and drink me down."

He grabs my face in his hands. "Do you understand me?" he commands.

I nod, arousal screaming through my body like never before.

He drags me to his desk and pushes me over it; he tears my dress up and I hear the zip of his fly. Gone is the sensitive lover I've had of late.

Elliot Miles is here in all his glory.

Fuck . . . *I've missed him.*

With one hand gripping a handful of my hair, he slams in hard.

The burn of his possession stretches me, burns like never before.

My mouth falls open as I try to deal with him, my face mangled into his desk.

Up close and personal.

His hands go to my shoulders as he rides me hard, the sound of our skin-slapping echoing.

They'll know.

He moans, and from the guttural sound he makes, I know he's close.

He pulls out and in one movement, pulls me up and pushes me down to my knees, slides his cock down my throat and with his two hands gripping my hair, he comes in a rush.

I nearly choke; he's a lot of man to take like this.

His dark eyes hold mine as he slowly pumps my mouth, completely emptying himself into me.

His chest rises and falls as he gasps for air, his grip on my hair loosens.

I lick my lips. "Happy birthday, sir."

A trace of a smile crosses his face as he realizes we're still in role play, and he zips up his trousers. "Stand up, Miss Landon."

I stand and he pulls my dress down and straightens it, pulls his fingers through my hair to neaten it.

I lick my lips again, excited that he called me here to get a blow job at work. "Will that be all, sir?" I whisper.

His dark eyes hold mine. "For now."

He walks around and sits behind his desk, leans back in his chair.

Arrogance personified.

"I'll . . . get back to work, Mr. Miles."

He nods as he picks up his pen.

I pick up my bag and walk toward the door.

"Miss Landon."

I turn back toward him. "Yes sir."

"Well done." He tilts his chin to the sky. "Excellent reporting skills."

I smirk. *Bastard.*

"I try my best, sir."

I leave and walk down the corridor and out into the reception area, and with their boss literally on my tongue, I bid his secretaries goodbye.

The car pulls up in front of a huge house and I peer out. Elliot squeezes my hand on my lap. "Ready?"

I fake a smile. "After the day I've had today, who knows?"

"Did I tell you, I love my present," he whispers as he kisses me.

"About a million times already."

I took a photo of Elliot outside near his lake the other morning. It's from behind, he's in a suit, and staring out over his enchanted estate. The ducks are gathered around his feet and the mist is rolling over the hills. It's a beautiful shot and I had it framed for him.

What do you get the man who has everything? Now I know. Sentiment.

He loves it because it's sentimental. It means something to him, just like he means something to me.

Being here in New York with his family has given me a little more insight into the mercurial man. He's not just difficult with me, he's difficult with everyone.

And I can't tell you how good that feels to know.

It's not me, it was never me, it's him.

We park the car and walk up to the front door; Elliot knocks as I hold my breath.

Tristan opens the door in a rush. "Hello." He smiles as he looks at us in turn, bends and kisses me on the cheek. "Come in."

Elliot takes my hand and we walk into a large living area, a hive of activity.

"This is Emily," Tristan introduces me, "Jameson's wife, and this is their son, James."

"Hello." The little boy looks to be about three. He has dark hair and blue eyes like his father.

"Hi." Emily smiles, leans in, and kisses my cheek. "Lovely to meet you." She's heavily pregnant. "Our daughter Imogen is around here somewhere." She smiles. "She's twenty-three months old."

"Oh, you have your hands full."

"As if dealing with Jim isn't enough." Tristan smiles. "And this is my wife, Claire."

"Hi." Claire smiles; she isn't at all what I expected. Naturally pretty, with dark hair.

He takes a baby dressed in pink from her. "This is Poppy and we have a two-year-old daughter around here somewhere, her name is Summer."

A bunch of kids go running and screaming through the house.

"That will be her," he says. "Noisiest tiny human you ever met."

I giggle. "Hello."

"Boys," he calls. "Come here please."

I look up to see two teenagers and a small boy walking over.

"These are my sons, Fletcher, Harrison, and Patrick."

"Hello." They all shake my hand politely. "How do you do?"

"Come out and join the party." Tristan smiles as he holds his hand out.

I look into the back living-room area to see everyone chatting and laughing, completely relaxed, and I let out a sigh of relief.

Maybe this won't be so bad after all.

If heaven was a week, this would be it.

I put my head on Elliot's chest as we ride up to his apartment in the elevator, his strong arm around me, and I feel completely safe and protected.

We've danced and laughed, made love and fucked.

Spent time with his wonderful family, and to say that Elliot Miles has romanced me around New York is the understatement of the year.

In a few days we go home to London, and I never thought I'd say this, but I don't want to.

I want to stay here, where we have privacy and Elliot has his brothers, and I have their wives, and we don't have to hide under a cloak of secrecy.

In London it's just us, but here . . . there's family. And I know they aren't mine, but they're his, and they've made me feel so welcome.

We arrive up at the apartment and Elliot leads me by the hand through to the kitchen, opens the freezer, and removes a silver ice bucket.

"What's this?" I ask.

He pulls out two Cornetto ice creams and hands one over; emotion overwhelms me as I stare at it in his hand.

"I thought we could toast New York."

I stare at him through tears, and I know that if I didn't already love him before . . .

I honestly do now.

I watch as he unwraps mine and he passes it over. I take it and wait for him to unwrap his, then he leads me out onto the balcony and we sit down on the day bed.

He holds his Cornetto up. "To New York."

I smile and tap my ice cream with his. "To New York."

He kisses me tenderly and then licks his ice cream and I could just burst out crying as I watch him.

So thoughtful.

"Don't worry," he says casually as he licks his ice cream. "I'll lick you next."

I burst out laughing. "You idiot."

ELLIOT

I lie in bed and toss and turn. Kate is asleep beside me and it's late.

My phone beeps with a text and I frown. Who's that? I pick it up and read the message: it's from the private investigator that I hired.

We found her.

What?

I sit up in a rush and walk downstairs to my study, close the door, and dial his number. "Hello."

"We found her."

"Where is she?"

"Nice."

I smile broadly. "Does she still have the paintings?"

"You're not going to believe this."

"What?"

"She isn't ninety at all."

"What?"

"She's twenty-nine and drop-dead gorgeous."

I frown. "What do you mean?"

"I'll send you an image of her right now."

I open my computer and wait. The email comes through, my heart drops.

A blonde woman, with red lipstick. Beautiful in every way.

Someone I already know that I'm attracted to.

I know this woman, I've seen her at auctions before, and I've chased her, knowing deep down that I was supposed to meet her. That something was there.

The ballerina.

Panic runs through me.

"I've organized for you to meet her next week in Paris," he says. "I know how long you've searched for this woman, I can't imagine how excited you must be."

"Yes," I reply as the world spins on its axis.

No . . . why now?

"I'll send through the details tomorrow."

"Okay."

"Goodnight sir."

I hang up and walk back into the bedroom in a daze, my heart beating hard and fast.

Is this the sign I've been waiting for?

I climb into bed beside Kate and I take her into my arms as sadness fills me.

"El," she murmurs in her sleep.

I hold her tighter.

"I love you," she whispers.

I close my eyes in regret.

Fuck.

I let out a deep exhale as I watch the game on the screen. I'm at a bar, sitting at a high bench seat near the back, waiting for my brothers. I'm carrying the weight of the world on my shoulders and fuck, I need to hash it out.

I see them amble through the front doors, deep in conversation, and then make their way over to me. Jameson heads straight to the bar.

"Here he is." Tristan slaps me hard three times on the back as he falls onto the seat beside me. "What is so damn important that we have to meet you in a bar at"—he glances at his watch—"eleven-fifty in the fucking morning?"

I roll my eyes. "Everything."

Christopher frowns across the table. "What's wrong?"

"Destiny is fucking me up the ass, that's what."

Tristan raises an eyebrow. "Strap-on, or cock?"

Christopher chuckles as he turns his phone off and puts it on the table.

"Will you shut the fuck up," I snap. "Trust you to make a joke of my life."

"It is comical," he says dryly. "And you are a clown."

Jameson arrives with a tray of beers, places them in front of us and falls into a seat, looks over at me. "What?"

"My life is a fucking disaster," I scoff.

He rolls his eyes. "So dramatic."

"What now?" Christopher says.

"Well, I'm happy."

They nod.

"And you know that I'm obsessed with Harriet Boucher and have had a private investigator searching for her for over six months?"

"Yes," they all reply.

"And you know how I've seen that beautiful blonde woman at her auctions for years and have never been able to find her afterwards? And that I've felt a connection to her as if she is someone I should know?"

"The ballerina?" Tristan asks.

"That's her." I take a gulp of my beer; this story is nothing short of horrifying.

They all sit back as they listen.

"I got an email from the private investigator last night, he found Harriet."

"That's great." Christopher smiles.

"The ballerina is her." Their faces fall. "I'm supposed to meet her in France next week."

Jameson slumps back in his chair. "Well, I'll be fucked."

"And Kate told me that she loved me last night."

They all blink, shocked.

"So, all along I've been waiting for a sign from the universe. I believed I would have that destined meeting or whatever that was. I've been obsessed with one woman, and searching for another woman's paintings. And I find out that they are the same person on the night that my new girlfriend . . . there, I said it . . ." I hold my fingers up and air-quote the word ". . . *girlfriend* . . . tells me that she loves me."

Their faces fall.

"And, I think I love Kate . . . Actually," I correct myself. "I know I'm in love with Kate."

"Fucking hell . . ." Jameson winces.

Tristan's eyes widen and Christopher puffs air into his cheeks.

I look at the three of them as I wait for their reaction. "Well, are you going to say something?"

Jameson curls his lip. "You're fucked."

Tristan and Christopher nod in agreement.

"Well, what's your thought process?" Tristan asks.

"I haven't slept. All night I've been going over different scenarios."

"Such as?"

"What if Harriet is the woman I'm supposed to be with? I've known from day one that I saw her painting that she was special. I've adored the ballerina from afar and to find out they are the same person is . . ." I pause as I try to articulate my words. "Mind-blowing."

They all listen intently.

"But then there's Kathryn. We hated each other for so long. I was never attracted to her. One day it was like a lightbulb went off and I could think of nothing else." I take a depressing sip of my beer. "She is . . ." I pause. "Just so beautiful."

Jameson frowns. "You're the happiest I've seen you in a very long time."

"I am. Since Kate and I got together, we've spent almost every night together."

"Every night?" Christopher frowns. "Like virtually every single night?"

"Yep, I can't stand the thought of her going back to her house for even one night."

Tristan holds his forehead as he leans his elbow on the table. "You're completely fucked."

"Well, what are you going to do?" Jameson asks. "What are the options?"

"I can stay with Kate and always have regrets and wonder, *what if.*"

They all wince.

"Or I go to Harriet and try with her, and leave Kate."

"Can you just leave Kate?" Christopher asks.

"I don't know." I sigh sadly. "I know that if I leave Kate now I've been the biggest fucking asshole in all of history."

They all listen.

"I haven't played games. I've been completely myself and haven't held back at all."

They all wince again.

"This is why I'm never falling in love," Christopher snaps. "No way in hell am I giving my balls on a platter to a woman."

Tristan rolls his eyes. "That statement right there is why you aren't in a relationship. When you love someone, you give them your heart, not your fucking balls, you dipshit."

Christopher sips his beer. "My wife will be getting my balls, straight down her throat."

We all chuckle as we take a drink and then we fall silent.

"So . . . what now?" Jay asks.

"I feel like Harriet is destined. I know you all don't believe in fate. But I do, I always have."

"Look, I never believed in fate. I always thought that I would meet some beautiful young woman and it would be easy," Tristan says.

I listen intently.

"And then I met Claire, and everything I thought I wanted went out the window. Her kids hated me and I had to fight tooth and nail to convince her to love me. Never in a million years did I ever imagine my life as it is now. But I honestly believe I am where I'm meant to be. Claire and those kids were meant for me, and the bigger picture of my destiny was already mapped out. They were my family long before I even met them; perhaps before they were even born it was decided that they would end up being mine."

I exhale, more confused, and I turn to Jay. "What about you?"

"Well." He shrugs. "I thought Claudia was the love of my life." He sips his beer. "Turns out she was just keeping me company until Emily came along. Trust me, she isn't who or what I thought I would end up with either."

"Would you change it?"

"Not for anything in the world."

I turn my attention to Christopher.

He holds his hands up in surrender. "Don't look at me, I'm going undercover to meet my wife. I don't want no socialite."

"What?" We all frown.

"One of these days I'm taking a gap year," Christopher says.

"What does that even mean?" Jameson says.

"I'm going to hand over my credit cards, resign, and grow a beard," he continues. "Go backpacking for twelve months. A do-over of sorts. I'm going to come back with someone who loves me for me."

We all burst out laughing.

"You," I scoff. "That's the most ridiculous thing I ever heard. You in a backpacker resort?"

We laugh harder, imagining him there with the ferals and bed-bugs. Christopher is accustomed to luxury; he'd die without it.

Jameson's attention comes back to me. "What are you going to do?"

"I know I can't live my life with regrets or wondering what if." I sigh.

"So, you're going to go to Paris?" Christopher frowns. "Just like that?"

I stay silent, unsure.

"You're stupid if you fuck this up with Kate," he snaps. "That she likes you is unbelievable, the fact that she loves you is a fucking miracle."

My eyes rise to meet his.

"You have something special with her; grab onto it with both hands and don't let go."

"Agreed," Tristan says.

"I think you need to go to Paris." Jameson sighs. "You need to know, once and for all. Are you really going to live your life wondering what if? Is that fair to Kate to start a relationship with this already hanging over your head?"

My chest tightens as I look at my brothers and I know that there is no right or wrong answer to this.

I'm fucked if I do, and fucked if I don't.

Chapter 22

KATE

The car pulls to a halt on the tarmac and I look over at Elliot. He's pensive and staring out of the window. A million miles away.

He's been quiet for the last few days; it must be hard for him to leave his family.

The driver takes our luggage from the trunk and carries it onto the plane.

"You ready?" Elliot asks, his voice quiet and monotone.

I smile with a nod. "I guess." I lean up to kiss him and he pecks me quickly and opens the door. "They're waiting."

Oh. I exhale; since when does he care if people are waiting for him? I take it he's not in the mood for kissing, then.

He takes my hand and helps me out of the car and then leads me up the stairs and onto the plane. We take our seats and he stares out of the window, deep in thought.

"I'm going to watch my favorite movie today on the flight." I smile.

"What's that?" he asks.

"*The Greatest Showman.*"

He smiles as if amused and he watches me as he leans back on the headrest. "Why is that your favorite movie?" he asks.

"I don't know." I shrug with a smile. "It's about dreams coming true for the dreamers."

A frown flashes across his face before he quickly covers it. "Sounds boring."

"It's not, you'll see."

"I'll be moving to my desk after takeoff, I have work to do."

"Oh."

He takes my hand in his as the plane begins to take off down the runway. "You'll have to watch it alone."

I pick up his hand and kiss the back of it. "One day, I'll strap you down to watch it."

He chuckles. "Not if I strap you down first."

I put my head on his shoulder. "El."

"Yeah, baby?"

"Thank you for taking me to meet your family, they're more wonderful than I ever expected."

He nods. "They are." He falls deep into thought for a moment. "Although if I hear any of them knock twice on anything once more, I may strangle someone."

I giggle. "Can you believe that—that's how I met your mother?"

"A lot of unbelievable things have happened this week." He stares straight ahead, seemingly falling serious.

The plane takes off into the sky and I smile as I stare out of the window. I can't wait to message Ed and discuss the week.

I get 10 percent of my information from Elliot, and the other 90 percent of his feelings from Ed.

Although, I have to admit, the last two weeks have been a dream come true in Elliot's arms. I couldn't ask for a more adoring, tender lover.

Fun, too.

"I wonder how the girls are?" I ask.

A broad smile crosses his face, the first one of the day. "I hope they've been guarding the lake as instructed."

My heart swells.

"What is that look?" He raises an eyebrow. "What do you think about when you look at me like that?"

I drop my head and smile shyly. "It's not so much a look, as a feeling."

He stares at me.

"When you're happy, it makes me happy," I whisper. "When you smile, really smile, I feel it all the way to my bones."

He frowns and drops his head and stares at his shoes.

I kiss his shoulder. "You're very special to me, Elliot," I whisper. "You know that, don't you?"

He inhales sharply and sits forward in his seat. "I have to work." He gets up and takes his briefcase out of the overhead and moves his things to the desk a few rows behind us.

I lean around the chairs. "Last call to watch *The Greatest Showman*." I bat my eyelashes to try and make myself look cute.

"It's a hard pass," he says flatly as he falls into his seat.

I chuckle and put my headphones on and click the screen. Mr. Boring Businessman is in town.

The plane comes to a halt on the tarmac and I frown: Elliot is still back at his desk working. He hasn't come near me for the entire flight.

I mean, I know he had to work, but . . . it was unlike him.

He appears beside me and opens the overhead. "How was your movie?" he asks.

"Good, great." I smile. "Did you get your work done?"

"No. Not all of it."

He seems stressed. "Anything I can help with?"

"No." He holds his hand out for me. "Come."

He thanks the cabin crew and we make our way down the stairs; Andrew and the Bentley are waiting.

"Hello Kate." He smiles as he puts our things into the trunk. "I trust you had a good week away?"

"Hi Andrew." I beam. "We had the best week."

Elliot gets into the car and slams the door. "Dropping Kate home at her house please, Andrew."

Andrew's eyes flick up to him in the rearview mirror. "Yes sir."

I frown over at Elliot.

"I have work to do, sweetheart," he whispers.

"I don't mind."

He picks up my hand and kisses my fingertips. "I'm not having you sit there alone while I work. Go home and see your friends."

I stare at him: *something's wrong.*

"Is everything alright?" I whisper.

He stares at me as he presses his lips together, as if he's stopping himself from saying something.

My heart drops.

If there's one thing I do know about Elliot Miles it's that he can't lie. His inability to answer that question just cemented my concerns.

Something is wrong.

What is it?

Elliot's gaze goes outside and with his elbow on the window he watches the world go by. My hand is held tight inside his hand but he's not here with me, he's miles away.

I just don't know where.

We arrive at my house and Elliot climbs out and retrieves my suitcase.

I don't want to be here, I want to go to Enchanted to see the girls and check on Gretel the goat.

"I'll carry your suitcase up the stairs—" he says.

"I've got it," I cut him off.

He stares down at me, and I don't know why but I get the feeling he has the weight of the world on his shoulders. "Goodbye, darling." He kisses me softly. I lean into the kiss and he pulls out of it. "See you tomorrow."

I nod, and before I can answer he's back in the car and the door slams shut.

I wheel my suitcase across the street and the car pulls away. I frown as I watch it disappear.

What was that about?

I carry my suitcase up the steps and open the front door to the apartment. "Hello," I call. "I'm home."

Silence.

My shoulders slump. "Great, they aren't even home." I exhale and begin to drag my suitcase up the stairs.

Oh well, I suppose some time to myself will do me good.

I haven't done it in so long.

I'll put a treatment in my hair and a face mask on, get some Uber Eats. I smile as my little room comes into view.

One night without Elliot Miles won't kill me.

It's late and I lie in the darkness.

I messaged Ed earlier tonight when I got home but he hasn't yet replied.

Elliot hasn't called to say goodnight either. It's not like him, he's usually so attentive.

Weird.

Did he have something on? Was he going somewhere?

I've got this sick feeling in my stomach, like something is wrong but I don't know what. I mean, he was a little bit evasive today but surely not enough to warrant this anxiety.

Is my gut telling me something?
My phone pings with a notification and I smile. Ed.
I jump out of bed and grab my phone and flick the table lamp on.

> Hi Pinkie,
>
> Sorry I haven't messaged you in a few days. I've
> been away seeing my family.
>
> How are you?

I smile and reply:

> That's okay, I missed you.
>
> Tell me about your trip.

His reply bounces in.

> My trip was incredible, Kate came with me and
> met my family. Although I should have known
> it was all going too well.

I frown. What?

> Why, what happened?
>
> I got an email last night, I've finally found the
> artist that I've been searching for.

I smile. Oh my God. He found her.
Excitement fills me.

This is amazing!

No, it's not.

She's not an old lady as I thought, she's young and beautiful.

Unattached.

I frown. What does that mean?
I read on.

I know who she is, I've seen her at auctions and have wanted to chase her before to ask her out. I've always felt like she was someone that I was supposed to meet.

I searched for her, even made my brothers follow her once.

And now to find that it was her paintings that have been calling me for so long . . .

I fear my fate has come to find me when I've finally found someone who makes me happy.

No.
Wait . . .
I read that last message again and my chest constricts.
What?
I put my head into my hands; this can't be happening.

No.

You believe this woman, the artist, is your fate?

I don't want to have regrets.

I can't go forward with my life and always regret not going to her and finding out what may have been.

This woman has been in my heart long before anyone else.

The words blur as tears cloud my vision.

What about Kate?

I'm confused.

For the first time in my life, I'm happy with where I am, who I am with.

I feel complete, and yet . . . I can't stop thinking that I have to go to her.

To see for myself if this is where I'm supposed to be.

Why now?

Why have I only found her now when I've been searching for her all along?

> Why has fate been so cruel to deliver her to me
> when I care so much for someone else?

I sob out loud.

I'm going to lose him.

> What should I do, Pinkie?

I slam my computer shut.

The lump is big in my throat and painful, and I angrily wipe my tears away.

This isn't happening. Tell me this isn't fucking happening.

I begin to pace, back and forth. What do I write back?

The worst part is, I already know what a friend would say.

A friend would tell him that he should go to her, that he should follow his gut feeling and find out if she's the one he's been searching for all along.

That he's stupid if he ignores his heart, because it's never wrong.

How could he ignore this sign and be with another?

But I love him.

My chest hurts and I sob out loud.

A deep sense of dread fills my every cell.

I walk into the bathroom and turn the hot water in the shower on, climb in, and cry.

It's 3 a.m. I lie in the darkness.

A sense of dread is slowly pumping through my veins as if the hope is draining out, and I know that life isn't fair sometimes.

Over the last month I've been happier than I've felt in years. Elliot brought me into his home, shared his farm animals, and showed me what it felt like to be truly cared for. He introduced me to his family and for the first time in a long time, I felt included, as if I were one of them.

The thought of not seeing his family again is another dagger to the heart.

Elizabeth.

I know that I'm standing on the precipice of heartache, and I can't even begin to understand the depths of the darkness that await me if he goes.

I love him.

Maybe more than I love myself, because his happiness is what I want above all else.

I want him fulfilled, and what good is he to me if his heart is with her? I get a painful lump in my throat because, deep down, I know the truth.

It was always with her.

Oh . . . This hurts.

The worst part is, I can't even tell him that I know.

This stupid fucking game of online chatting we play . . . has come back to haunt me.

This is what you get for lying to someone, Kate.

I deserve everything I'm getting and then some.

I've deceived Elliot for weeks, and I knew it was wrong and I was going to tell him, but the right time never came around.

I thought it was harmless, I now know it's not.

With a shaky breath I get up and open my computer. I write to Ed.

You should follow your heart Ed.

A message bounces straight back. Why is he still awake?

I don't want to hurt Kate.

I screw up my face in tears. Too late.
The computer screen is blurred.

It's your heart that you have to live with, follow
it.

Kate would want you to be happy.

She loves you.

Xoxo

Hello darkness, my old friend.

It's been a while since you graced me with your presence, I can't
say that I've missed you.

I sit at my desk and stare out the window. It's 3 p.m. and I
haven't heard from Elliot.

I don't expect to.

A million emotions have run through me: sadness, regret,
anger . . . but mostly disappointment.

I can see it so clearly now—he and I had fun, but he was always
searching for the dream, the fairy-tale ending.

And I'm not talented or special, least of all extraordinary.

It was never me.

And I hate that for a brief moment I forgot that—it hurts.

I remember the love that we made, the laughter we had. The
tenderness we shared.

It felt so real.

Like a fairy tale to me, only better.

My eyes fill with tears and I blink them away.

Maybe he won't go?

Paul walks past and glances in and then stops in his tracks and comes back. "You alright?"

"Yeah." I fake a smile with a subtle shake of my head. "Sorry, just had some bad news about a relative."

"Do you want to go home?"

"No," I answer way too fast, I don't want Elliot to know that I know. "I'm fine. Just a bit teary, don't pay me any attention."

"There's some birthday cake in the staff-room fridge, you want some?"

I smile, grateful for the kindness. "I do. Bring the whole damn thing."

It's 11 p.m. and I sit at the window and stare out over the street.

The house is quiet for the night and my facade has dropped. I went out to dinner with Daniel and Rebecca tonight and had to pretend that everything was great between Elliot and I.

I couldn't tell them what I know or how, and I've been lying to them about my Pinkie persona too.

This situation is one big fucked-up deception and I deserve to have my heart broken alone.

And maybe if Elliot cared enough to want to see me, I would tell him so.

But he doesn't.

Because he's at Enchanted thinking about her.

My eyes well with tears and I close them in regret. I hate this, I hate the whole fucking thing.

A car comes around the corner and I watch it slowly pull in and park. Elliot gets out.

Oh no.

Shit.

I run and dive into bed, pick up my phone: five missed calls from Elliot.

I hear a knock downstairs and then Daniel's voice.

I pull the blankets up over me and pretend to sleep, my heart racing hard and fast, and I inhale deeply to try and calm myself down.

My bedroom door opens and Elliot comes in and sits beside me on the bed. "Babe," he says softly, "are you awake?"

I roll toward him and he takes my face in his hand and I stare up at him.

"Hi," he whispers sadly.

"Hi." I force a smile.

"I have to go to France tomorrow, sweetheart," he whispers.

My heart constricts. *He's here to say goodbye.*

I nod, unable to push a word past my lips.

"Can I stay?" he asks.

I clench my hands into fists; how am I supposed to do this?

Say goodbye with love when he's breaking my fucking heart?

I should be kicking him out, I should be punching him square in the face.

I should hate him.

He takes his clothes off and climbs in beside me. His lips take mine, and I can feel the heartbreak as it radiates out of him. He's right here in hell with me.

This isn't his fault, he's a good man.

His eyes search mine. "Tell me you love me," he whispers. "Just once."

My heart begins to ache and I know this is it, our last dance together; his silhouette blurs. "I love you."

We kiss, and my face screws up against his.

Don't go.

For a long time, we kiss, until my heart can't take it anymore. I need this goodbye over . . . I can't do this.

I'm not strong enough. "I need you," I whisper.

He crawls over me and slides in deep, his head buried in my shoulder, and I screw up my face as I stare at the ceiling.

He moves slowly, carefully, as if I'm breakable. He always said that he loves me when I'm vulnerable.

Here I am in Imax; I've never felt so unprotected in my life. Defenseless.

His body heats up and he moves slowly to bring himself closer. He spreads his knees and wraps my legs around his hips, but I have no chance of climaxing tonight.

How could I possibly feel physical pleasure when I'm in such pain?

He may as well be stabbing me in the heart, it would feel the same.

He holds himself deep and shudders as he comes. His lips run up and down my neck, a tender love song of affection.

I stare at the ceiling, lifeless.

I feel the hot lone tear roll down my face and into my ear.

He rolls off me and falls onto his back, glances over and sees my tears, and throws his forearm over his eyes, as if to shield himself. He's unable to deal with me.

Or unwilling.

After a while, "Go to sleep, sweetheart," he whispers.

I stay silent and stare at the ceiling, my heart shattering into a million pieces.

Go to hell.

The dawn light peeks through the side of the blinds, and I watch him put his suit on from my place in bed. Gone is my tender lover from last night.

Elliot Miles is here this morning, and I'm glad. Because he's easier to hate.

"When will you be back?" I ask.

"I'm not sure," he says as he pulls his jacket over his shoulders. *He can't even look at me.*

He pats his trouser pockets as he checks he has everything; I should ask him if I can have my heart back before he leaves. He's had it in his possession since the first night we spent together, unashamedly so.

His eyes find me across the room and I force a smile. "Have a nice trip."

"I don't want to go," he whispers.

"But you will."

We stare at each other and eventually, as if making an internal decision, he closes his eyes. "Goodbye, Kate," he murmurs.

"Goodbye, Elliot."

He walks over to me and takes my face in his hands and kisses me, and this time it's his face that screws up against mine. He knows, he knows that if he does this then we are done.

Without one word, he turns and walks out, and the door clicks quietly behind him.

I inhale with a shaky breath.

He went anyway.

/

Chapter 23

ELLIOT

The rain comes down heavy and hard, and I walk on to the plane like it's a galley.

"Good afternoon, Mr. Miles." The pilot smiles.

"Hello." I shake out my umbrella and fold it away.

"We are scheduled to take off in fifteen minutes, sir. I trust you'll have a pleasant trip."

"Thank you." I walk through the plane and take my usual seat.

Just fucking go, already.

My phone lets off a ding and I glance at it. Kate.

I open up the message and frown.

It's a song, "Never Enough" by Loren Allred.

Fuck.

I drag my hand down my face and eventually, curiosity gets the better of me and I put my headphones on and hit play.

It's a slow song, of love and loss.

I put my head back against the headrest and exhale heavily; I want this over with.

Just fucking go already.

"Mr. Miles." The waiter smiles. "We've been expecting you, sir. Miss Boucher is waiting."

I nod. "Thank you."

"The private dining room is this way." I follow him through to the glass atrium; there are fairy lights strewn across the top of the glass and the table is candlelit. I see her sitting alone at a table for two by the fire.

She looks up, and our eyes meet.

"Hello." She smiles softly.

My heart flips in my chest.

She's absolutely breathtaking . . .

"Hello." I frown—she makes me nervous—and my stomach flutters. "Sorry I'm late."

She smiles up at me with her big eyes. "Better late than never."

KATE

I sit at the window seat and stare out over the road as the rain comes down.

Even the weather is miserable. Like a dark heavy blanket of sadness.

I glance at my watch, Elliot will be in France now.

I get a vision of the two of them sitting in a romantic location, staring into each other's eyes.

I'm in a literal hell.

"Is everything alright with your meal, ma'am?" the waiter interrupts me.

"Oh." I look down to see my untouched cold dinner. "Yes, I'm sorry . . . I'm . . ." I pick up my fork. "A little distracted."

"Perhaps some wine?" The waiter smiles hopefully.

"Yes." I nod. "That would be lovely."

He raises his eyebrow as he waits for something.

"What is it?" I ask.

"What wine would you like?"

"Oh." I shake my head, embarrassed. "Surprise me."

"Very well." He disappears into the kitchen and I take a forkful of pasta into my mouth.

Ugh, my stomach rolls and I clench my teeth to stop the gag reflex.

I make myself swallow; food is the very last thing I can handle tonight.

I don't even want to go home to my roommates, because then I have to pretend that everything is okay . . . or tell another lie, or worse still, tell them the sordid truth.

Neither of the tasks I feel capable of while I'm this weak.

I'll just wait until everyone goes to bed, it's easier that way.

It's 9 p.m. and . . . in a few hours, I will know.

Elliot will either call me . . . or he won't.

I know he will . . . he loves me, I know he does and I believe in us. He will call me.

He has to.

I'm not in this alone. I haven't imagined this entire thing. We do have something real.

I know we do.

I can't be this gullible.

I force another mouthful in and my stomach rolls and I heave.

I think I'm going to throw up.

One a.m.

I walk up my street toward my house in the rain. With two bottles of wine under my belt, I should be happy.

What I am is . . . devastated.

He's with her.

I take out my phone and check it for the ten thousandth time tonight.

"Call me," I whisper angrily. "You fucking call me, goddamn it."

I screw up my face in tears. Why is this happening? What on earth did I ever do to deserve such fucking shit in my life? I lost my parents, my sister is the devil, and now the man that I love . . . doesn't even love me back.

"Why?" I cry out loud. "What have I done to deserve this?"

I get to my apartment and I can't face going inside, because then I have to sleep.

And then it will be morning, and too late to go back on what happened last night.

And I will know what he did.

I get a vision of Elliot and her waking up in bed and him being all witty and charming and wowing her with his sexuality and her falling madly in love with him.

How could she not?

There's a lot to love about Elliot Miles.

I drop to sit on the bottom step and I stare into space. And as the rain comes down on top of me, wet, afraid, and alone . . . I cry.

It's the silence that kills you. The things that aren't said.

The closure you never got.

Three days.

Seventy-two hours. Four thousand, three hundred, and twenty minutes.

Too many seconds to count.

The clock ticks in my office. It's like a megaphone, loud and annoying, reminding me of how time's going by . . . with not a word.

Not even a text.

He's with her.

I know that now, but that doesn't make it any easier to swallow.

I really thought he loved me.

My faith in humanity is smashed to smithereens.

Did he even care about me at all? He couldn't have . . . nobody could treat someone that they care about like this. The joke of it is that he doesn't even know that I know what he's doing in France.

Was that his plan, to just disappear on a business trip and ghost me . . . let me down easy? Push me to end it with him?

Maybe I'll never hear from him again . . . nothing would surprise me any more.

It's like I'm grieving a death all over again.

I still haven't told my flatmates . . . I can't.

I don't feel strong enough to talk about it . . . so I avoid going home.

I've been going to the movies, loitering in restaurants. Spending five hours in the gym. I'll do anything rather than bring this up and show everyone how weak I really am.

I hate myself for being so weak, I thought I was stronger than this.

Wednesday.

"Knock, knock." A soft tap sounds on my office door. I glance up to see Christopher and I instantly get a lump in my throat.

Go away.

"Got a minute?" he asks softly.

No.

I force a smile and gesture to the seat at my desk. "Sure."

He sits down and leans back and crosses his legs; his eyes hold mine.

He knows something.

"What is it?" I ask.

"Have you heard from Elliot?" he asks, his voice soft, cajoling.

I press my lips together hard. "No."

He narrows his eyes.

"Why do you ask?"

"We haven't been able to reach him."

I frown.

"I'm a little worried, to be honest."

I turn back to my computer and act busy. "You don't need to worry, he's in France with his artist."

He stays silent, so silent that I look back.

His eyes hold mine, and I know that he knows just how broken I am.

My eyes well with tears. "I'm sorry. I just . . ."

"It's okay—"

"It's not," I cut him off; this is the most degrading moment of my life. My boyfriend's brother coming to comfort me after he ran off with another woman.

I just want to be out of here, away from all these . . . snakes.

"I'm giving you my notice."

His face falls. "Kate, no."

"I can't be here, Chris."

His haunted eyes hold mine.

"I just . . ." Words fail me, because there are none. None that will make sense anyway. "Today is my last day, I'll be out by close of business."

"I don't want you to leave," he whispers. "Elliot wouldn't want you to leave."

"Elliot is not here, is he?" I snap sharply. "I'm sorry." I shrug. "I don't mean to snap at you but . . ."

"It's okay." He watches me for a moment. "What are you going to do?"

"I don't know." I sigh. "Get the hell out of London for a while."

He leans his face on his hand as he watches me. "Mom's upset."

That makes two of us.

I nod, unable to push out words in fear of a full-on meltdown.

"Can I help you pack up?" he asks as he looks around my office.

I smile sadly, Christopher is so kind. "No, I'm okay."

"Are you?" His eyes hold mine.

"Not really." I smile through tears. "But . . . I will be."

We stare at each other for a while. "Kate, for what it's worth . . . I know he'll—" He cuts himself off as if reconsidering what he was going to say.

"What?"

"He'll regret this."

"I know. I do."

He frowns. "Do you?"

I puff air into my cheeks. "Actually, that's not fair, I can't say that. Elliot showed me what it was like to feel again. I've been numb since my parents died, so in a way"—I shrug—"I have to be grateful for that."

He smiles sadly. "You're a pretty cool chick, Landon."

"Ha." I smirk. "You should probably leave now then, before you get the jilted-lover-psycho-smashing-up-the-office version."

He holds his hands up and laughs as he stands. "Yeah, I'm leaving her well alone."

He puts his hands in his expensive suit pockets, and his eyes hold mine.

I reach up onto my toes and kiss his cheek. "Thank you."

"For the record." He twists his lips. "He's a fucking idiot."

I smile, grateful for his kindness. "Tell me something I don't know."

I lie in the darkness in my bed; the world is a dark and lonely place.

I feel like this hurt is just going on and on.

I opened up and told Daniel and Rebecca everything tonight and it's torn down the last of my defenses.

Now that I don't have to act brave, I'm falling apart. I can't stop crying.

Howling-to-the-moon heartbreak, where he's not coming back and I feel like my whole future has been snatched from my

418

grasp. The life I saw us having, living at Enchanted, his animals, the laughing and loving, his family . . . all gone.

My eyes are red and swollen and I've taken three showers tonight to try and make me feel better.

I'm sobbing, my chest wracked, and for the life of me, I can't stop it. To the point that I think I'm going to have to take a sleeping tablet or something to calm myself down.

I remember this kind of grief all too well.

I feel the bed dip and Daniel crawls in behind me; he's wearing boxer shorts and is bare-chested. "Baby," he whispers as he pulls me close.

"I'm sorry," I murmur.

He tightens his grip and I close my eyes, grateful for the warmth.

For a long time, he holds me as I cry, and every now and then he pushes the hair back from my forehead as he looks down at me. "Tell me how to make this better?" he whispers, his body snug up against mine.

"You can't."

He wipes my tears and holds me. He's warm and big and a closeness runs between us. My head is on his chest and his arms are tight around me; he kisses my temple and I feel something move down below.

I frown.

He holds me closer and I feel it again.

What?

He's hard.

"Let me make you better, baby," he whispers.

I stare up at him in the darkness.

"Let me take away your pain for a little while."

I frown again and he takes my hand and runs it down over his rippled abs, and lower into his shorts.

419

We stare at each other, my breath catches, and I feel his pubic hair and then hard cock; my hand closes around it instinctively.

"Let me love you," he whispers. He kisses me softly and I screw up my face against his.

He kisses me again and rolls me onto my back as he leans over me, and I feel his body up against mine. "Stop," I whisper. "Daniel, stop." I sit up in a rush and pull away from him.

What the hell?

"I don't want this; my body isn't even mine to give to you," I stammer in a panic. "It's Elliot's."

"He's with another woman, Kate, he's not coming back for you. They're probably making love right now."

I wince as I get a visual.

"I'm trying to help you," he whispers.

"You're trying to sleep with me."

"To make you forget *him*."

"Please . . . don't."

He gets out of my bed and puts his hands on his hips. "I was trying to help you."

I turn my back to him and stare at the wall. "I know."

He sits on the chair in the corner. "I'm not leaving you alone."

I nod, grateful that he isn't leaving but he's out of my bed. I would have never forgiven myself . . . not that it matters to anyone anyway, I guess.

But I would know.

I wasn't lying—my body belongs to Elliot, whether he wants it or not.

I sip my coffee in a crowded café on a Sunday morning. I got up early and went to the gym; I have a chocolate muffin in front of me and I'm feeling a little better today. I had a talk with Daniel and I believe him, he was just trying to be of comfort.

And maybe on some level I should have done it, maybe it would have helped me to move on and forget *him*.

I hear the familiar ding of my phone and my blood runs cold. Ed.

I ignore it for a moment, and it dings again.

I don't want to talk to Ed, because I know he's going to tell me about her.

I'm cutting ties with him too.

I'm sick of all the fucking lies. No more charades, it's obvious I can't handle this game.

It dings again and I close my eyes.

Go away.

With a shaky hand I lift my coffee to my mouth. It dings again. Fuck it.

May as well get this over with . . .

I take out my phone and click on his message.

Hi Pinkie,

Sorry I haven't been in touch, I've been busy.

I've missed you.

His sweet words open it all back up, emotion overwhelms me, and the tears I so gallantly told myself that I no longer had, appear once more.

I go to type but everything is blurred so I put my phone down on the table and angrily swipe them away.

No, I have to know.

I type:

How is your artist?

A reply bounces back.

I don't care.

I frown and write:

Why?

Because, she's not you.

What?

What are you talking about?

I love you . . . Pinkie . . . or should I say, Kate.

My eyes widen and I sit back in my chair—what the hell is going on here?

Are you going to eat that chocolate muffin, or will I?

I look up and Elliot is sitting at a table across the café; his eyes search mine as he gives me a soft smile.

And something snaps inside of me and I'm furious and I hate him, so I stand and march out of the café and down the street.

"Kate," he calls as he runs after me. "Kate, come back here."

I don't want to hear his lies, I don't want to be anywhere near him.

I walk quickly across the road to the park, needing to get as far away from him as I possibly can.

"Kate." I can hear his voice getting closer.

I get to the park and I run.

"Kate," he cries as he takes chase. "Kathryn, stop." He grabs my arm and I turn and take a swing at him.

"Get away from me," I scream like a maniac through tears.

He pants as he tries to catch his breath; his eyes are wide. "I love you."

"Don't you dare say that to me!" I cry.

"I had to go," he whispers. "I had to know."

"And now you do."

"It's you."

"It took you a week in her bed to find that out?" I hiss.

"No." He pauses as if choosing his words carefully. "There was no chemistry."

"Is that supposed to make me feel special . . . you fucking asshole?" I cry.

His chest rises and falls as he gasps for breath.

"Should I feel flattered that you didn't feel something?"

His shoulders slump.

"You are *always* going to be this person, Elliot," I whisper through tears as I take a step back. "You are always going to want the fairy tale . . . the artist or the dancer . . . the singer." I screw up my face in tears. "You want extraordinary."

"You are," he whispers.

"No, I'm not," I cry. "I'm just a hot piece of ass that you happened to like in a netball dress."

He shakes his head as if lost for words. "We can get past this."

"No."

He dives for me and holds me against my will as I struggle to get away from him. "I love you," he says. "I fucking love you, don't do this." We struggle as he tries to hold me. "Don't do this."

"It is done," I cry as I break away from his grip. "You did it, the moment you got on that fucking plane. It is over. I'm nobody's second prize, Elliot."

He stares at me.

"Least of all yours," I sneer. "You think I could honestly be with someone who I know will throw me to the side every time he finds something shiny and new?"

We stare at each other, me in full-blown tears and him with flared nostrils as he battles for control.

"I swear to you . . ."

We hear the click of a camera and we both turn to see a photographer taking photos of the whole thing.

"Give me that," Elliot growls.

Oh no.

The guy with the camera begins to run and Elliot chases him.

He wrestles him to the ground and people around them scream. Elliot snatches the camera from him and smashes it into a million pieces.

The photographer gives him a mouthful and goes to stand and Elliot punches him hard in the face.

He punches him again, and again.

What the hell is going on?

I turn, and I run.

Chapter 24

Elliot

"Your brother and solicitor are downstairs, they've posted your bail," the police officer says as he writes something on his pad.

I clench my jaw as I stare at him. "I did nothing wrong."

He exhales heavily, clearly frustrated. "We've been through this, ten times today already, Mr. Miles. You cannot smash someone's private property. Nor can you assault them. Now stop wasting my time with your blatant disregard for the law."

"What about my rights? Where is my protection? I don't want my photo taken, are you telling me that he has a right to do something against my will and I'm unable to react? I was protecting myself and my loved ones. It's my rights that have been compromised today."

"Look." He sighs. "Stop playing dumb. You know how this works, you own a media company, for Christ's sake." He hands me a ticket. "You've been charged with assault and vandalism, get your solicitor to fight the arguments in court. I don't make the laws."

I snatch it out of his hand. "What you do is protect criminals." I stand.

He rolls his eyes.

"And don't roll your fucking eyes at me," I snap.

"Do you want to go back to the lockup? Is that it?" He gestures to the door. "Just go, before you overstep the line for the tenth time today."

I'm led downstairs and into the reception area, where I see Christopher and our lawyer sitting and waiting. I glare at them and turn to the police officer. "I want my possessions returned."

"Your phone, belt, and keys are in the tray over on the counter."

I take them and put them in my pockets. "Let's go."

"Thank you, officer," Christopher says.

"Don't fucking thank him," I snap. "It's a joke that I was even arrested." I storm out of the front door of the police station.

"Will you stop being such a fucking prick?" Christopher calls from behind me. "It's not his fault you had a brain snap."

"Shut the fuck up," I whisper angrily as I march down the steps. I turn toward them. "Thank you both for coming. Go home, now."

"You go home too, Mr. Miles," Edward, our solicitor, says. "You are in no state to be in public."

"I'm fine."

"You are not fine. Go straight home before you make your situation worse."

"It can't get any fucking worse," I snap.

"Believe me, it can. Christopher, drive him home and stay with him tonight."

"I will, don't worry."

"Fuck off the both of you." I turn away in disgust. "Actually, drive me back to my car."

"I had Andrew pick your car up earlier," Christopher says. "I'm driving you home."

I stare at him. "Fine." I shake Edward's hand. "Thank you."

"I'll be in touch. Stay home, Elliot. I can't stress to you how important it is that you don't get into any more trouble."

"I won't let him out of my sight," Christopher says.

I exhale heavily and we walk over to his car. I slam the door shut. "Take me to Kate's."

"I am *not* taking you to Kate's."

"Fine." I open the car door to get back out. "I'll fucking walk." I march down the street in the direction of her house.

"She doesn't want to see you," he calls.

I carry on walking and he drives the car up alongside me and winds down the window. "Stop being an idiot."

I keep walking.

"Elliot, you are all over the news right now. They'll be camped out the front of her house."

I stop on the spot and my shoulders slump. "I've fucked it."

"I know." He sighs. "But you can't be acting like a lunatic. Go home and call her. I'll go pick her up myself, I promise. You cannot just turn up there unannounced."

I stare at him.

"What if she won't let you in?" he asks.

"She will."

"Will she?" he says. "Because I saw the footage of her on the news taking a swing at you and she didn't look like she was too happy to see you."

My heart drops. "You saw that?"

"Everyone's seen it, it was filmed from a phone." His eyes hold mine. "Just get in the fucking car, man." He sighs sadly.

I look up the street.

Fuck.

I get in the car and slam the door and we drive in silence.

Eventually he turns on to the motorway and we head to Enchanted.

I stare out of the window with my phone in my hand. What do I do?

I close my eyes in regret.

I fucked up . . . bad.

"She's not going to forgive me," I say as I get a vision of Kate from today, the look in her eyes. "I know her, she's too stubborn . . . if you saw how hurt and angry she was."

"Do you blame her?" Christopher says as his eyes flick over to me.

I clench my jaw as anger surges.

"What the hell were you thinking?" Christopher snaps. "You had it. For the first time, you actually had it in your hand. A woman who made you happy . . . and you go off on some stupid fucking tangent chasing an artist."

"It's not stupid to me," I cry. "I'd only been with Kate for a month." I kick the dashboard.

"Don't kick my car or I'm kicking you out, and you can fucking walk, prick," Christopher yells.

"I had been searching for this artist for years. I've been obsessed with her, I thought there was something there."

"Did you sleep with her?" His eyes move between me and the road.

I stay silent.

"Did you fuck this artist or not?" he yells.

"No!" I scream. "As soon as I got there I knew I had done the wrong thing."

"So why then . . . did you stay?"

"I stayed one night."

"So . . . you *did* sleep with her?"

428

"No." I shake my head, regret swimming through my body. "She was full on into me and . . . I faked a headache and went back to my hotel room. I didn't even get through the first dinner date."

He frowns at me.

"I was confused," I cry. "I thought it was a sign, that she was the one." My nostrils flare as I try to get a hold of my emotions. "The beautiful woman I had been searching for, for years, was right in front of me, but then when I looked at her . . . she wasn't Kate."

Christopher shakes his head in disgust.

"I told her the next morning that I'd made a mistake and was going home. I bought the remainder of her paintings and left."

"Then where have you been for a week?"

"I believed in fate. The destiny I had dreamed about and thought I wanted wasn't even real. It took me some time to see that what I had with Kate was real. She's the woman for me, she's the one that I love."

Christopher exhales and we drive in silence for a while.

"Please, take me back to Kate's, I have to see her."

"You're an idiot."

"You think I don't know that?" I shout. "Take me to Kate's."

"Shut the fuck up," he yells as he hits the steering wheel. "You've fucked your relationship up with Kate, and now you're hell-bent on getting arrested again. You're all over the news, Elliot. Go home and sort your shit out. I am not in the mood for dealing with your mental fucking breakdown over a woman."

"She isn't just a woman," I yell. "She's the one."

He huffs with an exaggerated roll of his eyes. "Now you discover that . . . after you've completely annihilated the relationship." He shakes his head. "What a fucking idiot."

"Shut. The. Hell. Up," I scream.

We drive the rest of the way in silence and pull into the driveway. "Drop me off and go," I snap.

"I wish I could," he sneers. "I've got better things to do than babysit your ungrateful ass."

"Then don't."

"I promised Jameson I would. That's the only reason I'm here putting up with your tantrum. Go inside, and go to bed."

He stops the car and I get out and slam the door hard, and march inside.

Fuck this day.

KATE

I sit on the couch with Daniel and Rebecca, horrified as we watch the news.

> *In breaking news, Elliot Miles, CEO of Miles Media, has been arrested and charged with assault and criminal damage after an altercation with a photographer this afternoon in Battersea Park.*

> *Mr. Miles, who appeared to be in some kind of domestic incident with a mystery woman, turned on a bystander when he was being photographed.*

> *He was apprehended and arrested at the scene.*

The footage goes to Elliot holding me against my will and I'm screaming at him to let me go, then he turns and we see the photographer, and Elliot begins to chase him as he runs away.

I put my hand over my mouth as I watch in horror. "Oh no, who took this footage?"

I already knew it was bad . . . but it looks even worse.

Elliot catches him, breaks his camera and then the man says something to Elliot who then proceeds to beat him. I can be seen in the footage running away from the scene.

Daniel's horrified eyes find mine.

I stay silent.

My phone buzzes on the coffee table and the name Elliot lights up the screen.

Tears fill my eyes.

"What's going on?" Daniel demands; he reaches down and turns my phone off. "Did he hurt you?"

"No," I snap. "It's fine, he came back and told me he loved me, that was the fight we had."

"He looks angry," Daniel says.

I roll my eyes. I can't imagine how dead Daniel would be if Elliot ever found out what happened last night between us in the darkness.

Not that I care, of course.

"He was."

I lie on my bed in the darkness; my phone has been off all night.

He can't be still arrested, he called me. What if I was his one phone call and I didn't answer?

Stop it, stop thinking of him. He doesn't think of you.

I turn my phone on.

Twenty-six missed calls . . . Elliot.

I close my eyes in regret and switch my phone back off.

"Kate," I hear Daniel call from downstairs. "I think we've got another problem."

"What?" I call.

"You better come and see this."

I drag myself out of bed and walk downstairs to see Daniel still watching the news.

> *In a breaking news update, the mystery woman involved in the domestic incident today with Elliot Miles has been confirmed as Kate Landon, until recently an employee of Miles Media.*

It has been alleged that Elliot Miles is involved in a sordid love triangle with Kate Landon and her partner, Daniel Stevens.

Landon, who lives with Stevens, was photographed with Miles in New York last week but has since returned to her home and partner. It is thought that Mr. Miles is upset with her returning to her partner, thus the altercation this afternoon in Battersea Park.

It flicks to photographs of me and Daniel holding hands and Daniel with his arm around me. A few of us arriving at various balls in different locations, each one strategically shot so that it looks like Daniel and I are together.

Then there are photos of me and Elliot in New York together last week, holding hands as we walked out of a restaurant. Another where he is kissing me in the car. Another of us in a shop and Elliot buying me lingerie. Another shot of me with Elizabeth Miles at our lunch date.

"Get fucked," Daniel whispers in horror.

"What the hell?" I put my hands over my mouth.

It goes to a shot of our house. Our eyes meet. "Hang on a minute, how did they get that?" He slowly gets up and walks to the window and his face falls. "Shit."

"What?" I run over and peer through the curtains to see a sea of photographers all set up on the pathway opposite our apartment. Cameras facing the house, waiting for their shot.

"Oh my God." I put my head into my hands. "This is a disaster, what do we do now?"

He hands me his phone. "Call him and find out. He does own a media company, after all. Surely there's a law about making up lies about people."

I exhale heavily. "I don't want to call him."

"Have you got a better idea?" Daniel points at the window. "Asking him what to do in this situation is not taking him back, Kate."

"You're right. Ugh, fine. I'll call him from my phone." I head toward the stairs.

"Let me know what he says."

"Okay." I trudge up the stairs and pick up my phone, turn it on. Thirty-six missed calls from Elliot.

I sit on the bed and hold the phone in my hands. I really don't want to call him.

What is there to say?

My phone rings in my hand, causing me to jump and fumble with it. It's him.

"Hello," I answer.

"Kate . . . hi." His voice is soft, cautious.

I stay silent, unsure what to say.

"I'm sorry about the press, I'll handle it tomorrow."

"How?" I ask. "How will you handle it, Elliot?"

"I don't—" He cuts himself off.

"The love triangle . . . with pictures as proof." I get a lump in my throat as shame overwhelms me.

He lets out an audible sigh. "Don't cry, sweetheart, I'll fix it."

"If I could believe anything that comes out of your mouth, then maybe I'd believe you," I spit. "You can't fix this, Elliot."

"I'm coming to get you."

"You *are* not, there are fifty reporters parked out the front."

"I'll get Andrew to collect you. I'll meet you at my apartment in town. I'm relocating there tomorrow anyway."

"Why?"

"Because I don't want to be followed to Enchanted Estate. I don't want them knowing where I live."

434

"These stories are lies. I'm not with Daniel," I spit, except I accidently nearly was and I'm mortified.

"I know that."

"But—"

"They don't care," he cuts me off. "Just stay there until Andrew arrives."

"No. Nothing has changed, Elliot, I don't want to see you."

"We *need* to talk."

"There's nothing to say."

"I'll come myself," he splutters.

"And I will kick you out in front of the press. Do not come here, Elliot, I mean it."

"Kate, that isn't fair," he snaps. "You know I need to see you, don't hold me hostage to the reporters outside your house. I want to talk to you."

I shake my head, disgusted. "It's always about you . . . isn't it, Elliot?" I whisper. "What *you* need, what's best for *you* . . . *your* dream girl. What *you* want."

"Enough," he barks.

"Okay. Fine." Exasperated, I hang up.

The phone rings immediately and I answer it. "Do not hang up on me."

"Fuck you." I hang up again.

It rings again. "What?" I cry. "What do you want?"

"I want to talk to you."

"I have nothing to say."

"Please." His voice softens. "Baby . . . I need to see you. We can sort this media mess out, but we need to be together to do it."

I screw up my face in tears. When his voice is soft like that, it reminds me of the man I care about.

"Kathryn," he says sternly. "Let me send Andrew, and come and meet me at my apartment."

I listen.

"At the very least it will get you out, they can't follow you into my building, you're safe there. Regardless of what happens with you and I, you need to leave your house or they will hound you to death and make up more lies."

I close my eyes. "I don't want—"

"I just want to talk, Kate. I promise."

"But . . ."

"Pack a bag so they know you won't be back soon. That way they will leave."

I pace back and forth as I think, pull the curtains to the side and peer out at the crowded street.

Reporters are sitting on fold-up chairs and smoking cigarettes. Settled in for the night. I get a vision of them staying for weeks and accosting Daniel as he tries to go to work. This isn't fair to Daniel or Rebecca.

Fuck.

He's right, I need to get out of here, regardless. He's the only one who can make that happen.

"Fine."

"See you soon."

I hang up and march downstairs.

"What happened?" Daniel asks as he sits up.

"Elliot is handling the press tomorrow, Andrew is picking me up. They won't leave until I go."

Daniel's face falls. "So you're just going to go to him? Just like that, he snaps his fingers and all is forgiven."

"No, I'm not stupid. I'm getting the hell out of here and he's the only way I can do it."

Daniel rolls his eyes.

"Have you got a better idea, Daniel?" I cry. "Because if you do, please let me know it." I throw my hands up in the air. "If I stay

436

here, tomorrow morning they follow me wherever I go and make up more lies."

He stares at me.

"Oh, and don't forget, you are the boyfriend I'm supposedly cheating on, so expect them to follow you too."

He pinches the bridge of his nose. "This is a fucking nightmare, Kate."

"You think I don't know that?" I cry.

Rebecca comes out of her room, half asleep. "What's happening?"

"Daniel and I are in a relationship, and I've been sleeping with Elliot behind his back," I tell her in frustration.

Rebecca scratches her head as she looks at us both. "You are?"

"No!" we both cry in unison.

"Oh." She frowns. "What a relief, thank fuck."

Daniel shakes his head. "Go back to bed," he snaps.

"Okay, shut up then, will you both? I'm trying to sleep here." She walks into her room and closes the door.

I run up the stairs to pack my suitcase and Daniel follows me. "What are you going to do?"

"I don't know." I throw my suitcase onto the bed; I already know what I'm doing but I don't want to tell Daniel just yet, not until it's done.

This is my decision, and mine alone; I don't want anyone to cloud my judgment. After Daniel and I crossed the friendship line last night, I know I have to think on my own from here on in. I begin to pack clothes into my suitcase at speed, run into the bathroom and pack my toiletries. I throw in my shampoo and conditioner, hairdryer. I put my hands on my hips as I look around. I take my framed photographs of me and my parents and put them in my suitcase.

"How long are you going for?" He frowns.

"Until things die down."

His eyes are wide. "How long will that be?"

"I don't know. I'm going to stay in a hotel or something for a few days. I'll call you when I know where I'm staying."

"Okay."

"Are you working tomorrow?" I ask.

"I think." He frowns again. "Maybe . . . I might go to my parents' for a few days too."

"Alright." My eyes hold his. "I'm so sorry to drag you into this."

"Hey." He smiles as he puts his arms around me. "It's not your fault." My eyes search his and he cups my face. "Just be careful with him . . . okay?" he whispers.

"He'd never hurt me."

"He already has."

I drop my head. "I know."

My phone beeps with a text.

Kate, it's Andrew.

I'm coming around the corner now.

Stay inside until I come to the door to get you.

Ask Daniel to stay out of sight.

I text back:

Okay, thanks.

"He's nearly here, he said for you to stay out of sight."

"Shit, okay. I'll go to my room." His eyes hold mine. "Be careful, babe." He hugs me.

"Call you tomorrow. When are you going to go to your parents'?" I ask.

"First thing in the morning."

"Okay."

With one last look he disappears down the stairs. A sense of urgency fills me and I quickly text Brad.

Are you home?

Can I get some things dropped at your house?

A reply bounces back.

Yeah sure,

I've been waiting for you to call.

I've seen the news.

What the fuck is going on, Kate?

I shake my head.

A whole lot of lies,

I'm fine.

Fill you in tomorrow.

Love you.

X

A reply bounces back.

Love you too, see you soon.

X

Ten minutes later I hear a knock on the front door and I open it. Andrew smiles and walks in and closes the door behind him. "Hello Kathryn."

"Hi."

"Are you ready?"

I nod.

"I have security with me."

My face falls.

"They will block the photographers and let us get to the car. I'm going to hold this umbrella up in front of you and you are going to put your head down and walk straight to the car. Do not look up, do not acknowledge anyone. We will both get into the backseat and security will drive us away."

Nerves dance in my stomach. "Okay," I whisper.

"Do you have a jacket with a hood?"

"Yes."

"Put it on."

I run up the stairs and whizz through my closet at full speed. My heart is hammering, I feel like I'm about to rob a bank or something. I put on my big jacket and walk back downstairs. "Ready."

Andrew gives me a kind smile and lifts my hood up over my head—my scared eyes hold his. "Don't worry, they'll all disappear as soon as another scandal arrives. This will all be over soon."

"I'm not in a relationship with my flatmate, Andrew."

"I know, dear." He takes my hand and opens the door just a little; two huge security guards stand at the edge of my porch. "Ready," he calls.

"Ready." They spread their legs wide as if preparing for battle.

Andrew opens the door and puts a black umbrella up, facing it toward the paparazzi who are running across the street, effectively blocking their view of me.

"Now," he snaps. He pulls me by the hand. "Keep your head down."

"Kate," I hear them all cry as they clamber around us. "Miss Landon, how is your husband?"

A million questions are being screamed as I am whisked at speed along the pavement.

"Back off," one of the security guards yells. He pushes a photographer hard in the chest and he falls onto his backside.

I begin to get jostled from side to side as they close in. "Run," Andrew yells.

My heart is hammering in my chest, and we make it to the car and I dive into the backseat. Andrew climbs in behind me and the door slams shut.

The photographers all surround the car as they yell out to me, and the security guards jump in and one begins to drive. "You're going to hit them," I cry.

He doesn't reply, and he doesn't stop. He just drives straight through the middle of them and somehow, they part and let us through.

I look back at my apartment and sadness fills me; how the hell is Daniel going to get out? "Can you please go back and help my friend Daniel out tomorrow?"

Andrew nods. "Yes, of course."

I wring my hands together nervously on my lap. "After you drop me at Elliot's, can you deliver my suitcase to my brother's house?"

"Yes, of course."

I nod as adrenaline surges through my body like a freight train.

We fly through the streets of London and, for the first time, I understand why Elliot guards his privacy so stringently. Why he doesn't give them an inch to work with.

This is an absolute fucking nightmare.

We drive into the underground parking lot at Elliot's luxury apartment; the security gates close behind us and the car pulls up in front of the elevator. The guard parks the car and we all get out. "Thank you," I whisper.

The burly guards walk over to the elevator. "I'm fine from here." The guards ignore me and walk into the elevator. "What are you doing?" I ask as I look at them in turn.

"We've been instructed to deliver you in person, Miss Landon."

I stare at them and Daniel's words from when I first met Elliot Miles come back to me: *he's a powerful man and not someone I would mess with.*

Suddenly I'm very aware that if Elliot Miles wants me delivered in person, I no longer have a choice. If I told them that I wasn't going up to his apartment right now, they would make me go, regardless.

A million things are running at full speed through my head, but the blazing emotion is . . . loss of control.

We ride to the top floor in silence and the doors open into Elliot's foyer, where he's waiting. His eyes find mine and he smiles softly, as if relieved.

"Thank you," he says to the guards; he opens the door to his apartment and I walk in.

I stand in the middle of his living room, determined to be strong.

This man has brought me to my knees for the last time.

Elliot's eyes hold mine and he stares at me as if I'm a wild animal, about to run at any moment.

"I'm sorry about that," he whispers.

I nod.

"Can I get you . . . anything to drink?"

"No."

He puffs air into his cheeks as if lost for words. "Are you going to sit down?"

My eyes hold his and I just want to hurt him, for hurting me.

For putting me through this fucking bullshit.

"We need to talk, sweetheart," he whispers.

"For God's sake, Elliot," I yell, "don't call me that. It's no longer a term of endearment, it makes me a laughing stock. It's you, taking advantage of my affection. Do not ever fucking call me sweetheart again!"

His face falls. "I had to go . . . you know I had to go."

I stare at him.

"You told me to go," he cries. "I asked you what to do, and you told me to go."

"I told you to follow your heart," I scream.

He clenches his jaw, unsure what to say.

"How long have you known it was me? How long have you been lying to me?"

"You knew Edgar was me all along, you've been lying to me," he says. "I told you who I was immediately."

"How long?" I throw up my hands.

"You told me all about Edgar Moffatt the night when you were high on meds. You even showed me his messages on your phone."

My face falls.

"Of all the people in the world, I couldn't believe it. I told you the next day. You found out the very next day that Edgar was me," he replies calmly.

"Why are you so honest with Pinkie?"

"Because *she* is easy to talk to . . . *she* doesn't judge me. *She* is my friend."

"So . . . you lie to me?"

"I knew I was talking to you, I never lied to you. Not once. I told you I was going to France to see her."

"But you didn't tell *me*," I yell in outrage. "You knew I couldn't say anything."

"Because you were lying to me all along," he cries. "And you fucking know it."

I drop my head, this is pointless. I sit on the couch and he falls to the floor on his knees in front of me. "Nothing happened with her, I promise you. Not even a kiss."

My eyes hold his.

Is that true?

"Kate." He sighs sadly. "If I didn't go, I would've always had that *what if* in the back of my mind."

"I know. So . . ." I pause as I try to get the wording right in my head. "You spent the week with her?"

"No. We had the dinner and she made it quite clear that she wanted . . . more."

I swallow the lump in my throat. Do I even want to hear this?

"All I could think about . . . was you," he whispers. "I knew I'd done the wrong thing, but I also knew that I had to go to her and find out. I couldn't make a future with someone and always have a

444

doubt in the back of my mind. It was a double-edged sword, Kate. I did what I thought I had to do."

I drop my head; *don't cry.*

"There was no connection with her, nothing at all." His eyes search mine. "I swear to you—"

"What if there was?" I interrupt. "What if there was a connection, Elliot? Where would I be now?"

"There wasn't."

"But there could have been."

He exhales heavily. "You're not listening to me."

"And you didn't answer my question. Where were you all week?" I ask.

"I told her that nothing was happening, that I had someone back home."

"Something that you should have thought of before you went to her," I cry, still outraged.

"I'm here now," he yells as he holds his hands out wide. "I'm yours, Kate."

Are you?

"I took the week to think," he continues. "I needed to clear my head."

My eyes rise to his and the hairs on the back of my neck stand to attention. "About what?"

"About life."

"You mean . . . about falling for someone who's average."

He inhales sharply and I know I hit the nail on the head.

My eyes well with tears. "I'm not your fairy tale, Elliot," I whisper.

"Yes, you are." He stands. "It's all bullshit. All along I thought I had to have signs. I thought that my gut would lead me to my soulmate."

Oh . . . this man hurts me. I drop my head, unable to look at him.

445

"Kate, we hated each other for years." He takes my face in his hand and he dusts his thumb back and forth over my bottom lip. "You can't blame me for wondering if it was the real thing, or simply a physical attraction. You had to have had the same concerns."

My heart drops.

Never once.

I force a nod; I just want this conversation over.

He falls to his knees in front of me again and looks up. "I love you." He kisses me softly. "We can fix this. We can start again, and this time we know it's the real thing. Nobody makes me feel like you do, Kate."

More lies.

I pull back from his kiss. "I need a shower."

He smiles as he holds me in his arms. "Yes, let's take a shower."

"Elliot, I've had the worst day in history and I'm tired. Can we talk about this tomorrow, please?"

"Okay." He nods as he pulls me to my feet. "You're right, we have all the time in the world."

He leads me into the bathroom and turns the shower on. He slowly undresses me and I get in under the water.

I shower in a daze, somewhere between heartache and relief.

Now, I know.

I get out and he dries me with a towel as he showers me in kisses. "Thank God, you're here," he whispers. "I thought I lost you."

I stare at him in a detached state: *is he for real?*

He thinks he can say a few pretty words and all is well between us?

I feel nothing . . . I'm dead inside. It's like I'm talking to a stranger, one that I don't even like.

Whatever we had is gone.

We get into his bed and our lips touch; his kiss deepens and I pull out of it. "Tomorrow, babe," I whisper. "I'm not in the mood tonight. Honestly, I'm just too emotionally exhausted."

"Okay." He reaches over and turns the bedside light off and snuggles in behind me, his arms around me, his lips at my temple.

"I love you, Kate," he whispers.

"I love you too," I whisper back. We lie in the darkness, so physically close and yet I've never felt so alone.

If he knew me at all, he would know that.

A tear rolls down my face in the darkness; it's hot and salty and feels a lot like betrayal.

Elliot Miles isn't the only one who wanted a fairy-tale ending. I did too.

And sadly, I know this isn't it.

Chapter 25

Elliot

I wake with a start, a bang in the distance.

I look over to Kate, but I'm in bed alone. I sit up. "Kate," I call.

Is she in the bathroom?

"Kate?"

I get up and walk to the bathroom, it's empty. Panic floods through me and I flick the light on. "Kate," I yell as I look around. "Where are you?"

I march into the living room. "Kate," I cry with urgency. "Kathryn." I look around, where's her handbag?

Her bag is gone.

No.

I run from room to room, screaming her name as my heart races.

She's not here.

I dial her number, it rings out. I dial it again and it's switched off.

Anger surges through me and I kick the wall.

I dial security. "Yes sir."

"Where's Kate?" I growl.

"Um . . . she's with you . . . isn't she?"

"Explain to me . . . how the fuck she got out of here unnoticed," I yell.

"I don't understand, sir, we've been on the doors all night."

"You're fucking useless," I cry. "Find her!" I hang up and begin to pace back and forth, my chest rising and falling as I grapple for control.

I go to the window and look down over the street.

"Kate," I whisper. "Where are you?"

I sit in the back of the car and dial Kate's number; it goes straight to voicemail.

I inhale sharply—I've searched for her all night. She simply disappeared into thin air.

Not a trace.

She hasn't gone home, her phone is off.

"This is the house sir."

I peer in. "Are you sure?"

"Yes, this is her brother's house. We dropped her bag off here as she requested."

I get out of the car and march up to the front door, knock hard, and it opens in a rush. A young man comes into view, early thirties.

"Hello, I'm Elliot Miles—"

"I know who you are."

"Can I see her?"

"She's not here."

"I need to—"

"You've done enough," he snaps, goes to close the door, and I put my hand up to block it, push it open, and barge my way in. "Kate," I yell. "I know you're here."

"You're too late. She's gone." He sighs.

"Where?"

"She flew out first thing this morning."

The room spins. "To where?"

"That's for me to know and you to never find out."

"What are you talking about?" I throw my hands up. "She has to work tomorrow."

He screws up his face. "You dumb fuck, she resigned last Wednesday, she's taking a job overseas. If you'd have bothered to come back from your artist's bed, you would already know this."

The earth spins on its axis.

My nostrils flare as I battle for control.

He shakes his head, with a deep exhale. "Just, get out, man. You've fucked it." He glances at his watch.

"Where is she, tell me," I demand.

"You're too late, she will have already checked in."

My eyes widen, her plane hasn't left yet. "I can still catch her then." I turn and run for the car.

"I didn't say that," he calls after me. "She doesn't want to see you," I hear in the distance as I dive in the backseat. "Heathrow Airport, quick," I cry.

Andrew pulls out into the traffic with speed and I dial Kate's number. Ring, ring . . . ring, ring . . . ring, ring.

"Come on, pick up. Pick up," I whisper. It rings out and I dial her number again. I imagine her staring at her phone ignoring my call and my fury begins to boil.

At her, at me . . . at this entire fucked-up situation.

Why did she run out in the middle of the night, *what was she thinking?*

When this is all over, I'm going to kill her . . . that's if I don't have a heart attack beforehand. I peer through the windshield. "Drive faster."

"I am." Andrew huffs as he changes lane, then he changes lane again and I dial Kate's number with my heart in my throat.

Please pick up, baby.

It rings out again. "Answer your fucking phone, Kathryn," I yell as I hit my phone on the back of the seat in anger.

Andrew's eyes flick up to mine in the rearview mirror. "Don't fucking start!" I growl.

He puts his foot down and we fly through the traffic, and half an hour later we pull up at the airport.

I dive out of the backseat and run in, my eyes scanning the check-in lines as I turn in a 360.

"Where are you?" I whisper to myself. "Kate." I begin to panic that I'm not going to find her, there are too many people. "Don't do this, please." I run along the back of the check-in queues as I search for her. I get to one end and run back to where I began: perhaps she's already gone through.

I run to the security checkpoint and stand in line. "Come on, come on," I mutter. I look around the line to the security guards, working at a snail's pace.

Hurry the fuck up.

I run my hands through my hair in a complete panic. Every minute that ticks past . . . is a minute I've lost to stop her.

Finally I get to the checkpoint and walk through the scanner, and it dings.

Fuck.

"Just step back through sir."

"I don't have time for this," I stammer. I go back through the scanner, it dings again, and I bend and tear off my shoes and throw them to the side, rip my belt off and hurl it on the floor. I go back through the scanner and no alarm goes off.

"Thank fuck." I pick up my belongings and tuck them under my arm and I run as fast as I can, until I get to an intersection. Six huge corridors go in different directions leading to the departure gates.

No.

I swallow the lump in my throat as I look at my options: what way should I go?

Umm. "Which way?" I'm panting as I gasp for breath. "Right." I run to the right down a corridor. This is hopeless, I'm never going to find her. "Fuck's sake."

I keep running and I just happen to glance to the side and I see the back of Kate, just as she goes through the boarding gate. "Kate," I cry as I take off in that direction. "Kate."

She doesn't hear me and she goes through the double doors.

"Kate," I yell as loud as I can. People turn and stare and I get to the flight attendants who are doing the check-in.

I gasp for air. "I need to get someone off the plane," I pant.

"I'm sorry, sir, that's impossible."

"No." I put my hand on my chest. Fuck, I can't breathe. "You don't understand, it's an emergency."

"You're too late."

"No," I yell. "Kate. I'm here," I cry. "Come back."

Two burly security guards come and stand beside me. "Is there a problem here, sir?"

I look between them as I gasp for air. "My girlfriend." I pant, and point to the flight. "Need . . . to . . . stop . . . her."

The guards exchange looks and with an eye roll, one of them says, "Leave now or you will be escorted from the building, sir."

Deflation fills me and I drop my shoes and belt and put my hands on my knees as I try to catch my breath.

Fuck it . . . she's gone . . .

But where to? I glance up and see the flight destination.

Honolulu

Flight 245

American Airlines

I stand with renewed purpose, put my shoes on, and roll my belt into my hand. "Thanks." I march off. *Fuckers.*

I dial my security; he answers first ring. "Hello, Mr. Miles."

"Hi, have someone meet the plane, she's landing in Honolulu, American Airlines flight 245."

"Got it."

"Do not let her out of your sight! I want an address."

KATE

The transfer car pulls up in front of the villa, and the driver turns in his seat. "Here you are, Miss."

I peer out as relief fills me; looks okay. I always have that panic moment when I see a place I booked online.

I pay him and he takes my suitcase from the trunk.

Thank God I arranged all this last week.

When I hadn't heard from Elliot, *when he was with her* . . . the thought of seeing him at work was mortifying. I booked this holiday to give myself some space. I didn't tell anyone about it except Brad. Not even Daniel and Rebecca. If they didn't know where I was then they couldn't accidently tell anyone, and thank God I didn't. I had no idea how much it was going to be needed.

I'm on Lanikai Beach, Kailua, on the island of Oahu, Hawaii.

The sound and smell of the ocean overwhelms me, and I wave my driver goodbye and walk up the steps.

The keys are in a lock box and excitement fills me. A hot shower . . . and some sleep.

I've had a horrendous trip, and to be honest I was half expecting the Miles jet to pull up alongside us and hijack my plane, and for Elliot to board mid-air and drag me off.

To get here alone and safe is a relief. The key turns and I walk in and gasp.

Oh my God. "So beautiful."

It's a little villa, in the shape of a hexagon, on the edge of a cliff. Huge windows with views of the sea are everywhere you look, and palm trees are on the edge of the waterline.

This place looks straight out of a movie.

I smile, lock the door behind me, and look around: one bedroom, a small, tidy bathroom, and an octagon-shaped living and kitchen area with light timber floors. Through large timber French doors is a huge deck, and I walk out to feel the sea breeze on my face.

"Wow." I smile into the view, stare out for a while, and then my mind goes to Elliot back home . . . and I can almost feel his panic. I know he'll be worried.

But I can't think of him right now. For once in my life, I have to put myself first.

I understand what he told me yesterday, that he loves me and that he didn't do anything with his beloved artist. And maybe if he had come straight home after he saw her I would have forgiven him and moved on.

But he took a week to convince himself that he wanted to be with me. To talk himself into his so-called happiness. If he loved me as he said he does, there would have been no soul-searching to arrive at that decision. He would have come straight home . . . to me.

I hate that he didn't.

I get a vision of us laughing and making love and of all the wonderful late-night deep and meaningful conversations we had in bed, and my heart hurts.

For a while there, I let myself believe that we had something special.

I exhale sadly; but it wasn't to be.

Elliot Miles isn't the only one who wants the happily-ever-after with someone extraordinary . . . and guess what, I'm waiting for it.

Even if it kills me . . . and the way I feel now, it just might.

"Hello." I smile at the kind-looking waiter. "I'm here to see Steven about the waitress position."

I've been here for four days and can't stomach the thought of going back. I called the real-estate agent and the place I'm staying at now is coming up for long-term rent.

I'm going to stay for a while and put some roots down while I sort myself out.

"Hi." He smiles as he wipes down the bar. "I'm Steven."

"Hi." I feel so awkward, and I clutch my résumé in my hands with white-knuckle force.

"Have you ever waitressed before?" he asks.

"No."

"Ever been in hospitality?"

"Nope."

"What do you normally do?"

"IT." I twist my fingers in front of me. "Computer analysis."

He frowns. "What are you doing here?"

"Honestly?" I shrug. "I broke up with my boyfriend and ran away. I figure Lanikai is a pretty amazing place to stay for a few months while I lick my wounds and get my shit together."

Oh no . . . I wrecked it.

He smiles broadly. "It is. I did that five years ago and never left. When can you start?"

"Today."

The sound of the ocean laps at the shore and I smile into the sun as I walk along.

This place is heaven.

And not just because it was my escape plan.

For the first time in a long time, probably since my parents died, I feel proud of myself.

I've pushed myself way out of my comfort zone.

I didn't want to stay in London; my gut told me to leave.

There were too many questions between us, too little trust on my behalf.

Even though I wanted to stay and fight for us, I knew that I needed this time alone.

To regroup and find out who I am again.

It's as if I'm finally coming into my own. I've lived in the shadow of my parents' death for seven dark years . . . but somehow, this new heartache over Elliot has snapped me out of it.

For a long time, I wanted a change, but I was always too cautious and scared, then this happened and suddenly without hesitation I moved to the other side of the world. I was tired of IT so I now work nights in a restaurant.

Everything I've been pushing through over the last few years, the staleness and boredom . . . I don't feel it anymore.

I wake up every day renewed, a little sad . . . but still, excited for what's coming.

I've been doing yoga as the sun comes up on the beach; I swim in the ocean and lie in the sun. I go for a big walk and then have an afternoon nap. At night, I go to work in the restaurant. It's fun and easy and the people there are so nice.

"Lovely day, isn't it?" a man says as he rides past me on a pushbike.

"Sure is." I smile as I get to the row of shops in town. This place is so lovely and quaint, and I come here most afternoons to buy my food for the following day.

I walk past a hobby shop and stop and look through the window: what's in there?

I'll take a look, so I walk in and a bell rings over the door.

"Hello." An elderly woman smiles.

"Hi."

"Can I help you with anything?"

"Just looking," I reply. I walk through the cross-stitch section and smile sadly as I look at all the patterns. My mum would have loved this shop.

When I was a teenager we used to spend hours together in the garden house, and she would do her cross-stitch and I would paint. We would laugh and talk and listen to music. I smile as I remember making her play Taylor Swift on repeat for hours and hours.

I pick up a cross-stitch pattern of a duck and I smile as I think of Elliot and his girls. Maybe I should learn how to do cross-stitch? It could be an ode to my mum. I look through all the patterns, but end up back at the ducks.

I want this one; I liked those bat-shit crazy ducks of Elliot's. I remember the day they attacked him and it brings a smile to my face. I tuck the packet under my arm and keep looking.

"All the art supplies are marked down by fifty percent," the old lady calls.

"Oh, thanks." I keep walking. "I haven't painted since high school."

"You should start again, it's the best therapy." She smiles.

Hmm, I guess it could be. I mean, if I'm learning how to cross-stitch, I guess I could paint a picture too. I'm totally crap at it . . . but it would make me feel close to Mum, by association.

She always loved my paintings, said every new painting I did was her new favorite. Isn't that what all mums say to their kids about their hideous hobbies?

I pick up a packet of paintbrushes and a starter pack of ten tubes of paint, go to the back and look through the canvases. Shit . . . these are expensive.

Did Mum really pay this much? I smile, knowing exactly why she did: so that I would sit with her while she did her cross-stitch. There was a method to her madness, after all.

I pick up a small canvas, which will be easier to fit into the bin when I fuck it up.

I take my things to the cashier, and I feel really excited for tomorrow. When I get back from the beach, I'm going to start learning how to do my cross-stitch, just like Mum. How fun.

Elliot

"Your paintings have arrived, Mr. Miles," Andrew says from the door.

I look up from my computer. "What?"

"Your Harriet collection has arrived out of storage, I know how much you missed it."

I run my hand through my hair in disgust. "Oh." I pause.

I don't want to be anywhere near those paintings; I left Kate for those.

All they do is remind me of what I no longer have.

My girl.

"Umm." I pause as I try to articulate my answer. "My apologies, Andrew, can you have them delivered to my apartment in London please?"

Andrew's face falls. "But—"

"But nothing," I cut him off. "I don't want them in this house."

He frowns as he stares at me.

"That is all, Andrew," I snap, dismissing him.

"Very well, sir."

I inhale a shaky breath and go back to my computer.

This is fucked.

KATE

I walk up the road to my house and see a car pulled up outside. I frown and, as I get closer, I see it's a mail delivery van.

"Can I help you?" I ask the driver.

"Yes, I'm looking for a Pinkie Leroo, does she live here?"

My heart skips a beat; *he knows where I am.*

Is he here? My eyes flick around suspiciously. "What do you have for her?" I ask.

"A letter." He holds up a red envelope and I can see Elliot's handwriting on the front of it.

Oh . . .

"Yes, I'm Pinkie," I reply.

"Can I get you to sign here? It's certified."

"Sure." Damn control freak wants to make sure I got it. I sign for it and he hands it over.

"Bye Pinkie," he says as he gets into his car.

"Thanks. Bye."

I look at the letter in my hand.

Miss Pinkie Leroo

98 Grosvenor Street

Mayweather, Oahu.

I turn it over and look at the back for the sender.

Edgar Moffatt

Enchanted Kingdom

I smirk. Garbologist extraordinaire . . . idiot.
I walk back inside and put the envelope on the countertop.
I'm not reading it.

It's 11 p.m. when I walk in the door and I go straight to the envelope and pick it up. Work was so busy tonight and I was torturing myself the entire shift wondering what this says.

How does he know where I am?

I pick up the envelope and stare at it. What does he want? There's only one way to find out.

Fuck it.

I tear open the envelope.

My dearest Pinkie,

In light of my inability to call you, and not wanting to stalk you, serial-killer style, I have decided to go old school and write you a letter.

To receive a total package experience, please spray this letter with the spray that is enclosed in the envelope.

I frown: what the hell?

I turn the envelope upside down and a tiny spray bottle falls out onto the countertop.

I pick it up and read the little label.

Elliot Miles—Love Potion.

I roll my lips to suppress my smile, hold it to my nose, and close my eyes as a flood of memories runs through me. It's Elliot's aftershave.

Hmmm.

I read on.

> *I'm writing to you with the greatest of news, you are to be a GG, also known as a Goat Grandma.*

I put my hand over my mouth and burst out laughing. What the hell?

> *The veterinarian has just left and he has confirmed my suspicions. Gretel your goat is pregnant. The expected arrival date is in 40 days, and I can't wait.*
>
> *Finally, some good news.*
>
> *I hope you are well?*
>
> *I hope you know how much of my strength it's taking to not come to you.*
>
> *Please know how much you are missed.*
>
> *Forever yours,*
>
> *Elliot*
>
> *ox*

Short and sweet. My heart swells and I bite my lip.

I pick up the tiny spray bottle and hold it to my nose . . . smells like heaven.

Elliot Miles.

I read the letter again . . . and again, and then I do as he asks. I spray the letter with his cologne.

And with a big smile on my face, and the scent of Elliot Miles swimming around me, I read it again.

Chapter 26

I smile as I mix the paint in my palette; who knew I would love this so much.

It's taken me back to a time when I was happy and carefree . . . I also have to admit, Elliot's letter yesterday has lifted my spirits.

He gets it.

He could have come here and talked me around and dragged me home . . . but he's letting me work this out for myself.

I hear a car pull up and I go and look out of the window. It's the van. I smile.

I open the door in a rush to see the delivery driver get out of his van with another red envelope.

"Pinkie?" he calls.

"That's me." I beam.

"Two letters in two days, someone's getting spoilt. Sign here please."

I sign with a smile on my face. "What was your name?" I ask.

"Richard."

"Thanks, Richard." I take my letter and breeze up my steps and, once inside, I tear it open. Just like the last letter, I tip the envelope up and the little bottle falls out.

I read the label and giggle.

Elliot Miles—Love Potion.

My dearest Pinkie,

In light of my inability to call you, and not wanting to stalk you, serial-killer style, I have decided to go old school and write you a letter.

To receive a total package experience, please spray this letter with the spray that is enclosed in the envelope.

In light of your various fetishes, I will oblige you.

Enclosed is a picture for your personal spank bank, use it willingly and often.

I frown. What?

I search in the envelope and, inside, there's a photograph wrapped in white paper.

I tear it open and laugh. It's a picture of Elliot's bare feet, crossed at the ankles and resting up on an ottoman. He's sitting on his deck with the lake and his beautiful Enchanted rolling green hills in the background.

There's a glass of Scotch on the side table and he's wearing grey sweatpants.

I frown as I stare at it. Maybe he's onto something. This picture makes me want to be there. I keep reading.

I hope you are well, my days are long, my nights are longer.

You are missed, my love.

Forever yours,

Elliot.

xo

P.S. have you started knitting collars for your grandkids yet?

Apparently, twins are common. I'm not nervous at all.

I smile as my eyes linger on the letter; I pick up the little bottle and spray the paper.

I hold it to my nose and inhale deeply, and Elliot Miles in all his glory swims around me.

These quirky little letters that are so him, mean a lot.

I smile. It's a good day.

ELLIOT

Christopher pops his head around the door. "You want to grab some lunch?"

I glance up. "Umm . . ." I do, but I don't want him to see where I have to go on the way.

"I'm good, thanks anyway."

"You have to eat."

"I know that, I just . . ." I pause as I think of an excuse. "I have to go to the post office later, I'll grab something on the way there."

Christopher frowns as he walks in. "Why would you go to the post office?"

"To have an eight-course banquet, what do you think?" I mutter dryly as I turn back to my computer.

He sits on the edge of my desk. "Heard from Kate?"

"No." I hit my keys. "What makes you say that?"

"You haven't been out, you haven't seen anyone else. You've barely left your property other than to come to work."

"So?"

"She's been gone nearly six weeks, Elliot."

"And your point is?" I snap, exasperated.

"She's not coming back, man."

"Listen," I bark. "Kate is my business, and what happens between us is none of yours. I fucked up, and come hell or high water, I'm going to fix it."

"Then go to her and bring her home. You know where she is, what are you waiting for? This isn't like you."

"You don't know her. She's too stubborn and if I push her, I'll lose her in the end anyway. I'm giving her the time she deserves."

"Or the time to get over you."

My eyes rise to meet his.

"Come on, lunch. We can go send your love letter on the way."

I exhale heavily. "Fine." I open the top drawer of my desk and pull out a red envelope. He snatches it off me and reads who it is addressed to and he frowns.

Miss Pinkie Leroo

98 Grosvenor Street

Mayweather, Oahu.

"Why the hell do you call her Pinkie Leroo?"
"Long story."
He turns the letter over and reads who it's from.

Edgar Moffatt

Garbologist Extraordinaire

Enchanted Kingdom

"Huh? Who the hell is Edgar Moffatt?"

I snatch the letter from him. "I'll explain on the way." I put the envelope safely inside my suit jacket pocket. "Let's go."

Twenty minutes later I stand in line at the post office, Christopher next to me on his phone.

"Next," the cashier calls, and she looks up. "Oh, hello Mr. Moffatt."

I cringe. She knows me by name now. "Hello." I slide my letter over the counter.

"Same as always? International tracked and signed to Oahu."

"Thank you." I take out my wallet.

"I hope these are love letters." She smiles dreamily as she puts it through her computer.

Just ring it up, stupid.

"I mean, it's so romantic, you sending a letter to Pinkie every day for a month."

I glance back at Christopher and he gives a subtle shake of his head in disgust. "Loser," he mouths.

I twist my lips in disapproval as I turn back to her. Why don't you tell the whole post office, bitch?

"I wish I had an admirer as devoted as you." She smiles.

Shut the fuck up.

That's it, tomorrow I find a new post office.

KATE

I struggle up the road with my new canvas, which is huge. Like the ones I used to paint when I was just a girl.

I'm addicted to my new hobby and every day is better than the last.

The sun, the sea, my life here . . . Edgar's letters.

I have a new thirst for life, my old self is returning day by day.

There's no pressure, no grief . . . only happy memories and freedom. I'm going to call Elliot soon; his quirky letters have made me feel closer to him. I read them constantly and may even sleep with the box I keep them all in.

I want to fix this; he's worth trying for.

I come around the corner to see Richard's van parked out the front and I wave and smile. "Hi, you're early today?"

He holds up three red envelopes. "It's Monday, three letters today."

My broad smile nearly splits my face. Elliot writes to me every day.

And I know we didn't have a romantic beginning, but he's definitely making up for it. Not that his letters are romantic, they're weird and funny little stories from his day. He sends me photos and clippings. Each one makes me smile, each one makes my day that much brighter.

"Wow, that's a big canvas. You paint?" Richard asks.

"Oh." I shrug, slightly embarrassed. "Abysmally, but it relaxes me . . . so that's the main thing, right?"

Richard chuckles. "Paint a picture of me delivering your letters every day."

I laugh. "Okay, although you wouldn't be able to tell what it was."

"I'm sure you're underestimating yourself." He smiles, I sign for my letters and bounce up the stairs.

I read through the envelopes to find Saturday's letter, as I like to read them in order.

My dearest Pinkie,

In light of my inability to call you, and not wanting to stalk you, serial-killer style, I have decided to go old school and write you a letter.

To receive a total package experience, please spray this letter with the spray that is enclosed in the envelope.

I smile as I imagine Elliot pouring his aftershave into these tiny bottles. I wonder, does he use a funnel? And who makes these tiny labels?

I notice a photograph wrapped in white paper and I tear it open.

It's a picture of an open hand, palm facing up. It has terrible huge blisters all over it.

What the hell? What's he done?

I read on.

Actual footage of my right hand.

I burst out laughing. "Are you serious?"

My love, things are grim.

My body needs you.

It's been eight weeks since you touched me, it feels like forever.

I waited thirty-five years to find you.

How much longer must I wait to hold you again?

Forever yours,

Elliot.

xo

Emotion overwhelms me and I blink through tears.

I walk outside and put my canvas on the easel and pour myself a glass of wine, turn up Taylor Swift's song "Style" on repeat, and begin to fill my canvas with paint. I smile as I listen to the words.

ELLIOT

I sit on my deck and stare out over Enchanted. It's late, near midnight . . . but I can't sleep.

I haven't been able to relax in what feels like weeks.

I'm mentally drained.

Kate's in Hawaii . . . and all I want to do is go to her and make her come back with me, but her brother's words keep rolling around in my head.

I know I could go to her, talk her around, and bring her home . . . but she needs to want to be here.

She knows how I feel and yet, she still left me.

How could I have fucked this up so bad?

I think over the events of that first week after she left and, to be honest, I'm glad Kate didn't have to suffer it. I've had to lodge court proceedings to silence the gossip about the love triangle; it's been a media-circus nightmare.

I lift my Scotch to my lips and sip it slowly, and the heat burns my throat as it goes down.

I've been sending Pinkie letters, and baring my soul, but something's not sitting right.

I'm missing something in this puzzle.

I have no idea what it is, but as the days go by and still no word from Kate, my agitation grows.

I refill my glass of Scotch and light a cigar, blow out a thin stream of smoke into the crisp night air.

My mind goes back to the picture she had framed for me for my birthday and I smile. I go and retrieve it from inside and stare at it in my hands.

It's a photograph of me taken from behind, in a navy suit, staring out over the lake with the ducks around my feet. It's early morning and the mist is rolling on the paddocks in the background.

Such a simple image and yet somehow it feels so intimate—her secret view of me when I wasn't looking.

I turn it over and look at the back of the frame, and I wonder what the photo looks like without the glass on it.

I retrieve a knife and undo the frame and I take the image out, turn it over and see her handwriting.

Happy Birthday my darling,

I love you.

Always, Kate.

My chest constricts and I read it again . . . and again . . . and again.

Always, Kate.

Always means forever . . . until it didn't.

I lift the cigar to my lips and inhale deeply. I'm sad and forlorn, full of regret.

My hands are tied, I can't contact her. I can't make her come home, no matter how much I want to. I have to do this on her terms and respect her decision.

She has to want to come home to me.

And I hate it.

I tip my head back and drain the glass, then I fill it again so fast that it sloshes over the sides.

Patience isn't my strong point.

Two months.

I write to her every day . . . and yet, no word back.

Does she even get my letters?

"Thank you," Christopher says to the waitress as she puts a plate of fortune cookies down in front of us.

It's Friday night and Christopher has dragged me out for dinner.

I want to be anywhere else but here.

He passes the plate over to me. "Take one."

"Pass."

He shoves the plate in my face. "Fucking take one, you love this shit."

I roll my eyes and take one, crack it open.

There is no such thing as a coincidence.

I raise my eyebrow. Ha . . . once upon a time I would have believed that.

"What did you get?" Christopher asks.

I throw my note over and he smiles. "Well, if that was the case, your life is one massive fucking web."

I stare at him.

"You've got to admit, it's pretty fucking freaky that you've been chasing this artist for years . . . and she turns up just when you found a girl you fell for. And you and Kate meeting online . . . out of all the people in the world, you met her. The woman you were already seeing."

I frown as I listen. "It is weird . . . isn't it?"

"I mean, what are the chances of that actually happening?"

"Next to none." My mind begins to tick as I read the little fortune cookie note again.

There is no such thing as a coincidence.

I always believed in it, that everything happens for a reason. No event or person in your life happens by accident and yet, here I am.

I think hard . . . for a long time.

Why does it feel off, what am I missing?

But what if falling for Kate wasn't a coincidence at all?

What if this is all the grand plan?

I read it again.

There is no such thing as a coincidence.

Hmm.

The next day I knock on Brad's door. He opens it in a rush and his face falls as he sees me. "Hi."

I smile. "Hi. I was wondering if you had a minute? I have a pressing question and you are the only one who I think will know the answer."

"Umm."

My eyes search his. "Please."

He steps aside and I walk in and take a seat on the couch.

He sits down. "What's up?"

"So . . ." I pause as I try to articulate my thoughts. "I have a feeling that I'm missing something."

"What do you mean?"

"I believe I was meant to meet Kate."

He listens.

"And I also believe that I was meant to meet the artist, but for what reason I don't know."

He frowns as if confused.

"Do you believe in fate, Brad?" I ask.

"Maybe." He sits back in his chair. "Didn't think you would be the kind of man who would, though."

"Hmm." I think for a moment. "Is there something I'm missing?"

"What do you mean?"

"I don't know, I keep getting the feeling I'm missing something, but I don't know what it is."

Brad exhales. "She reads your letters."

"She does? What did she say?"

"Nothing, only that you write to her every day and that it makes her happy."

I smile as hope fills me.

"You know, for the first time since Mum and Dad died, she sounds back to herself."

"What do you mean?"

"She's working nights and learning how to cross-stitch like Mum used to do. She even started painting again."

What?

"She paints?"

"Oh, just mucking around, she definitely doesn't see herself as an artist. But she used to love it as a teenager."

"I never knew this about her," I whisper, fascinated.

"I think she'd forgotten all about it. Oahu and time alone has been good for her."

I smile as I imagine her painting at an easel . . . hmm. "She reads my letters, hey?" I should go. I pause, thinking of what else I can say. "Well, if you think of anything, can you call me?" I ask.

"I will."

I exhale heavily as I stand.

"I thought you would have given up on her by now," Brad says.

I turn to him in surprise. "I'm in love with her, why would I give up?"

"You did before."

"I never gave up. I had to meet that artist and I don't regret it; I never touched her and returned to Kate. Given, I did take too long to return . . . but still, my intention never wavered." I shrug. "I guess I just needed some time to get my head around it too."

He walks me to the door, and I hold out my hand to shake his. "Well, you've made my day, knowing she reads my letters means a lot."

"No worries."

"And if you think of anything . . ."

"Sure."

I turn toward the door and glance up and see a photo on the sideboard.

I walk over and pick it up, stare at it, my mind a clusterfuck of confusion.

What?

It's a picture of Brad and Kate, with Harriet Boucher.

My eyes meet his. "How do you know this woman?"

"Who?" He frowns.

I point to Harriet. "How do you know her?" I demand.

"She's our sister, Elanor."

Chapter 27

"What do you mean?" I frown.

"That's Elanor, our sister."

"Since when?"

"What are you talking about?"

"This woman." I tap her face on the photo. "That's Harriet Boucher, the artist I met in France."

"What?" He screws up his face in confusion. "What do you mean?"

"The artist, the one whose paintings I love, it's this woman." I tap her face on the glass again. "Her name is Harriet."

"No. It's Elanor, you're mistaken."

I stare at the photo. "I swear, it's her."

"It's not, you've got the wrong woman, maybe someone who looks similar. Elanor doesn't paint . . . not at all."

"Oh." I think on it for a moment. "Hmm, maybe it isn't her." I give an embarrassed shake of my head. "I feel like I'm going crazy lately."

He smiles. "That's okay."

I nod.

"I'll let Kate know you dropped by."

I give him a lopsided smile. "I just want her to come home."

"She will."

My eyes hold his.

"Give her time, she'll come back."

I smile, feeling a little better, and I shake his hand. "Thanks for listening. I'm completely out of my depth here with Kate, I don't know what I'm doing."

"You're doing okay, keep doing whatever it is that you're doing."

"Thanks." I walk back out to the car with a spring in my step.

She reads my letters.

Trust your gut.

I frown; why did that thought just come to me? Trust your gut.

It *was* Harriet . . . I know it was.

What if?

No . . . couldn't be.

I march back and knock on the door.

"What now?" Brad sighs as he opens it.

I bring up a picture on my phone and show it to him. "Have you ever seen this painting before?"

He screws up his face as he tries to focus on it. "I don't know."

I scroll through to another pic. "What about this one?"

He shrugs. "Not sure."

I scroll through again. "This one?"

"Hmmm . . . don't know."

"Fuck's sake, think."

"Why?"

"I think . . ." I pause. "I know this sounds ridiculous and maybe I am completely off track here. I think—"

"What?" he cuts me off.

481

"I think the paintings I've been buying off Harriet . . . are Kate's."

He chuckles. "You're delusional. And correct, that *is* ridiculous."

"Can you ask her?"

"What do you mean?"

"Without telling Kate why, ask her if she painted these pictures."

"Don't you think that if Kate was a famous artist, she would at least know?"

"Can you just do it? What's your number? I'm sending you the pictures now."

He finds his phone and saves the images I send him. "What will I ask her?"

"Um." I try to think. "Just say you found these pictures; does she know who painted them."

Brad shrugs and texts Kate.

Hey, I found these paintings in a charity shop.

They looked familiar, are they yours?

My heart is hammering hard and I pace. "What did she say?"

"No answer yet."

I close my eyes and walk back and forth as my hands run through my hair.

"She's typing, the dots are moving." He holds his phone out and we both stare at it, waiting for the answer.

Now, there's a blast from the past.

Yeah, they're mine. I painted them years ago.

God knows why Mum insisted on keeping them.

I can't believe Elanor thought someone would actually want them.

Lol, hilarious.

The air leaves my lungs and I grip the wall to steady myself. Brad drops to sit on the couch and we stare at each other, eyes wide.

"So this means . . ." Brad frowns as he connects the dots.

"It was always Kate," I whisper. "Of course it was."

KATE

I wait on the porch and look up the road. "Where is he?" I glance at my watch. Richard didn't bring me a letter yesterday . . . and he's late today.

I didn't realize how much Elliot's letters brighten my day . . . or how much they mean.

I twist my hands in my lap as I wait. "Come on," I whisper. "Where are you?"

What if he's met someone else?

Regret fills me that I haven't responded to him at all. I should have said something, if even only a thank you. What must he think with no correspondence back?

A car comes around the corner and I hold my breath—it's a different car.

Red.

It's not Richard. My shoulders slump with deflation.

The car pulls up to a halt outside my place and I frown as I watch. Who is it?

Elliot gets out of the backseat and my breath catches.

What?

He looks up and his eyes find mine . . . *Oh.*

Seeing him in the flesh opens old wounds and an unexpected rush of emotion sweeps through me. My eyes well with tears.

Glued to the floor, I stand and watch him as he leans in and takes out an overnight bag and pays the driver, and I want to run to him . . . and kiss him and tell him everything.

But my feet are set in concrete, frozen with fear. The hurt he caused me, magnified all over again. I thought my disappointment and anger were over—maybe not.

He stands on the curb with his bag in his hand, staring up at me, and as the car drives off, he gives me a soft smile.

And with my heart in my throat, I smile.

Oh . . . I've missed him so.

He slowly walks up the steps and I walk down them and we meet in the middle.

"Hi," he whispers.

"Hi."

"I came to bring you home." His eyes hold mine as he swallows a lump in his throat.

He's nervous.

My eyes well with tears, because suddenly everything is crystal clear: he *is* my home.

Elliot Casanova Miles is the great love of my life, and I don't know how it worked out that way, but I honestly don't think I can go on without him. I wouldn't want to.

"Took your time."

A slow, sexy smile crosses his face, and he wraps me in his arms and holds me tight.

And he squeezes me and I melt into him as our lips touch.

"Don't ever fucking leave me again," he whispers.

"Don't make me."

He kisses me, his tongue slowly sliding between my lips as he holds my face in his hands and, oh . . . the way he kisses. I had nearly forgotten.

Elliot Miles kisses from his soul.

Every chink in his armor, every weakness he keeps inside, all the passion in the world. I can feel it all. And fuck, do I love it.

We kiss again and he pulls me toward him, hugs me tight in his arms as the horror we've been through becomes too much.

The emotion between us . . . too much.

Sacred.

"We need to talk," he says as he takes my hand and leads me up the steps.

"I know."

His eyes flick back to me as if questioning my statement.

Huh, what was that look?

I frown as uneasiness runs through me: he's here to tell me something.

There's more.

Did he sleep with his artist?

My heart begins to race as I brace myself. Somehow, I don't think our reunion is going to stay happy.

We walk into the living area and he turns toward me. "Sit down, baby, I need to tell you something."

I drop to the couch without question.

Thump, thump, thump sounds my pulse in my ears.

He goes to his overnight bag and takes out a large, yellow envelope and passes it to me. "Images of Harriet Boucher."

"Who?" I frown.

"The artist I was looking for, these are the images that were sent to me from the private investigator."

"Why would I want to see who she is, haven't you hurt me enough with her?" I spit.

"Open it," he demands.

"I don't—"

"Open it," he barks.

I open the envelope and pull out the large A4-sized photographs, and I frown.

It's Elanor.

I flick through them—image after image of Elanor. Black and white, color, different locations.

I shake my head, confused. "I don't understand."

He passes me a white envelope. "These are the paintings I have bought at auction."

I screw up my face; what the fuck is he going on about? "Elliot, I don't—"

"Open it," he barks.

Jeez, psycho . . . I open the envelope and my eyes widen. I flick through the images, confusion takes me over. I know these paintings . . . I *did* these paintings.

My eyes rise to meet his.

"All those years, all that time . . . it was you," he whispers.

Goosebumps scatter up my spine.

He drops to his knees on the floor in front of me, takes my hands in his. "It was you who was calling me through those paintings."

My eyes well with tears as my world spins on its axis.

"It's always been you," he whispers. "I knew in my heart that I was called to them for a reason. It's you, Kate, you are the reason."

I drop my head, overwhelmed. "I don't . . . how . . . I mean . . ." I look up at him. "How did this happen?" I whisper. "I don't understand."

"Brad and I have pieced this together."

"Brad?" I frown. "Brad knows about this?"

He nods and leans up and kisses me tenderly as if to soften the blow, but I can't feel it. I'm numb.

"Elanor cleared out your parents' house to hide a crime."

My eyes hold his.

"She had been selling your old paintings from the attic at auctions using a pseudonym. And she knew that once you and Brad cleared out your parents' house, her crime would be discovered."

487

Horror dawns.

"What she didn't count on, was that one particular art collector, me, would become obsessed with the paintings and hire a private investigator to find her."

My chest rises and falls as I scramble for air.

"And she would have gotten away with it, too. If she hadn't got greedy and wanted the fame that my name delivered."

Elanor is the artist he met in France?

"She agreed to meet with the full intention of seducing me, but what she didn't count on was that I was already in love with someone else, and I wanted nothing to do with her plan."

I put my head into my hands. "Elliot," I whisper.

He hugs me and pulls my head to his. "I'm so sorry, baby."

A thought comes to me and I pull back to look at him. "How much did you pay for those paintings?"

He puffs air into his cheeks. "Around twenty million dollars."

I put my hands over my mouth as my eyes widen in horror. "You idiot. Daniel is completely right, you do have more money than sense. They're abysmal, Elliot."

His face softens, then he smiles and chuckles.

"I would have given you those paintings for free," I scoff. "Hell, I would have paid you to take them away."

He tips his head back and laughs hard, as if the weight of the world has been lifted.

"Oh no." I stand as another thought comes to me. "What about Elanor?"

He falls silent, his eyes hold mine.

"Elliot, what about Elanor?"

"She will be dealt with by the law."

"No." My chest tightens. "I don't want . . ."

He takes my hands in his. "We'll talk about Elanor on Monday," he says sternly.

"Monday?"

"For now"—he kisses me softly—"I just want to talk about us." He kisses me again as he holds my head to his. "Can we just fix us before we worry about your witch of a sister?"

Elliot Miles calling Elanor a witch brings an unexpected smile to my face, and I know it shouldn't, but it does.

"You think this is funny?" He smiles as his lips take mine; he walks forward and I walk back.

"This just confirms what I always knew," I reply.

"What's that?" He smiles against me.

"You are an idiot."

In one sharp movement, he bends and throws me over his shoulder. I laugh out loud and he slaps my behind. "Where's your bedroom, wench? You're about to get it."

"Aren't you all wanked out?" I laugh as I hang upside down. "I saw the blisters."

"Behave." He slaps my behind again.

He carries me into the bedroom and throws me on the bed, and I bounce as I land.

With his eyes locked on mine he takes his shirt off over his head. His chest is broad with a scattering of dark hair, his tanned shoulders and arms cut with definition, his stomach rippled with muscles. But it's his eyes that arrest me, filled with desire and love and a sense of belonging.

Home.

In slow motion he slides down his trousers and my breath catches. No matter how many times I see him naked, I'm never prepared for his powerful beauty.

Elliot Miles is a million things, but most of all . . . he's mine.

He crawls over me. "You owe me for the hell you've put me through," he says as he nips my hip bone through my dress.

"Oh." I sit up, remembering something. "Come."

489

"What?"

I jump up and take his hand. "I have something to show you." I drag him out into the other room and hold my hand up toward my easel.

It's a huge oil painting of the two of us together; I've been working on it for weeks. We are in each other's arms, staring lovingly at each other.

A moment of intimacy between us, captured in my memory.

His breath catches as he stares at it, and he runs his finger over the title of the painting at the bottom right corner.

Forever Enchanted.

His nostrils flare and he presses his lips together, overwhelmed with emotion.

His eyes find mine. "I love you," he whispers.

"I love you."

He kisses me and we melt together and, oh . . .

"Marry me."

I pull back to look at him. "What?"

"Marry me, Kathryn. I know this isn't the most romantic proposal . . . but our story and this painting." He wells up. "I just . . ."

Oh, I love him.

"Elliot Miles, are you asking me to marry you, buck naked with an erection?"

He looks down at himself and then breaks into a slow smile. "I guess I am."

He kisses me and pulls me close, and I can feel every hard inch that he has. "Well, what do you say, Landon?" He drags me over his hard cock.

I giggle. Only him.

He jerks me against him, demanding an answer.

"Yes. I'll marry you."

We laugh against each other's lips and he picks me up and carries me back to the bedroom, then he lifts my dress over my head and then takes off my bra and panties and lays me down.

He lies down beside me and spreads my legs; his fingers find that sweet spot as he kisses me deeply. My back arches off the bed as he works me harder, and harder. The sound of my wet arousal echoes around us but he doesn't stop, he pushes me.

"Elliot," I murmur.

"I have to warm you up, angel . . . because, fucking hell, I'm about to blow. Hard." His voice is deep, commanding, and I know he's running on pure instinct. The urge to fuck has taken him over and he's losing control by the second.

I slide my hand down and feel him: he's rock-hard with pre-ejaculate dripping from his end.

God, how did I ever think I could live without this? *Without him.*

"Now, El," I whisper as I pull him over me. "Please."

With his dark eyes locked on mine, he rolls over me and nudges my opening with his tip, and I feel the burn of his possession.

Every time with this man is like the first.

His size, unforgiving.

"I love you." His eyes flutter closed.

I smile against him and then he pushes in hard, nailing me to the mattress. Forcing my body to accept his.

His sweet words in vast contrast to his hard actions.

I cling to his broad shoulders and I close my eyes as I try to deal with him.

Ouch.

Elliot Miles was born to fuck, unapologetic, and hard.

He pulls out and slides back in, his eyes dark with want. He rotates his hips one way, and then the other. Stretching me, opening me up for his pleasure.

"You alright?" he murmurs, his eyes locked on my lips.

I nod. "I'm good. Go."

He bites my neck as his hips begin to pump, hard, thick, and fast, and oh hell.

I arch my back, his cock working at piston pace. His big hands grab my inner thighs as he holds my legs open, his knees spread wide, and I can see every muscle in his torso as it contracts. The sound of the bed hitting the wall with force echoes around us and I scream out as I come hard. I hold him tight, through the ecstasy, as all the pain from the last few months is washed away with love. He holds himself deep and I feel the telling jerk of his cock deep inside my body.

And he kisses me, tenderly, with so much love that I can hardly stand it, and my world stops.

And another life begins.

Mrs. Miles.

Elliot takes me by the hand. "Do you have everything, sweetheart?"

I look around the airplane. "Yes, I think so."

"Nice to see you, Mr. Miles," the pilot says. He turns to me and nods kindly. "Have a nice night, Kathryn."

"Thank you."

Elliot shakes his hand and leads me down the stairs where the black Bentley is parked. Andrew gets out, and he smiles broadly when he sees us. "Hello Kate."

I skip over to him and go up onto my toes and kiss his cheek. "Hello Andrew."

"I hear that congratulations are in order." He beams.

I giggle and hunch my shoulders up in excitement. "Can you believe it?" I gush.

"I can actually." He smiles as his eyes flick to Elliot, who smirks in return.

Elliot can't even act grumpy. In fact, that sexy-as-fuck smile hasn't left his face, and after the dreamiest five days in Oahu, we've landed back in London.

Elliot publicly announced today that we are engaged to be married, and in some kind of strategic plan he told me that I would be photographed tonight, which I'm guessing was code for . . . don't wear your sweatpants on the plane.

I did wonder why he changed into a full three-piece suit before we landed.

Andrew and Elliot load all of our things in the trunk and I get into the backseat. Elliot slides in behind me and picks up my hand and rests it on his thick quad; he always has to be touching.

"Are we still sticking to the schedule, sir?" Andrew asks as he makes eye contact in the rearview mirror.

"Yes," Elliot replies.

Schedule . . . there's a schedule?

We zoom off into the night and twenty minutes later we come around the corner into the street where Elliot's swanky apartment is; there are photographers everywhere. I feel my anxiety rise and instead of pulling into the private undercover parking lot, Andrew pulls the car up right next to them.

"What are you doing?" I whisper.

Elliot leans over and kisses me. "Giving them what they want."

"What?"

"Once they have the first photograph of us together, and it's published tomorrow, they'll leave us alone and we can go home."

I stare at my beautiful man. This goes against everything he is, but he wants me to be left alone, he's doing this for me.

The door opens in a rush. Andrew stands outside as the cameras flash.

Elliot gets out, takes my hand, and helps me from the car. I climb out to the blinding lights of flashes and the sound of photographers screaming over the top of each other. "When is the wedding?"

"Congratulations, Mr. Miles."

"Kathryn, who's designing your wedding dress?"

Elliot takes my hand and in slow motion lifts it to his lips and kisses it.

They go wild.

"Kathryn," someone calls. "How does it feel to know you finally tamed the elusive Casanova Miles?"

Elliot chuckles, our eyes are locked as electricity bounces between us, and he raises an eyebrow as he waits for my answer.

If only they knew that the supposed Casanova is a romantic fool.

I turn back to them and smile. "Wonderful."

We pose for a few shots and then he leads me into the building by the hand as they yell to us in the background. I get into the elevator with the love of my life.

He smiles down at me and I smile right back up at him.

Turns out I do believe in fairy tales.

And fate.

Never give up, he will find you.

Love always,

Kate.

Xox

The Epilogue

I sit at the desk with the glass screen in front of me, waiting to see my sister Elanor.

She's being held in custody until her court case, and although Elliot and I have had an almighty row over this, he refuses to drop the charges.

And I get it, I really do. Brad is working with Elliot and they're doing this together. Weirdly enough they get on very well and Brad spends a lot of time at Enchanted with us.

I won't testify against Elanor, not ever; she's my sister. They have agreed that I can stay out of this.

But I need to know why.

Elanor comes into view. She's in a minimal-security prison and wearing a grey pant suit. I smile and stand and she smiles in return as she takes a seat.

"Hi." I sit down.

"Hi." She clasps her hands in front of her.

I stare at her and my natural inclination is to apologize. After all, it is my fiancé who has put her here.

But then I remember what she's done and if anyone should be angry, it should be me.

What I am is disappointed.

"Are you going to say anything, or are you just going to sit there?" she says, void of emotion.

My eyes hold hers and I wonder what the hell went so wrong with her.

"Why?" I ask.

She shrugs as if she doesn't care. "It was always about you . . . wasn't it?"

I frown.

"The smartest, the prettiest, the sweetest, the most talented . . . Mum's favorite."

My heart constricts, is that how she saw it?

"I guess you'll have a perfect life now that you have him." She lifts her chin in defiance. "I read you're getting married." She smiles sarcastically. "Mrs. Miles."

I nod, my hands clenched into fists.

"It won't last." She smirks. "He'll be bored with you in twelve months, run off with someone." She readjusts herself on the chair as if proud of herself for being so mean.

"I would have given the paintings to you, if you'd only asked me," I whisper.

Her eyes search mine.

"I would have given you the world, if you had just let me in," I say.

Her eyes well with tears and for the first time since my parents died, I see the sweet little girl that she always was.

Grief works in different ways. Although always destructive, its effects changed her. This isn't who she really is.

"I love you, Elanor, and regardless of this whole mess, I will always love you and will get you the help that you need."

She inhales sharply as if shocked by my support.

I stand and turn to walk out.

"Kate," she calls.

I turn back.

"Send me a photo of you in your wedding dress?"

I smile through tears and nod. "Okay."

I turn and walk out. We have a lot of shit to work through, but I'm no quitter.

Elliot

A toast: I hold my glass up to my beautiful bride as she sits beside me.

We are now husband and wife, married in a white marquee in the grounds of Enchanted. My brothers are beside me, our closest fifty friends and family are here. "Kathryn." I smile down at her. "My Kate."

"Oh, fucking hell," I hear Christopher whisper to Tristan, "here we go."

Tristan chuckles as he listens.

"I could rattle on all night about how beautiful and intelligent and warm and loving you are."

She reaches up and takes my hand and kisses it from her seated position.

"I could tell you how I loved you from afar for years before we even met. How our love was fated, that you were my destiny."

She smiles.

"But none of that matters." Emotion overwhelms me and I pause with a frown, clear my throat. "Because waking up next to you every day . . . is the reason I am here."

Her eyes fill with tears and I have to stop before I get really fucking pathetic.

I hold my glass in the air. "I want you to all toast my beautiful wife. To Kate."

"To Kate." They all cheer.

It's dusk and I'm standing with Tristan, Jameson, and Christopher.

Kate is dancing with her brother, and it's been a wonderful day.

The best.

We are under the huge oak tree that's strung with fairy lights.

Patrick, Tristan's youngest son, runs up, panting. He looks out of breath and slightly panicked, and points toward the paddock.

Tristan frowns. "What's up?"

"I did a thing."

"What thing?"

"You didn't," Harry mutters under his breath.

"What thing?" Tristan asks more sternly.

Patrick points to his elder brother. "Harry dared me to."

"What did you do?" Tristan takes Patrick's hand and leads him away. I watch as they walk down toward the bottom paddock and I continue talking to my brothers.

"Ahh!" I hear Tristan's bloodcurdling scream in the distance. "What the hell?"

We all look down and see Humphrey the ram chasing the two of them back up the hill at full speed.

"What the fuck did you do, Harrison?" Jameson barks.

"I didn't think he would really open the gate!" he yells. "Everyone knows you don't do dares."

Everyone starts screaming as the ram runs toward us, then he stops and, seemingly distracted, begins to head-butt a tree at full force. The sound echoes like thunder.

Then he turns and rams into Daniel, who goes flying spectacularly in the air.

"Oh . . . *fucking hell*." Jameson winces.

The guests all run for their lives, screaming.

"Elliot," Kate cries. "Do something."

Christopher's eyes widen and then he bursts out laughing. "Best wedding ever."

Tristan is holding Patrick under his arm while he runs as fast as he can.

"Everyone, get out of the way," he screams. "This thing is a killer."

I clench my jaw, ready to explode. "Fucking Harry."

ACKNOWLEDGMENTS

It takes an army to write a book and I have the best army on earth.

I would dearly love to thank my mum Kerry, Nadia, Rachel, Amanda, Lisa, Nicole. Rena and Vicki, you guys have been my beta team since day one, you are my rock and I am so grateful for all that you do for me. You make me better.

To my amazing Montlake team, Sammia, Lindsey, and Nicole, thank you for being so good at what you do. Your help and guidance is a dream come true.

To the best PA in all of the world, my beloved Kellie.

Special thanks to my family for putting up with a wife and mum who is always writing . . . or thinking about writing. I'm annoying, I know.

And to you . . . my beloved readers, you are the reason I write.

You are all so appreciated, thank you so much for making my dreams come true.

xoxoxo

ABOUT THE AUTHOR

T L Swan is seriously addicted to the thrill of writing and can't imagine a time when she wasn't. She resides in Sydney, Australia, where she is living out her own happily-ever-after with her husband and their three children.